INDIAN LOVE SONG

Abby tried to make him understand. "No. No be squaw, Corn Dancer. No be squaw," she told him.

He looked puzzled. His eyes widened; his mouth dropped. But Abby persisted, repeating her gestures. She struck her bare chest with her fist, then swung her arm back in what she thought must be the location of their burned settlement, Westover.

"My man back there. My . . . my fireside . . . back there."

Corn Dancer stared at her a moment, then smiled. He shook his head, making a slashing movement with the edge of his hand as if wielding a weapon.

"Your warrior . . . he gone," he told her as he pulled a dirty bundle of hair from a bag. It wasn't Daniel's hair, but she knew what Corn Dancer meant. And she realized then that Daniel and her parents had been killed, scalped and that she'd never see them again.

She swayed and caught herself, but she could not help the tears that coursed down her cheeks. Then, not wanting to show weakness to these savages, she pulled back her shoulders and proudly straightened.

Corn Dancer roughly jerked her chin up and glared deep into her eyes. She met his stare with one equally as hard. Slowly, his expression softened, and he pointed to one of the rooms behind him.

"You be my woman," he said. "That our fireside."

THE TEMPESTUOUS TOLLIVER SAGA

BY ARTHUR MOORE

WHITEWATER DYNASTY
HUDSON!

BY HELEN LEE POOLE

ZEBRA BOOKS

KENSINGTON PUBLISHING CORP.

ZEBRA BOOKS

are published by

KENSINGTON PUBLISHING CORP.
21 East 40th Street
New York, N.Y. 10016

To
GLADYS MARCUS
of
Olean, N.Y.

I

The summer sky had barely lightened when Abigail Brewster threw aside the covers of her bunk bed built against the wall of the cabin and pulled the coarse weave of her nightgown down to cover her long shapely legs. Flames from the fireplace at the far end of the cabin silhouetted her mother, already bent over a pot. The planked cabin door stood open, so Abigail knew her father had already gone to the lean-to that sheltered the family horse and cow.

Her mother turned her head from the pot to look over her shoulder and laugh. "Well, sleepyhead! Did your dreams of Daniel keep you asleep this morning?"

Her voice held only warm humor but still Abby blushed as she grasped the rail of the short ladder at the head of the double bunks and climbed down to the cool, hard-packed dirt floor. Her dark, auburn-red hair hung wildly about her face, down over her shoulders and back. She hastily smoothed it away from her high, tanned forehead, gathered it and tied it with a strip of cloth at the back of her neck.

"Of course not, Mother. I never dream of boys."

"Not even of the one you're betrothed to and will marry soon?" Her mother turned to face Abby, and the older woman again had that moment of disbelieving wonder as she traced the mature, delightful curves of her daughter. How quickly the girl had changed from a gangling, awkward tomboy to this desirable young, nubile woman who hastily shed her gown and grabbed up her rough linsey-woolsey dress from a chest. In the few seconds it took Abby to lift the dress over her head and then drop it about her, she revealed fully rounded breasts, deep-cleaved, outstanding nipples of pink, a narrow waist that flared at hips and legs that would set any man's brain aflame. Mother Brewster smiled crookedly

8

and turned back to the pottage over the fire.

"I think you stretch the truth a bit, daughter. I can well remember how I thought and felt and dreamt when I was seventeen, going on eighteen, and I knew every young oaf in my village had his eyes on me from morning until night."

Again Abby flushed at having been caught so easily. How could Mother know everything so certainly, even thoughts and dreams of which Abby never spoke? Daniel Williams was always in her thoughts deep in the night when the only light in the cabin was the glow of dying embers in the huge stone fireplace. In the daytime she would often surreptitiously watch him, keenly aware of his wide shoulders and deep chest, of the muscles that rippled along his arms as he swung an ax or a scythe, and of the fluid ease with which he walked into the cabin to pay a call or out through the stockade gate to join the other men at ploughing or cutting trees to clear another few acres of land that later would become fields of corn or flax or tobacco.

The thought of him and her father already at work out beyond the village stockade abruptly turned her mind from dreams of what it would be like married to him. She couldn't woolgather! There was work to be done—always work, from dawn to dusk in this Western Connecticut wilderness.

She pulled on moccasins, bartered from a small village of local Indians nearby. Old Zeke Blaine, who had helped establish other frontier villages, had insisted on discarding the rough, homemade, heavy and awkward leather shoes for the Indian footgear and now everyone wore them, thankful for Zeke's knowledge of the forest ways.

"Injuns ain't fools," he had growled at the town meeting, then he brought up the matter of footwear. "They been living in these woods, I reckon, since time began and they've learned more of how to live out here than we ever will. You'll see."

So now Abigail gratefully pulled on her moccasins with their little circles of ornate quillwork and hurried out the door to the bench where the wooden water pail, washbowl and rough towel waited beside the bar of lye soap. She scrubbed her face, wincing at the bite and burn of the soap and the abrasive touch of the towel. She glanced up to the clear sky above the dark trees beyond the stockade. The pink and rose light of early dawn promised a beautiful day.

The peeled high stakes of the stockade restricted Abby's vision, except for the stout gate now open and swinging wide. She remembered that when she first came here some five years before, the gate was never open but closed, barred and guarded. But now there was no Indian threat as there had been a decade ago. The gate stood open from dawn to dusk so that horses, carts, farm equipment and the crops could be readily brought into the village compound. Soon Abby would lead the cow out to pasturage near the walls and she planned to hoe with the women in the cornfield a hundred yards beyond.

She turned back into the cabin, paused when she heard a distant sound from within the forest. That would be an ax blade biting deep into a tree. By next year the village of Westover would have more acres of farmland to cultivate.

Mother had placed a bowl of steaming porridge on the plank table that took up the center of the cabin what with its bench on either side. A tankard of milk, topped by a crust of golden, thick cream stood beside it. Abby sat down to her breakfast as her mother dried her hands on her long apron.

"Did ye hear the menfolk?" she asked.

"They're at work, Mother. The air is so clear and still, the sound of the axes is plain."

Her mother sat down to her own porridge and milk and she looked out to the stockade and the open gate, her eyes distant and thoughtful. At last she sighed, a long yet patient sound. Some subtle shift of the morning breeze brought the sound of the axes more clearly for a moment.

"Trees," Mother said. "Always trees no matter where you turn until our menfolk cut them down and we gradually get more and more open fields and farming land."

"Do the woods go on forever?" Abby wondered.

"I reckon as far as the land goes west, and there's no knowing how far that is. You and Dan'l and your children and maybe your children's children will be clearing woods and making new farms, building new settlements like

11

this one.''

"But there are cities back east, and not far away at that. There's Hartford and—''

"Boston up in Massachusetts Colony and towns in New York Colony as well as Rhode Island settlements. But your father and me, you and Daniel, face west and somehow that's the direction we have to go. I reckon the good Lord planned it that way for us.''

"We'll make our home right here,'' Abby said confidently. "Daniel and me plan it that way. We want to see Westover grow into a real town, maybe even a city as large as Darien or even Hartford. We want to be part of it and help it grow.''

Mother chuckled and reached across the table to stroke Abby's bare forearm for a moment. "You sound like me when your father and I were first married. We would settle down and help Bluefield grow, and here we are in Westover. It'll probably be the same way with you.''

"I know Daniel wants to set down roots, Mother. He likes it here and so do I.'' She nodded toward the open door and the forest beyond the stockade gate. "We want to plow and plant and garden. Someday build a real house instead of a cabin.''

"Glory be to that and may God forward the plan! But, Abby, before all that Daniel and the other men will have many an acre of woods to clean out.'' She added after a moment, "And Indians, too. I'm thankful those around us are friendly, but I've been besieged behind a stockade and tamped powder, wadding, and ball down many a musket that I handed up to my father and yours as red devils screeched just beyond the palisades. Be ready for anything, Abby, in these days and times.''

"I think I remember some of that,'' Abby said slowly. "It was more like a bad dream, though."

"You were less'n five years old the last raid we went through, so maybe it would be like a dream to you after these years and young as you were."

"But now Westover's peaceful and likely to stay that way."

"With luck. So long as our present Indians stay near us.'' Then her mother threw a swift, judging look at the sky and hastily arose. "We best get to work, girl. It's such a nice day, sunny and all, that you get out to the garden and I'll stay inside and do the cabin."

"Thank you, Mother. It *is* beautiful."

"And you'll get more of a chance to see Daniel."

Abby also stood and picked up her bowl and tankard. "Mother, whenever will the parson get here?"

"Not soon enough to suit you but too soon for me. I'll be losing a daughter, honey."

Abby swiftly circled the table and hugged the older woman. "You will not!" She pointed to the gate. "Daniel and I will be living right out there, and we'll both see you everyday."

"I know." Mother looked thoughtful, con-

13

cerned. "Yours will be the first house beyond the stockade. I'd feel better if it wasn't."

"But there's no room inside anymore, and besides, all's peaceful. You just said so yourself."

"That's true, and may it always be true." The older woman suddenly smiled, and the shadow of trouble left her tanned face. "But what with your house, your garden, children and all, you'll get too busy for me." She shooed Abby toward the door as the girl started to protest. "Out to your garden! Do you want the weeds to choke all those tender new plantings! Grab a hoe, and we'll be sure of a full table come summer and autumn."

Abby had been working hardly an hour when she heard the sharp screeching of an axle. She straightened and turned swiftly to face the gate. Sure enough, there was Daniel driving the cart with the water barrel. She could see the white flash of his grin even as horse and cart rumbled through the stockade gate and turned toward the low rock wall of the village well, its high sweep and dangling bucket dark silhouettes against the sunny sky.

Abby threw a searching look back at her cabin door. Mother was not in sight, but her laughing voice came clearly. "Why, Abby, what're you waiting for? It's been such a *long* time since you've seen or talked to your swain!"

"Mother! You're making me blush!"

Abby laughed as she dropped the hoe and managed a sedate pace toward the well where

Daniel filled the water barrel. As she approached, Abby again had that feeling of loving wonder as she matched Daniel's smile with her own. He stood a good six feet and more, and she knew, when she came close, she would have to look up into his face.

His black hair curled in a mad tangle over his head, two stray locks hanging down his forehead almost to his brown eyes that danced with soft lights as he looked at her. His head sat well and proudly on wide, powerful shoulders that strained at the rough cloth of his shirt. His chest, half exposed because he had loosened the three top buttons, showed a curl of the same black hair, and she knew that powerful muscles rippled just beneath his skin. His butternut work trousers concealed his strong thighs and stout legs. How, Abby wondered, had she been so fortunate to gain Daniel's attention when a dozen other village girls had tried so hard to interest him?

She didn't know, and she didn't care. Her heart was a constant song of thanks and gladness that it had happened. He extended his arm, the sleeve rolled to the elbow, to her, and she accepted his hand after a swift glance told her nobody watched them from any doorway. It was a bit too bold for an unmarried couple—even though betrothed and waiting only for the coming of the parson for marriage—to indulge in such an intimacy. Of course, there were times at a dance or a house-raising, or even at church where custom and politeness permitted such actions.

The physical contact was only for a moment but it was enough to catch her breath for a split second and send a wave of warm desire through her whole body. Daniel's slightest touch could always do that to her, and once more, Abby silently but fervently wished the parson would come soon. How much longer could she maintain her defenses against this man whom she so much desired?

They stood as close as possible while he filled the huge water cask and told her how the work went out in the woods and that Jamey Gray had a limp this morning, probably the ague that always bothered the gray-haired settler. Neither of these interested Abby nor Daniel but then it would be highly improper to even hint at their true thoughts.

At last the cask was filled and Daniel let the sweep lift the well bucket over their heads. Instead of climbing back into the cart, he walked beside her to the gate. Now she could get a full, sweeping view of the trees and bushes that formed a solid wall about the village, broken only by the newly made trail ahead leading to the workers and by the old, well-trodden one that circled the far corner of the stockade to meander eastward and, miles away, connect with a wider trail, sometimes called a "road," that led to Conneut and the older colony towns and settlements beyond.

"We'll work the rest of the day," Daniel regretfully told her. "At least, all but your father. He'll bring the water cart in this afternoon should we have need of it."

"You will. The day will grow warm as the sun lifts toward nooning." She frowned slightly. "Does my father tire easily, as he has of late?"

Daniel laughed. "Not this day! He's the one who tires those his age and even makes the young'ns like me sweat a good deal. Have no worry for him."

They had now progressed some distance across the already cleared land close to the mouth of the trail, and they halted. Daniel threw a hasty look back toward the open gate and moved toward her. She read his intent in his eyes and, though she wanted his lips, her hand on his chest kept him at arm's length.

"Nay, Luv. There's always eyes watching, though you don't see them. There'll be time enough soon."

"But how soon!"

She caught the frustration, longing and impatience in his voice, an echo of her own. "A day, a week, a month—no more—and the parson will wed us." Her face lit. "Why, it might even be this day he'll come riding around the turn over there."

His wide shoulders lifted and dropped in acceptance but she well understood that he disbelieved her false optimism.

"Not that soon and, mayhap, not even in a week or a month."

"And, pray, why not?" she demanded.

"A preaching back East, a funeral, or even another wedding could delay him." He hesitated a second. "Might even be Indians."

"Now, that is an addlepated thought! There has been no trouble in ten years."

"There's whispers the French stir up the northern tribes while the British quietly send musket and powder to the Six Nations."

"The Iroquois!"

Her eyes widened in alarm and he hastily squeezed her arm and smiled. "Old men's fears and whispers," he reassured her. "Like Zeke Blaine."

"Oh, him!" she sniffed. "He is always smelling danger and seeing ghosts."

"Aye . . . Well, we will talk tonight, eh?"

"Tonight, Luv, and don't forget."

"How can I?"

They parted then, Abby slowly walking back to the stockade. She turned at the gate and saw that Daniel, on his cart, had also turned to look back at her. He waved and she returned the gesture. A few moments later the cart made a turn and disappeared among the trees, though she could hear the squeal of its axle for a moment or two longer.

"I'll remind him to use bear grease," she thought.

Her sweeping glance circled the silent green wall of trees and bushes, a hundred or more yards away now but still seeming to tightly press upon the village.

She slowly walked back to the garden, picked up the hoe and considered the work to be done. There were little sprigs of green that indicated weeds rather than vegetables but, on the whole, the patch was clean. Abby and her mother took pride in that, as they would in their vegetables when the time came to pluck them.

Each cabin had its small plot beside the structure itself, a custom dating from the time when the most urgent business of Indian danger kept everyone within the walls. Now there was a huge communal garden outside that the men took turns in working. It was the forerunner of the corn and wheat fields that in time would sustain the whole settlement. Now that peace remained unbroken between Indian and settler, between tribe and tribe, that day could not be too far off.

Abby worked steadily for perhaps an hour or more, then straightened to relieve the strain in her back, and used her apron to wipe the sweat from her face and neck. She became immobile when she heard a single, distant sound. She could not be sure but she thought it was a rifle shot. When, after a few seconds, it was not repeated, she mentally shrugged—one of the men had bagged a squirrel or sighted a deer.

She turned to the garden and lifted the hoe, held it poised over the furrow. Another distant shot sounded, then a third.

She was yet to learn that those distant explosions signaled disaster and a complete change in her life.

II

Abby dropped the hoe and, in alarm, raced to the gate, hardly aware that women and a few men appeared in the doorways of other cabins. She dashed through the gate and a short distance along the trail leading into the woods, but saw no movement along its length to the first turn.

But more shouts sounded and she wheeled about to alarm the village, racing back toward the gate.

Behind her, beyond the narrow expanse of cleared fields, the bushes stirred wildly and suddenly dark, sinister figures appeared between the trees. Abby did not see them, her attention on the cabins behind the stockade, and she shouted wild warnings. Suddenly dark, bronze, nearly naked men darted out of the trees and raced across the fields at an angle to cut her off. Then she saw them. Bodies nearly naked except for breechclouts. Faces painted with slashes of crimson, blue and green. Heads shaven except for a single high-standing line of black hair from the top of the forehead back over the crown to the nape of the neck. She glimpsed lances, tomahawks and round-headed, heavy clubs. She saw bows in red hands and glimpsed, protruding over the shoulders of red backs, quivers filled with arrows. Some of the warriors held rifles, while powder horns and shotbags swung from bands crossing muscular chests, as horribly painted for war as the grimacing faces.

She came to the gate, sensed rather than heard the beat of moccasined feet behind her. She glimpsed her own cabin and in horror saw her mother framed in the door. She screamed a warning. Something invisible made a sibilant whisper over her shoulder. Like an evil apparition, a short, feather-tipped object plunged into her mother's chest. Then something grabbed her hair and her head was wrenched back and up. Greasy hands and fingers slapped over her face and eyes and she did not see her mother fall to the ground, face forward across the doorsill.

Something hard struck Abby in the small of the back and she flung out her arms as she felt herself falling blindly forward. A muscular arm whipped about her waist and the fingers taloning her hair wrenched her head further back. The greasy, odorous fingers slipped from her mouth for an instant and she screamed in terror and warning. But a calloused palm slammed across her lips, muffling the sound, and she was swung helplessly around.

She glimpsed a young, hawklike and cruel face, blood-red warpaint leading from the corner of the thin lips up to each ear. Black eyes bored into hers and she read murder in them. She had a confused feeling of milling forms close around and screams and shouts filled her ears. She sensed her captor's right arm lifted, muscles bunched and then knuckles slammed against her chin.

Everything instantly disappeared into swirling darkness as her consciousness snapped like a brittle twig.

Some kind of far distant pain slowly aroused her. She felt that in some strange way she clawed herself upward through darkness toward unknown sounds. Gradually she realized the pain was in her face and then localized it to her jaw, mouth and teeth. Her left ear felt as though some hard object had been jammed into it.

The sounds became louder, not a part of her but coming closer. Her full brain tried to encompass and understand it and then momentarily swept back into black silence again. But—and she never knew whether it was in a moment or an hour—the sounds gradually returned. This time they did not fade away but came nearer and grew louder.

She heard screams of agony made by both men and women. Guttural shouts fell like savage gibberish on her ears. She heard a constant crackling sound all about her and breathing became difficult. Wood burned somewhere close by.

Her eyes opened but she recognized only light—all else remained confused. But the screams and groans grew louder. She felt constricted, unable to move except for a slight roll from side to side. Then, as abruptly as darkness had fallen on her, full consciousness snapped back. Her sight focused and sharpened and she sucked in her breath with sheer fright and horror at what she saw.

Mary Tazey, just a year older than Abby, thrashed about on the ground close enough to be touched. But her eyes had turned into two bloody, burned holes and her head was bare of skin. Her long, golden hair had disappeared. Her dress had been ripped down to her waist but her full breasts had disappeared with her hair, her chest no more than a huge smear of blood.

Her mouth opened and scream after agonized scream beat at Abby's senses. Mary rolled over and her bloody body struck Abby with the blind force of a fallen, rolling log and the devil's face that once had been that of a beautiful woman sprayed a crimson coat over Abby's nose, eyes and face, blinding her.

Abby also screamed and tried to lift her hands to push the horror away. She couldn't so much as move an arm or a leg because of the tight bonds or thongs that held them against her body. Suddenly a muscular red arm appeared. Fingers taloned into Abby's shoulder just as a moccasined foot struck Mary Tazey's side, kicking her over and away. The girl jerked spasmodically, her body arched, then collapsed in upon itself and she lay still, the burned, sightless eye sockets holding Abby in paralyzed silence.

The painted, lean face of a young Indian filled her vision for a second and glittering eyes bored into hers. Abby saw high cheekbones, a mouth with red paint lifting from the lips over planed bronzed cheeks to the ears. Then the face moved out of her vision. But Abby had a stunned, vivid memory of it. She had seen it just before the blow to her jaw had whipped her off into darkness.

Flames shot out of windows and doors of the cabins and licked greedily at the roof shingles. The warrior crouched beside her yelled unintelligible, harsh words and she glimpsed more Indians racing between the buildings. Abby saw her own cabin aflame and also the prone form lying in the doorway. It had no hair on its head, but Abby knew the dress whose skirt moved slightly in the wind created by the flames. Just then the roof, a mass of fire, collapsed into the cabin.

Abby screamed. The Indian whipped about and his hard, open palm slammed against her cheek. But she didn't feel the blow. She had fainted.

When her eyes opened, she could again hear the crackle of flames but she heard no shouts or screams. She lay with one side of her face grinding in the grass and dirt. She heard men speaking in a language she could not understand, the words hardly more than garbled sounds and grunts. Then she heard a woman scream and she tried to get up. But someone slammed her head down again and a male voice spoke just above her. She sensed warning and at the same moment realized her hands had been thonged behind her back and her arms tied to her sides. But her feet and legs were free.

She fearfully moved her head a slight inch, just enough to lift her vision above the grass and leaves of the flower bed in which she lay. She saw only well worn, quilled moccasins and, above them, a pair of muscular, dark bronze ankles.

Again the voice called out from somewhere above her head and she heard shouted replies at a distance. Smoke was heavy in her nostrils and stung her eyes. She heard a cry in a voice that could only be Meg Warner's, who lived with her parents just four cabins away. It choked off and the harsh voice above her called again—and Abby sensed approval of some action of someone beyond her vision. Then a comparative silence except for a constant, low whispering movement.

Powerful fingers suddenly sank into each shoulder and she was jerked to her feet. She had only a dazed, whirling glimpse of fiery destruction, of sprawled, unmoving bodies and then a hard palm slammed between her shoulders, the force of the blow knocking her forward while she made automatic, stumbling efforts to keep her balance. Talons in her hair pulled her head back but restored her to balance.

Fierce, painted faces surrounded her and savage eyes flashed threat. Muscular, bare male bodies, shining with some sort of animal grease, pressed close. Then lips pulled back from teeth in wolfish smiles and she saw nostrils flare in desire.

Then she saw the women, a double-dozen of them perhaps, her friends and neighbors, mostly girls with here and there a young matron. Many of them stood naked to the waist and all bore the bruises of knuckles or hard palms. Their faces looked to be hardly more than masks of dirt and blood, hair all atangle. One bled from a knife slash the length of her cheek from chin to ear.

One cried out, "Abby! they murdered—"

A knife blade, already covered with blood, plunged into her back and she fell at Abby's feet. Abby's senses swirled once more and she felt herself falling straight forward onto her face. But something whipped about her waist and jerked her half around, knocking the wind out of her. But it acted as a counter-irritant to the faintness and by then she had been shoved beyond the still quivering body of the murdered girl.

Stumbling, often forced into a half run, constantly slapped or pummeled if she did not move fast enough or change directions swiftly, head down to watch her footing as best she could and her shoulders bowed to avoid the constant blows, Abby only dimly knew that the band of red raiders did not take to the trail Daniel, her father and the men had used earlier that morning. For a long time her dull brain held only that thought until, suddenly, she knew!

Her head snapped up but she could see only trees. She moved between two lines of painted warriors, some of whom wore only breechclouts of wide leather covering front and rear. Others wore skin trousers, caught by a band at the waist. These protected the legs and thighs from the whipping bushes.

But she could think only of her menfolk. What had happened to them? Then she saw the segments of bloody skin and long hair hanging from many of those belts. Horror widened her eyes. She could not believe her senses. This was a strange, living nightmare with all the sharp pain of reality.

Some distance ahead, a young buck stepped out to cuff a girl captive back into line. All Abby saw, however, was the powder horn hanging from a wide, tooled leather band crossing his back from one shoulder. That crescent and double star worked into it! Daniel's! Then she saw the thing loosely swinging back and forth from the other side of the man's belt. The hair was a light black and had once been made into a queue by the thin blue ribbon that still held it in place. Daniel's!

Her brain and senses could take no more shock and horror. This time, neither cuffing nor the sharp slaps that rocked her head could hold off the black curtain that snapped over and blocked out her senses.

She slowly, slowly awakened to a jolting, bouncing, torturing world. Her head hung down and she looked at heavily muscled legs and feet that rhythmically alternated forward and back. Her body bounced again and again on something hard and bony and a stout, muscular arm circled her waist while another held the thongs between her wrists. She was being carried!

As though her bearer had in some way read her dazed mind, movement halted and she was roughly swung off the shoulder and nearly slammed to the ground. She looked up at a face that had grown only too horribly familiar. There were the thin lips, the blazing eyes, the single line of stiff hair like a helmet plume atop the otherwise bald head and the two red lines slanting up from the corners of the lips to the ears.

He bent over her and grabbed the thong between her wrists, jerking her to her feet. He half turned her and she saw the double file of Indians, the stumbling, beaten girls between them.

"Go!" her captor said.

She stared. "You speak English!"

"Go!"

Once more came the hard push that sent her

stumbling ahead. She managed to catch her balance and she tried to turn. "You speak—"

His slap caught her squarely across the eyes and nose. She was blinded by tears from the blow, then she felt thick fluid flow from her nose over her lips. She tasted blood and, hands thonged behind her, there was no way she could staunch it. It flowed into her mouth and she managed, head bent, to spit it out before it strangled her. It continued to flow for what seemed to be an eternity of tortured, stumbling walk and a constant rain of blows. Then it miraculously stopped but her mouth and chin felt caked.

Bushes whipped at her, clawed at what remained of her dress and skirt but Abby hardly knew it. Instead of blows from fist or hand, she felt the cut of a whip across her back. She dully realized it was a switch cut or broken from the bushes.

She did not see the root and it probably would not have mattered if she had. Her foot slid under it and it smashed against her bare ankle. She toppled over and managed to partially twist about so that she struck the ground with her shoulder rather than her face. The impetus of her fall rolled her fully over onto her back.

She looked up into a strange Indian face, as fierce as the one she had constantly seen before. But the bronzed face held green and blue stripes along the cheeks, across the forehead and from the corner of the devil's eyes that glared at her. The man bent over her and she watched in dull, impersonal fascination as he lifted a feathered tomahawk to slam the blade into her skull. Abby didn't care.

Suddenly another bronzed hand came into her vision and she watched, as though in the slowest of motions, the red fingers encircle the wrist of the strange warrior. The tomahawk's descent was checked and her original captor appeared in her vision.

The second man looked up and twisted about, tried to free his wrist but could not. Harsh words crackled back and forth as both men crouched over her. The warrior with the crimson slashes spoke again, fast and harsh, commands in an unknown tongue that the second warrior answered with obvious protest. He pointed to her, swung his bare arm about in a sweeping gesture and again tried to free his weapon. But the other held on, slapped his chest with his fist and pointed down to Abby, and then slammed his fist once more against his chest.

Reluctantly, the second man slowly stood up, lowered the tomahawk and pushed its short handle through the belt about his waist. He spoke a few angry words, answered in kind, and he then strode away.

The warrior with the crimson warpaint looked down at her but Abby could read no mercy in his eyes. He roughly rolled her over on her face and his knee in the small of her back held her. She felt the thongs about her wrists loosened and then her hands and arms were free. But only for a moment for she was again rolled onto her back and her arms cruelly pulled forward. The thongs whipped about her wrists and the man swiftly slipped a second thong between them and lashed it tight. Then, using this further binding, he jerked her to her feet. His savage tug pulled her toward him but he wheeled about and Abby's arms were nearly pulled from their shoulder sockets. She screamed with the pain of it but the Indian did not bother to so much as look around. She cried out as he pulled her unmercifully behind him, but she might as well have asked for kindness from the silent trees and the cold wind that had sprung up.

III

The thick, never-ending arch of trees and leaves above the tangle of bushes, roots and grass hid the sky except for rare open glades where the sun could beam down unimpeded golden streams of light. Abby, concerned only with keeping alive and stumbling on to avoid the pain of the savage jerks of her arms, did not notice or care that very gradually clouds moved up from out of the mysterious west toward which her captives led her.

At last the clouds placed a thin gray veil across the whole of the sky, which darkened gradually as the wind increased. The captive girls and women barely knew what happened, even immediately around them, but the Indians began to look up between the boughs, judging the slow but certain change in the weather.

Abby's captor entered a long, narrow glade, stopped short and pointed upward. His fellow warriors, still keeping their bound captives between the double line, also stopped and studied the sky. The women had neither the strength nor the courage to lift their heads. The Indians grunted phrases and words back and forth, now and then pointing upward as the gray thickened and darkened, and clouds scudded almost due eastward.

The wind increased and became chilled. Abby's captor gave an order and the women were pushed, shoved and dragged to the far end of the open glade. Three warriors watched them while the others hurried to the wall of bushes and trees. Tomahawk blades flashed, limbs and bushes fell. Some high bushes and tall saplings were pulled in to form arches and stoutly thonged together, forming domes that the Indians covered with branches heavy with leaves. Small, rounded temporary shelters miraculously took shape.

Flint sparked on flint over small piles of dry grass and half a dozen little fires soon flickered along the glade. Some of the Indians had disappeared into the forest while others cut down the bushes. None of the girls were really aware of the activity nor, if they had been, would have known its meaning.

Abby's arm wrenched up and forward as the crimson-cheeked warrior jerked her toward one of the dome huts. An open space between two of the arched and tied boughs formed a doorway of sorts and the Indian jerked Abby through it, pointing to the ground. Abby dropped exhausted to the grass, senses reeling.

The Indian glared down at her and then, apparently satisfied that Abby would never move under her own power, he turned and went back through the break in the leafy wall. He tended the fire before the hut, building it up with old limbs that had long ago fallen from the trees. All around, other warriors appeared and soon each sat cross-legged before his own fire. They exchanged comments. One pointed back toward destroyed Westover and laughed; then, with a boasting air, held up three bloody scalps hanging from his belt. Then a long but muffled undulating cry brought all of them to their feet and they expectantly faced the woods as two warriors appeared carrying a slain deer lashed to a stout pole held across their shoulders.

With the easy, speedy efficiency of the wilds, the deer was soon skinned, cleaned and dressed, cut into portions that sizzled over the flames of the fires. The warriors ate greedily, completely forgetting their captives within the huts. Occasionally, while licking greasy fingers or gnawing on a bone, a warrior would look up to the sky, now almost black with scudding storm clouds.

The rain came first as a whisper deep in the trees and steadily approached the encampment. The whisper increased to a loud, sibilant noise and when it reached the camp, it fell on the flames that bowed and struggled for life, but soon flickered out in defeat. The warriors disappeared into the leafy huts, escaping the onslaught of the heavy spring storm.

Abby still lay where she had fallen, wrists thonged before her. Her brain had cleared just enough to register bruises and aches in every joint and over each inch of her body. She felt she would never be able to move again. She heard a peculiar whisper that she did not know was the rain striking the leafy roof and slowly beginning to find its way through. She sensed something or someone nearby and she opened her eyes to look at the quilled moccasins and muscular red-bronze ankles she had seen before.

Then fingers grabbed her hair and she was lifted to a sitting position with a long, cruel, pain-filled pull. She swayed but strong hands held her shoulders. She looked into the gleaming black eyes of her captor and dully noted the paint on his cheeks had started to dry and crack. But, sick thought of a battered mind, her awareness vanished instantly.

The man held out a hunk of grease dripping

meat to her. "Eat."

She turned her head, gagging, but steel fingers grabbed her jaws and pulled her head back around. "Eat."

"I don't want—"

His fingers entered her mouth, forced open her jaws and the half-cooked mess clogged her throat. She automatically tried to reject it but the fingers held the lump on her tongue and against the roof of her mouth. The fingers withdrew but before she could spit out the food his hand slammed against her jaw.

"Eat!"

To avoid further battering, her sore jaws moved and the meat juices streamed down her throat. She couldn't undestand why, after the first two swallows, that she continued to chew and eat. Her senses grew a trifle sharper and her eyes came in focus. The Indian now dropped to a cross-legged seat before her.

"Eat," he ordered. "Eat many more."

She choked down the mouthful but he had another ready to force between her lips. She could only helplessly chew and swallow as she fearfully studied him. She slowly realized he had more than a streaked crimson painted face and that his naked shoulders were wide and his upper arms, one circled by a metal band of copper, were muscular and supple. A broad strap of animal skin crossed his deep chest, supporting a sheathed knife and powder horn. She saw the blade and blunt head of a tomahawk in a beaded belt circling his flat waist.

She found her voice but feared for many minutes to use it. Finally she took the risk. "You speak English?"

"I speak," he nodded. "Many time trade at post on big river."

"Big river?"

He answered with an Indian word that meant nothing to her. She risked his anger again. "Who are you?"

His fist thumped proudly against his chest and his chin arrogantly lifted. "Corn Dancer, me. Me Pine Tree Sachem someday soon." She knew his sweeping hand indicated whatever was beyond the walls pressing so close about her. "Lead little war band this time. Bigger next if Mother like—I big warrior." He struck his chest again. "Corn Dancer *orenda* strong . . . big . . . strong. Mother know soon. *Owachira* know."

"*Owachira?* Mother?"

He made a disgusted sound, glared and abruptly slapped her down onto the ground. She fearfully looked at the figure towering above her. He suddenly pulled his knife from the sheath at his belt and she saw the evil, dark stains on the blade that could only be blood. He bent over her, knife close to her face and she tried to shrink away. He grabbed the collar of her dress and the knife blade flashed. She closed her eyes in sheer terror, felt the knife against the base of her throat. The blade turned and suddenly ripped the whole front of her dress. He pulled the cloth back over her shoulders on

37

either side and down her arms.

Her breasts lay exposed. She tried to lift her hands to cover them but, with a growl and harsh word, he jerked them away. She could only submit to his slow examination and felt the blush rise to her cheeks and face. His close and critical gaze moved from her breasts to her waist.

"No!" The thought came unbidden to her numbed brain. "Not you—Daniel!"

His fingers touched her bare stomach and she knew that in a moment her skirt would be ripped away and she would lie fully exposed before him. A screaming "NO!" wrenched out of her throat and she squeezed her eyes tightly shut in horror, her whole body tense against the onslaught that would come any second.

Instead, she felt and heard him move, stand up. She held her breath. He would be untying his girdle, dropping his animal skin trousers. She knew it and her body grew even more stiff and wooden. Nothing happened. He did not move. She could hold her breath no longer and had to expel it in loud gusts. Her eyes opened despite her will. He stood over her but the knife was no longer in his hand but back in its scabbard.

"You fine . . ." He groped for the word, shrugged and said it in his own language. She knew he meant either "woman" or "squaw." To her stunned surprise he stepped back and dropped to his cross-legged seat and considered her across the short distance between them. Abby knew his attack had only been deferred but he made no move to prevent her from covering her breasts with her crossed arms.

He tried again. "You fine . . . " but once more failed to find the English word.

Abby moistened her dry lips and, as though the word had the deadly hypnotic fascination attributed to a poisonous snake's charm, she said "Squaw?"

His face lighted as he grunted assent. "Squaw. I hear that at trade post. Squaw."

They sat in silence, staring at one another. But his glittering eyes moved over her from the crown of her head to her moccasined feet protruding below her linsey-woolsey, rumpled, muddy skirt. She fearfully tried to guess his thoughts but could not. But she knew beyond doubt that in a matter of minutes she would be raped. It was the Indian way. Then afterwards? Her sickening thoughts veered away. Searchers from Westover might find her body before the wolves but . . .

His movement broke her thoughts. He thumped his fist against his chest. "Me Corn Dancer." He pointed a long finger at her. "You?"

"I—I'm Abby."

"Abby?" He pronounced the name as though it had three b's and half a dozen e's.

"Abby," she nodded. "Me." Her loud, crying plea wrenched from her throat. "Take me back. Please! Corn Dancer! Back. Oh, in the name of God, please!"

He stared blankly at her and, in despair, she knew he might have understood his own name.

But no more. Sobs shook and strangled her and she bent over, pulling up her knees and resting her head on them.

"Abbbeee?"

Her head lifted and she choked back more sobs, scouring her fingers across her eyes. "Yes, Corn Dancer?"

"Me Corn Dancer." His fist struck his chest in the familiar gesture and once more his finger pointed at her. "You Abbbeee. You Corn Dancer squaw. You come me." He swung his arm about, turning partially with it so that he indicated the west. "Over Big River. You . . . me. Mother see you. Shaman see you. They say you *orenda*—" He broke off, lost for another English word, then his face brightened. "They say you good *orenda,* you stay Corn Dancer squaw. You be Onondaga. Long time stay Corn Dancer. You be *owachira* squaw, yes."

He stood up then and stepped to her. But only to check her wrist thongs and then pull her knife-slashed dress over her shoulders. She understood and the lump rose in her throat. Her old life lay burned back of her in the ashes of Westover. She broke into a loud crying and Corn Dancer simply watched and listened to her. The rain came down harder and now a stream of water penetrated the leafy dome of the hut and poured down the far wall.

Corn Dancer turned his head to look at the thin stream as dispassionately as he had Abby's tears.

IV

The storm that swept over the forest and the miserable leaf huts continued eastward, finally out across the Atlantic Ocean, hurried on by the black clouds that pushed out of the west behind it. It gathered strength and wind and, as night fell, howled out over the high-breaking waves and rough seas as it turned slightly north.

Hundreds of miles out, it struck the bare masts and furled sails of the *Demoiselle de la Gironde* and the waves snarled and roared at the hull of the French merchant ship. The stubby craft lifted to the crest of the waves and then, almost standing on end, plunged into the troughs. Masts swayed from side to side and at times threatened to pull right out of the caulked oaken deck. But they held and so did the high castle at the stern of the vessel, though it creaked and groaned, as did all of the ship. The steersman gripped the wheel, his face astream with the whipping rain, his clothing soaked through to his cold skin. Above the beat of the rain, the howl of the wind and the creaking of the vessel, he listened for a lesser but more ominous sound that would signal shift of the full cargo in the hold. Not daring to release the wheel for a second, he mentally crossed himself and prayed they would raise Cape Breton instead of plunging into the ocean depths on the way to hell.

Below the deck, Edouard de Fournet gripped the rails of his bunk, bracing to the roll of the ship and wondering if he had escaped the royal executioner or life incarceration only to be drowned somewhere in this damnable ocean. He ripped out a Gascon oath when he heard the roll of the metal wine tankard across the floor of the boxlike cabin. Why in the name of a thousand devils couldn't the thing jam itself in a corner or under a bunk or settle!

Lightning flashed outside across the thick, rain-streaked glass of a small porthole. Why in the name of many more thousands of devils did this storm have to blow up when just this morning the captain had said they would sight New France on the morrow? Morrow, as Edouard felt certain now, would never come—or at least *he* would never see it. Well, perhaps the fishes would find him a tender morsel.

His aching fingers took a stronger grip on the bunk rails as the ship made a steep pitch, bow down . . . and down . . . and down. *Dieu!* was this the final—?

His breath eased out as the ship lifted and then slowly began a terrifying dip to the stern. His feet came level with his eyes and then moved higher and higher above his head. Lightning flashed again and he had a brief glimpse of the lamp above the bolted-down table swing far out on its chains. Suddenly the tankard made a clattering roll across the floor and slammed against the far wall—bulkhead, he corrected himself and then didn't give a damn what sailors called walls or anything else.

Now the stern began to rise and the bow to dip. How long would this infernal threat to plunge to the bottom, either head or feet first, continue! Thank *le bon Dieu* he had somewhat gained his sealegs soon after they had sailed from Bordeaux and had weathered two storms before this third, the greatest of them all, had struck. Was this some indication or omen of what his life would be in New France—if he ever managed to land there?

He suddenly became aware that the howl and shriek of the wind had lessened, though nothing within the cabin became stable or held to an even keel. Rain still angrily drummed on the deck outside, though no longer in the steady drumroll of the preceding dark hours. Now it came in slamming, gusting blows and whispers. Over soon? Edouard could not believe it but clung to the bunk rails with each pitch. But they, too, were not as steep and came less often. This simply must be what the sailors called "the eye of the storm," that false calm within the very heart of all wind, rain and waves. Oh, it would start again! He'd wait before he ventured from the relative safety of the bunk.

Waiting, he fell asleep as the ship's tossing became more like a soothing rocking.

Something awakened him. His eyes snapped open and his right hand made an automatic whip across his body, fingers reaching for his sword hilt. Then his mind snapped fully awake. He still lay in his bunk and realized that calm had come to the restless ocean. The cabin door stood open and he could look out on a sunny deck and watch half a dozen sailors holystone the planks. He saw the shadows of the great sails move with the gentle sway of the vessel.

"Bon matin, Milord."

Edouard's head turned and his cabin steward smiled, touched a finger to his knitted cap. The table with its rail that kept metal plates, tumblers and utensils from rolling off onto the deck even held the blasted tankard that had rolled cease-lessly about all night.

"Hot rum, *Milord,* as *l'Anglais* have it? Or perhaps a mulled wine—maybe cognac?"

Edouard blinked his surprise and swung his long legs out of the bunk. "A *soupçon* of cognac now to warm my bones and then a bath. What time is it?"

"The sun's three hours up, *Milord.*"

"Get the bucket. I'll meet you on the deck."

"*Et pour le déjeuner?*"

"Later, *mon ami.* We'll decide later."

"*Eh, bien.*"

Edouard dropped to the deck, crossed to the heavy chest that held his worldly possessions. He used a heavy brass key to turn the lock and lift the lid. Then, as the steward left the cabin, Edouard stripped off his rumpled clothing that he had worn should the storm have created an emergency. He raced stark naked out onto the deck and heard the captain's laugh and greeting from the quarterdeck above.

"After last night, Sieur de Fournet, we can consider you a sailor, eh?"

"After last night, *mon Capitaine,* I want to see no more ships—not even a rowboat on the Gironde."

The captain's left brow lifted to a high, black arch and a peculiar expression came over his face. He looked down at Edouard but it seemed almost as if he searched deep into Edouard's body or brain.

"Is something wrong, *Capitaine?*"

The man shook his head as though releasing himself from some invisible grip. He studied Edouard but this time in a strange manner of curiosity. "Far back, *mon Sieur,* my family were Albigensians."

"And they evaded the Inquisition long enough to start a line of descendants? A miracle!"

The captain's smile was uneasy. "So it might be said. But it is also said that the gift of foresight has descended, somewhat watered down, to my generation. It came just then as you spoke."

Edouard stepped further out on deck so that he could fully see the man above him. The captain no longer leaned on the rail but he still eyed Edouard, who demanded, "And what did it say?"

"That you would see many ships and many waters, *mon Sieur* . . . that your children, their children and *their* children will live in ships, boats, on oceans, lakes and rivers. It came like a clear flash."

"Sun in your eyes, *mon Capitaine,* or in your brain," Edouard laughed and turned to the sailor holding the wooden bucket of water. *"Eh bien, commencez."* His laughter choked off as the cold water splashed over him and he gasped, *"Mon Dieu!"*

A second bucket again took his breath and he raced back into the cabin, snatching a thick towel from a chest by the door. Vigorous rubbing and towelling brought warmth and the flush of blood to his skin, and then the steward handed him a steaming mug of coffee that nearly burned his tongue as he tried to gulp it down. The steward finished drying him and Edouard hastened to don his clothing.

Then, fully dressed from buckled slippers to open throat cambric shirt and knee length, heavy trousers, he sat to the table and the food the steward placed before him. Now there was only the normal roll and pitch of a ship sailing over a calm sea. The morning ritual of bath, dress and breakfast had been finished once more.

Edouard dropped back in his chair and stared moodily through the doorway out onto the busy deck where sailors constantly handled the thick ropes adjusting the sails to the order of the captain's raucous voice coming from the quarter-deck above. How many more morning rituals? Edouard wondered. How long before New France? And would he be safe even there from the jealous vengeance of that old goat, the Duc de la Verre? Edouard's long lips curled disgustedly when he recalled what Elenie had told him of the old man's different ways of arousing his fading sexual ardor.

Edouard's dark brow arched high once more as vivid memory brought Elenie to disturbing life. Petite, the crown of her golden-yellow head just the right height for his lips to touch before they nibbled gently at her ear or made delightful tracery down the delightfully short length of her nose. And her lips—*ma foi!* Her breasts—small like the rest of her proportions—spheres that fitted so excitedly perfect in his cupped hands. And when he bent his head to nuzzle the outstanding pink nipples, she would always hold him tightly and move his hand down to her stomach and the golden triangle of hair that formed a tangled, wiry bush between her legs.

Elenie! Would to God he had her with him— in this very cabin. No . . . over there in the bunk, twisting and arching to meet his thrusts, long fingernails biting into his shoulders, gasps and moans issuing from her lips when they weren't crushed against his, tongue darting in and out to the rhythm of her body.

His thoughts grew too vivid and he abruptly left the table and strode out onto the deck. Sailors' fingers touched their forelocks to him but Edouard hardly noticed. His restless glance swept the horizon. There was nothing but ocean and a clear sky if he peered up between the huge canvas wings of the sails that blocked the direct strike of the sun's rays.

He walked in long strides to the bow, climbed to the restricted deck that the sailors used and stood looking west and north, futilely straining his eyes for a landfall. There was not so much as a gull.

He clasped the rail, leaned slightly forward, still looking out over heaving water and small, chopping waves. But his thoughts remained back in Gascony and the Chateau de la Verre. What would Elenie be doing now? This minute? He hastily turned his thoughts to a question of more moment to his own well-being and health. What had the ancient duke with the scrawny, wattled neck of an ancient rooster done?

That question brought up Edouard's present position aboard this lumbering merchantman out of Bordeaux. He had no doubt he was lucky to be here instead of in a royal jail in Marseilles or Paris, or in a grave somewhere in Bearn minus his head. Edouard had always prided himself that his long, supple-bladed duelling sword or his brace of pistols in their velvet case could always get him out of danger. But not this time.

When he had met Elenie at the Vicomte d'Oleans' *bal masqué* and had immediately plunged into a mad love affair, he had neither brains nor time to realize that dukes related to the royal family would no more consider meeting a person of minor title on the field of honor than he would meeting the serf who tended his estate's pigs. Dukes did not bestir themselves, no matter how their honor was clouded, to face a young fool who bore only the "de" of a knight or lowly baronet. They had other, more efficient and less strenuous means.

Edouard had, mistake of mistakes, forgotten the *lettre de cachet,* the blank arrest warrant that so well served nobles of high rank. These were arrest forms bearing the king's signature and seal, needing only the name of the culprit to be added. That would send the enemy to prison, the galleys, guillotine or prison. That had been *le duc's* way for Edouard. Praise God, Elenie's seamstress had heard the whisper from her own lover and warned them.

Edouard left the Chateau de la Verre immediately and without ceremony. Elenie, confident the old rooster lusted too much for her, refused to flee with him. *Le Duc* would not harm a single golden hair of his *chére amie* and mistress. Now there, Edouard thought sourly as he gazed unseeing out over the rail, was a lesson in fidelity almost too dearly learned.

A *lettre de cachet* being the king's own order to arrest, the royal soldiers would move very, very fast. So Edouard had kicked up the dust of the many leagues from the chateau to Bordeaux, since he was certain the royal minions would believe he'd flee for the nearest escape port, Marseilles. He had a purse filled with *louis d'or* thanks to *le Duc's* poor whist during the month and more Edouard had been at the chateau, and those golden coins smoothed the way, paid for two or three hours snatched each night at a hostel, traded a jaded mount for a fresh one and finally placed him aboard the *Demoiselle de la Gironde* just moments before she cast off and sailed away from the Bordeaux dock.

Captain Jouvier had immediate questions for this passenger who had come aboard so hastily but the golden coins silenced them. Besides, the expanse of water between ship and dock widened by the moment. They had cleared the port and the breakwater without a glimpse of hard-riding, royal cavalry.

Only that night at dinner at the captain's lonely table did Edouard give any consideration to more than the immediate moment. "Where do we sail?"

"Would you like a French port, *mon Sieur?*" the captain asked and grinned crookedly, continuing dryly at Edouard's startled reaction. "I see you would not. Chance, I think, placed you aboard the right craft. Our port of call is Quebec in New France. We will also call at Montreal. We will then be far from the ocean, you understand. Those towns along the St. Lawrence River can be profitable. We supply their needs in exchange for furs and pelts that come from somewhere west of north. We scratch one another's backs, *vous comprenez?*"

But they had not sailed on a direct course. As Jouvier explained and Edouard knew, there had been almost a half century of war between France and England, so the *Demoiselle de la Gironde* had pointed her bow directly west to keep as far as possible from the English Islands and a chance British man-of-war. Once far to the west and south of England, Jouvier sharply changed the course, turning northwestward. They had to chance crossing the well-traveled sea lanes between England and her colonies, but the odds then lay with Captain Jouvier.

After a time Edouard tired of the empty sea and worked his way across the busy deck, avoiding the seamen who constantly climbed up or down the rigging as they manned the sails to the shouted orders of the captain or mates, but he had no more than climbed to the quarterdeck to join the captain and the steersman handling the huge wheel than a shout came from the crow's nest on the mainmast.

"Sail ho! Four points east by north off stern."

Edouard wheeled around with Jouvier, whose telescope was already to his eye. Edouard stood tense, searching the ocean, seeing nothing until at long last a faint movement on the horizon indicated the sails of one or more ships.

"What flag is flying?" Edouard asked.

"I cannot yet tell, *mon Sieur*. *Prie Dieu* they are not English or I have lost my ship."

Edouard breathed to himself, "*Prie Dieu* they are not French or I've lost my liberty and my life."

V

Jouvier remained, back to Edouard, eye glued to the long telescope. He called up to the nest on the mainmast. "Can you see her colors?"

"*Non,* but she comes on fast. Perhaps man-of-war or, from her look, pirate or privateer."

Jouvier snapped the telescope into its folds. "To your cabin, *mon Sieur,* and stay there."

"To my cabin! But—" Edouard sputtered and waved his arm toward the speck on the horizon. "That ship—British or pirate we fight."

"We run, *mon Sieur.* We clap on sail and hope we can show our heels. We have only two small guns, no match for a fighting ship. So, to your cabin, *s'il vous plaît.* My men need all this deck for themselves and coiled lines. They will be up and down the rigging, everywhere. You will only be in the way."

"But—"

Jouvier's patience broke. "To your cabin! That is an order. If you want to fight that craft with your sword and pistols, go overboard and swim to meet her. I give you a minute to decide to fight her yourself or move out of our way."

Edouard's face suffused. He had never been ordered about like this by a *bourgeois* such as Jouvier. Then his reason returned and he clapped a lid on his foolish, prideful anger. The captain was right and his word as much law as the king's own aboard this craft.

"*Vous avez raison. Excusez moi.*"

"*Oui,*" Jouvier grunted and shouted an order that sent men racing up the rigging.

Edouard entered his cabin, darted across it to the passenger dining room. On this second deck of the superstructure, the windows towered outward high above the water line. He could not see the far distant ship that had so alarmed them all, but he felt the surge of the *Demoiselle* as sail must have piled on.

He returned to his cabin, checked the flints in his pistols, hefted his powder horn. Its weight told him it was full. He opened a heavy leather bag, poured shot into the pockets of his jacket and dropped it back onto the settle. He bowed the slender blade of his sword and released it, reassured by the high, vibrating sing of the steel. That done, he could only look out on the deck and await the outcome of the race.

Men swarmed everywhere, coiling ropes, jumping into the rigging to disappear somewhere above his line of vision. But Jouvier's bellowed commands sounded like trumpet calls. Edouard wished he could see the distant ships but another visit to the dining room, for all his peering through one large window after another, proved futile. Back in his cabin, aware of the frantic activity on the deck, the increased speed of the *Demoiselle* and Jouvier's right to demand implicit obedience, he no more than pushed his head out the door. That proved to be even more futile than the windows he had just left.

So he returned to his bench at the table. All sails set and trimmed, the *Demoiselle* took the wind in her teeth and Edouard could envision the pluming waves to either side of the bow as the ship sped ahead. He simply could not sit and do nothing, so he paced for a time and then returned to the table and once more checked his pistols and the temper of his sword blade. His head lifted and he twisted fully about to face the cabin door and the deck beyond when a voice came from high on the mainmast.

"Captaine! Two ships. They gain on us.''

''What ensign, you dolts!''

''Can't see yet . . . Wait . . . *mon Capitaine,* the Lilies! They are French royal men-of-war! *French,* praise God!''

''Certain?''

"Oui. Oui!"

Edouard started to sigh with relief but it died in his throat. The *lettre de cachet!* He could be made a prisoner in the middle of the Atlantic as well as in Marseilles, Toulouse or Paris. The power of Louis XV extended wherever French authority existed. He had jumped to his feet but, with the thought, he dropped back on the bench. If the captain of either of these two royal warships knew of the *lettre* or of Edouard de Fournet, he would be in irons below decks as quickly as the sailors of the warships could transfer him from the *Demoiselle.*

Jouvier's shouted commands broke Edouard's grim thoughts. At the same moment, the shadows of sails shifted on the deck outside and the *Demoiselle's* speed fell off. They were coming about or lying to! Edouard swept the small cabin with a swift turn of his head. Nowhere to hide—nowhere to flee. He choked down panic and, as the activity on the deck slackened, he ventured out.

''Eh, *mon Sieur,''* Jouvier called and smiled broadly down from the rail above. ''We had fear for nothing.'' He indicated the stern. ''They are the King's ships of the line. They are protectors, not foes.''

56

Edouard climbed to the quarterdeck as the sails were trimmed. He saw the two ships quite plainly now and realized that, no matter what their nationality, the *Demoiselle* could never win a race with them. A puff of white smoke appeared beside one and then Edouard saw the splash of a shot across the *Demoiselle's* bow and he heard the distant dull thud of the cannon.

On Jouvier's snapped orders, the helmsman brought the *Demoiselle* around even as the last of her sails were furled. A seaman hurried to the stern and soon the French royal Lilies snapped into the breeze above the red and blue house flag of the merchant owners of the *Demoiselle*. Now Edouard could plainly define the figureheads on the fast approaching ships.

"Mon Capitaine," he started, but Jouvier's impatient gesture silenced him.

"A moment, eh? We must prepare to receive at least one inspection party and its officer."

The men-of-war, sails full of the wind, came on much too swiftly, looming larger and larger by the moment and more and more threatening and full of doom.

He could see the black maw of each cannon projecting through its port and he had the insane thought that all of them had been aimed directly at him. The utterly ludicrous idea brought him to his senses and his panic vanished. Edouard de Fournet did not have the importance—except to the half-senile old Duke—to stir up the whole realm merely because a *lettre de cachet* demanded his arrest.

But as the warships came up on either side of the *Demoiselle* and he heard shrill whistles blowing the commands of the petty officers to the men in the rigging, his confidence diminished. Now the two ships, spars almost bare, bobbed in cannon range. A heavy boat swung out from one, was lowered to the ocean with its officers, oarsmen and armed sailors. Oar blades flashed rhythmically in the sun as the boat swiftly narrowed the distance to the *Demoiselle*.

Edouard moved to leave the quarterdeck and the captain to return to his cabin. But with the first step, he knew that boldness alone would serve. That, of course, gambled that the junior officer approaching or even the captains of the menacing huge crafts to either side would know nothing of Edouard de Fournet or the Duc de Verre.

So he waited for Jouvier and then followed the captain down to the main deck to receive the boarding party. The officer proved to be an ensign, younger than Edouard, somewhat downy-faced but quite obviously filled with the importance of his rank and his duty. He came over the rail and onto the deck, thrust out his chin and swung his sword to the proper angle at his side, pulled himself to full height and arrogantly eyed Jouvier and Edouard. At their salutes, some of the stiffness left the ensign's shoulders and he returned the courtesy.

"I am Ensign de Launy, *Capitaine.*" He gestured over the rail to the warship looming against the sky like a huge storm cloud. "His

Majesty's ship, *Orleans,* and I am on official, royal business.''

''Welcome aboard, Sieur de Launy,'' Jouvier answered and the young officer's slight smile revealed his pleasure at the personal rather than official address. ''This is my passenger, Sieur de Fournet.''

The ensign gave Edouard a sharp, sweeping glance, curtly bobbed his head and turned back to Jouvier. ''Your home port, *Capitaine?* and whither bound?''

''Bordeaux, *mon Sieur,* and bound for Quebec in New France.''

The armed sailors now had all come up over the rail. De Launy's swift, sharp eyes made certain that each stood at stiff attention. He turned directly to Edouard. ''What is your business in New France, *Sieur* de Fournet?''

Edouard managed to overcome a slight quiver in his voice. ''I am recently *Capitaine* of the Royal Regiment of Bearn, Ensign.'' The young officer's expression subtly changed to one of momentary respect.

''You do have identification, *Capitaine?*''

''Of course. In my cabin.''

Jouvier gestured up to the quarterdeck. ''And my registry and bills of lading are in my cabin, where I also have some excellent wine, if it pleases you.''

De Launy did not make a direct acceptance but bobbed his head toward his marines who had come aboard with him. ''My men would appreciate a round, *Capitaine.* I shall be in your cabin shortly. But first—"

Edouard smiled thinly, stepped aside and gestured toward his cabin. "If it pleases you, Ensign."

"*Après vous,*" De Launy answered, eyes sharp.

Edouard led the way into his cabin, gestured de Launy to a seat at his table. He then bent to his bunk and tugged out his small traveling chest. In a moment de Launy scowled importantly at Edouard's commission and his father's written attestation of Edouard's birth and lineage. His face finally cleared up and he swept up the papers, and extended them to Edouard.

"Gascon, eh?" He smiled at Edouard's nod. "One of our national fire-eaters. *Dieu!* but France needs more like you in the royal armies. Have you resigned your commission, *mon Sieur*? Do you make this voyage on official business?"

"I have not resigned as yet. And I travel more on family business, *mon Sieur*. There are certain interests in the fur trade out of Quebec, *comprenez vous?*"

De Launy made an easy, dismissing sign. "I understand." He sobered. "It might be best, *mon Sieur*, if you made your stay in New France brief. There are hints in Paris that we again will be at England's throat before long."

"Another war! How long must we wait for peace again. It has now been almost a century."

De Launy sighed. "I suppose until the Hanover kings of England stop muddying the waters of Europe. If they would only forget they're German and try to be English and stay on their little island!'' He returned to the official questioning but now suspicion had left his voice and he sounded almost bored. ''You will present yourself to the Royal Governor in Quebec?''

''But of course, *mon Sieur*! It is formal, a required courtesy.''

''And Quebec so small a settlement, I understand, that a stranger would be immediately noticed.''

''You have not been there, *mon Sieur*?''

De Launy flushed and answered with a touch of gruffness. ''I am but a year out of the naval school, *mon Sieur*, serving in the *Mediterranée*.''

''Then we both see New France for the first time. A pity it cannot be together.''

''Indeed. The *Orleans* is first bound for Martinique.'' De Launy shrugged and reluctantly rose. ''I suppose I must sample the captain's wine.''

''You'll find it is not bad, *mon Sieur*. Be assured the crew does not get nearly as good.''

''That helps.'' De Launy bowed. ''I hope to see you on deck when I leave, *mon Sieur*.''

''*Merci*. I will be there.''

In less than half an hour Edouard and Jouvier leaned on the rail watching the longboat of the man-of-war pull away from the *Demoiselle*. As the crew across the water attached davits, Jouvier pushed up from the rail.

''That is over, thanks to God! No matter how clean the cargo or correct the papers, an inspection like this makes me feel all my nerves. Join me at wine to soothe my mind?''

Edouard watched as the long boat was pulled to the deck of the distant warship and swung inward. He thought of the *lettre de cachet* and wondered what would have happened had Ensign de Launy known of it.

"When will the next ships that carry royal dispatches and orders sail for New France?"

Jouvier, puzzled, turned to look at him then shrugged, "Who is to know? A packet could carry important and immediate orders and news. It could sail at any time—a few days, a week, a month. A man-of-war? Well, not likely for some time since those two are in these waters."

"A packet. I had not thought—" Edouard broke off, realizing he could easily say too much. He clapped Jouvier on the shoulder. "I'll drink of your wine to the end of our visit of royalty."

"But he was only an ensign—"

"The ships?"

"Ah, *oui,* and we're well rid of them."

VI

For two days after the heavy rainstorm had passed, the war party moved steadily westward. Had anyone survived the raid on Westover and could see Abby Brewster, she would never have been recognized. The clothing she had worn in the stockade village had deteriorated into hardly more than fluttering rags and she had long since stopped trying to conceal her partial nakedness. Not only was it futile but Corn Dancer led at such a pace that neither he nor his warriors thought of her as more than one of many prisoners they battered, jerked and pushed along.

Three more women had paid the final penalty for weakness, stumbling and constantly falling. Their bodies lay back along the trail, probably already prey to the forest animals. For long periods, as Abby staggered along at the end of the thong Corn Dancer held, she thought the dead women were lucky. Certainly further torture and fear could not touch them. But despite the thought some inner, barely smoldering core kept Abby moving, stumbling, catching herself and moving on. Life had been reduced to only the effort to place one foot ahead of the other, to keep some sort of balance no matter how much or often she swayed.

The days and nights became a horrid blur of sunlight, darkness, rain now and then, more sunshine and then darkness once more; an endless repetition of a meaningless round of sensations. She fell to the grass when Corn Dancer called a halt. She came to her feet when the thongs jerked her wrists. Now and then her vision cleared and she saw Corn Dancer's stalwart from just ahead or she caught his sharp appraisal from dark, narrowed eyes. Even if her wits had been clear, she could not have read the expression on his immobile face. But she did realize that quite often he spooned some sort of meat into her mouth as they sat before an open fire that had appeared from out of some unknown place in her brain's raggled awareness. Now and then he would place his cupped hands to her lips and she would swallow a few drops of precious water. When there was need, he would lead her out of the line and impassively watch her relieve herself or he would take care of his own needs. She had neither the strength nor wits to protest or feel any reaction but a hard determination to keep drawing breath and stumble on.

Suddenly even her dull mind registered that the seemingly eternal forest had an end. Without warning the war party broke out of the trees and Abby blinked against harsh, golden bright sunlight. She stood swaying, closing her eyes against the new torture of light. She heard the guttural conversation of the Indians about her, vaguely sensing that they no longer spoke in the swift staccato of flight and tension. She felt a tug on her bonds and then a heavy hand fell on her shoulder. She forced open her eyes, now like a pair of slits but, even so, the sun stabbed like knives into them. She saw a peculiar dancing and rippling light about her, especially when she looked down to avoid the direct blow of sunshine.

Corn Dancer spoke at her shoulder. "Big River we come now. We go other side. Safe then." He spoke her name, again with all the B's and E's, and she turned her head toward him, forced her eyes to open a trifle wider. His face came in focus. Somewhere, sometime, he had removed the old slashes of crimson paint on his cheeks and replaced them with new bars. He pointed and she turned to see that the party stood on the bank of the widest river she had ever seen.

She stared dully, swaying slightly. Corn Dancer's hand steadied her. "Abbbeee, you strong. Fine woman. Good squaw, You *good.*"

She dully thought his accent on the last word must mean some sort of compliment, though for what she didn't know—or care. She heard other noises as the rest of the war party and its remaining captives came up. Some of the Indians headed directly to what seemed to be a wall of bushes. But they clawed them aside and soon reappeared, two warriors to each of the five long canoes that had been hidden behind the foliage. Corn Dancer and two companions walked to the bank and searched the river as far as they could see both north and south. At last Corn Dancer issued guttural orders, motioning toward the captives.

The captive women stumbled under harsh prodding to the craft and each of them had to be lifted and placed in a prone position below the narrow, thick boards that served as seats. The warriors took their places, picking up paddles and, one by one, the frail birchbark crafts were pushed out into the current.

Abby sank to the ground at Corn Dancer's feet. He merely glanced at her and then out to the river where the first canoe sped across the stream at an angle determined by the current. It made the trip alone, bronze powerful arms and muscular backs made the paddle blades flash in a constant rhythm. The rest of the party remained on the bank, the warriors still watching the river in both directions. Abby could only see the paddlers, the captive women out of sight below the gunwales.

When the craft made the far bank and was dragged ashore, the captives were hauled out. They and the canoe were swiftly carried to concealment amidst the brush and trees over there. Only then did Corn Dancer signal the second canoe, already loaded, to launch.

So, one by one, four of the birchbarks made the crossing. There remained only Corn Dancer, Abby, another woman and Corn Dancer's remaining warrior. He bent to Abby; but instead of jerking her upright, he placed his hands under her arms and lifted her to her feet. Then he held her as she weaved across the gravelly bank and managed in some tortured manner to step into the canoe and sink to the floor. Corn Dancer pushed her prone, the crown of her head against the soles of the the other girl's blistered, scratched and bleeding feet.

Corn Dancer took his place on the seat in the bow and Abby could see him above the tips of her worn moccasins. His back muscles rippled as he lifted the paddle, looked over his shoulder to the man in the stern. His teeth flashed in a wide triumphant grin and he spoke a few words with a laugh that sounded like proud, brief praise.

Then the canoe suddenly moved and Abby saw Corn Dancer's paddle swing and his shoulder and arm muscles bunch as the current caught the canoe and he directed it across the water. They had progressed but a few yards when suddenly Corn Dancer spoke urgently, pointing northward.

The unseen man in the rear answered and instantly the speed of the canoe lessened. Corn Dancer spoke in harsh haste and received an answer. Corn Dancer then let his shoulders slump and his paddle moved with slow, easy strokes. Abby felt the canoe's speed lessen. Corn Dancer spoke without turning his head.

"Abbbeee, hide. Down! . . . hide. They find . . . you dead." His hand went to his knife scabbard at his belt and now he turned, threw her a look filled with scowling threat. She managed to nod that she understood.

"Tell other squaw. Now!"

Abby passed the warning and a voice helpless with bone-weariness answered, "I understand, Abby."

She tried to place the voice, familiar and yet unknown. But she knew the speaker was someone in the cabins that had stood near her own. Then Corn Dancer's sudden hiss of warning brought her attention fully on him. He lifted an arm high in a signal to someone that the high birchbark walls of the canoe hid from her.

"How!" Corn Dancer called.

"Hey, Redskin! Ain't you kinda far from home?"

"Me hunt. Me trade."

"On the east bank of the Hudson? I never knew you Injuns went clean over there."

Abby wanted to lift herself into sight and scream for help, but she knew Corn Dancer would instantly plunge his knife in her chest. And also the girl whose feet she touched would instantly die. She forced herself to lie rigid and silent, her mind screaming silently that she'd have later and better chances to escape.

"Good trade," Corn Dancer answered the question. His paddle lay across the canoe thwarts as he sat seemingly unconcerned.

Now the other voice seemed to recede and Abby knew the river's current swept it on downstream and away. "You Injuns gonna fight for us or them Frenchies?"

"Fight?"

"Warpath, Redskin—for us or the French?"

"No warpath us now. If so—maybe you."

"Better be, Injun."

Then Abby heard only the constant slap of water against the canoe. Corn Dancer remained slumped on his seat but his head slowly turned so that Abby knew the other craft had swept on by to the south. She dully thought, "So it's the Hudson. We're in New York Colony. Where do we go?"

Corn Dancer suddenly lifted his arm high and waved his paddle. Then he straightened and once again bent to a swift rowing rhythm that sent the canoe skimming across the water. He spoke over his shoulder to his companion, who answered with a series of short grunts.

She heard a scraping sound along the bottom of the craft. Corn Dancer jumped out and Abby felt the canoe tugged into shallow water and then onto gravelly sand. Motion stopped and Corn Dancer appeared again. He bent to lift her to a sitting position.

As she had guessed, they had come ashore on the west bank of the mighty river. Mountains loomed high just beyond the forest that recommenced many yards back from the river bank. Corn Dancer leaned close, the lines of his face hard and grim. His eyes glittered as they bored into hers.

"Abbbeee, now maybe you walk good? But me close." He whipped out his knife and placed the blade to the thong that bound one of her wrists to the other. "Me close. You no . . . run, eh?"

She understood and nodded. The blade slashed through the thong and her arms fell free to her sides. Then Corn Dancer bent and in a second the thongs about her ankles fell away. Abby could only stand and rub her wrists, still feeling the deep bite of the skin binding that had held and chafed her arms. Corn Dancer watched her, knife still in his hand. Then with a satisfied grunt he sheathed it and turned to the beached canoe.

Abby, stumbling because of weariness and lack of circulation in her feet, managed to turn with him. The Indian in the stern had also vaulted ashore and now lifted the second prisoner onto the bank. The slender woman was nearly naked, her dress shredded and ripped, her long hair falling over her face as she stood swaying, her head bowed.

Corn Dancer gave a short, barking order and the Indian jerked the captive's head up. Abby gasped when she saw the girl's scratched, dirty face and the dried blood on her right shoulder.

"Marion! Marion Barth!"

Marion had lived back of Abby's own home and closer to the rear wall of the village stockade. Now the girl's head dropped forward again and the Indian started to pull his hunting knife from its sheath.

"No!" Abby cried and then screamed a second desperate "No!"

She took a step toward Marion but her strength would permit no more. Her knees started to buckle and Corn Dancer caught her as he gave more commands to his companion. The man scowled but jerked Marion's head up again. His knife cut her thongs instead of plunging into her body. The girl's gray eyes looked blank and dead, unseeing. Her bare breasts hung nakedly from what was left of her dress but her matted black hair momentarily fell across them.

Corn Dancer turned Abby toward the forest, gave another order and both Indians picked up the canoe, carrying it to concealment in the nearby bushes and trees. They left the two girls alone, swaying, unable to move, hardly able to even stand. They did not have the strength to attempt escape and the Indians knew it.

In a moment they returned to the exposed beach. Corn Dancer searched the length of the river in a long, sweeping glance, then he faced Abby. He pointed to the forest, to himself, her, his companion and Marion Barth.

"We go now. There my town far . . . far. You follow Corn Dancer, eh? Maybe soon come my fireside."

She nodded that she understood. Corn Dancer spoke to his companion and then fully turned his back on Abby and stalked toward the woods. Abby took an uncertain step after him, then another. The movements started the blood circulating in her legs and arms and, though her steps were short and uncertain, at least she made progress of a sort.

But, behind her, the Indian called to Corn Dancer, who checked his stride and wheeled about. Abby saw that Marion simply could not take more than a few steps and again the other Indian fingered his knife handle. Abby looked fearfully at Corn Dancer. He stood hesitant and she knew he tried to decide Marion's fate.

"She my friend," Abby risked speaking. "She rest a night, better tomorrow. Walk then. Understand?"

Corn Dancer's eyes jumped to hers and now she saw to her horror that he, too, touched his knife. She spoke more urgently, pleading, one hand extended toward him, the other to Marion.

"She good squaw." Abby almost choked on the word but Marion's life stood in a delicate balance. "Just rest . . . understand?" She made a sign of eating. "Food. Need food. Then she strong."

Corn Dancer had watched her closely, each movement of her hand to her mouth, to Marion and then to the other warrior. Abby then lay down and Corn Dancer's eyes widened as she put her palms together, then placed both hands under her head and closed her eyes. She looked up at him.

"Sleep. Please? One night sleep and then she'll walk tomorrow when the sun comes up." Abby made a gesture to the sky to signify the sun setting then rising tomorrow morning.

Corn Dancer's face suddenly lit up as he understood. He nodded to Abby and turned to his companion. Abby could not understand his words as he explained in the Iroquois tongue, gesturing to Marion.

"She's lost her strength. She is hungry and needs rest. She will be well and walking by morning. Get her food. We camp here tonight."

"Out here? On the beach?" The Indian motioned to the wide river. "Anyone who passes would see us or the fire. This is a paleface idea to trap us."

Corn Dancer answered shortly, "Pick her up and carry her into the woods."

"Me? A squaw! Better I kill her and we will not be slowed."

His hand jumped to his knife. Abby had not understood a word but tones and gestures had been enough. She tried to block the Indian but her legs and feet betrayed her and she only succeeded in falling across Marion, who stirred slightly and moaned. The warrior completely cleared his knife from its sheath.

"No!" Corn Dancer jumped to him, grabbed his wrist and forced the knife back in the sheath. Then he laughed, taking the bite out of his words, making a joke out of the incident. He pointed at his companion's breechclout. "Is your weapon so small you're not sure of it. Why else would you want to kill a woman so young, with such nice tits? And look at those legs! Are you afraid they could hold you too tight, eh? Let her rest—eat. We will camp a few miles back and no one will see. Eh, Sees-the-Sun, give yourself a chance to show you are a man!"

Sees-the-Sun, anger still showing clearly in his face, stared at Corn Dancer. Then he pushed the knife back into its sheath with a decisive thrust.

"I will show you what I can do with a squaw."

"Good! But not a half-dead one." Corn Dancer scanned the river. "Throw her over your shoulder and let the trees cover us from sight of the river and the white faces."

He turned then to Abby and with a short, abrupt motion signalled her to follow him.

VII

A half-formed hope filled Abby's mind that because Sees-the-Sun carried Marion over his shoulder like a heavy sack the day's march would not be as hard or as long. But the Indian only shifted the girl's weight from time to time and matched Corn Dancer stride for stride. It may have been that Corn Dancer imperceptibly slowed his pace but Abby was not aware of it.

They moved deeper and deeper into the forest and soon came on the warriors and captives who had waited for them. The warriors squatted in an alert circle around their captives. The girls and young women had, in sheer exhaustion, thrown themselves prone on the ground in the small, open glade. The men came lithely to their feet when Corn Dancer and Sees-the-Sun appeared and some roughly kicked the girls with their moccasined feet. But Corn Dancer stopped them.

"We camp here. White squaws no good for travel, cooking or nothing." He pointed to Sees-the-Sun who carelessly let Marion fall off his shoulder into a near lifeless heap at his feet. Corn Dancer swept his arm about the glade.

"This is a good place for us. Safe from whites and from Huron. Game in the forest—rabbit, deer, bear. That is if there is a hunter among you. We'll eat, dance and each tells us how he took a scalp or maybe more, how many he killed, how many women he will add to the Long House at home. We'll have a little war dance but—" he added swiftly "no drums, no victory songs. That would be loud and who can tell how many out in the shadows could hear us?"

"That's not as it should be," a warrior protested, striking his own chest with his fist. "We are warriors now and we have proof—captives and scalps."

"That is true, Tall Bear, but we are not yet

home. For yet a while there will be enemies all around us. Who knows how many or when they will strike? They could steal our new squaws, take our own scalps. No, we will practice tonight what we will tell at Onondaga Town among the *owachira,* and we will know what the Mothers will say to us—proud of their sons and warriors—if we're alive. No, now we build fire, make camp and hunt. Maybe some of the squaws are strong enough to find good fire sticks for us, eh? I, Corn Dancer, can already hear a tale in my head about my bravery. Hurry! Let's make camp, eat, and then there will be stories to hear—many of them.''

He had fired them, though Sees-the-Sun started to protest. But the other warriors grinned like wolves, snatched up bows and quivers and turned to the woods. Others kicked the women onto their feet, though three of them instantly fell back down into senseless heaps. Corn Dancer blocked the blow of a club aimed at one helpless girl and then turned to jerk Abby erect.

Signs, guttural words and shoves made Abigail understand after long, dull moments he wanted her to gather the fallen sticks and branches for a fire. She and a few of the other girls moved slowly but, gradually, a pile of wood formed in the center of the glade. Corn Dancer watched Abby, saying nothing, expression unreadable. He made no move to help, nor did the other men assist the tumbling, staggering girls with their burdens.

Suddenly one of the hunters appeared and

held up a freshly killed rabbit. Corn Dancer smiled. "One for our cook pot, Silent Owl. A little more and we will feast, eh?"

Silent Owl nodded and started to skin his prey. Before long another Indian appeared, this one with a squirrel. Suddenly the Indians jumped to their feet and faced the forest in the direction of an ululating yell that held an unmistakable note of triumph. Corn Dancer and his friends called a reply, then with one accord turned to the laboring women.

Corn Dancer struck Abby's shoulder, pointed to the wood already gathered and then made a circling motion. "More! Bring more!"

"I can't—"

But his open palm struck her shoulder, spinning her around to face the trees. "More! Bring more!" His shove sent her stumbling and made his meaning doubly clear.

Four warriors emerged from the woods, bearing two long, bare branches on their shoulders. A freshly slain, small deer hung from the poles, lashed by its feet. Corn Dancer raised his voice in a call that echoed through the woods and it was answered immediately from several different directions. Now even some of the warriors themselves gathered up wood while the others cleaned the game just beyond one side of the clearing. Other hunters returned, each of them going over to inspect the deer. They laughed, made little hopping jumps and slapped one another on the back.

Men used flints to spark a huge pile of dry

grass into flames that soon caught on the small sticks of wood and then ignited the thicker branches. The glade became aglow with dancing firelight. A branch was trimmed, pointed at one end and was instantly skewered through a haunch of the deer. A second followed, then squirrels and rabbits, hanging from small branches, were suspended over the flames. The captive women did such cooking as was possible. Corn Dancer and the warriors squatted on their haunches, muscular backs straight and proud.

The odor of cooking meat filled the glade and Abby suddenly became ravenous, tortured by hunger. She surreptitiously sucked her greasy, bloody fingers, casting cautious glances at the Indians, especially Corn Dancer. But the warriors paid no attention and Abby continued to steal the juices of fat, meat and blood that dripped onto her fingers. Twice she severely burned herself but she hardly felt the heat, hunger driving her.

At last, according to some unknown, savage standard, the cooking was over. The meat was simply swung off the flames onto leafy branches that formed tables of sorts. Corn Dancer and his friends hunkered down immediately and grabbed up food. Abby started to reach for a rabbit leg but Corn Dancer struck her wrist with the hard edge of his hand.

"You wait. Squaw wait. Always."

Abby fell back, catching herself on her elbows. Corn Dancer glared at her a long moment and then, though Abby could not be sure, the flashing anger seemed to leave his eyes. His stabbing finger indicated a spot beside him. "Sit—here."

She obeyed and he gave her no more attention, though the others laughed derisively. Corn Dancer answered them in a few words and then Abby was completely dismissed from mind. She could only sit and watch, listen to her stomach growl and feel the drooling in the corners of her mouth. She had to clench her fingers until her nails cut into her palms to keep from snatching a morsel of meat as Corn Dancer gnawed on it, licked his fingers and then threw the bone, bare to gristle and tendon, carelessly over his shoulder. Abby heard a scrambling sound. Marion and two other girls fought over the knuckle and cartilage.

When the warriors had at last finished, Corn Dancer motioned her forward and indicated the few morsels that were left. "You eat now. Squaw eat last. Man first, then his woman. Understand?"

She nodded and he made a magnanimous, sweeping gesture. "Eat. Come to me then. I be there."

He indicated a spot several yards away from the flames and stood up. He glared at her a second and stalked off. The other warriors straggled after him and then, with a rush, the starved white captives swooped onto what was left of the food. Abby ate as fast as her jaws could move, her mouth filled and empty. She nearly choked twice and that slowed her pace.

Still, she could not get quite enough.

A wave of intense nausea abruptly swept over her. She choked it down but then a second wave came, stronger than the first. Her stomach heaved and her throat filled. She jumped to her feet and started to run to the edge of the glade. She never made it. She managed to grab a small tree and hold on tightly as she bent over and all the food she had choked down came gushing up and out of her throat. Cold sweat broke out all over her. She vaguely heard roars of laughter coming from all about her. She was too sick to care.

At last she could carefully straighten though she had to cling to the tree. She felt emptied, sick. Tears of agony left her eyes and she saw that many of the other women had also been stricken. She became aware of the bronze-red warriors squatted in a huge circle, watching and laughing. She brushed the back of her hand across her lips and felt the greasy mess on her knuckles. That made her sick all over again and her stomach heaved. But it was empty and she could only retch miserably.

At last she could breathe after a fashion and she dared release the tree. She wavered on her feet for a moment, then strength and balance returned. She realized that she had become hungry all over again and that not one bit of the food she had gorged had remained with her. She tentatively turned to the fire but knew she could not so much as look at another piece of meat. She once more choked her stomach back in place.

"Abbbeee!"

She looked around to see Corn Dancer grinning at her like a red devil from his place in the circle of warriors. He motioned her to come to him and then spoke to his companions, who nodded and laughed on a high note of glee that somehow frightened Abby. But by now, through blows and bruises, she had learned to obey and she stumbled toward Corn Dancer.

The other bucks called guttural orders that their captives did not understand. Only Abby continued a slow advance to Corn Dancer. The others scowled and jumped up. Many already had knife, tomahawk or club in hand. Corn Dancer instantly called a warning in the Iroqouis tongue.

"No more dead or we'll have no captives to show our Mothers and *wachiras* when we come home. This is for us. Let us see what is the worth of these squaws, eh?"

The girls were jerked into a line before the warriors and were left standing and swaying as the men dropped back to their seats. Abby looked down at Corn Dancer, whose sharp eyes met hers and then slowly moved over her body from the crown of her head to the tips of her moccasins. Even in her dulled state she understood his weighing, questioning examination.

"No. Please! No!"

"Dress," he grunted and made a motion that she should remove her tatters and throw them aside. Instead, she instinctively crossed her arms tightly across her body.

"Dress. Gone." He repeated.

She shook her head and hugged herself the more tightly. With a lithe, fluid movement he came to his feet directly before her. He snatched her arms aside and then his fingers roughly ripped down her front, destroying and casting aside the last pitiful remains of her clothing. She stood completely naked before him and the other men. She made futile, aimless movements to cover herself but Corn Dancer cuffed her jaw and jerked her arms away from her body.

Abby faintly heard women cry out to either side and saw one knocked flat because she had not stripped speedily enough to suit her captor. Sensing the uselessness of resistance, knowing that would lead to more blows or even death, Abby dropped her arms to her sides.

"*Aieee!*" Corn Dancer laughed and stepped back to give her a more thorough examination.

She submitted, feeling the burning weight of his eyes, shivering to the crawling sensation as he looked from breast to breast, nipple to nipple and then down over her stomach to her groin and the thick thatch of wiry, auburn hair between her legs, and then down to her ankles and feet. He stepped to her and, before she could even so much as flinch away, cupped her right breast in his hand, jounced it as though estimating its weight. His thumb and finger traveled over her nipple and then his palm moved along the curve of her breast.

Suddenly his hand was between her legs and his fingers explored her. His breech stirred and his hand lifted to his belt to loosen it. His blazing eyes bored into Abby's and she knew hers held fear and she could not check her backward step.

The feral gleam left his eyes and his lips twisted in a sardonic grin that she somehow knew was directed at his own thoughts instead of at her. His foot kicked at the dress remnant and he abruptly turned away.

"I see. That is all. I see. Later, maybe. No more now."

Hardly believing what she had heard, Abby snatched up her rags and hurried out of the ring of warriors and struggling women. She managed to pull on her tatters, had just tied her worn collar at the back of the neck when a scream brought her whirling about.

She instantly saw the struggling group off to her left. One of the girls had been thrown to the ground while three men held her naked, thrashing legs and arms. A fourth had discarded his breechclout and crouched, waiting, as the others forcibly spread the screaming girl's legs. Suddenly, she managed to free an arm, twist about and half rise. An Indian grabbed for her arm but her hand streaked down to his belt. Abby saw the wicked gleam of steel.

Corn Dancer called a warning but the blade plunged down and one of the Indians toppled. The girl tried to recover the knife but another Indian snatched up a club. It made a sickening, crunching sound as it struck her skull with the force of sinewy, savage muscles behind it. The girl pitched forward onto her face, quivered and then lay still.

Corn Dancer had moved a second too late. His angry yell froze the struggling group as though some magic power had acted instantaneously. Corn Dancer looked down at the dead girl, at the warrior who had bludgeoned her and then about at the unmoving men and women, who stood as though hypnotized.

Corn Dancer barked orders and even Abby understood the scorching anger in his guttural words. He pointed to the dead girl, made a contemptuous sign to the woods and then stood spread-legged, proud, defiant, hands on hips, one grasping the hilt of his knife. He looked slowly from warrior to warrior and each almost visibly shrank as he met Corn Dancer's eyes.

He barked another order. Two men scooped up the dead girl and disappeared among the trees. The others resumed their seats and Corn Dancer slowly turned about.

"Abbbeee, tell squaws they dress. Tell squaws all over now. We come to Onondaga town—then maybe more. Not now. Tell squaws."

Abby stammered out some sort of garbled version but fear instantly left the captives as they hurried to crouch around her.

"It's all right," she assured them.

Marion shook her head. "No, Abby, it will never be all right—ever again. All of us are dead. It's only a matter of time."

VIII

At the first faint touch of dawn the warrior guards aroused the others and the whole camp came alive. The women had to pull themselves to their feet once more and they were immediately forced to build up the fire and gather wood. Though the routine seemed to be familiar and a normal one for a war party in a strange territory, there was a subtle change. Abby saw more than one warrior throw a covert, angry look at Corn Dancer.

If he was aware, he showed no sign of it but gave sharp orders that sent the men out into the forest for more game, set a few to watch the women captives and keep them stumbling at their tasks. At Corn Dancer's order and gesture, a few warriors started back toward the wide river. They returned before long and tension left Corn Dancer and the others as reports were made. Quite obviously there had been no signs of pursuit or discovery.

This morning, Abby found that although the sight of half-cooked meat made her want to close her eyes, her stomach had become too demanding. She choked down a mouthful, then a second. She could not keep the bloody grease from dripping over her mouth and chin and had to wipe it off with the back of her hand or with a pitiful remnant of her dress. But her hunger mounted and mounted. She tried to hold it in check, forcing herself to slowly chew and swallow. Even so, she half expected the nausea that had filled her the night before with each bite. Once she caught Corn Dancer watching her and, to her surprise, he flashed a wide smile and bobbed his bald head with the high crest of greased hair in approval.

"Abbbeee good. Eat slow. Keep meat here." He patted his stomach. "Not there." He pointed to the ground. "Maybe bye-n-bye you good squaw. Maybe."

The Indians ate fast, constantly watching the forest about them as though fearful of foes or a sudden trap. Like Abby, the women captives had learned their lessons in allaying ravening hunger though now and then, also like Abby, they found themselves cramming their mouths. But they controlled themselves and, unlike the night before, only now and then one of them choked.

Abby never saw the signal Corn Dancer must have given but almost as one every Indian came to his feet. Some rounded up and thonged the captives while others smothered the fire with dirt until there was only a dark mound to mark its place in the glade. Corn Dancer came to Abby. He held out a thong but, instead of tying her, pointed westward.

"You good squaw, eh? Walk?" He held up the thong, "Not tie, eh?"

"Where do we go?" Abby asked and Corn Dancer looked puzzled. She gestured westward as he had and then formed her hands into a triangle resembling a roof. "Town? We go town?"

"Ah! Long house. Yes. Corn Dancer live Onondaga Town. We go there." He jabbed his chest with his thumb. "My town. My family. My *owachira*. You come—walk? Me tie?"

"I walk," Abby said and turned to face the west.

Corn Dancer instantly tucked the thong in his belt. He then took three steps, stopped, pointed back to where he had started. "You squaw. You my squaw for now, eh?"

"I—guess so."

"Good, eh?" He held up three fingers, took three more steps and then pointed back, swung his finger to Abby. "Squaw walk there, eh?"

"I walk there." Abby took her station and once more Corn Dancer's smile flashed. "Good Lord!" she thought. "If he wasn't a bloodthirsty savage, he'd be a handsome man!"

He turned then and motioned her to follow. "Come. Be good squaw. No . . . No . . . How you say?" He doubled his hand into a fist and struck the air, then touched the hilt of his knife in its sheath at his belt. "No . . . ?"

"Trouble?"

"That word, huh? No trouble?"

"No trouble." She nodded agreement and, satisfied, he turned his back fully on her and started off on the new leg of the journey.

The other Indians called out to him and Abby heard the warning note in their voices. But Corn Dancer only waved dismissal and then threw his arm forward in a signal to march. Abby kept her three paces behind Corn Dancer's back but she looked around now and then. The other women had been thonged by their individual captors. She saw Leah Bates stumble and then fall headlong as her captor slammed his fist between her shoulder blades. He jerked her upright.

Leah looked at Abby, who gasped in a horrible start of surprise at the hatred in the young matron's eyes. "You're a whore of Babylon.

You've cozened that savage. Have you laid with him?''

"Leah!"

"Oh, it's plain enough. All of us have seen. If any of us manage to live, it will be you, because you have no shame. You're a harlot.''

Abby felt unable to breathe for a moment. Then she saw the other captives glaring at her. Until that moment Abby had not realized how the others must have interpreted Corn Dancer's treatment of her as compared to their own lot.

"Marion! Tell them. Leah, it's not true!

Corn Dancer wheeled about, scowling at her and then at the others. Abby made a pleading gesture to him. "Let me talk to them.''

"Talk? Who?"

"My friends. You listen to what I say and then you talk to your warriors.''

"What I say? What you say?"

"Me talk to them.'' She pointed to Leah and the others. "Please!''

He scowled, then shrugged. "You talk— okay.''

"Tell your men to untie them, please.'' She made motions of removing thongs from her arms and wrists. Corn Dancer's frown deepened. Abby continued, "You talk them, I talk women. We march faster—more.'' She pointed to the east and then made a sign indicating the sun's travel across the sky. She moved her fingers across her palm to indicate legs walking, then increased the speed.

Suddenly she saw the light of comprehension

in his face. "You talk. Me talk. Make good march, eh?"

It took a good deal of discussion back and forth among the Indians but at last they cautiously herded the women around Abby, then themselves formed a wider, watchful ring to listen as Abby spoke. She doubted if they understood half a dozen words but it didn't matter.

Leah still glared at her, mouth forming a contemptuous sneer. Abby knew she herself would be the key, the one who could stop the senseless thongings, falling, beatings and even murders if Leah could be brought to understand.

"Leah—all of you—please, oh, please listen! We can't act toward these savages as we would to our men back home—if we had a home."

"Do we crawl under a blanket with them like you?" Leah demanded.

Abby choked down angry resentment. "No, Leah. But we're women and so, in the way they think, we're squaws. We do the work. We jump when they order us. We cook, gather wood, make fires. We say nothing unless they speak to us. We go where they point. We stand, sit, turn as they command. We have to do it."

"And what do they do besides tear off our clothes, sit loafing around the fire? They fight and loaf and, I suppose in time, rape us and we do nothing?"

"It's all we can do now."

"You *are* a harlot!" Leah blazed.

"I have only been knocked around, undressed

and cuffed. Corn Dancer has not done more to me. But, Leah, oh, all of you—we have to stay *alive* until our men or those from the other towns catch up with this war party. Then we're free."

Marion exclaimed, "Will they come? Will they truly find us?"

"Of course," Abby answered with an assurance she did not wholly feel. "You know they won't allow a band of scraggly Indians to keep us prisoner! Just do as the Indians say."

Leah wanted to retort but was no longer quite sure of her accusations. Abby pressed the point, indicating Corn Dancer with a slight bob of her head and dart of her eyes. "He's beginning to trust me. He'll tell the others to take a chance with each of you as he has with me. We'll all live. Marion, Patience, Leah—don't you see? We have to play for time so our men can catch up with us."

The women exchanged, long, uncertain looks. The girl, Patience, suddenly spoke up. "I'll risk it, Abby. I think I already have a broken rib, and my Indian would as soon knock me in the head with a club as pull me to my feet if I fall again."

"Marion?" Abby asked.

"I—don't know. I'm tired of thongs and kicks and fists."

Leah thoughtfully rubbed a dark bruise on her temple, scowled at Abby and then shrugged. Her tone was conciliatory and Abby began to have a sense of triumph. Leah dropped her hand. "You make sense but I ain't so sure you've told all the truth. Seems funny your Indian lets you walk free and easy while we—"

"But she *told* you why!" Marion cut in. "Besides, I'd say it's worth a chance."

Leah glanced over at the Indians whom Corn Dancer harangued in a near barking voice. Just then Corn Dancer stepped back, looking from one warrior to the next around the circle. Some growled, some scowled and one man even lifted his voice in sharp anger. But at last silence fell. Corn Dancer barked a word that sounded to Abby like a question. Again he eyed each warrior in turn and then nodded. He turned and strode to Abby.

He studied each captive woman as he had his warriors and then looked at Abby. "You talk squaws. I talk warriors. What squaws say?"

"They say they will march. They will make camp, gather wood. Warriors bring game. Squaws cook. No trouble so long as no tie 'em up. So long they not beaten."

"Like you—me?"

"What? Oh, you mean like we were this morning. Yes, they be good squaws. I be good squaw. No tie. No beat."

Corn Dancer motioned toward the woods and the thick tangle of bushes, the occasional open glades that made natural pathways. "No—what you say?—run, eh?"

"No run," she promised.

Corn Dancer returned to the Indians and again the harsh words of the Indian tongue jumped from man to man. Several times Corn Dancer pointed to the women and the argument continued. At long last he returned to Abby, stabbed a long finger at her and then jabbed his own chest.

"You—me walk." His finger swung around the circle, pointing at each woman a second. "Squaw, they walk with warrior. You," he indicated Patience, "walk your warrior. Three steps." He lifted his fingers and then indicated a spot behind him. "You walk there, eh? You—" Leah jerked nervously as the finger pointed to her and then her own captor. "You walk him—three back, eh?"

Leah looked at Abby. "No bonds? No fists?"

"Be a good squaw," Abby nodded, "and no thongs nor blows. When we stop for camp, we gather wood and make up the fire. That squaw work, Corn Dancer tells me. No trouble then."

"How about bedding 'em?"

Abby started to answer, shrugged. From the many admiring glances Corn Dancer had given her, she did not know how to answer. She held out her hands, palm up. "I honestly don't know. It hasn't happened yet, but it might. None of us can tell what these savages think."

After a long moment Leah sighed. "Well, you're honest. I'll say that. And I take back what I said before, Abby."

"No need to apologize. None of us have thought straight or used our heads other than to keep alive and moving since we left Westover. Lots of us are dead because we didn't. Maybe now we can gather our wits about us while we march.''

Leah half smiled, then her lips pressed together and she was one of the first women to move to the side of her captor and then wait until he had taken a few steps before she followed. The other women exchanged uncertain looks, then Patience took her place behind the warrior who was her captor. Marion followed and the marchers lined out. Corn Dancer looked at Abby.

"You do good. You make'm march, eh? Be good squaws to warriors, eh? Do squaw work come night until we reach Onondaga Town.''

"I'll try. That's all I can promise.''

"Good word,'' Corn Dancer nodded. "Abbbeee say, Corn Dancer believe. Squaws believe, eh?''

"Oh Lord, I hope so!'' she breathed.

The Indians and women lined out for the march, each in the right place. Corn Dancer made an imperial sign to Abby to step behind him and then he headed the line. Abby dared a question.

"Corn Dancer, what happens when we come to Onondaga Town?''

He spoke over his shoulder. "Up to keepers of the Faith and the Mothers of the *wachira*. *They* say. We lose plenty *orenda*. Maybe you— them—take place. Maybe die. The Keepers and the Mothers say.''

"But what about the chiefs? the warriors?''

"They do what Mothers and Keepers say.'' He added curtly. "Squaw talk too much.''

IX

The remainder of the march through the woods and occasional open glades lasted only a few days but even that short time was sufficient to establish the routine. The Indian braves lolled at ease over their pipes and stories after they had returned with the day's catch of game or fish.

The women labored at camp tasks and then, thankfully, the day truly ended and they could all seek whatever rest they could find on hard ground, thick grass or masses of leaves that formed crude beds. Abby found no difficulty in finding sleep. Her eyes closed and her senses left her the second she stretched out beside Corn Dancer.

There were times as she marched behind him when she wondered why he had not molested her, or why the other Indians left the captive girls alone except for that one tense time when Abby knew all of them would be raped and perhaps murdered afterward. But Corn Dancer had stopped that and he held his men under tight control. In one sense Abby was grateful, but in another she wondered at the reason for the discipline. During the raid on the town, rape had been as much of the horror as the killing and scalping so Abby now wondered if there was not some sinister reason why control had been imposed. Was it a means of building up male desire so that when restraints were removed, there would be unlimited licentiousness and death? She would fearfully push the thought out of her mind with a shudder.

But the other women evidently shared Abby's fearful line of thinking. Marion expressed it one night in a whisper to Abby and Leah. "What's to happen to us? Why do strong young bucks like these leave us alone like we're cattle or something, not women?"

"Well!" Leah whispered, "listen to our clean-mouthed young lady! I'd not have believed it."

"Hush, Leah," Abby whispered fearfully. She's right. Why do they leave us alone?"

"The more time they have to think about it, the more they'll enjoy what's between our legs when the time comes. That's how I figure it."

"So do I," Marion almost wailed. Her warrior awakened, growled a word or two, slapped her and immediately fell asleep again.

No one spoke the rest of the night.

The long march ended surprisingly and abruptly. There had been no indication of a break in the forest. The ever present mountains, their slopes dark with pine and oak trees, loomed higher and more ragged. Abby noticed the party now moved with less caution. Suddenly one of the warriors pointed ahead up through the oak trees to a gap in the serrated wall of the jagged barriers lifting high into the sky. Instantly the Indians shouted and smiled at one another. The march halted at a word from Corn Dancer.

The women once more had to scout for wood for a fire to be built in the glade. The hunters did not go out. They squatted about the fire and Corn Dancer indicated to Abby that the women pick berries, varied flowers, dig up indicated roots. Before long, each warrior, using the ingredients the women had brought, had mixed paints of varied colors. As Abby watched, the warpaint, long missing, returned to the red faces, the chests and muscular arms. Abby thought the Indian braves looked much like women preparing themselves for a dance or a meeting with their swains. Not that she had ever witnessed such a scene, but she had read of them in surreptitiously acquired novels that the parson had called "the devil's works," and she had heard of them in rumors trickling back to Westover from travelers who had been to distant Boston or Hartford or, now and then, from an itinerant trader out of New York or from far up in Maine.

At last Corn Dancer, the crimson slashes again on his cheeks making him once more grim and frightening, all warrior and no longer the savage who could be pleasant, smile and call her "Abbbeee" at times, stood up, club in one hand, knife in the other.

"Onondaga—*ohwachira.*" He pointed to a young warrior. "Take the news to the Keepers of the Faith, our Mothers and our *wachiras,* Long Houses and Town that Corn Dancer has returned with scalps, prisoners, squaws. Our *orenda* is good. Our *orenda* is filled again when the ceremonies are over. We will come—" He pointed to the sun and made a small sign that indicated an hour of elapsed time.

The young man wheeled about and raced down the glade to disappear among the trees at the far end. Then Corn Dancer lifted his arms high, face turned to the sun, and began to sing, repeatedly using a single musical phrase. The other warriors joined in and for a time the forest echoed and rang with their voices.

The singing stopped as abruptly as Corn

Dancer had started it and now Abby heard a distant throbbing, a steady beat in a savage rhythm. Corn Dancer lowered his arms and without a word started off down the glade, Abby instantly taking her place behind him. But he stopped, looked at her, and then pointed to the other women whom the warriors pushed and shoved into a single line.

In the new order, the march resumed down the glade and under the trees. The sound of the throbbing grew louder and Abby realized she must be listening to drums.

Suddenly the procession broke clear of the forest and Abby stumbled and cried out in surprise. Corn Dancer instantly wheeled around, club lifted as though to strike. But Abby instinctively knew the weapon would not descend. She regained balance and Corn Dancer turned away but not before she caught a gleam of approval and pleasure in his eyes.

She looked out ahead of Corn Dancer onto a great expanse of fields, planted with Indian maize or corn, as it had been called for as long as Abby could remember. Further sections of the field held other growing plants. She saw the round shape of melons, high stalks of tobacco, tall bean poles. It was a veritable farm, unbelievable in this wilderness.

But beyond the fields she saw a stout stockade, the pointed, peeled trunks standing at least fifteen feet high, placed so close together that Abby could not see even a single thin space between them. The heavy stockade stood as far as she could see to either side, broken only by a single, wide gate as thick and stout as the walls. The way was now filled with warriors, women, children, old men and squaws and some women whom Abby momentarily believed to be white. But that, of course, would be impossible.

Then she saw the six people who stood before the main group in the gate. Three women and three men wearing high headdresses, beads and ornaments of strange design hanging about their necks, held instruments that seemed combinations of weapons and ceremonial instruments. The six stood without moving, as though ignoring Corn Dancer and the approaching, victorious warriors.

Corn Dancer stopped his little prancing step of triumph. He sobered and stepped forward to the six with a slow, measured step. While still some feet away, he threw his tomahawk on the ground, drew his knife, held it high so that the sun glinted from the blade and then placed it at the feet of one of the women, the three of whom stood slightly in advance of the three statuesque men. He then swung bow and quiver of arrows from his back and placed them before the other women. He half turned and took a half step backward so that his warriors and the line of prisoners could be fully seen.

Abby could not suppress a shudder when next Corn Dancer pulled the long-haired scalps from his belt and placed them beside the weapons as though adding to the tokens of triumph. He then stepped farther back and one by one his warriors approached the proud six and repeated the performance. During all the time not a word had been said and the three "Keepers of the Faith" had not moved a muscle as far as Abby could tell.

One of the women spoke and the other two nodded. The men stood as silent and statuesque as when Abby had first seen them.

Leah, beside Abby, whispered, "Hey, do you—?"

"Sssh!" Abby hissed a warning as one of the three proud women looked toward them with a sweeping scornful glance that made Abby wonder if she and her fellow captives were considered human at all.

The woman spoke to Corn Dancer, who held out his hands palms up, his body slightly bent in something close to a bow. He answered her, then a second and third question. Then, surprisingly, one of the men barked a single questioning word. Instantly Corn Dancer straightened proudly and commenced what seemed to be a long, boastful harangue. All the Indians listened, the warriors of the party grunted a "hai!" now and then as though confirming whatever Corn Dancer was narrating.

Then the six parted, the men moving in one direction, the women in another, and wheeled about and faced one another. At an imperious gesture from one of the women, all the rest of the Indians moved to form an open path straight into the village.

Abby again gasped. This was no ordinary

savage encampment! She looked down a wide street lined by long houses with low, curved roofs, sealed with what appeared to be elm bark, bound from base to peak of roof with stout limbs bent to the curve of the structure. Each house had a single door and Abby saw wisps of smoke escaping from vent holes in the roof. She wondered how many people each house could accommodate. A single sweep of her eyes told her there must be at least twenty of these structures, for she could glimpse the roofs of others and see wisps of smoke over and beyond those immediately in sight.

But the street down which she marched ended in an open area where something like a high, huge altar had been built. There was also another of the long houses, this even larger than the others she had seen. The three men and women made a commanding gesture to Corn Dancer and then, ignoring him, came together as a group and marched sedately ahead of the returning war party and the women captives. Abby paced down the street following the six and Corn Dancer, who closely trailed them.

They arrived at the open space and halted. Abby looked up on a wide platform, an evil looking, stout post protruding from its center. Ashes and fragments of burned wood in a circle about the stake, the height of the whole structure above the ground, gave her a hint of what it might be and suddenly her whole body turned cold. That structure was an altar of sacrifice, of torture and death. Were all of them, one by one, to be immolated in flames up there?

The prisoners were halted at a command. Now everyone in the town moved slowly to either side of the line, closely examining each captive. One man touched Abby's chin to lift her head but Corn Dancer immediately jumped to her side and the intruder moved on with a single, contemptuous word. One of the ceremonial women instantly called out and Corn Dancer almost jumped to stand stiffly before her.

They exchanged many sharp, staccato sentences and Corn Dancer looked contrite while the woman seemed mollified. The crowd about the captives increased. More warriors, most of them older than Corn Dancer's band, pressed close. The women gathered, pushing in closer, scowling as they examined Abby and her friends in obvious feminine suspicion and jealousy. Children of all sizes, boys and girls, naked for the most part except for moccasins, mingled with the rest, some coming up boldly to the captives, others rather fearfully peering at them from around a squaw or a warrior.

The six Keepers of the Faith slowly and solemnly moved to a spot that had obviously been kept clear for them. Indian women hurried up and spread animal robes on the ground. When the three women and men sat down, a rustle sounded through the crowd as the others found seats wherever there was room. Long pipes appeared, the bowls filled, the contents lighted and ceremoniously offered to the six. A dead silence fell on the entire crowd as small puffs of smoke ascended from the pipes, puffed in turn to each of the major directions. Corn Dancer, like the captives, remained standing before the Keepers of the Faith, arms folded across his body, head held high.

Abby began to believe that one of the three women of the Keepers of the Faith was something like a high priestess. She was slightly younger than the other two but as tall and lithe as a warrior. Her full deerskin blouse, gathered at the waist with a wide belt of varied colored beads, could not fully conceal the thrust of her breasts. Her coarse black hair did not hang carelessly over her shoulders but had been combed and brushed smoothly back from her dark face to hang in a glinting cascade down her back. She had bound it about the forehead by another, narrower band of wampum. Abby had heard that shells composing the wampum served as money among the savages. If so, this woman wore a small fortune. A necklace of polished bear claws made a wide ring about her neck and her blouse bore a strange emblem strangely patterned in a soft blue weave.

She spoke to Corn Dancer in the Iroquoian tongue as she made a sweeping hand motion toward the captives. "All women, Corn Dancer? No white warrior whose strength and bravery can be tested there?"

She pointed to the platform with the short charred post that Abby believed to be a torture altar. "We would have liked to see how the white skins meet death."

Corn Dancer lost a touch of his pride and assurance. "Mother, they met death bravely."

"We did not see it."

"I did—and my warriors—Mother. Not one of the white skins stopped fighting until a knife, lance, hatchet or club killed him."

"That is true?" she asked.

He turned to his warriors and they answered in a chorus, "Hai!"

Leah nudged Abby and started to whisper, "It's the *women*—"

"Tell *that* one to be silent!" the regal woman ordered angrily, "or her tongue will leave her mouth. Tell her."

The young Indian beside Leah slammed his palm across her cheek and mouth, rocking her off balance against Abby, who caught and supported her. Leah needed no further instruction but stood silent, head bent, rubbing her cheek and lips. A trickle of blood made a wavering line down over her chin and along her neck.

The Keeper of the Faith glanced at her companions and then turned her attention back to Corn Dancer. "Can these be trained to become Onondaga women?"

"Let us ask our Mothers of the families. They will know. Try the test of the clubs and switches. That will also tell. The *orenda* of our town needs new strength—women who will bear warriors."

"Wise words," the woman said, "from one so young and back from only his second or third war trail as a leader. Take the women to the

Mothers, each man's captive to his own family.'' She pointed upward. ''When the sun has made a hand's length in the sky, bring them all out here to us.''

Corn Dancer lifted his hand, palm out in acknowledgement and salute. He took Abby by the arm and turned her toward one of the long houses. Other warriors followed him, but some moved toward the other houses.

''Abbbeee,'' he said in a low voice, ''my Mother look at you. She nod or maybe she shake her head.''

''What happens?''

''She nod, you become of our family maybe. She shake her head—'' His suddenly grim, tight-pressed lips told the story.

They entered the narrow door and Abby was at first blinded in the comparatively dim interior. Then she slowly regained her sight. She stood at one end of a long passage that led from the door across the darkness to the far end of the building. She saw the ashes of many fires spaced along the passage and what appeared to be rooms opening off to either side of each fire. Most of the fires were merely ashes but here and there tiny flames licked at the bottoms of metal vessels in which food of some kind bubbled and steamed. Women and girls tended the pots, looking up as Corn Dancer circled each fire as he moved deeper into the building. They spoke to him and he answered. He pushed Abby ahead, caught her once when she stumbled and almost fell on a naked baby cooing and kicking on the ground.

He finally halted about halfway down the corridor. A woman who had crouched over the fire slowly arose. She asked several sharp questions. In answer to one, Corn Dancer touched the scalps at his belt. Another time he drew out his knife and then his tomahawk, struck a blow in the air with each. He replaced the weapons, extended his bare arms and rubbed his hand over his chest. The woman, face expressionless, rubbed her hands along his arms and across his body. He extended his legs. She looked, nodded and her dark face lighted. Then she looked at Abby.

Corn Dancer again spoke rapidly and Abby heard her name in his speech. The woman came close to peer into Abby's face and then looked around at Corn Dancer. "Abbbeee?" she asked.

Corn Dancer nodded. The woman, her face barely touched with wrinkles and with only a trace of white in her long black and glossy hair, suddenly taloned her fingers into Abby's shoulder and whirled her about.

So stunned with surprise she could neither cry out nor move, Abby felt the woman grab the remains of her dress collar and rip the whole thing away. Then the woman fondled and weighed each breast, stroked her stomach and prodded down into the groin. She smacked Abby's buttocks, whirled her about again.

She spoke shortly to Corn Dancer, whose face lighted as he looked at Abby. "Mother say *orenda* good. You fit family if Sachem and Mothers say."

"Orenda?" Abby asked.

Corn Dancer's brows raised as his jaw dropped as though he had been stunned. Then he closely searched her face and Abby repeated the word as a question again. *"Orenda?"*

He touched himself and then pointed to his mother and the children who had gathered in a silent, wondering circle about them. *"Orenda. All them have, I have. Here."*

He touched his chest above his heart. He pointed to the house walls but Abby knew instinctively he indicated the whole world outside. *"Orenda.* Everything has. I die—*orenda* gone. Get back someone else."

She frowned and then suddenly understood. "Oh, you must mean something like soul."

"Not know 'soul.' Know *orenda.* All your friends—the squaws—each has *orenda."*

"And mine's good?"

"Mother think. Know later, eh?"

"Mother chief family?" Abby asked.

"Mother chief. Mother chief *Owachira."*

"Owachira?"

Corn Dancer pointed to the rooms along the hall. "Brother—sister. Mother—father. All Mothers sisters, eh? *Owachira*—all same blood.'

Corn Dancer must mean, Abby decided, that everyone in the long house was related in some way through the mothers and she began to understand that the mothers or women ruled despite the fact that the men did the fighting and hunting, were the big chiefs or "sachems," as Corn Dancer called them, or were little chiefs just starting a career as she gathered Corn Dancer must be doing.

A shout from outside ululated through the house, hardly muffled by the walls. Corn Dancer turned Abby toward the narrow, long house entrance.

"Find out now you *orenda*—other squaw *orenda*. Now." As he led her to the door following his mother and the other women of the long house, he said in a low voice. "Run. Fast. Run. No fall. You dead. Run."

Abby thought he meant immediately and lunged forward only to be jerked back by Corn Dancer. "No—later. Run fast."

She didn't understand until she came out of the long house. Now the street leading to the distant stockade gate was lined with men, women and children for the whole distance. Abby saw that the largest and most muscular women stood in a long double line, facing one another. Each carried a thin limb peeled of leaves, as supple and as dangerous as a buggy whip. Some carried heavier weapons, almost like clubs.

Leah, Marion, Patience, Abby were roughly pushed into a line along with other captives. One of the statuesque women Keepers of the Faith faced them. She pointed to the captives, to the distant gate and then to the waiting, armed women. She spoke imperious words, echoed by the other Keepers and then by the crowd.

Corn Dancer translated. "You run gate. Get whip . . . club. You fall, you dead. You reach gate, you strong . . . you have *orenda*. Take place squaws who gone—dead. You maybe become Iroquois—Onondaga. Maybe. First, reach gate.''

The rounded, dark red face of each squaw in the double line told Abby that not one of them would lessen the strength of her blow and that many of them hoped to down at least one of the captive women. She felt the blood leave her face as a cold chill moved up her spine. This would be an ordeal and the gate looked so far, far away. Shouts lifted and words came shattering at her in taunts that could not be mistaken.

The female Keeper of the Gate stepped aside and pointed down the double row as Leah gasped, ''My God! We're to run the gauntlet. I thought they did that only to men!''

The priestess spoke and Corn Dancer yelled.

''Run!''

X

The *Demoiselle* had been sailing into the wide mouth of the St. Lawrence for a day and at dusk it still looked to Edouard to be an ocean bay. He retired to his cabin wondering when in the world he would get a glimpse of New France. It should be soon. But the gray sky blended with the gray, choppy waters and he sensed rather than saw a faint, faint hint of sun somewhere far above and far ahead.

To his surprise, the captain's steward brought an invitation to sup that night in Jouvier's cabin. Edouard accepted, wondering what had caused this break in the routine of the days. When the steward threw open the door to Edouard's knock, Jouvier greeted him by thrusting a tankard of wine into his hand.

"Bienvenue, mon Sieur. The wine might be better but it is all we have for greeting New France."

"New France! But we'll not be there in—"

"We are already well inside Anacosta Bay, Sieur de Fournet. You *are* in New France even though—this accursed weather—the clouds, the fog keep us from having even so much as a glimpse of land. But it's always this way."

"So the voyage is about over?"

"Almost, *mon Sieur."* Jouvier lifted his tankard. "Here's to your new life in a new land."

Edouard lifted his tankard to respond to the toast but scowled at the gray cloud curtain outside the porthole. "Not a bright welcome."

"It will be better as we work up the river. But let us be comfortable, if it pleases you."

They dropped onto the padded settle that had been built the entire length of the stern windows. Edouard could see only a hint of the wake the *Demoiselle* made in the cold gray waters of the bay—river?—ocean? He still felt that they were at sea except that he sensed a subtle new stress as the ship seemed to be fighting an unseen current.

"Jacques will soon have sup on the table," Jouvier said and chuckled. I'll be glad to taste the last of ocean fare, *mon Sieur*. Before long we'll have fresh fish and venison and beef. Even milk. Now that will be a change!"

"Indeed! and welcome."

Jouvier refilled the flagons, dropped back against the settle. "After we cross the Gulf, *mon Sieur*, we can touch at Bersimis, if you like, or at Tadoussac."

"Is there reason why I should? What are those places?"

"Posts along the river. Hardly more than fishing villages, places where the Indians bring in peltry from the country north of the Laurentian Mountains. There is a chapel at Tadoussac if you wish to see a priest."

"*Le pêtre* would hardly be interested in my sins." Edouard smiled but suddenly grew sharpeyed. "And how could I err aboard such a craft as the *Demoiselle*?"

Jouvier made a face. "I'm afraid to ask that of anyone since the less I hear the less I know."

"I wish all men were like you, *mon Capitaine*. If I have sinned at all, it has only been in thought."

"Some say that is enough." Jouvier took a deep pull of his wine. "Then we will go right on to Quebec or Montreal, whichever pleases you."

"What would you suggest, *mon ami?*"

Jouvier shrugged. "It depends upon what you plan to do now that we are in New France. Of course, you will first report to the Governor. Strangers are so rare, he'll know and be curious about you before you set foot on the *quai*."

"This Quebec and Montreal are small, eh?"

"For France, yes. But here they are main cities. Several hundred Frenchmen, perhaps, and fewer women. But they both swarm with Hurons and trappers—*courriers du bois* and *voyageurs* coming and going from the far interior."

"What supports them?"

"Peltry, *mon Sieur*. Furs—of the finest quality. Many fortunes have already been made in skins—beaver, lynx, bear, otter."

Edouard pursed his lips thoughtfully but just at that moment, after a discreet knock, Jacques entered with the first covered dish of the supper. Edouard absently watched the man scurry obsequiously about the table and then hurry out, closing the door behind him.

"Furs," he said suddenly and Jouvier stared uncomprehendingly at him. "Furs—peltry. I had not thought of that."

The captain spoke slowly and carefully, swirling the wine about in his tankard. "I had not thought so, *mon Sieur*. I saw at first that your first thought was to leave Bordeaux, the Gironde and perhaps France itself."

Edouard suppressed his start of surprise and touch of fear at the captain's shrewd guess. *"Pourquoi, mon Capitaine?* A man travels as he sees fit."

"Vraiment, mon Sieur. But he may also travel as *le Roi* smiles or frowns, eh?" Jouvier hastily lifted his hand to prevent anger. *"Mon Sieur,* you are not the first I have seen board an outward-bound vessel in haste. However, I did not see any *gendarmes* or *soldats* in pursuit or search. So perhaps my first thought of a *lettre de cachet* was in error, eh?"

"Oui . . . perhaps."

After a silence, Jouvier said, studiously eyeing the gray fog beyond the windows. "I have heard the arm of His Majesty is long. But sometimes it moves very, very slowly. There was no sign of trouble when we were boarded and inspected by the officer of the *Orleans, non?"*

"No."

"So the *Orleans* sailed for Martinique far to the south. When will another royal ship or dispatch boat come into the bleak St. Lawrence? And who wants anything but furs in New France?"

"You're saying—?"

"In New France the Governor *is* the king, but it is often months, sometimes a year, before he knows what is happening in that part of his realm back across the ocean. Furs are a royal monopoly, and the *courriers* and *voyageurs* seek them only by license of the Governor. Once the license is granted, who is to search all the wilderness west and south for the hunter?"

Edouard grunted and again Jouvier refilled his tankard and lifted it ceremoniously to Edouard. "When we dock at Quebec, present yourself to the Governor. If you have a purse of any size, it might be well to share a few *louis d'or* with His Excellency. The permit, eh?''

''And then the woods!''

''Not so fast, *mon Sieur*. You must meet with the *courrier* and learn what is needed to wear in this frigid country of New France. It is not Gascony—far from it.''

''But if a packet—''

''A long chance, *mon Sieur*.''

Jacques returned with more of the supper and Edouard looked with new respect on the captain, who grabbed up knife and long pronged fork to tackle the food. Edouard touched his sleeve and Jouvier checked the move of his knife to his mouth, a bit of skewered meat dripping sauce.

''*Mon Capitaine,* my purse may also have a *louis d'or* or two for you. *Eh bien?*''

Jouvier chuckled. ''*Eh bien et merci, mon Sieur.*''

He gulped down the meat.

There was still no sight or even sound of land in the dense fog as Edouard returned to his own cabin that night. Dawn light was drab and gray but the clouds had lifted when he dressed and went out on deck. He stopped short. Half formed, perhaps even half dreamed, he thought, he saw off to the north a faint shadowy line slightly above the waters about him. The mountains?

He walked to the rail and looked down at the water, still ocean-colored and still choppy with small waves, but now he saw a current moving from the *Demoiselle's* bow to disappear in the swirling fog beyond the stern. A current could only mean a river, particularly when so swift and well defined.

Edouard looked northward again to that uncertain, uneven line along the horizon, more certain than ever that it marked mountains. He whirled about and grabbed a seaman's arm as the man moved by him. He pointed to the horizon.

"Are those mountains?"

"They are the Laurentians." The sailor shrugged, dismissing them. "But I hear there is nothing beyond them but snow and what is called 'tundra' for perhaps a thousand miles."

"But land, eh?"

"If you wish to call it that, *mon Sieur.*"

"You are sure?"

"I have never been ashore along this stretch of coast and can only say what I have been told. But that is what I have heard."

"Thank you, *mon ami.*"

The sailor touched finger to the edge of his knitted cap and moved on along the deck. Edouard remained grasping the rail, looking northward. He still could not fully believe the sailor. The great expanse of water had not narrowed and it appeared that the *Demoiselle's* bow cleaved ocean rather than river.

Then he realized that there was a change in the air, something subtly different. What was it? He sniffed, turning his head this way and that. One way, he caught the usual ocean smell and taste of salt. The other, the salt taste remained in his nose and on his lips but . . . what else?

He turned about and looked up to the deck of the stern castle as Jouvier called down to him. "No, *mon Sieur*, you are not insane. What you smell is wind from off land—and from trees. Before long you will see them."

"Then it is truly New France? The voyage is over."

"Almost, *mon Sieur*. By tomorrow or the next day you will put your feet on land, the *quai* at Quebec."

Edouard looked back over the rail and the northern hint of irregular horizon. He recalled the man-of-war, *Orleans,* and felt a touch of danger. As Jouvier had said, the vengeful arm of the king could be long.

"Are you sure, *mon Capitaine*? There have been no royal craft passing us?"

"Certain, *mon Sieur*." Jouvier grinned. "You may present yourself to his Excellency the Governor, with no fear."

"Why should I fear?" Edouard demanded, then laughed and threw off the masquerade with a shrug. "His Majesty will be much too busy with the lovely Madame de Pompadour to give me or even New France a thought."

"Ah, that is true. I hear *la Madame* can well make a man forgetful of many things." Jouvier pointed down to the entrance of his own cabin. "Now that you are certain, *mon Sieur*, perhaps you will honor me at table once more? This

119

time, you can swallow honest, good wine in good cheer, eh?''

Shortly afterward, Edouard and Jouvier banged their empty tankards down on the table before the settle and the captain bellowed to Jacques for a refill.

''Is it still Quebec, *mon Sieur*?'' he asked Edouard.

''This peltry business intrigues me.''

''Only His Excellency can license you, *mon Sieur*.''

''Who is the Governor?''

''The Marquis de la Gallissonnière, *mon Sieur*. I hear he is a man of reason and he will be eager to hear news of home.''

''Gascon?''

''I don't know, *mon Sieur*. But whether you be from Rouen, Lyons, Paris or Grenoble, you will be welcome.''

Edouard slapped his hand on the table. ''Then I shall ask for a license.''

''*Bien!* When you have it, find Pierre Leduc in the Lower Town. He has trapped and traded as far to the west where I have heard there are lakes as large as oceans. Pierre is a friend of mine—we are both Picards. He will not only tell you what you need but equip you.''

Edouard lifted his newly filled tankard. ''*Merci, mon Capitaine, et à 'votre santé'*. I will keep my promise about the *louis d'or*.''

''Speaking of *l'argent, mon Sieur*, I hear His Excellency has somewhat of a fancy for such stray pieces as may come his way. So does Jacques.''

As Jouvier had predicted, the *Demoiselle* fought wind and current upstream. At last Edouard saw banks, trees, hills and streams to either side of the wide, watery path they traveled. This was truly a river, truly the St. Lawrence and he had truly reached the temporary haven of New France. Even so, he often stood at the ship's rail and watched the solid forests of beeches, birches, and evergreens wheel by on either side. Now and then the solid forest would be broken by a clearing and three or four times by small villages, the typically French farmhouses huddling about a small chapel, its stubby steeple and crude cross a defiant point against the sky.

Then suddenly he saw Quebec. His first impression was that the immense, towering rock and the cluster of the town at its base was surely only a fantasy from a dark and grim folktale, centuries old. He had to throw his head far back to get even a glimpse of what appeared to be walls or palisades crowning the neolithic rock. A road wound its steep way upward, springing from the center of the town below as a spiral of smoke would spring from a fire. It *had* to be fantasy! But the *Demoiselle* turned her prow in toward a *quai* that was a substantial structure combined of solid rock and timber. He saw carts and wagons, a gathering of men, women, children, a few soldiers, Indians, men in buckskin garments. They must comprise every element and inhabitant of the town—city, he corrected himself.

The *Demoiselle* pulled into the *quai*. Sailors vaulted over the rail and caught lines tossed down to them. Jouvier, from his high deck, bellowed orders. Sails dropped and were swiftly rolled and secured. Hawsers noosed over bollards on the *quai* and Edouard heard the splash of the anchors into the rushing waters of the St. Lawrence. Suddenly all action and voices ceased aboard and ashore. The ensuing silence seemed deafening for a second—and then it resumed.

A squad of soldiers in the blue uniform and brass buttons of the royal army pushed through the crowd. A chill traced down Edouard's spine and he hastily retreated to his cabin. Jouvier called down to him from the stern castle.

"Mon sieur! What frightens you about the king's uniform? They have been sent by his Excellency, the Governor, to check my papers, our identification—just as we were stopped by the *Orleans*. It is nothing more."

Edouard looked up at Jouvier then back at the approaching soldiers. Just a squad, flashed through his mind, headed by a sergeant. There would have been more if the Governor had to capture a man wanted by His Majesty. Edouard eyed the clustered houses, shops and narrow streets of the town here at the base of the mighty citadel.

He looked back at Jouvier. "Perhaps they bring me an invitation from *le Gouverneur*. I should dress properly for the occasion."

Jouvier grinned. *"Eh bien, mon Sieur.* It may

be His Excellency seeks only news from France and the royal palace."

"And it may be," Edouard muttered in a half whisper to himself, "to dungeon me until the next ship leaves for France."

He entered his cabin and closed the door. He opened his chest and removed his velvet coat and the knee-length trousers with the silver trimming. Then he took his curled, formal wig from its box and picked up his sheathed, bejewelled court dagger and buckled it about his waist. His hat, its broad brim curled up and pinned to one side of the crown with a small jewel, he placed on his head. He smoothed the long, luxuriant white plume.

Whether he would meet His Excellency as guest or prisoner, it would be in style, he thought wryly. He called loudly for Jacques to come help him dress.

His Excellency would find Edouard, Sieur de Fournet, a properly accoutered *chevalier* of the realm.

XI

The gangplank was lowered to the *quai* but as Edouard stepped forward, the sergeant placed himself squarely in his path. The soldiers made an armed ring behind him, their muskets held ready to aim and fire on a second's notice.

"And what is this, Sergeant?" Edouard

demanded as he pulled up short. "I am le Sieur de Fournet and I wish to have audience with His Excellency, the Governor."

The sergeant saluted, fingertips smartly touching the brim of his cocked hat. The river wind riffled the short feathers of the white cockade that adorned it. "*Mille pardons, mon Sieur*, it is inspection, you understand. His Excellency allows no craft to land or anyone ashore until all papers and identification are examined and approved.

"It is procedure," Jouvier called down from the stern, "a formality . . . but generally there is more than a sergeant. His Excellency must think little of us."

"*Au contraire,*" a new voice answered from the rail and a lean-cheeked, tall man, with just a hint of gray in his dark brown hair, descended to the deck. He wore the same blue uniform but his coat buttons were of gold, with white trim along his high uniform collar, sleeves and edge of his coat. His left hand rested on the pommel of a sword at his belt and the other touched the polished walnut grip of a flintlock pistol tucked into a wide tasseled sash at his waist.

He stepped onto the deck, made a short bow to Edouard. "*Sieur* de Fournet? *C'est mon plaisir*. Allow me. I am Captain Maltrot of His Excellency's guards."

Edouard returned the bow, the curls of his wig momentarily concealing his reaction. Maltrot gave him the impression of having been in New France and perhaps Quebec itself for decades and Edouard also had the certainty the man had been a captain far too long. Had he been in France, the man should have easily advanced to a much higher rank. But perhaps Quebec and its distance from palatial influence explained it. Or—and Edouard thought of his own situation, Captain Maltrot had gained the disfavor of someone in power and dared not return to France. It would not be a *lettre de cachet*, but a pistol ball, a poignard, a hired cutthroat could be as effective, and much more swift.

The captain arrogantly looked up to the stern castle, but Jouvier had already scurried down the steps, struck the deck with a thud of his heels and swept off his hat in a low bow. "If the captain will honor me and my cabin, there is some wine from Burgundy . . ."

Maltrot pulled a golden snuff box from his coat pocket and inhaled a pinch as his inclusive glance swept the deck from bow to masts to the stern castle. His piercing eyes rested momentarily on the sailors almost as if he expected to recognize a felon in each. At last he replaced the snuff box.

"*Eh bien*, Captain. The ship's registry and manifests, of course, then your own and that of Sieur de Fournet—*that* will, of course, be a mere formality. May I ask what brings you to New France. His Excellency will want to know."

Edouard laughed. "Do you recall the old saying that a Gascon has only a *sou* and pride in his pocket, *mon Sieur*? It is said New France offers opportunities."

Maltrot's lips twisted for a second into an expression of acid satire. "Much is said of our country, *mon Sieur*. I have found fortune as fickle as a whore here as elsewhere. But let us sample the Burgundy."

He cast a faintly disdainful look about Jouvier's cabin when he entered, shifted his sword enough to drop onto the most comfortable spot on the settle beneath the window. "Your manifests, Captain?"

Jouvier had already spread the papers on the table before the officer, and Jacques popped through the doorway with a clay wine jug that he held to Maltrot for approval. The officer nodded faintly at the data baked into the clay jug and Jacques poured the wine into tankards he placed before each man. Edouard excused himself and made a hurried trip to his cabin for his identification, silently cursing his own obtuseness. In a moment he was back but not before Maltrot with the ease of many, many such inspections had completed the registry and lading of the *Demoiselle*.

"I see you have not forgotten our Ursuline Sisters, Captain. They will appreciate French cloth for their habits. The local product is inferior and coarse. And lace! *Ma foi!* For His Excellency's collars—and every gentleman and officer will praise this day for all our sleeves and cuffs! Captain, every scrap of yellowing, stringy lace in Quebec will be burned by sundown!"

"*Merci, mon Sieur.*"

"No thanks to me but to your merchant

adventurers who made up the cargo. I see there is also cloth for pantaloons, for skirts—hatchets for our savages and couriers. They will need them in the western and northern wilds. Ah! and knives! Needles! Necessities in this God-blasted, Devil-blessed corner of nowhere!''

In something of a miracle, the dour harsh look had left his face and he accepted the papers Edouard extended, merely glanced at them and thrust them back. "No need, Sieur de Fournet. And now the wine, eh?''

He swept up the tankard Jacques had filled, made salutation to Edouard, a flick to Jouvier and downed the liquid in a series of deep gulps. When he thumped the pewter mug on the table it made a hollow echo. He stretched out his legs and looked to Edouard. "What news of France? Of Europe? We hear rumors there may be war with England again. True?''

He listened to the news and gossip that both Edouard and Jouvier poured into his ears. Jacques made constant trips in and out to keep Maltrot's tankard full but the man always demanded more. He grew thick of speech, then maudlin, then confidential. Edouard felt certain Maltrot's exile had been caused by his inordinate love of the jug. He would be, in a sense, what the English call a "remittance man"—paid to remain not only out of sight but out of the country. The Maltrots at home did not want embarrassment.

Edouard cut in a few times on his rambling, disconnected speech. "What sort of man is His Excellency?''

"The Marquis de la Gallissonnière is one of the best families of France, *mon ami—the best*—unless it be the Maltrots. We are of ancient lines and ancient times, Sieur de Fournet, and as close to the Bourbons of Versailles as any."

"But you, out here in the woods—"

Maltrot placed his finger beside his nose with a wet smile that abruptly vanished as his eyes darkened and his face became an angry thundercloud. "I am in this pesthole on family business. We have investments in depots where the couriers bring peltry. His Excellency and I made certain neither the Crown, his family or mine are cheated by the scoundrels who roam these woods. Oh, yes! I am most important to those back home." His expression grew mournful. "Too important, *mon Sieur*. They can trust only me and so—I must stay year after year."

"His Excellency?" Edouard tried to stop the flood of accusation and recrimination he sensed would soon spew from Maltrot.

The officer peered suspiciously about the cabin, eyed Jouvier with a moment's suspicion and then leaned forward, a move of his thumbs bringing their heads close to his. His voice dropped to a whisper.

"*Marquis*, eh? Peasant! Canard! That is more like it. Show him a louis d'or and he'll lick your ass for an hour to get it. That's His Excellency."

Jouvier and Edouard exchanged frightened, startled looks. This was treason, *lèse majesté*, for here in Quebec the Governor *was* the king—all of royal France. Edouard made a sharp, fierce signal that Jouvier instantly understood. He spoke in harsh protest.

Maltrot stared with surprised, unfocused eyes. "*Canaille!* I'll have you strung up by the thumbs! Have you no respect for an officer of the King! The Hurons will cut off your nose, like they do to an unfaithful squaw."

"Huron," Edouard grabbed at the word to change the topic and soothe the inebriated captain. "Indians? I saw some out on the quai."

Maltrot forgot his anger and all that had been said before. "Huron. Indian." His face lighted. "Ah *mon Sieur*, you have been too many weeks at sea, eh?"

"Too many."

"Then you have need of a woman. Huron girls squirm under you like a fish." He grinned, drooling, "I can tell you that myself, eh? They like a man's muscle and a thrust like the blade of a rapier. Would you like?"

"Of course . . . before long."

Maltrot waved his arm in a wide sweep toward the dock and the town beyond. "I could take you now to Spotted Doe and, *ma foi,* you will never after forget her."

"It might be best, Sieur Maltrot, to first present myself to His Excellency. I'm sure he wouldn't want to be considered second to an Indian girl."

Maltrot grinned crookedly. "Now there you have correctly read our most excellent governor. He has but two superiors in all the world—

money and the King, and in that order, depend on it. Even His Holiness would not excel those two nor the ego of our Marquis.''

He did not notice Jouvier's fearful expression. He banged his empty tankard on the table and pulled himself to his feet. By some strange magic he instantly became tall, impressive and military. He made a curt bow to Edouard, glanced at Jouvier and rapped a knuckle on the ship's papers. ''All is in order. Sieur de Fournet, I will convey your request for an audience to His Excellency. He will send an escort for you.''

''But won't you . . . ?''

''I am not assigned to the palace, *mon Sieur*, God be praised! I command the garrison of the Lower Town and that's to my liking. If I were on the staff of the Marquis, there would be a duel within a week.''

''With the Governor!'' Edouard exclaimed.

Maltrot cocked his head and sniffed contemptuously. ''*Vous avez raison, mon ami*. He would not dare. I would be shot, knifed, garotted or shipped to Martinique.'' Maltrot bowed and caution momentarily flicked through the wine fumes. ''This has all been between us, eh, *mes amis*?''

''Between us, Sieur de Maltrot.''

He saluted them, turned and marched to the rail and his waiting guard with only a faint hint of waver in his stance. The sergeant helped him overside but before leaving himself turned and saluted Edouard. He looked uncomfortable and apologetic.

"I beg, *mon Sieur*, that you forgive and forget the captain. It is one of his bad days and I fear he will not long be with us. We—*soldats* and no more—he treats with kindness and understanding. That is rare in the army, especially in this far post of France, *vous comprenez*."

Jouvier nodded with a grimace of distaste, shrugged and sighed. "It is the wine that mellows him, Sergeant, and that also ruins him. I will forgive and forget, as you say."

"So will I," Edouard added then checked the sergeant's move to leave the ship. "Is there a good, clean hostel in Quebec?"

"Three or four for *gentilhommes*—the rest for traders, trappers and ordinary travelers. Try the Snow Fox, *mon Sieur*. I hear it is clean, comfortable and the food and wine are excellent. Some few stay at the Ursuline hospice but—?"

"That would be too austere."

"Then the Snow Fox. I will send men to handle your luggage, if you wish." He hesitated. "If you have need of a maid—there are the Indian girls for an evening or so as long as you wish—Huron or Algonquin. They are not fair of skin as *mon Sieur* might wish—more bronze-dark with coarse black hair and their faces are sometimes like moons. But they are lively if the *sous* are plentiful."

"At the Snow Fox!"

The sergeant grinned. "We are far from home, *mon Sieur*, and you will soon discover that most of Quebec and Montreal, even all New France, is mostly men without families. That ex-

132

cepts the Indians, of course, and the Good Sisters are above the thoughts of ordinary men. So, a Huron girl discreetly serviced may be known but never mentioned and seldom seen. It is well for us that way."

Edouard lifted his hands, palms up and out in a typical Gallic gesture and turned to his cabin. When all the soldiers had left, Jouvier knocked on the door and entered as Edouard dropped his shoes on the deck and propped his stockinged feet on the far bench of the table.

"And what do you think of Quebec, *mon Sieur*? Will it be difficult to find your place here?"

"*Qui sait?* This port is easy and liberal enough, depending—" Edouard lifted his eyes toward the ceiling and the huge rock that he knew towered above it—"on His Excellency of whom we have varying reports."

"A lonely man, the Marquis, governing a million miles of forest, plains, mountains, ice, Indians and wild *emigrés*. He must answer to men in France who have never so much as seen the St. Lawrence, a voyageur or a *courrier de bois*. If one thinks on it—"

Edouard sighed, finishing the captain's unspoken thought, then looked about the cabin. "Can Jacques pack my belongings to go ashore? Strange, I think I am going to miss the *Demoiselle* and you, *mon Capitaine*."

"And who would have believed it!" Jouvier laughed, reopened the door on the deck and bellowed, "Jacques!"

The curious crowd on the dock had not dispersed when Edouard gave Jacques a generous *pourboire* and watched two soldiers, his trunks and boxes on their shoulders, push through the motley group on the dock and trudge to the street that by now was almost hidden by the *Demoiselle's* unloading cargo.

A brawny man with wide shoulders, bow legs and muscled arms came up and respectfully swept off his fur cap as he stepped before Edouard. "You are le Sieur de Fournet? Captain Maltrot said that you would need the hostel and his sergeant has just reported that you favor the Snow Fox."

"Word travels swiftly," Edouard commented.

"*Oui, mon Sieur*. Also Captain Maltrot has caused our Spotted Doe to bathe and prepare your room."

"Spotted Doe?"

The man grinned, the movement of his leathery lips making his face move like a rubber ball. "She is very good at changing a cold bed into a very warm one, *mon Sieur*."

"Eh, so?" Edouard caught Jouvier's twinkling eyes and laughed, then sobered. "Does His Excellency—?"

"The Marquis hardly knows she exists, *mon Sieur*."

"Ah, then, no *lettre*—no jealousy?"

"None."

"*L'amour,*" Edouard sighed pleasurably, "It is everywhere, eh?"

134

"Even here, *mon Sieur*, if you like it a little red of skin and smelling slightly smoky from her village campfires."

XII

Quebec proved to be a town of greater proportions than Edouard had thought and it
seemed to grow immensely from the moment he
set his feet firmly on the actual land of New
France. Now that his vision was no longer
limited by the view from the *Demoiselle*, he saw

that the street beyond the stone factories' buildings was only the first of several, each of which curved out of sight around the base of the moutain to the left and right.

Except for the exotically dressed trappers and Indians, he could easily believe himself to be in a large marketing town anywhere in France. A fat woman dressed in coarse black, her white kerchief tied in a bow, the ends dangling over her ample bosom, smiled courteously as she passed. She carried a woven wicker basket on each plump arm and Edouard saw the golden-brown ends of loaves of bread peeking from under the coarse but clean cloth that covered them. But his rubbery-faced guide did not allow an easy stroll. The man knew his station in life but he had an ability to hurry Edouard right along, threading through the passersby—most of them dressed in smocks, their feet encased in moccasins which, rather than shoes, seemed to be the principal footgear of all Quebec.

They constantly came upon Indians—men who walked with a lithe forest dignity, women in fringed buckskin blouses and wide, shapeless skirts of the same material. Edouard noted that all of them wore buckskin leggings, wrapped about thick, powerful limbs that peeked from under the skirts.

Solemn-faced workers and artisans merely gave him a curious look as they passed, each intent on some destination and project that, from the expressions, required their immediate presence and unqualified attention. How often he had seen the carpenters, brick masons and tradesmen of Bearn stride by in the same unseeing, intent manner! Nuns walked by, two by two, but with unhurried dignity, beads of their rosaries swinging and clicking from the narrow dark belts about their waists. They had the other-world, distant vision of *les religieuses* in their calm eyes and placid, assured faces.

Indians seemed to be everywhere, mingling with the French *habitants* with the ease of long familiarity. Some of them even wore soiled smocks over their buckskin trousers, their coarse, braided black hair swinging down loose over their shoulders. Edouard's guide tried to increase the pace but Edouard at last refused to be herded along like some of the donkeys he met, the poor animals nearly buried under huge loads of firewood or bearing great woven *paniers* hanging from stout wide leather straps passing over their backs, the containers bulging with everything from vegetables to squawking chickens and ducks. Edouard's guide turned in surprise as Edouard abruptly halted.

"*Mon Sieur*, is there something wrong?"

"What is your name?"

The man's cap instantly swept from his head. "Robert, *mon Sieur*."

"And, Robert, is there some danger of the Snow Fox burning up or sliding into the river?"

"No, *mon Sieur*. Madam Demain would never permit it."

Edouard stared and then burst into laughter. "This Madam Demain must be quite a woman."

"She allows no nonsense, *mon Sieur*."

"I can see that. So, then, why do we hurry? I would like to look about as we go to my new home."

Robert's ugly face lit up. "Ah, *mon Sieur*, I had forgotten you are newly come. I have been here so long that I hardly see anything any more."

Edouard nodded curtly. "Then set your pace to mine but lead the way."

Able now to stroll as a gentleman should, Edouard saw that Quebec had been built for permanence rather than as a wilderness outpost that might easily be abandoned by the end of the year. The houses were of stone, or a combination of stone and wood. Chimneys smoked atop high gabled roofs and everywhere Edouard saw the narrow windows with lead diamond glass panels set in them. Stout, thick doors, banded with iron, decorative straps of reinforcement suggested many he had seen in France and he suddenly felt in full force the nostalgia of the exile. Would he ever see Gascony again? Oh, damn the Duc de la Verre and his scrawny neck!

The Snow Fox proved to be an impressive three-storied edifice, the stone street floor occupied by a tavern, and a shop separated by a low arched, wide entrance to the hostel itself. Robert tugged a bellpull and without pause, pushed open the iron-banded door of thick oak planks. Edouard judged only a battering ram would break it down.

But his speculation instantly ended when an

immense woman in a dark blue dress, keys rattling from a huge ring at her waist, came striding
to them. She fairly filled the short hall, her
shoulders so wide they nearly brushed each wall,
her bosom so large and full that Edouard judged
it must surely march ahead of her by moments.
Her heavy voice boomed in the narrow space of
the hallway.

"*Bienvenue, Sieur* de Fournet."

"You know my name!"

"Certainly. Captain Maltrot often visits us."
She slightly inclined her massive head to a door
that led into an interior entrance to the tavern.
She wore a coarse, high cap trimmed with pink
ribbon atop the high pile of her graying brown
hair. Now, his eyes adjusted to the interior light,
Edouard saw that she was probably the ugliest
woman he had ever seen. Her face was bony,
angular, the skin sallow and pitted, her nose a
hooked beak, a hairy wart at the base of the left
nostril.

"What news of France, *mon Sieur*? Is it true
we will soon again war with the lobsterbacks?"

"Lobsterbacks?"

"The English, *mon Sieur*. Many of our men
lumber and trade in Maine Colony, over beyond
the south bank of the river, and many live there.
We have heard the people call the English
soldiers 'lobsterbacks' because of the red
uniforms they wear."

"French working alongside the English? And
there is talk of war!"

"Ah, these are American, *mon Sieur*, as they

call themselves, and they do not like the soldiers. We of Quebec and those of Maine are friendly enough—there have even been marriages between us. But if war comes—" She broke off, shrugged. "But you would know more than we since you have just come from *la belle France*, eh?"

"I have heard rumors, Madam Demain, many of them. But nothing more definite. But England is always at our throat and it would not surprise me. I will say there is more dark and threatening talk lately, but—" Edouard shrugged "—wagging tongues love the words of doom, eh? The *Demoiselle* kept well south of British shipping lanes and we were stopped by two of His Majesty's men-of-war bound for Martinique."

Madam Demain's ugly face lit up. "Ah, so! Then they patrol. We have heard His Majesty sends is an army and a general to garrison Quebec since we lost Louisburg in the last war."

Again Edouard helplessly shrugged. "I would not know, Madam. Now . . . about lodgings?"

"For how long? And are you alone?"

"I am alone. How long? I do not know. I want to see His Excellency about dealing in peltry and perhaps to travel west."

"If you have money, His Excellency will not detain you for long. If not . . . it could be months."

"I have a few coins."

"Then a week, two at the most. You will be traveling to our Fort DeTroit, *mon Sieur*, or

141

perhaps Michilimacinac many leagues beyond on the Lac du Huron.''

''Northward?''

''The English would drive you out, *mon Sieur*. They have a factory on what is called Hudson's Bay and their trappers and Indians allow no trespassers. No, it will be DeTroit.'' She thoughtfully placed her finger on her ugly mouth. ''I would judge a month with us at the Snow Fox.''

''But if it's just a matter of days—''

''Still a month, *mon Sieur*. I furnish bed, meals and service of all kinds. You will not lose, I assure you.'' She made the smile of a gargoyle. ''And there could be companionship, *mon Sieur*. Indian maids work for me and they are friendly, if I permit.''

''Ah, yes—Spotted Doe.''

''Among others. But you have heard of her?''

''Very much.''

She extended her hand. ''Then a month it is. If you will sample our wines in the tavern, I will have Spotted Doe prepare your room *immédiatement*. Robert will take care of your luggage. Leave it here with me.''

He paid her and her fingers snapped tight on the coins the moment they touched her palm. She smiled again, indicated the tavern door. ''Robert will find you when all is ready and—*mon Sieur*—the first tankard of a guest at the Snow Fox will cost you nothing. It is our custom.''

''*Merci,* Madam.'' He started to turn but a

thought struck him. "Madam, this American colony—Maine. Do I need his permission to cross the boundary?"

"Of course! That is, should your tongue slip and he learn of it. Otherwise . . . eh, many of our own go and come."

"In case of war that you are so certain will come?"

"Then everything will change, *mon Sieur*, if the day *should* come. No American colony to the south would be safe for a Frenchman or Canadian."

The tavern's host made him welcome and Edouard sat at a small table beneath a leaded window. Across the small room, at another larger table in a corner, three army subalterns in blue uniforms merely gave him a curious glance and returned to their animated conversation. Edouard accepted the flagon of wine and glass placed before him and listened to the young officers as he slowly sipped his wine.

They spoke of doings of the garrison-fortress atop the mountain and most of it was mere gibberish to Edouard. But his attention suddenly grew sharp when one of the men, his voice carrying clearly across the small room, spoke of a march he would soon be making.

"To follow Celeron's route, *mes amis*. It will be all river, forest and Indians—and mosquitoes. Sieur de Celeron discovered those damnable English have built a fort at the forks of *La Belle Rivière* with that other stream—what is it? —ah, *oui*, the Monongahela. How those Indians can make tongue-twisting words!''

"A fort? That close to us!'' a second exclaimed. "But all that country was long ago claimed for our King!''

"We're to make that most plain and certain to the English. They call the place Fort Prince George now, after their next Hanover ruler.''

"Well! And what do we do if they will not listen?''

"Drive them out, I understand.''

"That will be war!''

"Of course, but then, when haven't we been warring with England, or Spain, or Austria, or some other idiotic country that grabs all it can and hopes that no one will make a challenge. But this time, we will.''

Suddenly the wigged heads came close as the officers leaned toward one another and Edouard strained his ears. He heard but a few words " . . . sends us an army . . . Montcalm . . . on its way now. We will have Fort George. Soon there will be . . . ''

One of the men looked up, saw Edouard closely watching them. He hastily said something under his breath and instantly the young men straightened in their seats, backs like ramrods, young faces tight and grim. One of them pushed back from the table and with a step close to a swagger crossed to Edouard's table. Edouard judged him to be a Norman. The officer made a barely perceptible bob of his head.

"You are new to Quebec?''

"I have just arrived aboard the *Demoiselle*.

144

Allow me, I am Sieur de Fournet of Bearn.''

The stripling looked startled. "Gascony! Do you know the Duc de la Verre?''

"I am fresh come over from a month as guest at his Château, *mon—mon Sieur de—*''

The lad then bowed. "De Valerain, *à votre service.*''

Edouard arose and returned the bow, then impulsively asked, "Are you on His Excellency's staff?''

"Of course, *mon Sieur.*''

"I would like to present myself to the Governor and pay my respects.''

"That is easily arranged. I myself assist Colonel Louvet, who makes the Governor's appointments.''

"Indeed! I am fortunate. Would it be possible to have audience say—oh, say tomorrow? You see, there is a matter of license to deal in peltry of great interest to my family and friends in Bearn and Toulouse.''

"My pleasure, sir, though I cannot speak for His Excellency. But I could send a messenger if Colonel Louvet finds the Governor is free. Are you staying here at the Snow Fox?''

"*Oui,* Lieutenant. Someone spoke of it by chance.''

"The best hostel in Quebec, so you are fortunate again.''

Edouard glanced at the officers at the table across the room. "In appreciation, Sieur de Valerain, would you do me the honor of accepting the best wine of the house. Perhaps your friends would also honor me."

De Valerain bowed. "There is no need—"

"I insist."

"Better yet, Sieur de Fournet. Join us. All of us would like to hear the latest news from home."

In a matter of moments Edouard was introduced around and a place made for him among the young officers. Madam Demain appeared in the doorway, but was unnoticed by Edouard and his new companions. She saw a servant with a tray of tankards move from the bar to the table and she instantly stepped back into the hall with a faint clank of keys on their ring. Francs spent on wine could be quite plentiful and certainly just as good as the comparatively few that could be spent in lodgings.

For his part, Edouard learned much about this strange new country. Talk confirmed the riches that could be made in furs, but de Valerain cautioned Edouard to establish what was called a factory—a post where Indians and trappers who brought in the peltry would quickly spend the money Edouard would pay them on bad wine, water-weakened whiskey and gin, a taste learned from the English to the south.

"So you have your coin back at a profit, then?" Edouard asked.

"A hundred times over," the soldiers assured him. "Your own Indians and men stack and pack them in bundles of the prescribed size with the Royal seal and send them on here or to Montreal. His Majesty's tax which His Excellency deducts assures shipment on to your factories in France, or local dealers will pay you louis d'or in hand.''

Edouard dropped back in his chair in amazement. ''That is all, once I have the permits. I can simply go out into the forest and be in the fur business!''

They laughed and de Valerain signaled for another round of wine. ''Not that easy, de Fournet. There have already been so many for a century that you will have to travel far beyond Fort de Troit, deep in the western wilderness. But it will be well worth all the time and money needed for the trip, to build your post and hire your workers. Have I discouraged you or do you still wish to beg license from the Governor?''

''The license.''

''Then I shall see Colonel Louvet. You'll hear from the palace by tomorrow at the latest.''

Edouard ordered another round of the wine to the pleasure of the young officers and then, despite their protests, left them. Madam Demain, seated with all the dignity of an extremely ugly duchess in a high-backed ample chair in the hostel's common room, arose when he appeared.

''Your room is ready, Sieur de Fournet.''

She led the way up wide stairs, along a hallway for a few feet and then stopped. She pointed ahead to a thick door that obviously opened on a room overlooking the street.

''You will find it fit for a man of title, *mon Sieur*. The maid is still—how is it said—cleaning up the corners. You may dismiss her . . . that is, if you like.''

She detached a key from her ring and gave it to Edouard. ''For the lock, but you will find the inner bolts secure. The girl will show you the closet and the bellpull should you need anything. I think you will find her most helpful and agreeable. If not, tell me.'' Her mouth suddenly shaped fearsomely like a dragon's. ''I will take care of impertinence, should there be any.''

''I'm sure there will not be any.''

''*Vraiment*—the Snow Fox is yours, *mon Sieur*.''

He thanked her and walked on ahead to the closed door. He looked back as he touched the knob, but Madam Demain already descended the stairs and he saw only the lace of the cap she wore before she disappeared. He opened the door, stepped inside, closed and slid a heavy bolt home. He turned—and froze.

The sharp bright sunlight of this northern country streamed in the lead-paned windows and fully on a tall, shapely girl with a slightly red tint to her dark skin. A leather band decorated with beadwork held her hair back from her slightly round face with high cheekbones, and her black eyes gleamed and danced as she saw his mouth drop open in stunned surprise. The beaded headband and moccasins were all she wore.

She spoke in a husky voice. ''La Madam say I be good to you. Me Spotted Doe. Tub hot water in there.'' She pointed to a closed door near the

148

canopied bed. "You bathe." She turned to the room's small fireplace and picked up a metal bedwarmer with a long handle. "I warm bed, eh?"

He could not stop from staring at her shapely legs, full hips and rounded breasts. He gulped, found his voice.

"Oui, you warm bed . . . plenty!"

XIII

The narrow way between the long houses of
Onondaga Town echoed and re-echoed to the
yells of the men, women and children onlookers.
But the double line of grim-faced women, each
with her switch or club, remained silent. The
captive women stood immobile, frozen with fear

as the shouts and yells roared about them. The six Keepers of the Faith stood imperious and unmoving, and Abby noticed the contemptuous curl of their lips. She looked far down the street to the distant gate, wondering if it would be at all possible to reach it on her feet—and alive. Certainly not unscathed, for the hard faces of the waiting, armed women assured her of that.

The High Priestess, if that was what she truly was, grew impatient and almost barked a single word. Instantly, one of the warriors seized his captive woman by the arm and with a powerful push and swing placed her between the first of the waiting women.

Instantly, the switches descended and the girl screamed as the whips struck, cut the skin and drew blood. She started to run, arms outstretched as though endeavoring to touch the gate even at this far distance. But the second pair struck her and she wavered to one side. Abby watched in numbed disbelief as she saw the girl viciously whipped across the face and pushed toward the opposite squaw whose lips drew back from her teeth as her own switch slammed and cut across the girl's ribs.

By now the second girl had been started through the devil's line. Yips, barbaric yells, pleased shouts rose on every side so that Abby's mind became overwhelmed and confused. The third girl suddenly stumbled forward, a blow on the back propelling her into the gauntlet. But Abby saw, on down the line, the first girl struck on the shoulder by one of the clubs and she thought she heard the crunch of the bone as the girl's arm dropped limp and broken to her side. She tried to wheel away, but one of the squaws scooped up a handful of dust and threw it directly into her face, blinding her.

Patience abruptly screamed as her captor whirled her about by her arm and almost literally threw her between the first pair of waiting switches. But Abby's eyes swiftly cut back to the blinded girl with the broken arm who could only alternate trying to rid her eyes of the blinding grit, and at the same time grope forward. But she lost her footing as a squaw adroitly jammed her thick long tree limb between her legs and pitched forward. Instantly, with a shout of triumph, several of the squaws sprang to her. The clubs and switches lifted and fell. For a moment the struggling group became hidden by a small but thick cloud of dust out of which came one blood curdling scream of pain.

The cloud began to settle and Abby saw warriors push a way between the squaws. The fallen girl lay in a grotesque heap on the ground, body twitching. But Abby saw the slowly spreading stain of blood and knew the girl was dead.

Leah breathed in a horrified whisper. "O my God! What chance is there for us!"

Abby started to answer but just then Corn Dancer came to her side. His strong fingers sank into her arm and she knew she would be catapulted to the waiting Indian women in a matter of minutes. Corn Dancer spoke under his breath.

"Abbbeee . . . you see . . . run . . . fast."

But so did the others, flashed through her mind as Corn Dancer propelled her forward. The switches instantly cut across her back and she bent herself against them, hugging her elbows to her side, her legs pumping her forward. Switches hit, some missed, and then she saw the first of the squaws with the clubs just ahead. The woman bent to fling the club between her flashing ankles to trip and throw her.

But Abby bent down with her and before the woman could prevent it, she grabbed the club and wrenched it from the squaw's bronzed hands. As she whirled about the weapon struck another squaw in the ribs with a bone-cracking thud. Without breaking stride, Abby reversed her turn even as her legs pumped her closer to the gate. Another Indian woman went down, the blow on her head knocking her unconscious. Now Abby felt a fierce vengeful joy as her club swung about again and again.

She only dimly heard the rising clamor about her, the shouts of alarm and amazement. She had her full attention on the open gate, now much nearer, though several women blocked her way. But lips pressed and nostrils flaring, Abby bore down on them. Club lifting and falling, flailing left and right as hands grabbed for her. The remaining Indian women suddenly dropped their switches and fled and the way to the gate, now but a few yards away, was unobstructed. She heard thudding steps behind her. She whirled about, club again lifted.

But someone grabbed her from behind. She struggled but other hands snatched at her and strong arms encircled her. She twisted fearsomely to escape but could not. Then she heard laughter—male laughter!

She could no longer take a step and her arms were jerked back of her, the club torn from her fingers. She struggled and twisted but to no avail. Laughter and shouts were now all about her.

Corn Dancer suddenly appeared before her, smiling. That sent a shock through her. Would he be laughing as he killed her? Or would he allow the squaws to have their vengeance? She suddenly realized that only men were pressed about her—the warriors. They held her as Corn Dancer stepped close. He, too, grabbed her arm and then her shoulders.

"Abbbeee! Abbbeee! Good. No hurt you. Nobody hurt you. You brave woman. I proud you my woman. Hah! Corn Dancer *orenda* great when he take you. Your *orenda* strong. See . . . there."

He pointed beyond her and she turned and gasped at what she saw. The double line of Indian women had vanished. Several of them lay sprawled on the ground, unmoving, and Abby had the fearful thought her swinging club had killed them until she saw two of them stir and then realized the others breathed but she had knocked them unconscious. Far back, at the point where she had started, the six Keepers of the Faith stood unmoving. But even as she looked, the stately woman with the higher head dress moved toward her and, a step behind, the others followed.

Instantly the men around Abby stopped their laughter and talk. A silence fell on the whole street, except for an occasional moan from one of the fallen women. Abby saw Leah, Marion and the others in a group guarded by warriors. Nearby, Patience, her legs, arms, back and stomach an interlacing of bleeding switch cuts, sobbed, and the girl with the broken arm sat beside her, nursing it and rocking back and forth in pain.

The Keepers of the Faith approached and stopped so close that Abby might have reached out and touched the leader. The stately woman looked at her slowly, from the crown of her head to her feet. Her high planed face held no expression but Abby caught bright gleams far back in her eyes. She slowly turned her head and spoke to Corn Dancer.

"Abbbeee," he replied to whatever she had said, thudded his fist against his chest and spoke rapidly again. Abby gathered that he claimed her for himself and she looked again at the woman.

Abby shook her head when the woman spoke directly to her, shook her head again when the woman evidently repeated herself in a sharper, more imperious tone. The woman looked at the other Keepers of the Faith and spoke several sentences, pointing to Corn Dancer and then to Abby. The others gravely nodded in apparent agreement. Then the woman pointed back to Leah and the other captives, speaking again. Once more the others indicated agreement and the woman turned to Corn Dancer.

She spoke at some length, making many gestures and signs both to Abby, her friends, Corn Dancer and his companions of the raiding party on Westover. Corn Dancer stood straighter and his expression was stern but it was also filled with pride. The woman then looked at the squaws who had formed the gauntlet. The few who still held switches and clubs threw them away as though suddenly their hands had been burned. They looked cowed, answered in a monosyllabic word and turned to help those who sat or lay on the ground.

Corn Dancer spoke then and the woman imperiously nodded, answered at some length and all six of the Keepers turned away, moving back along the street with slow dignity. For long moments, Corn Dancer watched them. One of his warriors started to speak but Corn Dancer fiercely motioned him to silence. The Keepers stopped before one of the houses, slightly separated from the rest. They turned, and with high lifted arms made a sign that Abby assumed to be some kind of salute or blessing. Then, they turned and disappeared into the house.

The second they vanished speech exploded in words, shouts and yells along the street. Corn Dancer flung off the hands of his companions and whipped around to face Abby. His bronze face was lit up and his smile as wide and flashing as Abby had ever seen it.

"Abbbeee! You Iroquois soon! *Orenda* strong. You be my Fireside. Mother say 'Ha!' you my Fireside—my squaw."

She stared at him, caught her voice. "Me? Iroquois?"

"Hai! You Corn Dancer woman. Clean out white—you Onondaga woman—Corn Dancer's."

Now she saw that the other warriors had taken the arms of the other women, who looked frightened and turned as one to Abby. Leah threw off the hand of the Indian who held her. "What do they mean?"

"I don't know for sure. I think we're to become Indian women—all of us."

"Not me!" Leah almost shouted and again flung off her warrior's detaining hand. He scowled, looked to Corn Dancer. Abby spoke hastily and fearfully.

"Leah! Better that than dead!"

Leah's eyes widened as the statement struck home but then she frowned and shook her head. "Why? What caused this? I thought they'd kill and scalp you when you started using that club on those greasy, fat women. I thought we'd all be dead."

Abby turned to Corn Dancer, touched herself and then pointed to the other girls, pulled at her hair and made a sign indicating a knife circling her head. "No kill? No scalp? All of us?"

"Keepers say you squaws good *orenda* for Onondaga Town. We make you Iroquois—all

157

squaw Iroquois.'' He pointed to her and then himself, to Leah, Patience, Marion and the warriors who had captured them. ''All Iroquois. All Onondaga. I take you my Fireside.'' He pointed to a warrior and then Leah. ''He take her his Fireside—our Mothers say 'haa!'' *Orenda* our firesides, our *owachira,* our clans. Big *orenda.''*

''I'm white—pale skin,'' Abby tapped herself. ''How Onondaga?''

''You see. Now we go Mother my fireside.''

He suddenly gripped her wrist and, smiling at her, led her back to the Long House she had first visited. Abby began to have some inkling of what was happening. When she had grabbed the club and started flailing about her in a last, desperate and hopeless effort to save her life, her action had amazingly gained the admiration of these savages. It had saved all their lives. She had not known that courage and fighting fury gained the admiration of her captors, evidently from women, men and warriors alike. But she had little time to think of anything clearly before she again stood at the small fire in the middle of the Long House, facing the woman who was obviously Corn Dancer's mother.

The older woman's demeanor had changed. Now she no longer scowled and withdrew from Abby, but came to her and touched her heart and forehead with her fingers. She rubbed Abby's skin at both places and then studied her fingers. She slowly touched the rags at Abby's throat and gently pulled apart the shreds of her blouse. Abby's breasts looked doubly white, full and rounded. The woman pulled her arms and hands down when she tried to cover herself. Still smiling, she slowly turned Abby about and stroked her buttocks and thighs, stepped back and looked at Corn Dancer.

He spoke to her and Abby heard *orenda* among the words. It was repeated by both several times. Now a tall, wrinkled man and some children came from one of the rooms to one side of the fire and Abby instantly saw the resemblance between him and Corn Dancer. Again the unintelligible words flew back and forth between the two men. The newcomer spoke to the woman who turned to Abby and again pulled open the tattered blouse. Abby instinctively lifted her hands to cover herself but the woman spoke sharply.

Corn Dancer said quickly, "Abbbeee—no hurt. Just see you fine squaw. No hurt."

Abby reluctantly dropped her hands, feeling shamed and embarrassed under the old man's careful scrutiny of her breasts. He ran his hands along her buttocks and Abby could not help her flinches as his fingers traced down her thighs to her knees. Then she gasped as he suddenly grasped the band at her hips and pulled down her skirts. She whirled away but Corn Dancer and his mother instantly grabbed her, turned her back around.

They held her wrists and arms immobile as the father moved his hand over her stomach down into her groin and for long, intolerable seconds his fingers probed within her. She struggled to free herself but the older man stepped back and nodded to the mother, obviously his wife.

He spoke quickly and incisively and both the mother and Corn Dancer nodded again and again, Corn Dancer quite openly proud and pleased. The father shrugged, turned away from Abby and returned to the room he had just left. The children remained, staring at Abby with great rounded dark eyes.

Corn Dancer's laugh broke the tense silence and Abby knew the ordeal had been finished. Corn Dancer said, "You good *orenda*. Keepers say you make good Onondaga. You be my woman."

"*Your* woman! Don't I have any say? Any right? I don't want to be your woman!"

Corn Dancer frowned, puzzled, not understanding and shook his head. "You say no meaning."

She tried to explain but again he shook his head and she patiently tried another means but he still did not understand. His mother looked from her to Corn Dancer, back to Abby and then her son again. Abby heard the note of puzzled question in her voice and Corn Dancer answered something, shaking his head uncomprehending. Suddenly Abby had an inspiration.

She touched the woman, who instantly swung around to her. Abby touched her again and then pointed to the room where the older warrior could barely be seen, seated in the heavy gloom against the far wall. The woman followed the gesture with her eyes and then Abby's hand as she touched the woman, pointed to the man again. Then Abby pointed to Corn Dancer, then touched herself and shook her head.

"No. No be squaw Corn Dancer."

Shock instantly widened her eyes and Corn Dancer himself looked stunned, his mouth dropping open. Abby persisted, repeating her gestures and this time her voice fairly echoed in the long corridor, now filled with curious women and children who had gathered about the ashes of the other fires.

"No be squaw Corn Dancer." She struck her bare chest with her fist, then swung her arm back in what she thought must be the location of burned Westover.

"My man back there. My . . . my . . . fireside . . . back there. No be squaw Corn Dancer."

She had her first insight to the Iroquois way of thinking and acting then. Corn Dancer stared at her a moment and then his lips pulled back in a tight, hard smile that had no hint of humor. He shook his head and made a slashing movement with the edge of his hand as though wielding a weapon.

"You no squaw white warrior there." He, too, indicated distant destroyed Westover. "Your warrior . . . gone." He stepped around the fire and entered the room where his father had disappeared. He came out an instant later and Abby shrank from the bundle of hair he held in his hand. It was gray and she saw the dirty, filthy, once blue ribbon that held the queue. It was not Daniel's but she knew what Corn Dancer meant. He held it up toward her and she retreated a stumbling step.

"Your warrior lose—what you say?—hair, scalp . . . like this." He half turned and contemptuously pitched the horrible trophy of some older raid back in the room, pointed to her and then slammed his fist against his chest. "You Corn Dancer squaw. Keepers say. You brave. Big *orenda*. You be Onondaga."

He glared at her and then, as though all discussion had ended, he spoke again to his mother. The woman watched Abby closely, her dark face suddenly as tight and cruel as Corn Dancer's.

The fact that Daniel had been killed . . . scalped . . . and that she'd never see him again slammed into her consciousness with the stunning force of a thunderbolt. She knew in that flashing, instant of doom what she had not really acknowledged through all the days and nights of her journey to this Iroquois town. Daniel was *dead*. Her mother and father were dead and probably Westover completely destroyed. There would never be rescuers now—never a familiar face except those of the girls and women, such as Leah, who had managed to survive the ordeal of the journey.

She swayed, caught herself but could not help the tears that coursed down her cheeks or the sobs that clutched at throat as she tried to choke them back. Then, not wanting to show weakness to these savages, she pulled back her shoulders

162

and proudly straightened. Muscles worked in her cheeks and throat as she mercilessly killed all thought of Daniel for the moment or for any other moment that even one of these savage children might be watching her.

The mother's expression slowly changed and she spoke over her shoulder to Corn Dancer. He made an imperious gesture to Abby to follow him, led the way down the long hall to its very end. Abby saw two of the rooms to either side of a bare spot where a fire had not yet been built. Corn Dancer roughly jerked up her chin and glared deep in her eyes. She met his stare with one equally as hard. Slowly his expression softened and he indicated one of the rooms.

"When you Onondaga—that our fireside."

XIV

Abby looked in on the dark, bare earthen floor of the compartment that seemed hardly more than a cave. She had the frightening thought that they were to move in immediately and start whatever the Iroquois called a family. But Corn Dancer's smile only widened and he turned about and walked back to the fire where his mother waited. Abby followed, relieved. But that lasted only a moment. There were too many unknown things that would be done with or to her—perhaps immediately, perhaps in a matter of hours or a day or so. Uppermost in the list of her unknowns in her mind remained the wonder as to how she would be "made" an Onondaga.

Corn Dancer spoke to his mother, who listened with several sidelong looks at Abby. Then she spoke a long series of words but Abby could only shake her head. The woman scowled, angry, but Corn Dancer spoke quickly and her face cleared.

He explained to Abby, "I tell Mother you speak whiteface talk. Not speak Onondaga. You not Onondaga . . . yet." He pointed to his mother, "You do she say, eh?"

What else, Abby wondered as she dubiously nodded. Now both Corn Dancer and his mother smiled and Abby, gaining a touch of courage, pointed to the woman. "What's her name?" Corn Dancer looked puzzled so Abby touched herself. "Me . . . Abby. Who she?" and she pointed to the woman.

Corn Dancer's face lighted. "She Moon Willow. She Mother our Fireside." He pointed beyond her and when Abby turned she saw an ancient crone huddled near the fire close to the door. "She Mother *Owachira.*"

"What *owachira?*"

Again he pointed to the old crone and then made a gesture that included the whole building even to the empty rooms that he had said would be "their fireside." "All . . . all Firesides here." At that moment a naked toddler came out of one of the rooms nearby. Corn Dancer jumped to him and swept him up in his arms, held him out so that the small brown face was practically in her own. She could read fright in the child's eyes, but, Indianlike, it did not show in his face—a small, bronze oval of impassivity. Corn Dancer lifted the boy higher, then put him down on his feet. The child looked up at him, at Abby, and then as though nothing had happened to him, waddled away on fat bow legs. Corn Dancer pointed to him and then came the familiar gesture of his fist hitting his own chest.

"Corn Dancer . . . him . . . we same *owachira*." He then indicated the other fires and rooms, the long length of the passage and again struck his chest. "All *owachira* . . . me . . . all same *owachira*."

Abby began to understand that *owachira* must mean some sort of family group and that everyone she saw in this Long House was, in some way, related to all the others. So then, she thought, if she and Corn Dancer were to establish the "fireside" far down the passageway, all the Indians she saw about her would be indirectly related to her. It would be as though she became the cousin, aunt, daughter or sister of everyone in Westover. Here she would soon have a whole tribe of relations when . . . How would they make her Onondaga returned to her thoughts to worry her.

But she had no time to dwell on the returning uncertainty. Moon Willow, with crooking finger, beckoned Abby to follow her and led the way to the single door of the Long House. They stepped out into the street and instantly all about stopped to curiously eye Abby and make unintelligible speech to one another—obviously about her.

She didn't quite know how to act, so she kept her attention on Moon Willow and followed the woman out beyond the stockade and into one of the cultivated fields. Now she saw that narrow little pathways divided the field into sections and Moon Willow pointed to one nearby, struck her chest and pointed again. Abby understood that this was the section that was owned or assigned to Corn Dancer's family.

Moon Willow walked along between rows of sprouting corn and, at the far end, bent to pick up a hoe lying on the ground, the metal rusty except for the bright cutting edge, proof that it had been used. Moon Willow handed it to Abby, picked up another for herself. She pointed to a line of corn shoots pushing up through dry earth, then at Abby and herself. She turned then and started breaking up the dry clods.

For the first time since she had come to Onondaga Town, Abby needed no explanation. How often had she done this same work back in Westover? Tears dimmed her eyes as she bent to the work and she barely heard Moon Willow's pleased tone when she said a few words. Then Abby saw the other women scattered over the fields, each apparently working the section assigned to her. Hoeing corn, Abby thought as she bent to the work, proved to be no different on an Iroquois garden patch than in the fields of Westover.

The sun slowly settled toward the western mountain ridges but Abby paid attention to it only when she would occasionally pause, straighten and stretch to work the cramp and ache from her back and arm muscles. Each time, Moon Willow would also stop, turn and twist her own body, smile at Abby and then bend to the work again.

When the sun touched the mountain ridges, Moon Willow suddenly spoke, indicated to Abby to follow her, and returned to the spot where they had found the hoes. Moon Willow threw hers down on a small pile of other instruments and nodded when Abby followed her example.

As they walked toward the stockade gate, Abby saw the other women also leaving the fields and converging on the town. Now warriors stood by the gate, lances, clubs and even a rifle here and there in their hands. They watched the distant edge of the forest rather than the women, though they covertly and curiously eyed Abby as she passed. The gate closed when the warriors themselves followed the women into the stockade and huge wooden bars were lifted by main strength and placed in brackets. Just as Abby entered the Long House, she looked back to see that some of the warriors remained by the gate; then Moon Willow urged her into the house.

Now the long hall was alit with the fires that glowed all along its length except at the far end where Abby and Corn Dancer would establish their own fireside—when she became Onondaga. That still puzzled her.

She saw Corn Dancer and his father seated before the family fire that had evidently been lit some time before and had by now become a small but wide circle of glowing coals and embers over which rabbits roasted on heavy skewered sticks. Following Moon Willow's gestures and Corn Dancer's broken English translations, Abby stirred some kind of corn mush mixture that the older woman prepared in a big clay pot. She also placed ears of corn in the coals. Apparently the work for all the men in the Long House had been completed for the day because Abby saw all of them squatted before the fires along the passageway. Long pipes with ornamented clay bowls spiraled tobacco smoke as the men talked among themselves.

Then the meal was ready. To Abby's surprise, Moon Willow instead of her husband was the first to start eating—a distinct change from what she had seen during the camps on the long, torturous flight from the raid on Westover. But Moon Willow's precedence seemed to be ceremonial, for she had no more than taken a few bites when the men also began eating. Abby reached for an ear of the roasting corn but Moon Willow painfully slapped her hand away.

Corn Dancer answered Abby's surprised, questioning look. "You white squaw. You not Onondaga. That be . . . soon." He had found the English word. "Then you eat fireside—" he pointed to the far end of the hall. "You be Mother my Fireside."

Abby sank back on her heels, pushing out of the circle of the family. She felt famished but could not touch the food until she had permission. Her muscles ached from the hours in the field and she longed simply to sleep. But hunger and the constant lift and fall of voices, the cries of the children as they played, created a din that deafened. She had not known that Indians, alone in their own towns and villages, could be so much like the inhabitants of Westover, old and young. She began to sense that there would be much she'd learn in a very short time.

The single door opened and a half a dozen warriors came in. Abby recognized one of them as the man she had seen guarding the gate and the stockade and she watched him, in surprise, stride beyond the fire to one down the corridor. Corn Dancer, happening to look around, saw her puzzled expression. He tapped her knee, catching her attention, pointed to the warrior, and then to the roof.

"How you say . . . night? . . . No fight . . . night. Fight come sun." Again he pointed to the roof and then placed his hand over his eyes. "Night no see. Night . . . bad. Night . . . how you say? . . . dead man's."

His gesture indicated all the dark world

beyond the walls of the Long House. Abby nodded that she understood. Another Iroquois custom learned, she thought.

She was finally permitted to eat and then as the men sat comfortably by and watched, she ate and then cleaned away the food scraps and ashes from around the fire as Moon Willow directed with signs, grunts and strange meaningless words. Then the woman pointed to one of the rooms and to Corn Dancer. Abby's eyes rounded and fear gripped her. Obviously the time for sleeping had come. Was she to be with Corn Dancer? In his savage way would he at last take her as a woman?

Her fright mounted when Corn Dancer came to his feet and held out his hand to her. She involuntarily shrank away and Corn Dancer's father frowned at her, looked at Corn Dancer. He spoke sharply to her.

"Abbbeee . . . Mother want to know what you do. Father want to know. Howling Wolf say white squaw do what told. Moon Willow say."

Abby looked wildly about her to find that her fright and hesitation had called full attention to her. Everyone in the Long House at all the fires, she thought in panic, stared at her, faces stern and eyes hard. The worse were the women, "Mothers" of all the Firesides. The scowls grew more fierce and Abby saw one woman lean forward and pick up a knife, her piercing, angry gaze never wavering from Abby. Corn Dancer . . . or death, she thought. No other choice.

She slowly pushed herself up and saw the sea of bronze faces slowly grow softer. Corn Dancer still held out his hand but he moved impatiently. Howling Wolf spoke sharply and angrily once more.

"Abbbeee . . . you come, eh? Mother . . . Father . . . me . . . no like you wait. Come."

She accepted his hand and he immediately turned into the room to the right of the fire. She slowly entered. She saw what appeared to be a pile of cloth along both sides and the back of the room. Corn Dancer pointed to one pile. "You there." He pointed to the pile at the back of the room. "Me there. Mother there. Father there." He indicated the piles to either side.

"Dark. All what you call sleep, eh?"

It frightened her but she had to ask the question, so she touched herself and then pointed to him. "You? . . . Me?"

"Eh?"

She repeated the signs. "You warrior. Me squaw. You . . . me?" She pointed to one of the piles. "There?"

He understood and his grim countenance broke into a wide grin and laugh. He shook his head. "Not this dark. You still white squaw. You be Onondaga then . . . you . . . me . . . back there. Our own Fireside."

So she had been saved at least for the night and it was though bonds had dropped from her body and mind. She walked to the back of the room. The cloths turned out to be thick-furred bearskins. She sat down on them but Corn

Dancer shook his head and pulled her back on her feet. Then he signed her to lie down on the remaining skins and carelessly threw a thick bearskin over her. She instantly felt its warmth and what little added protection it gave her. She pulled it to her chin. He stood over her a long moment, smiling down at her and then turned to his own pallet. She heard approving grunts from Moon Willow and Howling Wolf, who curled up together under a huge pile of skins near the door. The room became darker as the fires in the long passage outside died down to little red diamonds of hot embers. Abby did not know when she went to sleep.

Her eyes suddenly snapped wide open, her whole body tense. She knew she had slept but could not tell how long. A sound had alarmed her and her nerves still vibrated throughout her body. The small area was pitch black, even the last embers of the fire long dead, and she could hardly see her hand before her face. But the alarming sound continued, muffled through the thick covering over her head.

She lay quite still, afraid, trying to define the moving sounds that had jerked her quivering into full consciousness. They continued and she thought she heard a woman moan and then a series of almost growling grunts. She slowly worked her hand up under the robe and pulled the edge of it down so that her head and ears were free.

Now the sounds came clearly and at first she could not place them. For a long time she even felt confused as to where she might be. Then the picture of the narrow corridor in the long house came to her, and the dark cubicle of a room. The sounds came from over to one side of near the entryway of the room. Again a woman moaned and once more she heard a heavy panting and grunts. Alarm mounted. If the darkness had not been so stygian and the cubicle so strange, she might have obeyed her impulse to throw aside the bearskin and run out into the corridor and along it to the door and escape to the outside.

But she would only encounter more of the horde of dark red savages who must be all about her, inside the Long House, in the streets and the other houses. There would be guards at the stockade and the gate. She had no place to run. She had to do something. She sat up, pulling the bearskin up to her shoulders as the threshing continued not more than an arm's reach from her.

A low chuckle from another direction nearby caused her to start and twist about in defense. Corn Dancer spoke in a whisper from out of the dark and she heard the laughter in his tone.

"Abbbeee? Sssssh!"

"But what—?"

"Sssh. It is Father and Mother. They play—how you say—try make papoose. Old now but . . . Ssssh!"

Her pent-up breath escaped in a low "Woosh!" Feeling foolish, she sank back and pulled the bearskin back over her head but not before she heard Corn Dancer's second low, almost whispered chuckle.

174

XV

Stirrings again awakened Abby but this time the noise sounded throughout the building. The Long House came awake to meet the new day, literally as well as figuratively. The cubicle was only slightly less dark and the corridor outside still held many of the lingering shadows of night.

But she saw Corn Dancer and Howling Wolf striking flint sparks over a small mound of dry grass out in the hallway and it caught, smoked a second and flamed even as she watched. Then Corn Dancer added small twigs and leaves until the flames grew larger while Howling Wolf pulled over larger sticks ready to build the main fire.

Moon Willow threw aside the robe that had covered her, looked at Abby with a frown, then spoke a few words and pointed to a clay pot in the corner and then out into the corridor. Corn Dancer appeared at the entryway at that moment.

"Abbbeee . . . water." He indicated the pot and then pointed to the Long House door. "Water . . . there. You see. Go. Mother make eat'm here, eh?"

Abby grasped the thought, picked up the clay pot and left the cubicle as Moon Willow said something to Corn Dancer that sounded like approval though she couldn't be sure. When she stepped out onto the street, she saw little more than a hint of dawn but many women and girls carried their pots along a side street toward a far row of other long houses. They looked curiously at Abby but said nothing or made no indication of either friendship or dislike. Abby fell in with the procession, ready to jump back and away at the first hostile sign. But none came.

Two streets over, she saw the crowd of women gathered about a well, its low wall, high wooden arm sweep and suspended bucket so like the one she'd known at Westover that a lump formed in her throat. She fought to keep all expression off her face. Two women manned the sweep and, one by one, the girls and women held up their pots to be filled. Abby fell in line and no one tried to push her aside. When her turn came the water dispensers filled her pot as readily and with as little concern as they had the others, though one hesitated slightly and her eyes faintly widened. Abby hurried back with her burden.

The older woman had been working at a shallow bowl filled with corn kernels and now she indicated them to Abby, held up a smoothly worn stone grinder, crushed more of the corn and handed the smooth stone to Abby.

Abby instantly understood. How many times had she herself ground up corn, adding water now and then, to make mush! She went to work without hesitation, happened to look up to catch Moon Willow watching her in both pleasure and surprise. Abby swiftly looked back to her bowl and grinder, knowing that she had gained a touch more of the mother's regard.

Soon the mush and water had reached the right consistency and Abby held it out for Moon Willow's inspection. Seeing her approval, Abby dipped her hand into the gritty batter and started forming it into flat cakes to be baked in the ashes near the edge of the fire. But Moon Willow's clawed hand stopped her and she indicated the kettle of water boiling over the flames. This would be a gruel, Abby realized, and she nodded, pouring most of the compound into the kettle. Then she pointed to the residue, herself, made a patting motion with her hands and looked questioningly at the older woman.

Without waiting for sign of approval, Abby formed the flat cake and dropped it in the ashes. She found a piece of wood that was almost flat and at the right time turned the Johnnycake over. Moon Willow watched curiously, looking down from the flat cake to the gruel simmering in the pot. When the cake was sufficiently cooked, Abby used the flat stick to remove it. Moon Willow reached for it but Abby checked her, blew on her fingers and shook them to indicate heat. Moon Willow sank back on her haunches.

Just then Corn Dancer and his father returned from a pipe smoking conversation at another fire and Moon Willow spoke rapidly to them, pointing to the bubbling pot and the cooling corn cake. Abby touched it with a swift dart of her finger and then, though it was still uncomfortably warm, broke off a piece, put it in her mouth, then extended a second piece to Moon Willow, making signs for her to taste it. She did and then looked up in pleased surprise at Abby, around at her son and husband, her head bobbing in approval. Soon all of them sat about the fire, alternating between the gruel in the pot and the Johnnycakes that Abby continued to bake.

Moon Willow called down the long corridor and curious women came forward. In a long harangue, unintelligible to Abby but easily followed by the women's gestures, they all nibbled at Abby's cakes, tentatively at first and then with increased speed and pleasure. They apparently asked questions, for Moon Willow spoke to Abby, who had to look to Corn Dancer.

"Mother say you . . . show'm. You . . . make? Show'm."

And Abby had instituted a cooking school of a sort in this wilderness town of the Onondaga. A look about at the pleased faces of the women told her that the first lesson, at least, was a success.

The other women returned to their "firesides" and, as had happened the day before, the process of cleaning the hallway and sweeping the ashes into the dying embers began. They had just finished when Abby heard a faint, distant and rhythmic throb. Instantly everyone down the hall straightened and turned to the far door. Corn Dancer came to Abby's side and so did Moon Willow. Her palm touched Abby's bare arm and—a miracle—she smiled. But she instantly turned as the door opened and a naked warrior, body painted from forehead to ankles in red and blue whorl designs, spoke several words in a loud voice. The answering "Hai!" from everyone in the corridor was almost deafening. Corn Dancer looked at her.

"The Keepers of the Faith come . . . for you. Make you Onondaga . . . Iroquois."

Abby could not check the instinctive catching of her breath. What would they do to her?

Would she be mutilated in some way by knife or lance? Even by fire? Moon Willow quite evidently saw her distress, for once again she softly touched Abby's bare arm, then turned to the far door and stood almost rigid.

The painted herald, if that was what he could be called, stepped to one side of the door and became as straight, unmoving and rigid as all the others in the Long House. In a moment or so the sunshine streaming through the door was suddenly blocked and Abby saw the stately woman with the high headdress enter, followed by one of the men, then alternately woman and man until all six stood in a proud, silent line, dark red faces now touched with vermillion, blue and green paint along cheeks, nose and forehead. Only their eyes moved but Abby knew that they looked the full length of the passage, at each person standing before the room of his fireside.

Then, without saying a word, the tall woman led the way with slow, dignified steps down the corridor, the others following. They halted before Abby as Moon Willow, Corn Dancer and Howling Wolf stepped back a pace. The woman addressed Moon Willow directly but her gleaming dark eyes rested on Abby.

Moon Willow answered her and the woman gave place to one of the men, who also eyed Abby from head to toe and asked something of Moon Willow. Each of the Keepers of the Faith repeated the process until, at last, the woman leader stood before her. But now she looked beyond Abby, her gaze moving from person to person, resting long on the women of the Long House. She asked another question.

"Hai!" came the loud answer from every throat. The other five of the Keepers also asked a question to be answered by the loud "Hai!"

The woman gave an order, turned on her heel and marched back to the door. Suddenly the other two female Keepers stood with Abby between them. The young man with the painted swirls of color lifted his voice in a sing-song series of words or sentences. The woman on either side touched her bare arms with what appeared to be short ceremonial lances and then pointed to the door, giving an order Abby could not understand.

With a questioning look at the tall woman and upon her nod, Corn Dancer said, "Abbbeee, Moon Willow say you be one . . . our Fireside, eh? You be Onondaga, eh?" He gestured to the pressing, silent crowd behind them. *"Owachira* say you be one of our *owachira,* eh. You come her . . . and her." He pointed to the female Keepers who stood at her side and then at the door. Abby nodded, though she did not really understand all the words, movements and actions. But she moved between the two proud women along the corridor, out through the door and then stopped short as the women suddenly placed their arms before her as a barrier.

The space before the Long House and all the street as far as the gate had been filled by every inhabitant of the town, Abby thought. The tall, proud woman suddenly lifted her arm high, palm out, and a dead silence fell on the throng. Speaking slowly, the Keeper spoke, pointing to Abby, to Moon Willow, Howling Wolf and then Corn Dancer. She must have asked another question for the "Hai!" resounded again.

She turned now and spoke to the women who flanked Abby. They turned to her and before her protest could hardly pass her lips the sharp edges and points of the ceremonial lances they held had torn every stitch of clothing from her body. The Westover rags lay twisted among the bits of Indian clothing that had been given her on the march and by Moon Willow here in Onondaga Town.

The women of the town had scurried away, darting along the long houses on all the streets. The few who remained lifted her feet by sheer brute force and the tattered, dirty moccasins joined the rest of her clothing. The twisted and now dirty white band that had held her hair back from her eyes and face whipped off her forehead and dropped to join the other remnants.

Abby tried to cover herself but the two Keepers grasped her arms and pulled them away from her body. One grabbed her chin, forcing her head up and back and she was held pinioned in a rigid, upright position, every inch of her body disclosed. Shame and embarrassment, mingled with broiling anger, flooded her as she saw warriors and old men of the town study her. For the most part their faces showed no expression, but she could not miss the fire that seemed to flame in each pair of male eyes.

The women who had scampered away now re-appeared. Some carried what seemed to be twisted roots, other bits of coarse, rough toweling, other twigs and sticks used to build fires. All of the women now circled Abby, cutting between her and the male spectators, a temporary relief at least. But their examination of her was just as full and minute as that of the men. Once more the stately woman Keeper lifted her arm high and spoke a word.

"Hai!" came the shouted answer and the Keepers moved Abby back as the women cleared a side space before the Long House. Flint struck flint, grass flamed to the sparks, then licked at small twigs, little branches and finally three or four fair sized tree limbs. Abby saw other women pushing through the crowd and they carried baskets of leaves that they dumped on the fire. The flames bent low in momentary surrender and then sent red tongues up again as the leaves curled, caught fire. Now a huge cloud of smoke spread out over the bare space, enveloping the crowd. Abby coughed, fought for breath with the rest of the women.

The two Keepers on either side now grabbed her arms again and propelled her to the fire. Abby looked with horror on the small, licking flames, tried to twist free but couldn't. In a moment she would be shoved into the very center of the fire!

But suddenly she was lifted by the armpits. Her kicking, bare feet cleared the ground and rose higher as the two Keepers rushed her right through the smoke to the far side of the fire. They whirled her around and again she choked and strangled as she passed through the smoke. The calloused soles of her feet were licked by the flames for a second and then thudded on cool bare ground. The process was repeated three times before the proud, assured Keeper barked a command. Abby was dropped and her feet struck the earth with a thud that vibrated up her legs and spine and into her skull. Suddenly she stood alone, eyes streaming tears, the moisture half blinding her and smoke in her lungs and throat choking her. She could not stop coughing for long, long minutes.

She was left alone to recover her breath, wipe the tears from her eyes, and finally, slowly straighten. As her vision cleared and her lungs renewed their regular pattern of breath, she saw the six Keepers once more standing in a stern, proud line before her. The leader spoke, spoke again a bit impatiently and Moon Willow answered. The Keeper's lips softened faintly and she spoke to Corn Dancer.

"Abbbeee, fire . . . how you say? . . . clean you. Now wash away white mans you have." His faint hand movement indicated her naked body. "No white mans Onondaga . . . Iroquois. All Onondaga, eh? Our womens clean, eh?"

Before she could fully decipher his meaning, the women had pushed him aside and now surrounded her. Even the Keepers had been forced to step aside. Hands grabbed Abby—arms, sides, hair, upper thighs. Suddenly a path opened to the far stockade gate and the whole crowd of women propelled her forward. When she involuntarily stumbled, rough hands jerked her upright.

In a mad rush, she was raced, pushed, half carried out beyond the stockade, along the path through the fields to a line of saplings and trees that bordered a small stream. There was no stopping. Before she could protest or check herself she and a dozen or more women stood waist deep in the flowing water.

Now she understood the reason for the roots, if that was what they were. The moment water touched them and they were rigorously rubbed, a white soapy sap appeared. It was immediately slapped all over Abby—into her hair, blinding and stinging her eyes, over her body. Female hands spread her legs and more of the substance stung her crotch and buttocks. The women did not miss so much as an inch of her.

As abruptly and swiftly as she had been rushed into the stream, the women now pulled her out to face the Keepers of the Faith. Dripping water from hair, chin, elbows, legs and hips, she was solemnly examined, once more inch by inch, turned this way and that. At last, swaying slightly to catch her balance, she again faced the six.

The tall leader looked at the other five, asked a question and received ''Hai!'' in reply.

At a signal, Moon Willow came up and the stately Keeper pulled a knife from a bead decorated sheath at her belt. Moon Willow lifted her arm, the deerskin sleeve of the smock falling back to bare her wrist. The Keeper grasped it, made a short cut with her knife that brought blood. Then the Keeper turned to Abby, grasped her wrist and the knife made a dart of pain. Blood welled up from the short but deep cut. Instantly, the Keeper placed Abby's wrist over Moon Willow's so that the two cuts touched each other and the blood mingled on their wrists. The woman beckoned Howling Wolf and made the incision and again the blood was transferred. Then the Keeper made the cut on her own wrist and placed it on Abby's. She held the wounds together with her free hand as she looked about at the women and then at the men of the Town. She spoke at some length before dropping Abby's wrist. She then pointed to Corn Dancer and held both hands high to the sky, lifting her face to the sun. Her voice lifted and changed and Abby heard the irregular lift and fall of a chanted song or prayer, she could not tell which.

The Keeper stopped abruptly but still held arms and face to the sky. The pressing crowd answered "Hai!" and then the Keeper dropped her arms. She beckoned to Moon Willow, asked a question and was answered. Then Howling Wolf replied to another question and was answered. The Keeper then turned to Abby, apparently asked a question that Abby did not understand and the Keeper beckoned to Corn Dancer, who literally jumped forward to Abby's side.

Abby shrank back, again shockingly aware of her nakedness and once more tried to cover herself. But Moon Willow forced her arms apart and down to her sides. Corn Dancer met her alarmed, questioning gaze.

"You Onondaga. Your blood is our blood." He pointed to the wounds that had been pressed against Abby's own cut wrist. You my mother's family. You no white . . . all gone . . . fire . . . water. Onondaga, Iroquois you . . . me. You one with Onondaga."

The Keeper spoke shortly again and Corn Dancer quickly, eagerly translated. "You be my woman, eh? Keeper of Faith says you Strong Woman . . . That your Onondaga name . . . Strong Woman. Soon get real name."

"Real name?"

"Real name give you squaw secret. Later . . . you speak better." He tapped his temple. "You know what words we use, eh?"

"Oh, understand?"

He nodded but hurried on. "Now you Onondaga, you . . . me . . . man . . . woman."

"Yes," she nodded. "You man . . . warrior. Me woman . . . squaw."

He made an impatient, negative gesture, frowning. Then his eyes lighted and he pointed to Moon Willow and Howling Wolf. He pointed to himself and Abby. He thumped his chest with his fist and then pointed to Abby again.

"Corn Dancer . . . Strong Woman . . . warrior . . . squaw." His arm swept around and pointed to the bare space at the end of the corridor. ''Fireside . . . our fireside . . . Strong Woman be Mother new fireside, eh?''

Then she understood. They were to be the Indian equivalent of man and wife. She sucked her breath in with surprise, stepped back but Moon Willow and the tall woman Keeper blocked her. Both women pointed to the bare spot and then Corn Dancer. He held out his hand.

''Come. We make new fireside. Add *orenda Owachira*.''

He took her hand and led her back along the corridor, around the ashes of the older fires. The Indians crowded at the entrance to each room on either side of the fires, the men grinning, the children round-eyed and the women critically examining Abby, their faces almost wholly expressionless. Abby became more and more aware of her nakedness and covered her lower stomach with her free hand. Corn Dancer made no effort to pull away her arm but strode ahead. Abby became aware of the Keepers of the Faith, Moon Willow and Howling Wolf pressed close behind.

They came to the barren space and Corn Dancer stopped, turned. Now he saw that she tried to cover herself and he pulled her hand away so once more she was completely exposed. But the proud Keeper came to Abby and now she held leather bands, each bearing a simple design of wampum beads. The woman fitted one on Corn Dancer's head and then one on Abby's. She stepped back, held her hands before her, palms up. She looked up to the roof, spoke rapidly in a sing-song chant. When it ended she turned to face the crowding inhabitants of the Long House.

"Hai!" came the shout.

The woman smiled, the first time Abby had seen her do it. When the ceremonial, grim hauteur left her face, she became surprisingly beautiful. Then, like Moon Willow, she stroked Abby's bare arm with her palm, touched each breast and then her groin. She pointed to Corn Dancer, smile gleaming brighter and then to three or four of the small children standing in nearby doorways. Abby could not help but understand her and felt her face become fiery red.

The woman held up her hand, palm out, first to Abby, then to Corn Dancer. Then the other Keepers repeated the gesture, turned and walked away down the corridor, the crowd parting before them to make a path. When they disappeared through the far door, the crowd turned as one on Abby and Corn Dancer.

Even the warriors and old men gave their attention to Abby and she began to understand that, though Corn Dancer might be her husband, she would rule the fireside. It explained Moon Willow's attitude toward Howling Wolf and the deference the male Keepers paid to the women. Leah had guessed right long ago. The men might be the warriors and hunters but the women—the "Mothers"—controlled the fireside, and may be even the *Owachira*, perhaps even more.

Corn Dancer broke in on her racing thoughts.

"Make fire . . . new fire. There."

He pointed to a small mound of dried grass and stalks, the twigs, small branches at hand, the larger pieces of wood ready. Abby hesitated and he gestured impatiently. Not sure she did the right thing, Abby gathered the material into a small mound. Corn Dancer disappeared into one of the two vacant rooms, reappeared and handed Abby two pieces of flint. She struck the sparks and the grass caught on the second blow.

A murmur of approval swept the crowd just behind her and she knelt low to gently blow the flickering spark first into flame and then stronger red tongues as it caught the twigs and the wood. She came to her feet and stared down at the fire she had just made.

"Is this home?" she silently asked. "This . . . ? this . . . ?"

She looked around at the long corridor and the Indians who crowded in a ring a short distance away. "What else can it be?" her thoughts answered. No one alive at Westover—at least no one close like Daniel, her mother and father and many of her friends. She became aware of the small clot of blood on her wrist.

"Onondaga! Abby Brewster an Onondaga Iroquois Indian!" The thought struck like a hammer blow and in that second she knew there was never a chance to return to Westover, her friends and her old life. She was no longer Abby Brewster but Strong Woman. She had to accept it.

Corn Dancer came to her side and, looking

190

around at him, she wondered why she had never truly seen him before except as a fearsome warrior, a savage. He had tried to help her so many times on that long, nightmarish flight from the raided burning village and stockade to this spot in the Long House where she now stood. The other Indians had used tomahawk, knife or club when the girls fell or sank down with weariness. He had always helped her, intervened so many times when his warriors had demanded her death out of impatience or fear of close pursuit.

The memories raced through her mind. She had an intuitive knowledge that, savage or no, Corn Dancer had come to love her in his own wild way, uncouth by colonial standards but the only way he could know. She began to have some idea he might easily have antagonized his own people, because of his defense and protection of her, and it struck her that few of the young men of Westover, under equivalent stress as Corn Dancer, would have risked so much for her.

He smiled and his high-boned, dark face seemed to light up, grow softer. His eyes caressed her even as he touched her bare shoulder lightly with a finger and then pointed to the empty room to one side of the fireplace. His fist thudded against his chest, then opened and the hand stroked over the curve of her shoulder, down her shoulder to her bare breast. The touch thrilled through her and she momentarily revolted from her own action. With an Indian!

She saw the shadows gather in his face and

eyes and the repulsion passed. Onondaga Town would hereafter always be her home and there was no more handsome and muscular male among the Iroquois that she had seen.

She did not resist when he turned her to the empty room and stepped back to allow him to go first, as he had taught her on the trail. But this time he halted, shook his head.

"No. You . . . go there." He pointed ahead of himself and his smile grew wider when he saw her puzzled look. "Eh, *then* you whiteface squaw. Now you Onondaga woman—Strong Woman. You be Mother this Fireside. I be man who hunts, fights, but you be Mother. Go."

She entered ahead of him, turned for further instruction. He pointed to a long, deep pile of furs along one wall, to her and then made a sweeping motion that indicated her whole, naked body, then pointed to the furs again, thumped his fist on his chest.

"You . . . me . . . there. Make *real* fireside."

His hands dropped to the thin belt that held his leather breechclout front and back. In a moment he stood naked before her, wearing only the narrow headband and his moccasins. She gasped and her eyes fell to his groin. She stared, fascinated, frightened and yet, having the feeling for the first time, felt a hot flame of desire in her stomach.

Corn Dancer, from what little she had heard from girlish whispers and tales, was a man . . . a powerful man.

XVI

Edouard had seen several naked women in his life—from the peasant farm girls of his father's impoverished estate to the elegant ones at the receptions of the Duc de la Verre and the salons of Toulouse and Marseilles. But none quite so naked as this wilderness beauty before him. He had the fleeting thought it was the headband and moccasins that somehow added to the bareness of her body.

"I Spotted Doe," she repeated and Edouard had to force his whirling, surprised thoughts into some sort of coherence. He found his voice.

"I did not expect . . ."

She smiled. "Madam order me to serve you, *mon Sieur*. I think maybe you travel long and far and there is no squaw for maybe months and months."

"And you . . . ?"

"I see you come along the street when I look out the window. You need squaw, eh?" She took a deep breath and her breasts filled, berry dark nipples becoming desirable little points. Her supple body seemed to shimmer with each slight move and she looked at a chest in a far corner. Edouard saw a pile of soft deerskin clothing. She continued. "I have room ready. Now I have me ready. You like maybe?"

"Like!" he echoed inanely and watched her move with a rhythmic move of rounded buttocks across the room to a chair and indicate that he sit down.

"I take your boots, your coat, your sword. I see they are cleaned and brushed and polished, eh?" She pointed to a tall armoire and opened the door, turned and held out her hand for his hat, cloak and sword. "I keep them here when you want, *mon Sieur*."

Still somewhat stunned, he dropped into the chair and she turned her lovely smooth back to him, placed a leg over his and bent to remove his boots. She removed them with the ease of good training and, once the thick leather no longer covered him, he felt the warmth of her body, a slight but continuous move of her inner thighs along his limbs as she removed the second boot. Desire suddenly swept away all his paralyzing amazement. He swept his arms around her waist and she instantly fell back against his chest, moving his hands up to and over her breasts. But only for a second. Then she jumped up and across the room, slammed the hallway door closed and whipped about.

"Shirt, clothes not good for bed, *mon Sieur*. I take them, too, eh? Then . . ."

He fumbled for the buckle of his sword belt, but she stepped close, playfully slapped his hands away. As she loosened the buckle and let the sword and scabbard fall, pulled back his coat and began opening his shirt, she remained very close, face close to his, tawny eyes bright with invitation, thin lips moving to purse for a kiss and then swiftly turning her head as he tried to taste them. She knew how to drive a man frantic with woman hunger.

Working with his clothing, hands caressing each time she touched him, body pressing close against him time and again, she worked him back across the room. Twice she pulled his hands away from her breasts that proved to be soft and vibrant to his touch.

Suddenly the back of his knees struck the bed and, caught off balance, he fell back upon it and then she fell atop him, fingers moving now to his groin as she rolled over on her side and her arm about his neck pulled him down beside her. He felt her knowing hand guide him and then he had penetrated her. Her invitational teasing instantly ended and as his hands wrapped about her waist, pulling her close, she threw back her head, lips peeled back from her teeth. Her body writhed and moved and arched to meet his every move and she made a peculiar, almost whispered and constant moaning as he lunged deep. Her legs wrapped around his hips and her nails clawed at his naked ribs and back and then grabbed his buttocks, pulling him hard against her and holding him there as she squirmed, twisted, gasped as great tremors constantly shook her body.

Suddenly he exploded, felt emptied for a moment but she was insatiable, pulling him close again and holding him. He instantly grew strong and powerful once more, the pressure building up in his chest, stomach and groin. His breath came in deep gusty inhalations and her low-pitched groans resumed. Her white teeth glinted like fangs as her lips peeled back in lustful grimaces.

He had the hallucinated thought that he would never rid himself of the pressure that built up and up and up and now he forgot everything but the brutal male need to plunge deep over and over. He did not know that his clawed fingers pulled her coarse black hair back and down so that her head and neck formed a strained, tortured arch. Then as though a keg of gunpowder went off within his body, a second explosion shook him. He felt himself burst within her time and time again and she clawed at his backsides, then his ribs. He heard a strange sound and momentarily realized it was his own cry of completion.

Suddenly she went limp under him, her hands dropped and her arms fell away. She lay flaccid, breasts rising and falling erratically as she gasped for breath. Her arms had fallen to either side, flat on the bed, her hands open and limp, fingers fanned out.

Edouard had fallen off her to one side and for long, long minutes could do no more than gasp for breath, head buried in the pillow, eyes closed. He sensed rather than actually felt the Indian girl's body and movements beside him. He could not move nor wanted to open his eyes when he felt her twist about away from him. Another movement told him she had stood up and, still gulping for air, he opened his eyes.

For a moment he did not see her and then, hearing a faint sound, he slightly turned his head without lifting it. She stood at the chest across the room and now worked a soft deerskin smock over her head, letting it fall as her arms went into the sleeves. It came to well below her knees, a shapeless garment that well concealed the magnificent body upon which Edouard had just spent himself. She sat down and pulled on what looked to be skin pantaloons, working them up under the smock, then wrapped thin thongs around her ankles and legs to hold the under-garment in place.

She looked up, saw him watching her. She whipped a bead decorated belt about her waist, tightened it and now Edouard saw a faint suggestion of her delightful hips, slender waist. But the loose garment gave no hint of those soft, full and rounded breasts beneath the deerskin. She added a crude carved wooden comb and smoothed her hair, replaced the band about her forehead and then smiled at him as unconcerned as if she had just met him in the street.

"You like Spotted Doe?"

He nodded, nodded again and then discovered he had the strength to lift his head, continuing to stare as though he could not yet fully believe his eyes. She cocked her head a bit to one side, such a coquettish, feminine move that Edouard wondered if the gesture was not common to girls of all races, places and times. He caught his voice.

"Mon Dieu! Where did you learn—?"

"Every woman knows, *mon Sieur*. Have you not had the same treatment from . . . from . . ." She made a vague gesture to indicate the world beyond the closed door and the stout walls of the Snow Fox. ". . . Out there?"

"Ma foi! No! Never like that!"

"Merci, mon Sieur." Her smile was pleased and pert.

"You are Indian, *Mam'selle*?"

"Oh, no! Do not call Indian '*Mam'selle*.' We are servants only, *paysannes*. Madam Demain

198

would be very angry if she had heard you.''

Edouard came up on one elbow and dismissed Madam Demain with a flip of his hand and curl of his lips. "Forget Madam. I asked if you are Indian.''

"Oui. I am Huron." her chin lifted proudly.

"Huron?''

"The Algonquin people. We are fine, great people. Better than Iroquois.''

"Who are they?''

"Enemies of the Huron. We fight them since . . . since the sun came in the sky. Once one of your people help us—Sieur de Champlain. Huron always friend of the French. Iroquois friend of English. Eh, no matter, Huron still greatest people.''

"You speak excellent French.''

She almost purred. *"Merci.* I live in a town close to Quebec all my life. All of us speak French.''

She stood up, smoothed her smock and touched her hair now hanging down over her smock from each side of her face. She swept up his clothing, moving from spot to spot where he had carelessly thrown aside a garment as they had moved to the great battleground of the bed.

"Do you wear them, *mon Sieur*? Or do I find fresh ones in your chest?''

"Fresh ones . . . but first, a bath, *non?*''

"Oui, mon Sieur. I will bring the water.''

She left the room, closing the door behind her. Edouard pulled the thick coverlets and warm blankets of Indian weave and design close

199

up around his chin, glad for their warmth. The air of New France had a decided chill, even this late in the spring. Lassitude from blanket heat and his recent activity swept over him and he did not know when his eyes closed and he slept.

But he snapped instantly awake when he heard the door latch and a faint whisper of hinges. Spotted Doe had returned, bringing a large tin bathtub. Behind her an Indian carried a wooden yoke across his shoulders, big, heavy wooden buckets hanging from each end. Spotted Doe placed several thick, worn blankets on the floor and then lowered the empty tin tub on them. The Indian man poured almost steaming water out of one bucket into the tub and then more carefully poured from the second. Spotted Doe tested the mixture in the tub with her finger.

"Perhaps, *mon Sieur* will find the bath warm enough for him."

"Maybe too warm," Edouard replied, recalling the shock of cold sea water splashing over him as he stood naked and shivering to the wind on the deck of the *Demoiselle*.

"Please to try?" Spotted Doe asked and waved the man out of the room.

Edouard threw aside the bed clothing, jumped to the tub and stepped into it. The water, though it might be considered merely lukewarm to some, was comparatively hot to him. He sighed with content and sank down to his waist. Instantly, Spotted Doe loosened her belt and pulled her smock back over her head. Edouard had a glimpse of her dark breast that quivered slightly to every move, but she stepped behind him and in a second, she sponged water over his head and shoulders, down his bare back.

Then he flinched to the bite of some kind of harsh soap and the scratch of a very soft bristled brush. But his first surprise vanished, he gripped the edges of the tub, leaned forward and enjoyed the feel of water, of a body growing cleaner by the moment. Spotted Doe moved now in front of him to bathe his chest and stomach and now her breasts were almost in his face, moving, enticing, and he wondered at the inner source of the desire that steadily mounted.

Spotted Doe, rescuing the soap from the sudsy water, became aware of faint movement and she suddenly squatted back on her heels. "*Mon Sieur*, how much do you think you can do after . . . ?" She tipped her head toward the bed. She touched her temple. "You think up here, *mon Sieur*, not down there. You would not—"

"I know," he cut her short. "Finish quickly, *s'il vous plait.*"

She smiled, sighed but smiled again. Now she worked faster and before long he stepped out of the tub and into the huge, thick towel she held for him. When he had it wrapped tightly about himself, she pointed to the bed with a commanding gesture. "I bring you food, eh? You eat when you are dry and covered again."

She was back at the door before he could remonstrate. She clapped her hands and the Indian man reappeared to pull the tub to a rear window, open it, and pour the soapy water out upon the alley-way below. But by then Edouard again stretched out in the bed, the warm coverings close about him.

Once more he drifted off to sleep before he knew it and once more Spotted Doe awakened him, this time by her noise in setting a small table with heavy plates and bowls of food, the warm odor making him realize how hungry he had become. He swiftly dressed and sat down to a feast of French cooking such as he had not had since leaving the chateau of the Duc de la Verre. This was not food for royalty before him, certainly, but there were the crisp rolls, the thin, delicate crepes, the thick cream. Pottage bubbled in its small pot, the sauce thick and brown, and he had almost forgotten the taste of onion soup rightly prepared. The wine was hearty and red though a far cry from those in the cellars of the noblesses of Toulouse, Bearn and Marseilles. The meat was excellent but he could not quite place the taste or the texture when he closely examined it.

Madam Demain entered as he ate and she told him the meat was venison, freshly shot in the forests that pressed close on the town. She asked to his comfort and if Spotted Doe had proved satisfactory. Edouard was not exactly certain what she meant by that.

"She served you well?" the ugly woman asked impatiently. She looked about. "The room is clean, I see, but there are other things a young Huron maid can do for a man who has been at sea for a long time."

"Ah, *oui!* She is dextrous and pleasing."

Madam Demain's gargoyle face creased in a rubbery travesty of a smile. "I am glad to hear that, *mon Sieur*."

Edouard added to the dark red wine in his goblet as he asked without looking up at his hostess, "I had understood, Madam, that you did not allow men and . . . well . . . *les jeune filles* . . . ?"

She sniffed as she would at the question of a dolt. "A Huron woman or girl in New France, *mon Sieur*, is not a girl, a *French* girl, you understand."

"That is a closely drawn line, Madam."

"Not at all. Huron—and all of the Algonquin tribes of Indians—are *sauvages*." She made a sharp gesture of dismissal. "But that is enough to understand, *non*? I came to tell you Lieutenant de Valerain sent a soldier with a message for you."

"From the Governor!"

"*Oui,* so I believe, though the paper is not the quality of that of His Excellency." She pulled a wax sealed envelope from her ample apron pocket and Edouard almost grabbed it from her fingers.

De Valerain wrote,

Sieur de Fournet: His Excellency will be pleased to receive you within the next day or two if at all possible. Word has come that his successor as Governor of New

France, the Marquis Duquesne, will arrive to relieve His Excellency of his many and onerous duties as Governor after having faithfully and fully served so many years to the pleasure of His Majesty, King Louis. The Marquis' ship is expected almost daily so there is little time to dispose of such formalities as your arrival and report present. Will you send me reply by Sergeant Balzan who awaits it.

As though she had read the note along with him, Madam Demain said, "The oaf waits downstairs in the tavern, his rear on one chair, his boots on another and his elbows on the table the better to drink the wine I must serve the Governor's errand dogs."

"Ah, let him, Madam. I shall see you are not out a *centime* or *sou*."

Madam's rubbery face assumed as pleased lines as possible. "*Merci*. I will include it in the total when you leave, *mon Sieur*."

"Very well. But now I will see this Sergeant Balzan. Downstairs, you say?"

"In the tavern."

As she had said, the soldier sprawled at one of the tables, wine tankard in hand. He instantly jumped to his feet and saluted as Edouard came into the room. "Sieur de Fournet?"

Edouard nodded. "Tell Lieutenant de Valerain I would be honored to be presented to His Excellency tomorrow, if possible. No need to bring a reply, Sergeant. If I do not see you before the morning, I shall present myself to Lieutenant de Valerain.''

"Oui, mon Sieur."

"That will be all, Sergeant. Down your wine and report to the Lieutenant.''

Edouard returned to his room. Madam Demain had disappeared and Edouard dropped onto a chest by one of the leaded windows to look out on the busy street. But he hardly saw it as his mind raced with the new developments. A new governor and rumors bubbled everywhere of renewed troubles with England and her colonies on this side of the Atlantic. It was hardly possible that the Duc de la Verre's *lettre de cachet* would be among the papers of this Marquis Duquesne, but it was always possible—a risk. The sooner Edouard could legally strike out into the wilderness with the present governor's permit to seek furs, the better—the sooner the western country would swallow him up. His absence added to the margin of his safety.

He encountered Spotted Doe in the upper hallway, storing folded bedding into a huge closet. She looked around at the sound of his step and once more her smile lighted her dark, angular face. The sight of her and her obvious pleasure with him as a man made him speak impulsively.

"Do you know one Pierre le Duc?''

"Oui," she answered in surprise. "He was *courrier du bois* but a Mohawk musket ball crippled him. Now he makes skin clothing for trappers or the gentlemen hunters who venture into

the woods. You have need of him?''

''I think so.''

''When you go out on the street, turn toward the setting sun. His shop is not a far distance . . . only a short walk.''

''Will he have a sign over his door?''

''No, but on his windows what they call letters that I cannot read.''

''His name,'' Edouard said to himself. *''Merci,* Spotted Doe.''

She smiled once more and then looked archly at him. ''Perhaps you will be rested again soon?''

He laughed, turned her about and patted her buttock as he pushed her on down the hall. ''I will be rested. Tonight, eh?''

''So soon! *Mon Sieur!*'' She pretended a pout. ''Spotted Doe becomes old, *non?''*

''Decidedly no!''

Her pout grew more pronounced. ''Then you should be much *fatigué, non?* Perhaps I do not please you enough?''

He turned her about to face him and stroked the rich globes of her breasts and even from under the soft deerskin of her blouse felt the nipples. He kissed her and she gasped, looked fearfully along the hallway.

''If Madam Demain—''

''Would she care?'' Edouard smiled at her, and this time passed his hands slowly down her back and over her buttocks as he kissed her again. Spotted Doe broke away and stepped back, again searching down the empty corridor.

"Madam Demain would not care if we—how you say it? We have *le sex*. But *s'embrasser*! To kiss! She would beat me and then see that I could never live in Quebec again! That is true!"

"But that is foolish!"

"It is Madam Demain." Suddenly her eyes softened and grew subtly larger as she studied him. "You are the first, *mon Sieur*, the first of the gentry. The others, the louts?" She snapped her fingers. "*Pouf!* But you!" She took a deep breath. "Spotted Doe belong to you."

"*Un moment!*" he exclaimed, stunned and somewhat horrified by the result of his impulsive act. "I only kissed you."

"But the first of *les gentilhommes*. To all but you I am"—she sought the word and her lips curled as she found it—"I am furniture—a bed *pour le sex*." She broke off, quickly turned her eyes toward the distant steps and spoke in a low, hurried voice. "Madam Demain! She find us and—"

He understood and turned sharply on his heels, taking several strides before the tip of Madam Demain's huge lace cap appeared above the stairwell. He replied to her "*Bon matin, mon Sieur*," with a nod and a smile, then hurried by her down the stairs and out into the street.

He turned west as he had been directed. An impulse caused him to look back and then up as he caught a movement just above his head. Spotted Doe leaned out of an upper window of the Snow Fox. He smiled, gave her a slight wave. She looked hurriedly around and then gave him a swift, small move of her fingers.

Edouard turned to continue his errand. But he remained puzzled by the expression on Spotted Doe's face. The Huron Indian girl looked exactly like any moonstruck girl in love.

"C'est impossible!" he grunted and threw the thought from his mind.

XVII

Edouard found the shop with some difficulty, for a small line of letters within one of the diamonds of leaded glass had gone unnoticed until he had walked by the tiny building two or three times. He barely heard a bell from somewhere deep within the house when he tugged the forged iron pull beside the door. He waited so long he wondered if he had the right place after all. But Spotted Doe had been accurate thus far so he impatiently decided to waste another moment or two after his second pull on the bell.

Then the door opened inward and a grizzle-haired man, sun-brown of face and deeply wrinkled, looked at him from under shaggy brows. "What is your need?" he asked in a patois French, his voice and tone short, abrupt and almost without courtesy.

"You are Pierre le Duc?"

"*Oui.* What of it?"

Edouard's chin lifted in anger at the near arrogance of the man. He saw the gray eyes, keen and sharp; the puckered line of short knife wound along the left cheekbone; the tall body as slender as his own, rather than that of a man with iron gray hair that spoke of many years. Le Duc wore a shirt of soft animal skin, fringed along the sleeves and tucked into a wide belt around a slender waist. His breeches were also of skin and also fringed, the legs extending down to the ankles just above moccasins that looked to be of Indian work.

"I have been told you make clothes for wilderness travel."

The man's voice lost its irritating, sharp edge but his eyes remained sharp and suspicious. "What would you do in the forest, *mon Sieur?* I think you are *noblesse,* eh?"

"I am Sieur de Fournet, le Duc, and what I do

in the forest is my own business.''

For a long moment both men almost glared at one another and then, slowly, le Duc's thin lips took the faint shape of a smile. ''Eh, you have spirit . . . if not sense, *mon Sieur*. So the woods or the Indians may not claim our bones.''

''I shall have something to say and do about that. But what I do is still of my own business.''

''And mine . . . if it pleases me. Will you hunt? Do you go into the woods afoot or 'saddle—or, *mon Dieu!* by carriage as some high-born fools have tried?''

''I shall ask someone who knows how I travel, le Duc, and that, too, is my business.''

The man stepped back, throwing the door wide. *''Entrez, mon Sieur.* I would say you do very well in the woods. At least you sound bold enough.''

Edouard's nostrils flared in continued anger. ''I am not accustomed to such speech, le Duc.''

The older man laughed and touched the shaft of a heavy long knife in leather sheath at his belt. ''Accustomed, eh? You will be. This is New France, Sieur de Fournet. Only His Excellency, his soldiers, the blessed Ursulines, use *le politesse* of Paris, Rouen or *Avignon. You will not find it in courrieur or voyageur,* in Huron, or in Ottawa or Ojibway here or anywhere outside the towns such as Montreal or here. You are newly arrived.''

''On the *Demoiselle* from Bordeaux.''

''As I thought—new to us and our ways and speech. So you have my pardon though you'd probably get a knife or a pistol ball a mile beyond the town. *Entrez, s'il vous plaît.*"

He took another step back and now Edouard saw that le Duc limped badly on his right leg. The old man saw Edouard's quick look, grimaced and patted his right flank. "As you see, it happened to me. But not because of my mouth, *mon Sieur*. Because a thief tried to take a beaver from one of my traps. It was on Lac Eau Claire."

"The thief?"

"His pistol ball was faster than my thrown knife, but it did him no good. He died." Le Duc waved him in, this time with a touch of impatience. "Do I stand waiting for you to make up your mind? Enter or leave—it is all one."

Edouard choked back retort, knowing now that short and nearly insulting speech was le Duc's way. The man closed the door, circled Edouard and limped ahead down a short hall to a large room which was lighted by an inevitable diamond-pane glass window in the rear next to a closed door that must lead to yet other rooms. Le Duc waved to a long, wide bench covered with fur skins that extended along one wall. He limped to the door, opened it and called, "Goes Walking! Wine! We have a customer for once!"

He limped to the bench and sat down beside Edouard. Once more the sharp, shrewd gray eyes studied Edouard and gradually the wrinkled face faintly softened. "How will you travel, *mon Sieur,* and for how long?"

"I do not know the woods, so perhaps you

could tell me."

Le Duc shrugged expressively. "Some stay out there but a day or two and then find it much too demanding on their noble blood for even that short a time. Others stay a month—two—a year—some only return to the towns now and again. Some never—losing themselves, or their scalps to Indians, Huron or Iroquois, or their lives to bear or wolf pack, drowning, or a fall. Who is to know?"

"I won't lose my life. I'll stay as long as need be."

"What will you do?"

"I have heard that furs . . ."

Just then a fat old Indian woman waddled in through the far door, carrying a baked clay wine jug and two pewter tankards. Her black, beady eyes touched on Edouard without sign of curiosity; then she placed jug and tankard at le Duc's side on the bench. She waddled out and the door closed behind her.

"Goes Walking," le Duc explained. "My Ojibway woman. Been with her twenty years. Good woman, Goes Walking."

"Ojibway?"

"Algonquin tribe from beyond the farthest of the lakes west of here. She was captured in some Indian war and traded or sold from tribe to tribe. I met and bought her around Lac du Huron. But we are not talking of her, eh?"

"No, of suitable forest dress for me."

"Furs, eh? Do you know anything about them? Do you have the Governor's permit? It is supposed to be required. Do you have traps, guns, pistols, knives, camping equipment, powder and shot?''

''None of those things.''

Le Duc sighed with impatience, and Edouard knew it was of long standing and not directed specifically at him. He took a long draft of his wine, twisted half around to face Edouard directly.

''I can make all you need, from underclothing that is warm enough, to shirt, jacket, cap, boots and moccasins. I can buy the rest for you—and snowshoes for—''

''Snowshoes? *Mon Dieu!* won't boots—''

''They would sink you to your knees in one step, *mon Sieur*. You have yet to know one of the winters of New France. Over there, on the wall, you see two of them.''

Edouard saw two crossed objects that appeared to be grotesque, framed racquets with a cross webbing across them, surmounted by straps and having long wooden heels that looked like tails. Le Duc explained that they would keep him atop the snow, rather than in it to his armpits or over his head.

As he listened, Edouard began to wonder if he was at all wise to consider peltry. But how else could he be certain to avoid inevitable arrest when the *lettre de cachet* arrived? He suddenly remembered the rumor that a new governor would arrive at almost any day from France, probably from the king's palace itself, and then Edouard could easily and certainly become a fugitive. His racing mind fixed on an alternative.

"Perhaps I could cross the river and—"

"Be shot by Iroquois or the English colonists just because you are French. Our people are returning, *mon Sieur*. All of us know there is a war in the making—and soon. No, you would be safer in the woods even as a *fou* to its dangers. I will see you are equipped. I will tell you all I can before you leave."

"But perhaps His Excellency will not give me a permit!"

Le Duc's lips moved in a faint, crooked smile. "His Excellency finds *louis d'or* persuasive, *mon Sieur,* and it may be the new one will not, what with trouble brewing back home and here between us and the British colonies. If His Excellency refuses the permit then . . ."

"Then?"

"There is so much land in New France, *mon Sieur,* and most of it covered with trees. It is a wilderness traversed mostly by stream, river and lakes—oh, many of them! There are maybe million kilometers where many have lost themselves—alone, with the Indians . . . who knows? *Permettez-moi* to say, see His Excellency and then, no matter what he says, see me."

"You could be breaking the law if—"

Le Duc spread his hands, palms out, lifted and dropped his shoulders in the Gallic manner of France. Edouard felt a quick twinge of homesickness as the old man chuckled. "You have them made to wear and boast when you return to La Belle France, eh? How do I break the King's law?"

Edouard stood up. "Do you measure me now?"

Le Duc also arose. *"Oui,* it would be best before word might get to His Excellency. Gossip and whispers travel fast in so small a place as Quebec."

When he returned to the Snow Fox some hours later, his purse was lighter but he had left le Duc spreading out pliable, soft but warm deer hides on a table in an inner room and marking in crayon Edouard's measurements. He had leather bag for shot; a hollowed, carved tip of an antler for powder horn; had tested the heavy blade of a huge skinning knife and had his introduction to a weapon practically unknown in Europe.

"It is from an English colony far to the south of us—Virginia. It is not a musket, as you see, but there is rifling in the barrel. That makes the ball spin and fly straight and true instead of wobbling as it would in a musket. It is costly, *mon Sieur,* but it will pay for itself over and over again. I will show you how to use it."

So Edouard sat down to the table in his own room. Pleased with the day, the knowledge he had acquired about this new land—and hungry. He had met Madam Demain downstairs and asked to be served up here instead of in the main room and a man with wine jug and tankard had followed on his heels. Now Edouard slowly and contentedly drank the wine. He would see the governor tomorrow, but now, if le Duc's hints had been right, it wo̶u̶l̶d̶ ... had a permit for the ... perhaps he should be cau̶ ... he confirmed the crippled c̶ ... about the western country.

His eyes, idly moving about the ... on his rapier and scabbard, carefully ... corner near his bed. It struck him t̶h̶ ... would be no place for a weapon like that ṇ̶ ̶h̶is wilderness, but how could he give up a sword that his father had given him when he had finished his training with his fencing master! He had also blooded it, though not fatally, in two duels in Gascony, and the Duc de la Verre had almost tasted its blood. Thank the good God Elenie had prevented him from committing that foolishness! He would have been shot out of hand by the old fool's own minions.

He shrugged, sipped his wine, wondering now if that might not have been only justice for the old turkey-cock with his *lettre de cachet. Faugh!* That was not the problem now that the *lettre* had sent him flying to this far New France and this room and whatever adventures awaited him out there in the wilderness.

Thoughts of Elenie vividly brought up her picture as he had often known her—naked, shapely and afire in bed with him. He sighed. Those days were gone forever, too.

Just then the door opened and Spotted Doe entered with a heavy tray covered by a coarse white cloth. She moved with a wild, dignified grace as she placed the tray on the small table in

took off the napkin. Dark
, a fowl that looked like a chicken
smaller. He pointed to it and looked up
at her.

"Partridge," she answered. "It is good."

It was still hot and hard to hold, but he
managed to cut off a small piece and eat it. He
looked up into her bronze, reddish face and
nodded. Her smile flashed. She started to leave
but he stopped her.

"That is, if Madam Demain permits."

"I have more work downstairs, *mon Sieur*—"

"Edouard," he corrected.

She shook her head. "I would not care here in
Quebec, but beyond the town, in my village, the
woods—" her sigh of regret finished the
sentence.

"Then, later." His eyes cut to the bed, back
to her.

She smiled again. "But you were so
tired . . . Edouard."

"There! You said it!"

"But no one to hear, especially Madam." She
walked to the door, looked back over her
shoulder. "You will wait, eh? There is much
work."

"I'll wait." He pointed to the bed. "Over
there, *non?*"

"*Oui.* I will hurry the work."

The door closed behind her.

He turned to his supper then and thought of
what he had learned from le Duc as he ate. The
old *courrier* had told Edouard much of New

France in the years ... Champlain, whose men... appreciate.

"He was a great man but ... know the Indian, except the A... met. So he went with them o... against the Mohegans. He had a m... time—one of those so heavy it had to ... ...d on a support and he carried a burning ... e to light it. But it killed Mohegans and they ran away, but not before our Indians killed and scalped a few themselves."

"A big battle?" Edouard had asked.

"No, *mon Sieur*. But big consequences from that day to this. The Iroquois, the Indians of the Six Nations, from that day to this, have always been enemies to us. No Frenchman is safe in their country below the river. They kept us back this side of the St. Lawrence when we tried to explore. They would not trade. They allowed the British to settle and now it is a colony over there. They call it Maine."

"I see why I would not be safe."

"Do you need to be fearful of us here in New France also?"

Edouard caught the sharpness in le Duc's voice and he waved away the question. "I am French, too . . . that is if a Gascon is considered French. Some think he is more a boasting, swaggering fool."

"Fiery is better, *mon Sieur*."

Now Edouard pushed aside the table and the tray holding only empty scraps of food, the

ne bird. He finished the re-
of wine in the tankard and looked
across the room to his rapier in the cor-
er. He obviously ran certain risks south of the
huge river out there—a Frenchman among
enemies both white and red. He could not long
stay here in Quebec or—what was the other
main town?—ah, yes! Montreal. A new governor came and a French army. Strangers would
be looked upon with suspicion as they always
were in wartime. A spy might be a renegade
native, especially if he had but newly arrived,
and what would be his chance of freedom if a
lettre de cachet . . . ?

Edouard cursed under his breath and looked
at the bed piled high with thick quilts and topped
by furry bearskin robes. Ah, well! Spotted Doe
would ease off the weight of his problems.

She came, long after Edouard had blown out
the candles and climbed into bed. He heard her
and, when he moved, she made a hissing
whisper. "No candles! Madam Demain is in the
inn. If she should hear of a light shining through
the window, she would come to see all is well. It
would not be, eh?"

He softly laughed. "Not after you join me."

In but a moment she snuggled beside him
under the fur robe. His hand touched bare flesh
on her back and, when she turned to him, the
smooth satin of her breasts. He felt her legs and
thighs against him and then her hand smoothed
over his hip, along the inside of his thigh and
fastened around him. She strained to him and

and he has what you whitefaces call an iron hand. It is said he will make many changes, build new forts, drive out strangers who do not belong in New France."

"Strangers?" and now Edouard's voice held a note of uncertainty. "Who do not belong?"

"Spies, outlaws—they say and I do not know exactly what that might mean or who they are."

Edouard answered tightly, "I think I do. You are right. I won't be much longer in Quebec."

She turned eagerly to him. "You do not need to wait for a guide if you go to De Troit and Lac du Huron. I have travelled from that country and I could find my way back. I would know the Algonquins and the trappers. I would be your woman, *mon brave!* Please!"

"I had not thought on it. Let me think. But first, I will see His Excellency tomorrow when the audience is set for me. Then Pierre le Duc and . . . let me think on it."

"You would become one of my people—my husband, for I would see that you became a Huron. My people will listen to me, for they will be glad that I have escaped the whitefaces who stole me."

He placed his finger on her lips. "First, His Excellency, then le Duc. We will talk again tomorrow, eh?"

"Tomorrow," she reluctantly agreed.

If Edouard had expected elaborate ceremony in his audience with the governor, he quickly became disillusioned. He rented a horse, donned the best finery in his travelling chest and placed the cordon bearing the crest of his family about his neck. The gold and enamel coat of arms, though somewhat small, made a pleasing contrast to his plum-colored jacket and the white plume in his wide brimmed, low crowned cap that he wore at a jaunty Gasconade manner.

He glimpsed Maltrot, who brushed aside some dangling hairs in his wig and who gave him a twisted smile and flip of the hand in greeting. But the guards at gate and main door of the governor's residence evidently expected him for they came to stiff attention and brought their muskets to present arms as a sergeant appeared and bowed to him.

"Sieur de Fournet? Lieutenant de Valerain will receive you for presentation. If it pleases you, *mon Sieur,* follow me."

He led the way down a long, richly carpeted hall but stopped short of heavy, ornate doors that obviously opened on the main audience hall, if it could be called that in this afar provincial town of Quebec. Upon Edouard's entrance following the sergeant's announcement, de Valerain circled a small desk and formally bowed. He wore a dark, smooth brushed wig, the queue tied with a watered silk blue ribbon. A decoration—the insignia of some order unknown to Edouard—was on his left breast.

"*Bienvenue,* Sieur de Fournet." He gestured to a gilded padded chair beside his desk and indicated the crystal wine flagon and glasses upon it. "I suggest we be comfortable while I instruct you as to what His Excellency will do himself and what he expects of you."

Edouard sat, sipped the excellent wine and listened carefully to de Valerain. He gathered that the governor tried in his way to reproduce the Royal Court in France to at least some small degree.

"His Excellency is naturally eager of news from home, Sieur de Fournet, and will question you closely. It will be from natural curiosity and nostalgia, you understand, not from suspicion," de Valerain faintly smiled. "I have already told His Excellency what I know of your family in Gascony. He will probably ask about Toulouse and Marseilles. Avignon would also interest him for his early army days were served there."

"That will all be easy," Edouard said.

"Good! If it pleases His Excellency, you can then, on your part, ask for some favor. I think it would be granted." De Valerain gently cleared his throat. "May I add in confidence that His Excellency believes one should be duly grateful if His Excellency is—generous."

"I understand. But . . . to whom do I express generosity?"

"To me. Here . . . after we have concluded the audience." De Valerain arose. "So, if you are ready, Sieur de Fournet?"

The Marquis de la Gallissonniere, Royal Governor of New France, hardly seemed the person to fulfill the resounding impression of both his position and his name when Edouard faced him and bowed low, sweeping the plume of his hat to the polished parquet of the floor of the small room. He is more like this little room, Edouard thought as he straightened and regarded the small man behind the inlaid table, littered with papers and documents. This was obviously the place where petitioners or callers of little consequence were received rather than the formal salon buried somewhere deeper beyond heavy closed doors.

However, His Excellency proved pleasant enough in a somewhat overblown and lordly way; nevertheless, he made Edouard welcome to New France. As de Valerain had predicted, as soon as the formalities of meeting had been concluded, the governor spoke of distant France with a longing he could not keep out of his voice. Edouard answered question after question about Paris, the palace, the King, Edouard's own family and its connections while the governor listened with obvious hunger.

At last he eased back in his chair and his thin pinched faced broke into a smile. "It is good to hear all this news, Sieur de Fournet. It has been so long since last I saw Bourges."

"It is my honor to give it to you, Your Excellency."

"Yes, indeed, I am fortunate. Here you are freshly arrived—even though from Gascony— and my successor as governor will also be here very soon."

"It is rumored about Quebec, Your Excellency."

The governor made a wry face. "Quebec is as

filled with gossip as any village back home. In fact, it is not much else, eh?"

"The city? Perhaps not. But I hear New France itself is as large as two or three empires."

"That very well may be for all we know. No one has travelled west to the end of land . . . if there is such a place."

"You have a heavy and grave responsibility from the King, Your Excellency. Not everyone would be worthy of it, or strong enough."

The governor nodded smugly and toyed with one of the many golden, jewelled rings on his fingers. "But now, Sieur de Fournet, you say you have come to improve the family fortune in our colony?"

"If it pleases Your Excellency."

"We are in need of bold young men such as you seem to be. And what did you have in mind?"

"Furs—peltry."

"You hardly appear to be one familiar with such a wilderness enterprise."

Edouard ventured a small smile of acknowledgment. "I am not, Your Excellency. But I understand that I can find French and Indian trappers who would bring their skins to me if I had a post to receive them."

"True." The governor's fingers made a whispering beat on the inlaid table as he considered Edouard. "But there would be the cost of building the post, buying trade goods, hiring skilled workers such as gunsmiths, carpenters, blacksmiths—oh, a hundred different trades—

and horses, sleighs, clothing. It is not at all cheap to enter into the business, Sieur de Fournet."

"So I have been told. But I am prepared to meet expenses."

The governor pinched his lips and considered Edouard with a sharp, probing look. He dropped his hand, cleared his throat and murmured, "The peltry business is a royal monopoly, subject to my permit or denial."

"I've heard."

Silence then, that built up for moments as the governor unconcernedly picked up a document and began reading it. Edouard shifted his weight and the governor looked up at the slight movement, expectancy in his glance that swept over Edouard and then returned to the paper. Edouard cleared his throat and again the governor looked up.

"Is there something more, Sieur de Fournet?" His face lighted. "Ah, *oui!* Your permit to stay for a time! Say, a month in Quebec, a month in Montreal and a brief journey to the Falls of Niagara. That should be sufficient, eh? You would have much to tell when you return to Gascony."

"Your Excellency, I think of peltry."

"Expensive, as I've said," de la Gallissonniere returned to a study of his document.

"I am lodged at the Inn of the Snow Fox, Your Excellency. Lieutenant de Valerain might be able to bring me His Excellency's estimate of the cost . . . even before I left Quebec? That, of course, does not include the other items we have discussed.''

The governor ran the tip of his finger along his chin to the edge of the salt-and-pepper small spade beard that tipped it. ''You are persistent, Sieur de Fournet.''

''Interested, rather, Your Excellency.'' Edouard shrugged, regretful lift and fall of his shoulders. ''But, of course, every purse has a bottom. It is said in Paris that even His Majesty is often counting his coins.''

The governor closely studied him again. ''So I have heard, even out here. If only the days of the Sun King would return! Then, there was no dearth of gold, eh?''

''It is regrettable, Your Excellency. I often envied the richness of Louis XIV. But who can restore the past . . . for His Majesty or even such as I?''

The governor sighed and shook his head, toyed with the paper and then looked up over the top of it. ''I will give some thought to the matter, Sieur de Fournet.''

''*Merci,* Your Excellency. For that alone I shall be in your debt.''

The governor picked up a beautifully worked small silver bell and tinkled a few notes. De Valerain instantly opened the doors behind Edouard. The governor merely gave him a glance. ''Sieur de Fournet will be leaving us, Lieutenant. Does he have a carriage or mount to . . . where does he stay?''

''The Snow Fox of Madam Demain, Your Excellency.''

The governor turned his eyes on Edouard. "It is our pleasure to have received you, Sieur de Fournet. I will have my secretary send you the information. De Valerain undoubtedly will see you again."

"You have given me honor, Your Excellency, *une mille*. I offer my sincere thanks."

The governor's beringed hand waved him away and Edouard once more bowed and swept his plume to the floor then followed de Valerain out of the room. The heavy doors closed; the lieutenant asked, "It went well, *mon Sieur*?"

"If I said the right things."

"If you hinted of money for him, it went well."

"I left His Excellency with a problem," Edouard grinned. "Is the traditionally poor Gascon *always* a poor Gascon? He promised to resolve it."

"He will."

Edouard sobered. "I hear the new governor comes. When?"

"No one is certain. But he comes by fast packet ahead of the royal army." De Valerain also sobered. "That is a sure sign that we will soon be at war with the British Colonies. This will be bloody. The Algonquin and the Iroquois will also take sides and fight."

"Who commands the army?"

"No word on that as yet. But some say Marquis Louis de Montcalm but that can be a whisper, just as they guess Duquesue will be governor. Whoever and in any case, we face a long, long war, *mon Sieur.*"

Before returning to the Snow Fox, Edouard paid a visit to Pierre le Duc. The crippled trapper already had his coat and trousers cut from the deerskin and Edouard remained for the fitting. Goes Walking phlegmatically helped though Edouard was at first reluctant to strip. Le Duc laughed at him.

"*Mon Sieur,* my squaw has seen many a naked male body before! God knows how many a bearskin before she was traded to me. Please not to waste time, eh, and let us see how well she and I have worked."

Le Duc held the cut skins against Edouard's legs, hips and torso as Goes Walking made marks on the hide with a stick, one charred end glowing with embers. She cut the cloth that would make his underclothing, pulling it in a tight wrap about his body. Le Duc explained that was done to hold body heat in and cut cold air out. Edouard learned that in winter this land could become unbearably cold so that fingers could be stuck to metal and the skin torn away to release them. In summer, there would be humid heat that the cloth would absorb.

"You will thank Goes Walking a thousand times in the woods, *mon Sieur.*"

Edouard also examined and approved of the heavy, long and thick bladed knife with its incredibly sharp edge and the ornate bead decorated sheath. He learned that the rifle would not arrive for a few days.

"It comes from south over the river," le Duc explained. "It is made in the British Colonies. Would to God we had gunsmiths in New France nearly as good."

It was late afternoon when he finally entered the Snow Fox and had wine brought to his table. He sat on bench under a window and Madam Demain, rubbery gargoyle face working in what Edouard believed to be a pleased smile, came up to him.

"Eh, and so you had audience with His Excellency!"

"So I did."

"Did he say anything about a new governor?"

"There is one expected, so the rumors you've heard are right."

"I wonder what he will be like." As she pondered her ugly face grew even more twisted. "It will be more taxes. That is always the first thing a new governor imposes to show his power."

"Or to obey His Majesty, who always needs money."

"In a palace! In Paris! I don't believe such tales."

"There is never enough money for a king, especially if he has a mistress, besides a wife, to bedeck with jewels, fine silks and carriages."

Madam Demain's face contorted in an expression that only her words could translate. "Ah, those grande femmes! Yes, I have heard. They live on our sweat, eh? even here in New France."

"Talk like that, Madam Demain, coming to the governor's ears . . ."

She spoke hastily, *"Mon Sieur,* you mistake. I am not a *sans coulette* speaking of revolution. I am loyal to our good King. It is these women, the leeches, who cost the whole kingdom, eh? If one wife is enough for Jacques, the shopkeeper, why cannot one queen be enough for His Majesty?"

Edouard laughed. "Ask him!"

Madam Demain's lips twisted in what might have been a return smile and she smoothed her hand down over her skirt, making the keys rattle on their metal ring. "I am having my court dress made now, *mon Sieur.* When it is finished, I will present myself to our King Louis and ask him."

She laughed, pleased with her own joke and walked down the hall toward the huge kitchen in the rear of the building. Edouard climbed the stairs to his room, unbuckled his sword belt and carefully placed his plumed hat in its box. He turned at a light tap on the door. It opened and Spotted Doe stepped in. She wore deerskin blouse and skirt stained and spotted, and he saw a smudge of ashes on her cheek so he guessed she had hurried up the back stairs from the kitchen as soon as Madam Demain brought news of his return.

"Do you go west to the Huron country?"

"I don't know yet, little redskin lady. But I am more hopeful. I'll know in a day or so."

She stepped toward him. "Take me with you."

"What!"

"I know the country and I know my people. I would be your squaw and your woman at the camps and wherever you finally settle. I would also be your wife—your woman. Haven't I pleased you?" She added hastily as he hesitated, surprised by her offer. "I will come tonight, *non?* We will talk then under the covers. O, I will persuade you . . . all night long, if need be."

XIX

As soon as the last guests had left the tap room and the lights had been turned out, Spotted Doe entered Edouard's room with the silence of a ghost. He had already undressed and was sitting under the bearskin on the bed, the candle glowing on the small table beside him. Spotted

Doe listened at the door after she had closed it behind her; then she turned to slip out of her clothing. Once more Edouard admired her supple, desirable, dark bronze, full-busted body. But she darted to the bed, snuffed out the candle and snuggled down beside him in the darkness.

She wrapped her arms about him, bringing him tight against her. Placing his hand on her breast, she guided his fingers to her nipple. He completely forgot about peltry and westward travel, Pierre le Duc, buckskins, weapons, and the governor's peltry permit.

Only much later, when their breaths had resumed normal rhythm, Spotted Doe said softly, "I would be very good for you in the wilderness, eh?"

"You would," he agreed, "if I knew I'd get the permit, if I knew where I would travel, if I knew I could persuade trappers to bring their pelts to me."

She surprised him with a typically Gallic and derisive, *"Pouf!* You know you will go first to De Troit and then I will guide you on to Lac du Huron. My people will accept you because I accept you. The *courriers du bois* will bring you fur because you will build your factory near my people and so you will be close at hand. I speak French well, eh? I speak Huron and a dozen other Indian tongues. They know what my words mean from the farthest western lake here to Quebec and down the river to the big what you call 'ocean,' eh?"

"You have it all thought out," he said.

"Certainement! I want the forests and I want to be back with my people."

"But there surely are others who would have taken you."

"Oui. But something here." Her finger tapped his chest over his heart. "Something here made me wait. I don't know why until now. And you come. Now I know why." She snuggled closer and her hand once more explored his body and he could not check the slow tightening of his fingers on her sides.

Once more they had to wait until normal breathing returned. Her palm lay gently against his cheek. "Now I come, eh?"

"Let us see what the next days bring from the governor."

"It will be the permit," she answered confidently.

He did not voice his own feeling that there would always by the chance of refusal, or the governor would want too much. Instead, he asked, "How do the travelers go to Fort De Troit? By the river?"

"Never that way! West, there is the first of many big fresh waters. But before they feed the river, they roll over what you call 'Falls' named Niagara. So, travelers go straight across the land north of Lac des Eries."

"I have not been told of that one."

"It is the second of the fresh waters, far to the south—out of the way. So very few go that way. But straight west. There are few French white-faces around Lac des Eries. There are Seneca Indians south of it and they are enemies to the Huron."

"That country is filled with British colonies?"

"No, it is part of New France but no one thinks much about it. The land is a travel-way, a trail, you understand, to the far end of Lac des Eries where Fort De Troit is built, then north along a stream to Lac du Huron and the Lac of the Clear Waters."

"*Eau Claire*," Edouard translated. "I have heard of it. Good peltry country?"

"The best," she answered proudly. "My country, that of my People."

When Spotted Doe slipped out of the room late in the night, she and Edouard came to no decision. The next morning he waited at the Snow Fox though de Valerain neither appeared nor sent word. But there was increasing talk of the impending arrival of the new governor and also of mounting activity among the Indians—both in New France and in the English colonies to the south, greater indications of trouble stirring, as Edouard guessed. He grew increasingly nervous, what with the rumored approach of governor and armies and whispers from the south that the colonies also were restless. Word came that Louisburg, the fortress the English had captured in the war of less than twenty years ago, had been strengthened by a contingent of soldiers and that the Abenaki Indians of Maine grew more belligerent toward French and Algonquins.

That seemed even a stronger signal of trouble

close at hand, and Pierre le Duc confirmed Edouard's feelings. He had a flintlock rifle that Edouard examined with care.

"The last I can buy from below the river," le Duc said. "Trade lessen back and forth." The old man touched his game leg. "Perhaps more and younger men will get lead balls in their bodies just as I did."

But the old courier knew little more than rumor and the fact that trade seemed to be decreasing. Edouard's deerskin clothing had been finished and jacket, shirt, trousers, and leggings fitted him perfectly. At last he stood before a mirror and studied his image with something akin to stunned surprise. Who would have thought Sieur de Fournet, former Gascon officer in His Majesty's army, would be wearing a skin cap with a tail hanging down his back, much less a fringed sleeve jacket and skin trousers, also with fringes down the legs? Moccasins replaced his boots and, he admitted, felt far lighter and more comfortable. He eyed them dubiously.

"Will they hold up in the wilderness?"

Le Duc smiled. "Far longer than leather, *mon Sieur*. Even if by chance they should not, they will be easier to replace. Now, let us try the belt."

Goes Walking had done as expert a job on the belt as she had the rest of the clothing and it fit snugly. Le Duc then hung the thick hide strap that held the bullet pouch over his head, followed by a lighter strap with the powder horn attached to its end. The straps crossed over his chest and he accepted the rifle le Duc handed him. He returned to the mirror and once more his new appearance surprised him.

"Eh, once you get the tan and the look of the forest and the portages on your face and body, no one will be able to tell you were not born right here in New France, *mon Sieur*. You are ready for the trails at any moment you care to strike out."

Edouard paid him, surprised at how little these provincials charged for such good work and equipment. He had all but the rifle bundled up after he changed back to his old, familiar clothing and returned to the Snow Fox where he waited impatiently for de Valerain. But the hours passed and the governor's officer did not appear.

Madam Demain had eyed the heavy bundle Edouard carried up to his room but he merely nodded and closed the door on her curious eyes and twisting lips which were just on the verge of questions. However, when Spotted Doe brought him wine and cookies to break his fast until the evening meal, he had his buckskins and equipment spread out on the bed. She placed his tray on the small table and turned to examine the clothing.

"It will serve you well in the woods." She touched the polished wooden stock of the rifle and lifted the hunting knife so that the late sun glinted bright reflections from its wide blade. "Old le Duc has not forgotten what lurks in the trees and bushes out there beyond the town."

"Both animals and human," Edouard agreed. "White and red."

"The 'red' will be Iroquois—mostly Seneca, I think. You need have no fear of the Huron."

He smiled crookedly and gave her a mocking salute with his tankard. "I would wager not all Huron are saints and a lone traveller with a good rifle and a bundle of furs would be as tempting as he would be to an Iroquois."

She looked angry for a moment and then smiled slightly. "Perhaps I think too—what you call—highly of my people."

"As I do of Gascons above all other French. No offense, *ma petite.*" He glanced toward the window, closed against street noise. "But, of importance, is there word of the new governor?"

"A messenger in a canoe arrived two hours ago. We have heard he told His Excellency that Marquis Duquesne is near Cape Breton."

"That close!" Edouard whistled faintly. "And I have had no visitors?"

"Only me." She came to the table and smiled down at him. "Not enough?"

"Too much at times."

"Then I will not visit you tonight, *mon Sieur.*"

He stretched an arm across the table and captured her hand. "O, but you will! I meant there has been no one from His Excellency . . . not a message?"

"Neither. You do not like to wait, eh?"

He shook his head, thinking of the *lettre de cachet* that the new governor might be bringing with him. Then he shrugged. "But the mighty set the pace, the lowly can only wait."

"I wait. I lowly?"

"You! Ah, Spotted Doe, whoever thought of *you* as lowly?"

He still held her hand and now he pulled her around the corner of the table and she moved willingly. He held out his arms and she willingly started to come into his lap. A tap on the door startled them and Spotted Doe swiftly straightened, instinctively smoothing her blouse and skirt and taking a long stride to the center of the room.

"*Qui vive*?" Edouard demanded in a loud, vexed voice.

"From His Excellency," a voice answered, muffled by the thick door panels.

Edouard signalled Spotted Doe and she opened the door. De Valerain looked at her and then at Edouard in surprise mingled with admiration. "*Ma foi!* You do well very quickly, *mon ami.*"

Spotted Doe had swiftly cut back of him and out into the hall, but Edouard checked her hasty retreat. "Wine for my guest, *Mam'selle.* Your pleasure, *mon Sieur?*"

De Valerain answered with a twinkle in his eye. "Since I am His Excellency for the moment and right here, only the best in the house, of course."

"Of course, *Mam'selle.*"

"Oui, mon Sieur."

She closed the door behind her and de Valerain, at Edouard's welcoming sign, spun his hat across the room onto the bed and then pulled up a chair to the table. He looked over his shoulder at the closed door. "The most desirable Huron wench in all Quebec, that one."

"Her charms are well known, I gather."

"Somewhat . . . but most difficult to come by. That's one Indian girl who does her own picking and choosing. Few gain her favors."

"And Madam Demain profits?"

"That gargoyle! I would not wager a sous on it. Spotted Doe, unlikely as it seems from an Indian, gives rather than sells—or so I have been told."

"Then you've never . . .?"

"She hardly knows I exist except now and then downstairs when she occasionally serves at the tavern. She tends to the hostel guests—the important ones and even few of them gain real favor." De Valerain correctly read Edouard's expression. "Eh, but you feel better! I only spread gossip so far as I know."

Mollified, Edouard's face cleared and he asked eagerly, "You bring word from His Excellency?"

"Of course! De la Gallissonniere's rule grows shorter day by day, almost hour by hour, and he is not one to let even one *louis d'or* escape him." De Valerain pulled a small parchment from an inside coat pocket and held it up. "It is signed by His Excellency and I may give it to you if your offer is acceptable."

"I bargain blind," Edouard protested.

"His Excellency hopes you overbid, of course. So much the more for him." De Valerain lifted his finger to check whatever Edouard might say. "I shall see he gets no more than the lowest price he named."

"Why do you give me this favor?"

"Well . . . I have a regard for you and it increased when I saw Spotted Doe so willing to serve you. Perhaps after you have gone westward, she would manage to notice me. It is something for home, eh?"

"I can only hope with you and leave fulfillment to her. But what will the permit cost?"

De Valerain named a figure that, though Edouard inwardly gasped, was still somewhat below the price he had feared. He would at least have enough left to pay wilderness prices for wilderness work, and he reluctantly agreed. De Valerain handed him the parchment and at that moment Spotted Doe returned with the wine and glasses. The young officer had eyes only for her as she moved about, and Edouard fished the required number of gold coins from his purse without de Valerain seeing how flattened the purse became. Spotted Doe left the room as soon as she had served and de Valerain sighed. "Ah, you see! Her favors are all for you, not for me."

"But I will soon be gone. Let's have a toast to my early departure, leaving you with opportunities." Edouard kept his voice casual as he asked, "Is there further news of the new governor?"

"He arrives tomorrow, I understand, so de Gallissonnière's eagerness for your coins is understandable. The Marquis du Quesne also brings royal orders and edicts and I have heard there might be one or two in New France who will return in chains to Paris and the Minister of Justice." He did not notice Edouard's spasmic hand jerk or hear the faint clink of the wine glass against his teeth.

"Prisoners!"

"So the King wishes but that is little more than a wish even with the royal orders. There is much of New France that has as yet even to be seen. No one knows how far west the land extends—and even the known area is dense with forest that could hide half a dozen armies. The Marquis Duquesne, unless the fugitives are caught unaware, will report nothing but failure on that score. Already the trees hide many a man who should be in the Bastille."

Edouard felt a flood of relief. He refilled the glasses. "A pity. That report is an unhappy start to his new post."

"He will have more important things than fugitives, my friend. He has to prepare to receive Montcalm's army and to prepare for war. Fugitives will be the last thing on his mind unless one or more of them should happen to simply fall into his hands."

"Not likely."

"Not likely," de Valerain agreed, drained his

glass and arose. "But I must get back to His Excellency with your coins. Perhaps, after Duquesne has taken full charge, I could present you — if you are still in Quebec. Who knows but he might have a liking for you."

"Eh, qui sait?" Edouard agreed.

When de Valerain had left, Edouard dropped back on the settle, alarmed but feeling safe at least until the morning—or perhaps longer, since ceremonies would keep the old and new governors from official business for at least another day or so; Edouard could be far away by then. He looked at the armoire whose closed doors hid his wilderness clothing and equipment. He could rent a saddle horse and—his thoughts broke off as Spotted Doe returned for the tray and glasses. She would know if a mount could be had in Quebec.

"But why?" she asked and abruptly dropped to a seat beside him and her eyes darkened. She touched her heart. "Why do you leave me?"

"I have to travel fast, *ma petite,* and a horse is necessary. You can't go with me."

"Why not! I have told you I can help, *non*?" Her contemptuous gesture dismissed his ideas. "Who could not see a man in a hurry on a horse? They would remember and if any asked, what then? My people have trails that the whiteface have never seen. We could travel to the setting sun and no one would be the wiser. I have asked to go with you, eh? Why not?"

He looked blank, without an answer, having never thought of the escape route she suggested.

He recalled le Duc saying that many a trapper out in the wilderness caught peltry or dealt in them without the governor's permit and that many of them avoided the law's minions and the royal soldiers. She sensed his uncertainty and pressed on.

"Beyond the town and the last houses, I can step off the road and no whiteface would see me again unless *I* step out on the road again. It is that simple."

"In the daytime?"

"That is of worry, eh? It could be done at night."

"The patrols would—"

Her faint, derisive smile answered him and then her lovely face grew grim. "You fear. The new governor who is coming?"

He hesitated and then nodded. "He has some papers about me."

"Outlaw?"

"Officially, yes. But an old fool who dreamed he was young wanted me gone. He arranged it with the king's officers in the place where I lived and . . . I escaped."

Her eyes sparkled. "An old man wants a young buck far away, eh? Or maybe his scalp? Ah, it has to have been a squaw, non?"

He had the grace to blush and she laughed, pointing to the bed. "I have been with you there. It was not hard to guess."

"Why or what doesn't matter," he snapped impatiently, wanting to avoid further questioning. "There is the question of arrest—mine. I will be in the governor's jail or on the packet back to France and the King's Bastille where my head could soon be on a pike.''

''You would not be very pretty then.'' But she sobered immediately. ''This new Excellency arrives tomorrow, eh? Are you rested? Could you travel far tonight?''

''What else can I do?''

She arose. ''Go down to the tavern and have more wine. Show yourself. Drink a little, eh? When Madam Demain snuffs the candles, you return here and change to the clothes Pierre and Goes Walking made for you. Be ready for my knock.''

''You're going with me to Montreal?''

''Or beyond. Be ready.''

She gathered up the tray and left the room, ignoring his word of protest and restraining hand. He did not want to involve her but she entirely had the right of it—and who could want a better travel companion in this strange, immense country? He waited a few moments, then pulled on his boots and his coat and soon sat downstairs in the tavern, a glass of wine in his hand.

Much later, he had returned to his room. He changed to his buckskins by the light of a single candle, bundled up his discarded clothing, and left the garments on the bed along with his rapier and its scabbard still attached to the fine leather belt he had worn for so long. His plumed hat topped the pile.

That done, he snuffed out the candle, made sure of the coins in his newly made belt purse and sat down by the window to wait. He heard no sound in the building and out on the street he saw few passersby. The two men of the night patrol caught his attention for a few moments and he warily watched them as they moved slowly and heedlessly on down the street and out of sight. He looked off toward the river, hidden from his sight by intervening buildings on the curve of the road and then up at the high shadow of the rock. The Marquis de la Gallissonnière would be spending his last few nights up there as the King's law in New France. Edouard shrugged. The Marquis du Quesne could be just as dangerous if he brought a *lettre de cachet* for one Edouard de Fournet.

He started when he heard a small noise at the door. It silently swung open and he saw a shadowy figure. A second later, Spotted Doe moved noiselessly across the room.

"Ready? We go now."

She held his hand to guide him along the dark hall, down the rear stairs and into the kitchen where the only light came from the windows and glowing embers in the huge fireplace. A moment later they stepped out into a narrow way at the rear of the building.

Spotted Doe stopped then and her arm barred any step Edouard might have taken. They stood unmoving for long moments and then she said in a barely audible whisper, "No one. Make no noise."

She bent to something against the building, straightened and Edouard saw she carried a bundle of some sort. He reached for it but she swung away. "I carry. You make noise and we caught. Carry your musket so."

She took his rifle, illustrated her instructions and handed the weapon back to him. He held it, muzzle of the long barrel slanted down, his fingers grasping the rifle just ahead of the trigger guard and flint hammer. Satisfied, she touched his arm as a silent signal and moved out. He followed her.

Once they had to swing back into the black shadows between two buildings as the town patrol noisily turned a far corner, slumped along the cobbles and unknowingly passed them by a matter of paces. When the last sounds of their boots died away, Spotted Doe again touched Edouard's arm and they moved on.

Dawn found them several miles from the town. They had walked steadily along a well-used road but at the first hint of morning light, Spotted Doe led the way into the border of trees and underbrush. She found a deep depression in a natural clearing and stopped.

"We hide here. Watch whiteface trail back there."

"But we are still so near the town!" he protested.

"If we travel, we be seen—and you caught. Here we safe. Eat and then sleep, first you, then me. Watch all the time."

"I'll take the first watch."

"No! You go to Huron country—forest. You

be Huron and courier now. Act forest and Indian way. So squaw," and she tapped herself, "do camp, cook, help her man. You hunt, trap. That's the way we live from now. I wake you after time. Then you watch."

He tried to argue the point but she would not be changed, so at last he curled up on a pile of grasses she formed for him. He quickly discovered that he had long ago become unused to the rough life of a soldier, that even life in a tent could have some ease, more than the hard ground below the grass pile. He spent most of the time trying to find a comfortable position or spot.

Now and then Spotted Doe looked over at him but she made no comment. The sun moved higher but the trees broke its rays into flickering, moving spots of gold between the leaves moving in a light breeze. He turned on his back, looked up through the leaves at the clear sky, feeling drowsy but unable to do more than close his eyes for a few moments and then snap wide awake. Finally he could no longer simply toss and turn.

He came to his feet and could now see over the rim of the depression. He could see the main road far off between the trees and, as he looked, a small herd of cattle passed, driven by four men with long prodding poles and whips which they snapped at any one of the animals who started to move away from the others. He touched Spotted Doe, who looked up over her shoulder.

"I can't rest. I'll watch."

She judged the sun. "There is yet an hour."

"Not for me. You rest."

"First I fix to eat, eh?" But we have long time until night. Then we walk until sun in the morning. You will be very tired."

"Maybe. But the thought of food makes me wish we had some."

"We do. Spotted Doe find plenty at Madam Demain's." She dropped down into the depression and bent over the bundle she had been carrying. When she opened it, Edouard looked at several flat loaves of crusty bread, a haunch of meat wrapped in thick cloth and even some unbroken eggs. She smiled at his stunned surprise.

"Indians know how to steal and I know we travel a long, long way!" She turned the skin bundle again and he saw a clay wine jug, the lead seal still unbroken over its mouth.

"How did you—?"

"I make ready some, like wine, when you say you are going away from Quebec. I know I go with you. Spotted Doe decide good days ago." She tapped her head to indicate her planning. "Then today I see you leave may be quick, so I make up food for us. I ready to go when you ready to go."

He looked at her, at the food, back at her and then dropped to a seat on the grass before the bundle. He could only exclaim, *"Tonnerre!"*

Spotted Doe proved to be sparing with the food. Edouard still felt hungry when she rolled everything back up again, lashed the bundle and then used it as a pillow when she lay down.

"Your time watch. I rest." She smiled wickedly. "Best if maybe sleep now, if maybe not, no matter, you march tonight."

Spotted Doe proved right. By the next dawn, after hours of plodding westward, he could only drop onto the ground in a glade completely hidden from the road by bush and trees. He did not even want to eat but dropped off into drugged sleep immediately. She awakened him to take his turn as guard and he barely managed to hold his eyes open until she at last wakened and allowed him a bit more sleep while she prepared a meal of bread and cheese and a few bites of cold venison. Then the night march started.

But at dawn, before they left the road, she pointed ahead to the nearly discernible outline of a few buildings. "A farm—that how you say? Give me a little money and I will buy more to eat."

He shook his head. "You've done enough and more than enough. I'll go to the farm."

"We come close to Montreal. Town big like Quebec. People see me, they not think about Huron squaw. But a new whiteface in trapper skins who act like new to woods? They remember him if soldiers ask, eh? No, I go when we find place to camp."

He could not argue the point. They found a hiding place and he could do nothing but wait and worry until she returned in mid-morning with her bundle again bulging, smiling and then sighing wearily. "You keep watch. I rest this time, eh?"

So they moved westward, hiding and sleeping as they could by day, marching by night. Following Spotted Doe's advice, they made a wide circuit around Montreal, cutting deep into the woodlands. They felt more secure now but still did not lessen their caution until Spotted Doe at last felt they would be far enough from French villages, farms and people so they could resume the more normal procedure of traveling by day and sleeping by night. They even built small fires and Spotted Doe taught him how to set traps for rabbits, squirrels, and other small edible woodland creatures.

"Gun make noise," she explained, "and maybe courier hear, or Indian and come look."

"Would Huron attack us?"

"All kinds of Indian here now—Huron, Erie, even Seneca sometime." She pointed to his rifle, bullet pouch and knife. "They like those—and your hair. Some want woman, like me, eh? Whiteface no better. So we very careful until we come to De Troit. My tribe and clan close. Then we safe."

She thought of a future that was not to be.

Two nights later they had finished eating but instead of throwing dirt and ashes on the fire to smother the flames, Spotted Doe came closer to Edouard and her dark eyes bored directly into his. He read the message and his long dormant desire sprang to full life. He reached for her and she placed his hand on her breast. He could not help his sudden, cautious look around at the silent trees that circled them. She laughed.

"We are deep in woods. No one near. So we be man and woman again, *non?*"

She twisted away just long enough to pull her blouse up over her head and her full, rich and desirable breasts invited him. He grabbed her and she pulled his lips to one of her nipples, held his head close as his breath increased into an irregular rhythm. Suddenly she pushed him away, and with a laugh of sheer pagan, primitive anticipation, stood up and a second later her skirt dropped and she stood before him, clad only in her moccasins and headband. Just as he first saw her, he thought, as she dropped to her knees before him, her coarse black hair now free and cascading down either side of her face.

"*Mon Dieu!*" A strange voice came from among the trees beyond her. "*Quelle femme!* But that squaw looks more for me and my friends."

Edouard wheeled about. He saw a tall, old-faced man in dirty fringed buckskins. Then other figures appeared—Indians who looked as if their own kind would disown them—and two other couriers, knife-scarred with the mark of the outlaw upon each coarse face.

XX

In all of her life Abby had never questioned that her first experience as a grown woman would be with some handsome young man of the village in which she lived. As a small girl she had never been able to give him a face but then Daniel had come to Westover with the company, she had known it would be him. But here she found herself in an Onondaga Iroquois town, naked as the day she was born except for the Indian headband, facing an equally naked young Indian warrior.

This handsome bronze savage would make a woman of Abigail Brewster, the descendant of generations of proud yeoman English and colonial ancestors! But . . .

"Come," Corn Dancer broke in on her racing, incoherent thoughts. "You—me—make real fireside." Then he seemed to guess her thoughts for his eyes narrowed as he studied her and his voice softened. "You Onondaga now. You not Abbee. You Strong Woman. You mother this fireside—mine, yours."

He reached for her hand and she started to flinch away, then realized the full extent of her situation for the first time. She must have had some small ray of hope buried deep within during the horrid flight from Westover to this Long House deep in the woods and mountains west of the Hudson. But now it had disappeared and she knew it. She had no immediate choice and Corn Dancer's extended hand and expectant face told her it would be final and complete. If she rejected him, she had no doubt she would be killed, as the other girls of Westover had been along the trail. Or she could become this man's woman—wife—squaw—"Mother," as he had called her. With a sense of dread, she accepted his hand.

"Hah! You Strong Woman! You no afraid

Corn Dancer—Onondaga woman you known down. We make Fireside.''

He led her to the furs and as she lay down watching him, she wondered if fear plus imagination played tricks with her eyesight. Surely no man of *any* color or race could have such a musculature! But he dropped beside her and before she could even gasp she found herself held tightly in his arms. The fire in her body rose despite all she could do, despite all she had been taught to fear Indians, or any man who fondled her breasts, thighs and stroked the bush between her legs.

Suddenly, in the fog of her fear, she heard the increasing, excited panting of his breath and the push and strain of his body against hers. With a dextrous but powerful shove of his hand, he rolled her onto her back and then loomed above her, poised, glittering eyes first on her face and then traveling over her body. For a second she resisted and then surrendered to his insistent striving and her legs parted.

His fingers fumbled with her lips down there and suddenly she felt him, large and strong. She could not help her cry of pain and fear at his first thwarted thrust. Then it came again and she tried to twist out from under him but he held her close and suddenly something happened. He was entirely within her.

She tried to withdraw but his full weight came down on her. She gasped, cried out and then could not check the hot desire that flooded her as he filled her body. Without her own volition, her body moved and arched to meet him. She felt a spark within that seemingly exploded through her whole body, shaking her, making her senses reel. Her fingers sank deep into the flesh of his shoulders, then enwrapped him and pulled him close. She hungered—hungered—and more waves of hot flames shook her body from within. She only dimly knew the cries that sounded from far off actually issued from her own mouth until her lips pressed against him and she could only softly moan.

A new warmth flooded her, not her own, but she had no care as another spasm swept her and she could only cling tightly to him, unable to move, cry out, even think. She could only feel. Corn Dancer had suddenly gone limp and lay atop her like a heavy sack that miraculously breathed with a ragged, almost whistling sound. Then he rolled off and to one side. She lay unmoving, unable to, her body wet with sweat, her mouth dry, her lips crushed. Her limp arm dropped across his chest and she heard him say, somewhere far off. "Strong Woman! Ah, Strong Woman!"

His palm stroked down through the hair between his thighs and he held it up. She saw a dark stain but he suddenly jumped up and rushed out into the main passageway. She heard his excited voice and the pleased, surprised answer of his mother. Naked as she was, Abby did not want to show herself so she edged and moved around until she had a view of the doorway. Corn Dancer held out his hand to his mother and to his father as they bent over the fire. Someone had thrown more grass and twigs on it for the embers had turned to flames.

Then, as Corn Dancer turned to answer the question of his father, Abby saw that he displayed his hand, palm and fingers stained with her own blood. She felt the blood rush up her neck into her cheeks and anger shook her. Then, as she saw Corn Dancer's pride and the approval of his parents, she realized that these savages took such things as they would any natural phenomenon. In fact, both the mother and father looked toward the doorway and Abby shrank back out of sight but not before she saw the glowing approval on both their faces.

She sank back on the furs and pulled one of them up over her, still choked with embarrassed anger. But it slowly diminished as she thought of what often happened in Westover and other villages back in her home land. True, the young husbands did not show bloody hands but how many of them, or their parents, displayed soiled bed clothing as proof that the new bride had been untouched before by any man!

Suddenly Moon Willow appeared in the doorway and Abby could not help the catch of her breath as she choked back anger and once more the heat of shame touched her cheeks. Moon Willow spoke several unintelligible words as she came into the room, crouched down beside Abby. She spoke again but Abby could only shake her head to show she did not understand. Moon Willow impatiently spoke over her shoulder and Corn Dancer jumped through the doorway. He listened to the gush of his mother's words and then faced Abby.

"She say—good! You, how you say? Clean. No buck have you. Only me. That good. She say you truly mother of our fireside. You Onondaga—Iroquois—mother now. You good squaw—Strong Woman, eh?"

Abby held up his stained hand. "Because of that?"

"Hai!" He made a sweeping gesture of contempt that she understood took in far more than the small room, the Long House and perhaps even the whole town. "You—how you say?—only one, two—"

He stopped, frowning, searching for a word. "You mean not many of your squaws are virgin when they are married?"

"What is 'virgin'!"

Abby had to use many signs and pointings, many of them indecent according to her own upbringing, to get him to understand but at last his face lit and he nodded vigorously, smiling widely.

"Hai! Virgin! Hai!"

He spoke to his mother and then Abby realized that the doorway of the little room was crowded with the curious—and she gasped when she saw a small boy about four years old, completely naked, staring at her with round eyes, thumb in his mouth and his round, bronze baby face a picture of complete puzzlement. She twisted about, face over her hands.

"Corn Dancer," she said, voice muffled. "Go—those people—go."

"But—" Then he shrugged. "Mother say what is. You mother now this Fireside. They go."

He spoke swiftly and forcefully and instantly the crowd about the door melted away. Moon Willow patted Abby's arm, spoke to her and then Corn Dancer. He translated. "Squaws make you dress. We tell Keepers. They come . . . look . . . make, how you say? Sure. Then no more, eh?"

"Hai!" she answered weakly.

Within minutes only she and Corn Dancer lay under the furs. She edged away from him and rolled over so that her back was to him. He placed his hand on her thigh and she flinched. But he made no further move and Abby didn't know whether to move his hand or leave it alone. His palm was warm and light upon her. Then she heard his deep even breathing and, in relief, knew that he slept.

But Abby could find no rest. She started with every slight sound—Corn Dancer's sleeping gasp, a faint cry of a child from somewhere down the long central passage, a passing gust of wind that touched the wall and was gone. Her mind raced around and around and then swiftly turned to her experience with Corn Dancer and remained there. She wondered at herself. How often had she heard travelling parsons pound rickety pulpits in the small village churches and call down brimstone and the fires of hell on the sins of the flesh? How wicked it was! Even married grown-ups, as she had come to believe, including her own father and mother, were not totally cleansed in the "spirit" when they indulged in "carnality." What about her—and especially now that it had been with an Indian?

She felt a horror at herself when she knew that the act was not at all ugly and she wondered how many of the married women of Westover and other towns told the truth when they said or implied that they simply had "to put up with" the male animal lusts of their husbands. Recalling some of them now and her childhood impressions, she wondered if many of those women—fat, lean, dried-up, ugly and but few of them pretty—had not covered the real truth with the worn-out phrase. Perhaps more often than not it was the husband who had "to put up with."

Suddenly she had a vivid memory picture of the pages of the Old Testament she had read over and over again at the urging of her father, mother, neighboring women, or the dour-faced parson of the moment in the village. "Beget" she had read, a long listing of "beget." How often in the long centuries since the Creation had suffering God had to condemn "begetters" and turn them over to Satan to, if the parsons were right, "roast in hell." As she recalled, there had been some fairly important Biblical names among the "begetters." She smiled in the darkness, turned once more and suddenly plunged into deep sleep—mind, body and spirit worn out by the demands that had been made upon them. Her last fading thought was that, finally, she was safe. But she was too tired to dwell on that miracle.

As Corn Dancer had predicted, the next day the six Keepers came, marching regally down the long passage to the new Fireside Moon Willow had Abby build. They took her into the side room, examined her carefully. The tall woman leader finally touched Abby's stomach, smiled and said a few words in a pleased tone. She then spoke to Moon Willow and marched out of the house, her retinue following her.

Corn Dancer explained. "You Strong Woman. You good Onondaga. Good Mother. The Keepers of the Faith make you one with us. Maybe—how you say, quick?—you belong secret woman clan. That good. You get real name then."

The Keepers had come just at dawn and the fires in the long passageway glowed as the families gathered about them. The women held their arms up to the roof and the men stood silent, listening to a short rhythmic spate of words, then picked up bows, arrows, lances and rifles and marched out of the house. Then Abby began the life of an Onondaga. The women built up the fires, some left with clay jugs to return very soon with water. Moon Willow motioned Abby to her fire as other women came up. They carried skin blouses and skirts and leggings of varied sizes. Some were much too large, some too small but the women patiently continued to bring clothing. At last, bit by bit, Abby found herself clothed from soft shirt through sturdy moccasins to headbands.

Moon Willow picked up blouses and skirts that had fit Abby while other women brought cured but unblemished hides. They were pegged out and marked to the exact measurements that matched the models. Throughout the Long House there was movement and women's voices, and not a man was in sight. Then, after a long time had passed, a woman by the door lifted her voice to a single word and instantly all the cutting and marking ceased.

The men returned, each going to his own Fireside and dropping the results of the morning hunt beside the flames. The women instantly went to work, knives flashing as they skinned the game, cut it up and tossed chunks in the boiling water of the pots hanging over the fires. Abby then realized that the men had also gone to the cultivated town fields and now returned with corn, beans, edible gourds, even berries and fruit. The morning meal turned into a banquet of sorts.

But only the women did the cooking. The men now looked to smoking the strong tobacco that they grew in the fields, or they sharpened knives, checked weapons, and constantly chattered to one another. Abby wondered now where the idea that Indians were taciturn and with few words had originated. The men appeared to be as much gossips as their wives.

When Corn Dancer had returned, Moon Willow had pushed Abby after him and she found herself busy cleaning two rabbits, shucking corn, peeling and cutting squash into chunks and pitching the whole into the pot that Moon Willow had hung over the fire for her.

Corn Dancer also sat cross-legged and puffed at his long-stemmed pipe, the small bowl decorated with a motley array of bird feathers. Abby, recalling how she had been forced to trail after him on the march, see to his every need at the camps, finished the cooking and motioned him to eat.

He surprised her, shaking his head, dipping a bowl into the stew and held the smoking food to her. "Mother eat first. You mother, Abbbeee. You mother like other mother." He pointed down the long hall and she saw that, truly, the women ate while the men waited. She couldn't understand and then she recalled Leah's surprised exclamation on the trail.

"I bet you, the women rule!"

She looked at Corn Dancer, pointed to herself and held her arm out so that her hand was a short distance above the floor, and then at herself again. Then she tapped his knee and again held out her arm, her hand much higher and pointed at him. He frowned and she repeated the sign.

He still looked puzzled and Abby impatiently looked around, saw Moon Willow sitting near the fire using a primitive round stone pestle to grind up corn in a shallow bowl. Abby pointed to her, then struck her own chest. She stood up and held herself tall and proud. Once more she struck her chest, and pointed to Moon Willow. Then she pointed to Howling Wolf, like the other warriors sitting cross-legged, some working on arrowheads or shafts or simply nodding in a half doze.

She held her hand even with the crown of her head, then pointed to Howling Wolf and Corn Dancer, bent low to the floor and held her hand less than a foot from the ground.

"Me big?" she asked. "You little? Howling Wolf little? Warriors little? Squaws big? eh?"

His face lighted. "Hai! You mother now this fireside."

Abby sighed in relief. Leah was right, it seemed.

XXI

Abby discovered time had a completely different meaning to the Iroquois than anything she had ever known. It was measured, if at all, by the slow movement of the sun, the coming of night, the coming of dawn. There was no sense of wasted minutes or hours but this by no means signified idleness. The peculiar kind of "ever-lasting now" in which they lived was filled with activity—work of all kinds, in the fields beyond the Long Houses, a constant search for game by the warriors, and for the children's play that copied in a small manner the work the adults engaged upon.

Little naked boys played with small bows and reed arrows, lances also of reed. It grew rougher and more realistic as the boys grew and approached manhood. The same, in a manner, was true of the girls. They made skin clothing for dolls whose bodies were thick long corncobs or broken bits of wood. They were often called to help their mothers with small chores that would eventually prepare them to become future mothers of firesides themselves.

For many months Abby had held to a shred of hope that some means of escape would present itself and a few times she thought such a chance had come. She once watched several bearded white men ride out of the woods and down the trail between the fields to the stockade. But they had no more than appeared than the Keepers closed the single door of the Long House and remained almost as guards before it. Later, Abby learned that the visitors had been wandering traders and Corn Dancer told her they had been stopped only a few yards from the edge of the forest and several hundred yards from the high stockade by the warriors. After this had happened half a dozen times, Abby knew that none but an Indian would see her.

She believed that she would be held to the confines of the Long House but, gradually, she could feel restrictions relax. Now she could move to the area just beyond the door, then along the street. As day followed day, she learned more and more of the language, many of the women going out of the way to touch an object and pronounce its Iroquoian name. Her vocabulary of words grew and gradually she began to speak phrases, then whole sentences. Now she could converse fairly easily with any of the Indians.

She had feared to ask about Leah, Marion and Patience or any of the captives from Westover but at last she worked up courage enough to speak to Moon Willow. At first the older woman either pretended not to understand or refused to answer. Then she hinted that Abby's friends were alive but for some mysterious reason, she could not see them.

More and more, the ways of the life of the Iroquois became clearer to her. These Indians were proud, considered themselves the lords of the forests. "As far as any one has walked," Corn Dancer boasted, "the Six Nations rule all the tribes, all the animals, all the woods. The Master of Life made it so."

"Master of Life?" she asked.

He pointed to the roof of the Long House and then his sweeping circular gesture encompassed everything beyond the walls. "Master of Life rules everything—you, me, the Mothers, the Keepers of the Faith. Our *shamans* teach his way and you will be taught it when the time comes.''

"When will that be?"

He shrugged, looked uncomfortable and his voice lowered as he leaned forward to answer in a low voice. "The Keepers of the Faith know. They will come for you. You will become a sister to Moon Willow in her Society."

Abby was even more puzzled about the strange use of "sister" and she wondered what the "society" must be. She did not have long to wait for an answer. About two weeks later, the three women of the Keepers and the shaman of the town, a wild-eyed man who carried a staff and constantly rattled beads in a gourd, suddenly appeared at the door. The shaman pranced in erratic steps along the passageway. The women Keepers followed him at some distance, sedate as usual, proud and now their bronze faces were frozen, their eyes did not seem to move. But they performed none of the gyrations of the shaman, whom Abby had often considered as a little more than half crazy.

The procession brought everyone in the house to their feet. The children ran into the dark rooms on either side of the fires and, as though the shaman had waved a wand, every man had disappeared! The shaman continued his wild dance and the rattle of dried beans in his decorated gourd echoed in the narrow passage. He wore long, yellowed bearclaws about his neck. Half his face had been painted blue, the other half red.

The closer he came, the more Abby began to

fear him. She started to turn but Moon Willow had appeared at her side. The older woman grasped Abby's arm at the elbow and her fingers became vises that Abby could not loosen or break. Her voice came as a bare whisper.

"Do not move. Do not fear, Strong Woman. All the mothers have been waiting for them to come."

The shaman now moved and shook, stamped his moccasined feet in a beat on the hard ground that sounded like a drum. He glared at her, shook the gourd the harder and then his hoarse, crow's voice screeched throughout the structure. He had changed his random shouts and screams into a chant.

"Master of Life! Great Mother of Mothers! Strong Woman is your daughter. She is one with you. You are one with her. Mother of Mothers, purify her. Bring her before the Master of Life. Give her the secret name! Her true name! Let no man look upon what the Mothers do! Let no man see or be struck blind! This is the Mothers'! This is not man's!"

The three women Keepers came forward and one, standing directly before Abby said in a firm, carrying voice, "No man may see. No man may listen. This is the Mothers'. Strong Woman, we take you now. We wash you clean. This time we wash away man—all men! You get the secret of the Mother of Mothers. Do you accept?"

Abby did not know what to answer but Moon Willow's gnarled fingers pressed cruelly into her arm and Abby understood the older woman's fearful insistence. Abby had as little choice with this as she had becoming Corn Dancer's wife. This concerned solely the women, she instinctively knew and she wondered if it was also happening to Patience, Marion or Leah. But the Keepers still waited and Moon Willow's fingers became cruel claws.

"I accept," she said.

Instantly the Keepers stepped closer and Moon Willow, dropping Abby's arm, stepped back. A tall proud woman took position on either side of Abby and the shaman's dance now became a frenetic prancing, the beans constantly rattling in the gourd he shook all about her, from her head to her feet. Then with his wand he pointed at the door of the Long House.

"The way is open, the men and warriors have departed. Only the Mothers remain."

Hands again grasped Abby's arms but this time their grasp was light. She marched forward between the Keepers out of the Long House into the street. Not a male, boy or man, was in sight. The march continued to the gate, down the wide trail between the fields to the stream. She was told to strip and then she stepped into the water. Instead, the Keepers filled gourds with water and then poured it over her head or flung it upon her body. Abby saw all the women of the town standing along the bank, watching intently, and she heard a long, continuing murmur of approval.

The Keepers sang a prayer to the Mother of

Mothers and the women on the bank joined in as the Keepers began a chanted repetition of the invocation. They led Abby toward the bank but stopped when she was still ankle deep. One of the Keepers slowly looked from woman to woman along the bank, her gaze holding on each one in turn. Then she lifted her voice in a question that everyone in the crowd heard.

"Is she Woman? Is she Mother?"

She pointed to Abby's thighs and the thick, coarse hair, dripping water. The shouted reply came instantly, "She is woman. She can be Mother."

"Can she be Sister of the Owl and the Hawk?"

"Hai!" the shout answered.

The two Keepers now bent and, cupping water in their hands, splashed it on Abby's stomach and then each poured a full gourd into her bush. The Keepers turned to the spectators on the bank.

"She is ready."

The Keepers led Abby completely out of the stream and along the trail to the village. Now the guards along the stockade were women and Abby had the strange sensation that every Onondaga man had magically vanished. This was a world solely of women. They marched through the gate but instead of moving along the familiar street to the Long House the Keepers turned her to the left and they passed by several more streets of bark houses. Still not a male in sight and an eerie silence broken only by the shuffle of women's moccasins in the dirt.

They came to an area occupied only by a huge, round building covered only by a roof and a second, this one enclosed in bark and roofed but not nearly the size of the usual Long Houses. A third woman Keeper stood at the closed door and, as the procession approached, she lifted her arm, palm out. The hands holding Abby's arms tightened and she was halted in her tracks. Silence held the area, the whole town. Abby, looking beyond the Keeper at the closed door, saw the emblems of hawk on one panel and owl on the other and the design of a woman wearing a headdress of the Keepers painted on the door panel itself.

"Has she the signs and the words?" the guardian Keeper demanded. "Has she the secrets?"

"None," one of Abby's guides answered, "but the Mothers ask that she be shown the signs and told the secrets."

"Hai!" came the approving chorus and the guardian Keeper looked hard at Abby. "Strong Woman, there are things you will see and hear that are to be spoken to no man—nor woman— who is not Sister of the Owl and Hawk." She pulled a long hunting knife from its concealment within her blouse. "If you speak of them, you will have no eyes, neither tongue nor nose. You will be driven into the forest to live if you can until an arrow, knife or animal finds you. Do you understand?"

Abby, confused and now frightened, nodded.

The Keeper stepped aside and opened the door, gesturing for Abby to enter. "Come then. Be one with us, with the Mothers, the Mother of Mothers. You will hear your true name."

Abby found her tongue and stammered, "You said it is Strong Woman."

"That is your Onondaga name. This will be your Sister name, the name of the power of the Mothers, the Hawk and the Owl. Enter and become one with us."

So Abby had her induction into the secret society of the women of the town. She felt it was more of a school where by rote, ritual and chant the women were taught their status in the tribe, the functions of their bodies as differing from those of men, medicines for almost every purpose from fevers to the healing of wounds and for easing childbirth.

She quickly came to know that "initiation" was not a single ceremony except on special occasions and subjects, such as the first day, the story of the Mother of Mothers, and the true meaning of the Owl and the Hawk. She also learned her "secret" name that only the Keeper who whispered it in her ear and she would know: "White Woman Made Red." Abby was warned over and over again that anyone who knew that name had full control over her body, mind and spirit; could make her do anything commanded, and its disclosure would cut her off from contact with the Mother of Mothers. Abby did not know until many years later that this matter of a public name and a secret or real name was not only true of her secret society but of primitive tribes of every race and place over the world. But by then . . .

More important, she was instructed in the method of controlling the men and warriors and thus controlling the destiny of the Onondaga. True, the men were the *Sachems* of all the tribes making up the Six Nations and there were also the Pine Tree *Sachems* of especially brave or wise rulers, councillors and warriors composing a select group who could send a tribe to war or raiding with a single word. But the Mothers, Abby learned, could depose even these lordly beings if their acts or words gave rise to doubt as to wisdom or bravery. Truly, the women, or Mothers, controlled.

The last day of the closed meetings in the house of the Society, again turned to ceremony. Now the Keepers came to her and brought her before a crude kind of altar. Prayers were chanted to the Mother of Mothers and Master of Life. A small round pot containing a dark, blue fluid was placed before her and one of the Keepers drew a long pointed copper needle. She punctured Abby's right shoulder time and again and Abby bit her lips to keep from exclaiming against the small, painful bites. Then the copper blade was dipped in the pot and she saw the fluid on its point. The jabbing started over and again, and was finally finished. The Keeper then drew her blouse over her head and turned her back.

Abby saw the small tattoo in the shape of the Owl and the Keeper turned Abby to touch her back over the sore area the copper needle had just worked. She realized she had been tattooed with the sign as the Keeper and the other women looked at her with an expectant questioning air. They sought her approval for what they had done!

She nodded and instantly formality left the whole group. They formed about her, chattering happily, speaking to her of Corn Dancer, her own Long House and Fireside. She had become one of them, one of the secret society! She knew it meant far more than the scrubbing that had washed the white blood out of her, the blood ceremony making her one with Moon Willow's Fireside and all Onondaga. Now the women could speak freely to her of many things hitherto unspoken. This would be true wherever Abby should happen to travel among the Nations.

The door was thrown open and the half-mad shaman, who had been dozing in the huge structure that had no walls, immediately jumped up and sounded a whoop that brought every man and boy popping out of the houses. The ceremony had been completed and Abby had truly become Iroquois, Onondaga. She suddenly glimpsed Leah among the crowd and the woman looked at her with envy and hatred once more flaming in her eyes and her mouth curled scornfully. Abby could not work her way to her in all the close pressing crowd but she pointed Leah out to Moon Willow.

"Is she a member of the Owl and the Hawk?"

"Nothing," Moon Willow answered in a

careless, contemptuous dismissal. "She not Strong Woman like you. She make trouble. She work. She not have regular man like Corn Dancer. She never become Onondaga. Never!"

XXII

Abby found the days in the Onondaga town had an easy flow, even though each was filled with activity. As she grew more proficient with the language she came to a better understanding of her town, tribe and nation. They had forcibly adopted her but, bit by bit, she thought more and more like an Iroquois.

She immediately discovered why she had been taken into the Fireside, initiated in the women's secret society and given privileges that time and again surprised her. The Iroquois held courage as the greatest of virtue, courage whenever found and displayed. The fact that she had run only a bit of the gauntlet and then had, in sheer self-defense, grabbed a weapon and laid it about her had given her the name Strong Woman. Even the women who had been knocked unconscious or suffered broken arms, ribs and legs from her blows did not hold that against her. Rather, they admired her and felt contempt for Leah and the other captives who had made no attempt to strike back at their tormenters.

Not long after, Leah disappeared from the town after a visitation from dignified *Sachems* from another Onondaga town. There had been a great deal of ceremony in receiving the visitors. Drums beat in reception and then continued day and night, it seemed to Abby. She witnessed constant dancing in the bare area before the roofed but open house. Some were performed by young men, even boys. Moon Willow explained each as it occurred: this one celebrated hunting prowess; this one spoke of a secret society of the warriors, that of another; this one told of the beautiful women of one of the women's secret societies, this another. This one boasted of war and brave deeds of the warriors of Abby's own town; this of those of the other. There were meetings held under the roof of the open hut and Abby saw the long-stemmed ceremonial pipes called *calumet* that passed around the circle from councillor to councillor. Each took a puff or two, blew it upward and asked favor and wisdom of the Father of Life before the pipe was passed to the next. Then the discussions began.

Abby gathered it had something to do with a division of hunting and fishing areas between the towns but Moon Willow had grown impatient and pulled Abby away, back toward the Long House.

"They talk and they talk—then they decide. But if the Mothers do not agree, there is nothing but talk among all those men."

Early the next morning the word came to the women of the Long House to meet with the Owl and the Hawk. Shielded from eyes and ears by the walls of the Society's house, the women formed their own circle around a small fire. The crude, carved standards of the Hawk and the Owl guarded the door within while the wild-eyed, half-crazed shaman guarded it from without. One of the women Keepers presented the decision of the men's meeting after the *calumet* had passed around the circle and the prayers to the Mother of Mothers had been said. When half an hour of discussion had passed, the meeting approved of the men's decision and the Keeper made a second invocation, shapely arms raised in thanksgiving to the Mother of Mothers. Five minutes afterward, every woman had returned to her own Long House and Fireside.

Abby saw the proud Keeper walk to the open council house. She spoke a few words which, at the distance, Abby could not hear but the answering male chorus of "Hai!" told her that the towns had reached agreement. Even Moon Willow spoke a few sentences of approval on the return to the Long House.

"Now their *Sachems* will go and we will hunt and fish freely in our own streams and woods."

So Abby first learned one of the main reasons for the famed Iroquois League, of which she had heard so much when her father and the men of Westover spoke of the Indians, but now she more fully understood. The Six Tribes each conducted its own business, solved its own problems and the League as a whole did not interfere. One tribe could even conduct small raiding and war parties on another, but these could by no means be counted as war. They permitted the hot-blooded young warriors to prove their own cunning and bravery in combat. Now and then they would bring back scalps or captured weapons. There would always be a night of blazing fire, then, of feasting, dancing and boasting.

Corn Dancer left on these raiding parties twice and each time Abby found herself moving nervously around the Long House, fearful for him and trying to hide it. Moon Willow, the other women and even Howling Wolf scornfully dismissed her fears for him.

"He is a good warrior," Howling Wolf told her and Moon Willow added with a tartness that sought to shame Abby. "He is the best in this

Owachira. He is still young and he will someday be a great *Sachem,* a Pine Tree. He will be a leader of warriors and when he is old, the young warriors then will listen to him with respect.''

''If he lives so long,'' Abby tried to warn. ''He could be killed—or captured. Then what?''

The two old people looked at her as though they could not believe what they heard. Moon Willow grunted in contempt but then her voice softened.

''We forget you are not born Onondaga—Iroquois. To die in war is an honor. All of us would be proud of him. If he is captured, he will be brave no matter what happens to him. His enemies will know what kind of man and warrior he is. They might adopt him.''

''Adopt him!''

''Of course—if their *orenda* needs one of courage and pride. If not, they will blacken his face and he will still be a brave and mighty warrior.''

Abby did not see the faint shadow that passed over Moon Willow's eyes and she assumed that if a captured warrior's face was blackened, it was a mark of shame and derision. The idea of adoption held her attention. It was the first time she knew that Indians would bring a fighting enemy into their own village or tribe, or whatever it might be.

''But after he is adopted, could he come back to us now and then?''

''No. He would be enemy. If he did come, it would be with arrow, club, spear and fire. We

286

would have to fight him. Your fireside would be gone if he is killed or adopted. The *Owachira* would lose his *orenda* and we would have to find another to fill it.''

''That other—would he be my husband?''

''If you chose. Only then. If the *Owachira* and the Keepers might choose for you.''

By now Abby knew that an *Owachira* composed the firesides of all those related to one another, either by birth or by the blood-rite she had gone through. Every fireside along the passage in the Long House was related to all the others and even to those in the Houses to either side. That total made up the *Owachira*, and *Owachiras* in a complicated system she did not understand, made up the clans that composed this town and two others. Clans, in turn, combined to make up a tribe and the tribes a Nation—such as the Onondaga. There were other tribes she had heard Corn Dancer and Howling Wolf mention—the Maican, Mohawk, Oneida, Cayuga, Seneca and her own Onondaga.

Thinking on all she had been told, Abby thought she understood the ''adoption'' idea. Corn Dancer would merely become, say, a Seneca instead of Onondaga. Or they might, in scorn, blacken his face and send him home to face the even greater scorn of his own tribe and *Owachira*.

Corn Dancer and many of the young warriors left with the town warriors and *Sachems* to conduct the visitors back in honor to their own town and it seemed to Abby as though the town had emptied, leaving only the women to attend the fields and the older men to guard the stockade and the trails. The women returned to their primitive tillage in the gardens and time again began to drag.

The ceremonies and dances and songs welcoming the visitors had taken all of Abby's curious attention. Not that she had much chance to watch for the women constantly tended the ceremonial fires, constantly skinned and cut the game and the fish brought in to make the great feasts. She fell asleep instantly each night, pulling the warm furs over her. Sometimes Corn Dancer stayed on in the constant round of noise, shouts, chants and beating drums outside. More often he crept under the furs with her so tired that with hardly more than a gentle grunt and a caress on her arm or thigh he fell asleep.

But several times he pulled her hungrily close to him. The blood raced through Abby's veins and desire flamed through her body. She could not help herself and gave with abandon. Often she lay in drowsy thought afterward, wondering how it had happened that she loved this savage young man who was not even of her own race.

Once, drifting off, she heard her mother's voice in her mind, the words spoken clearly as though she still lived. "The Good Lord arranges our lives in strange ways, honey, and for His own purposes. I reckon some day you and Dan'l will find that out."

It was not Daniel, but Corn Dancer. Still, Mother's adage held true and the trail from the village where she was born to Westover, the raid and her torturing journey to this Onondaga town deep in the New York Colony wilderness mountains seemed, in retrospect, so highly improbable that she could hardly believe it even now. And what of the change in her own ideas and standards! She refused to consider them, uncertain whether it was God's will or her own carnal desires spawned of the devil that had caused the strange series of events that made her an Indian bride, an Onondaga Mother!

She did not see Leah, Patience or Marion in the fields the next day but gave it little thought. They worked for Firesides in other *Owachiras,* each in a different Long House. Slaves in a sense, rather than prisoners, the girls were not ill treated, though they did not have Abby's privileges. They could easily have been assigned to work in the various Long Houses for a time and would soon reappear with their crude garden instruments, digging, weeding, furrowing. But day after day passed and still Abby did not see them. Then, one night, half asleep beside Corn Dancer, the girls suddenly came vividly to her mind. She asked Corn Dancer why she no longer saw them.

"They are gone," he answered sleepily.

"Gone! Where!"

"The Council and the Keepers agreed to a trade offered for them by the other town."

"But—but that's slavery!"

"What is—how you call it?—slavery?"

"Selling or bartering human beings."

Corn Dancer moved irritably under the furs and answered shortly, "They are not like you—strong and brave. They are good workers. Maybe in the other towns they will be made Onondaga like you. Anyway, have babies and the *orenda* over there grows stronger, eh?"

"Breeders!"

"How you say?"

She explained in a shock that did not communicate to him. "Other towns lose warriors in raids and a sickness kill many. Need new *orenda*. Now maybe they have it in a year, eh?"

"But . . . but their husbands . . . ?"

He growled an impatient answer. "They are squaws and can have babies. Sure, they are whiteskin but babies be Iroquois because their fathers will be Iroquois. Now go to sleep, eh?"

She tried, lying quite still, her eyes closed. She had not known of this aspect of the Iroquois, or perhaps it was confined to the Onondaga. She could no longer contain herself.

"Will I be sold or bartered?"

He abruptly sat up, turning toward her. In the dim light from the dying fires on the corridor she could see his frown, and hastily added, "I am new to this life."

His frown vanished and he smiled, touched her cheek and spoke patiently. "No, that will not happen to you. Remember the washing and the blood ceremony? That made you one of us. Now you are mother of this Fireside and a Mother of the Nation. You belong to the Hawk and the Owl. You will always be here unless—"

He broke off and frowned. She ventured, "Unless . . . what?"

"There is raid with another Nation or war with the Algonquin and you are captured." Then he smiled and smote his broad chest. "I will not let that happen. I promise."

She pulled him back down beside her and threw the fur over them. "I know, Corn Dancer."

In the following days she often wondered what had happened to her former friends of Westover, but as time passed the question faded into the back of her mind but was never forgotten. Now and then she heard news of the other town or met hunters from it, once even a small raiding party bent on a foray against the Oneida. The Great *Sachems* of the Six Nations would not intervene, Corn Dancer assured her.

"See," he pointed to the group, "there are only ten young men who want to become warriors and the Oneida have fished and trapped off their own land. It will be over soon and finished. Someday maybe I will go again with another raiding party like the one where I found you."

She did not fully understand, nor did Corn Dancer fully explain, evidently feeling that she had somehow absorbed all the way of the Iroquois. She knew that the Indians had no concept of the white ownership of land, or tree, plant or animal. All belonged to the Great Father and was for the use of His people, the Iroquois. In fact, Abby had heard hunters pray and make sacrifice to the spirit of the Great Rabbit, assuring him that whatever animal of that species they killed would be food, a sacrifice of a bit of the *orenda* of the Great Rabbit.

A month later, she discovered the reason for the great house without walls. Corn Dancer informed her that the annual meetings of the Great Council of *Sachems* would be held within two weeks. Abby had never seen his dark bronze face so alight and eager as he hurried on.

"A chief of our whiteface allies comes with them. He asks the Nations to join with them in war against the Algonquin . . . the Huron. If the Great *Sachems* and the Nations agree, all of us will take the warpath."

Abby went through the motions and gestures of equal excitement and eagerness, even as Moon Willow and everyone in the Long House boasted of great deeds to be done. But deep in her heart Abby feared—for Corn Dancer, for her own people back in Connecticut Colony, for every settler and village out in the great forests. She had heard rumors before her capture that another of the series of wars with the hated French might soon erupt and, from what she had learned in this Indian tribal town, she felt it had at last come. She could only hope that the Great Council would at least keep the Iroquois, and particularly the Onondaga, out of the white man's quarrel.

A week later, the first of the delegations from the other nations appeared. They were Oneidas and they brought news that, to the north along the St. Lawrence and eastward along the Hudson, the whole land was astir. A great fleet had come to the French town of Quebec and the Algonquin tribes had sent runners to all their tribes as far as the western seas to come to council. French troops landed at Quebec and Montreal and their great Warrior Chief had also come.

The ceremonial drums beat a welcome and had ceased for only a day when a runner came from the Cayuga to announce their arrival and again the drums beat. At night the fires blazed high in the bare area before the roofed house and again the dancers pranced and chanted. Abby heard the bloody words of war and boasting. She had a glimpse of two bound white men, their faces blackened by ashes, hurrying into a small house, the door barred and guards stationed before it.

"They are French," Corn Dancer answered her. "The Cayuga captured them. We hope they are brave men."

"What will be done with them?"

"We save them for the Council of the Nations," Corn Dancer answered and hurried away to join the dancers.

The Tuscarora Nation was the last to arrive from the south and they brought word that the colonial town of New York had as much turmoil as Montreal and Quebec. "A great War Chief has come to them," the Tuscarora reported, "and soon one of his warriors will come here bringing the pipe of peace for the whitefaces of the Hudson and the pipe of War for the whitefaces of the St. Lawrence."

"And for the Huron and all Algonquin tribes?" the Keepers of the Peace demanded.

"We think so. But that red-coated warrior will tell you when he comes."

The next day a small band of Tuscaroras appeared and with them came the first white man Abby had seen since Westover. He wore the red uniform of the British colonial forces of New York Colony but that was about all Abby could see of him from her position far back in the crowd of women. Warriors of all the Nations danced, moved and shouted around the white man who rode so proudly on the horse that snorted and fought the tight rein the man held. It was frightened by the scent of the Indians and wanted to bolt.

The night passed in constant dancing and shouting around the great fires that seemed to shoot flames to the sky. Abby tried several times to work her way to the white soldier but each time found herself blocked, shoved aside by truculent warriors of the other Nations or ordered to some woman's task by Moon Willow.

Abby had not fully known how central the Onondaga Nation and this town of theirs was to the heart of the Iroquois. Now she understood the meaning of the Great House without walls. The *Sachems* gathered there and a sudden silence descended on the town. *Shamans*, rattling gourds, made ceremonial dances about the house, moccasined feet stamping an arrhythmic beat as they fended off evil spirits from those who would later consider problems that would shape the destiny of all the Nations. Then the Keepers of the Faith from every Nation and its town made invocations to the Father of All and the Mother of Mothers for wisdom.

The *calumets* passed around the concentric circles formed about a raised platform of earth whereon *Sachems* and honored warriors stood to support or harangue against propositions that had been brought forth. Abby swiftly learned from the women about her that this was the annual meeting of the Council. Here quarrels between the nations were settled by speeches and boasting instead of wars between them. Here the problems of other tribes such as Shawnee or Delaware were discussed and the answers sought—and found. Each nation, after all the haranguing on a particular question, cast one vote for the whole tribe, no matter how numerous its people. The voting would be done over and over until at last all the Nations had voted yea or nay. It had to be unanimous.

Days were spent on disputes between the Iroquois Nations until all had been decided. During the time, Abby continued to try to reach the white officer during the few times he was allowed out of his guarded house. But each time, she was fended off. Once the officer saw her at a distance. She saw him lift himself in his stirrups to stare at her over the sea of Indian heads with their high single feathers. His jaw dropped in surprise. He lifted an arm and waved at her and she made an eager reply. But he was hurried off. Even her shouts could not rise above the cacophony of Indian voices and she could only turn back to her own Long House in despairing disappointment.

Moon Willow, Howling Wolf and Corn Dancer reproached her that night, Moon Willow especially vehement. "No woman go to Great Council to be seen or to talk. No woman!"

"But we decide finally, don't we?"

"Only later," Moon Willow nodded, "about what our own warriors and *Sachems* say or do. But not at Great Council."

"You listen to her," Howling Wolf admonished, and added sourly, "or maybe you want to be whiteface squaw again."

Abby saw Corn Dancer's face then. Though he seemed impassive and expressionless, she caught an angry gleam in his eyes. "He's jealous!" she thought. "He doesn't understand how good it is just to see and speak to one of my own for only a few minutes. He's afraid I'll leave him."

A moment later his harsh order confirmed her thought. "You will stay in this house. You will watch the children and keep the food pots full and cooking. Moon Willow cannot do everything."

"But—"

"You will stay until last day of the Great Council. Then you can join the women of the Hawk and the Owl for the final ceremonies." He looked at his mother. "Do I speak right to her?"

"You speak right. Redcoat whiteface see her

today and make signs.'' She turned on Abby. ''Do you want to go back to your own whitefaces . . . you, an Onandaga!''

Abby knew she could never explain so they would understand and, suddenly, wondered if she could explain to herself. She watched all but Moon Willow leave and then began shucking corn for the night's feast and ceremonies. She could hear the constant sound of voices beyond the walls and, from a distance, occasional shouts. Once she heard a wall-shaking ''Hai!'' and knew that something of extreme importance had been settled.

Corn Dancer enlightened her late that night. ''The white-faced warrior in the red coat has called on us as old allies to help them. They war against the French and Huron, our old enemies. We have agreed.''

''War!'' Abby gasped. ''Big war?''

''Everywhere!'' Corn Dancer answered and thumped his chest. ''I have been made a war leader, a chief leading bands north to the head-water of the river the whitefaces call Hudson and then with their armies we will go to the river they call St. Lawrence. We will raid and pillage the Huron towns and the French places they call Quebec and Montreal. I will return a great chief—a *Sachem*.''

''You will return dead,'' Abby wailed.

Moon Willow exercised her *Owachira* privilege for the first time. She slapped Abby so that her head rocked and pointed to the room beside Abby's own fireside. ''Go! Beg Mother of Mothers to forgive you for weakening your husband's *orenda*. He is not destined to die even if you could have it so."

Abby, knowing the Onondaga codes and way of life, made no argument. She went to the room and sat down on the furs. She could hear Moon Willow's angry growls, Howling Wolf's guttural replies and now and then Corn Dancer would speak in her defense. But she knew that in her fear for Corn Dancer, she had broken a custom by which the Onondaga lived.

Not by deed, word, or thought, did anyone draw the energy of the Father of All from another's *orenda*.

A shadow fell over her and she looked up to see Corn Dancer standing in the doorway, his muscular body blocking out the firelight. He paused only a second and then swiftly crossed the small room and dropped by her side. He took her hand.

"I told my father and the mother that you had no evil in your mind for me—only fear and worry."

She looked at him and her eyes brimmed with tears. How little her people, the white-skin ones, knew of these Indians! He smiled at her.

"The Great Council ends tomorrow in ceremony. You will go with me."

"Of course!"

She reached for him and he gathered her into his arms. O, tomorrow she would be Strong Woman, Onondaga, Corn Dancer's pride among all the women of the town. Tomorrow!

It would change her life, though she did not think of her mother's words that "God moves in strange ways."

XXIII

The drums awakened her before dawn the next morning and flickering light from the family fires in the corridor made grotesque shadows on the wall as she hurried to dress and go out to help Moon Willow. The older woman's fury had lessened with sleep but she still frowned at Abby and answered her curtly, watching her narrowly as though expecting Abby to take flight at any moment. Abby waited until Corn Dancer and Howling Wolf came out to eat, though time and again she had to swallow an impulse to speak directly to Moon Willow.

As the families ate along the long corridor, the light seeping through the log and birch walls grew stronger and the tempo of the drums increased. Finally, Corn Dancer set aside his food bowl, licked his fingers and rubbed them dry along the legs of his skin trousers and then in the dirt to brush off the final grease and food particles. He started to rise but Abby spoke quickly and he sat down again, looking questioningly at her.

"This is the last day of the Great Council!" she asked and, at his nod, hurried on. "I would like to speak to the white-skin chief in the red-coat."

Moon Willow jerked around from the pot on the fire but Abby spoke before the woman could object. "I do not want to go with him, leave you, Howling Wolf or my husband. I am now Onondaga."

"Then why," Corn Dancer growled, "does the red-coat white-skin mean so much to you?"

"When Onondagas come from other towns, you ask them what has happened to their town or their firesides. You have friends among them. You talk to them. You ask about friends who have not come. Are they sick? Have they died? Have they been captured or killed by blood enemies or by Hurons or by accident? Has a bear crushed this one or has that one drowned? You ask. You are friends, eh?''

Corn Dancer looked at his father, then at Moon Willow, then back at Abby. ''You do not want to return to your people? You do not want to ask this white-face to take you away?''

''Once I was white-face woman, now I am Strong Woman, Onondaga, member of the Hawk and the Owl. I am wife of Corn Dancer who will become great chief before long.'' She took a short breath and then pointed to the fire around the small group and along the corridor. ''You are my family and my people now. The blood made it so. Why should I leave when the white has been washed out of me?''

Once more questioning look met questioning look around the fire. Decision among them was reached without words, a strange silent process that Abby had experienced several times before in minor ways since coming to the town. It was as though mind spoke to mind while the tongue did not move behind closed lips. Abby believed it to be some trick or ability of the Iroquois that white people did not know or possess. Whatever it was, the decision came quickly.

''The red-coated white-face leaves early,'' Moon Willow said abruptly and in a silent moment another of those strange messages without words passed between them.

Corn Dancer stood up. ''I will bring the red-coat here.''

''Does he stay for the Fire Ritual?'' Howling Wolf asked.

"I don't know, many whiteface do not."

"Then bring him now," Moon Willow ordered but lifted an admonitory finger. "He will answer her questions about her friends and that is all."

Corn Dancer strode down the passage and out through the far door. Abby could not quite believe her ears and choked back her eagerness. Only a few words and no chance to escape even if she wanted to. But she preferred being with Corn Dancer now and wondered if she would ever again fit into the life of settlements like Westover. The life here was free. The life back there had been tight and restricted by parson, gossip, constant strictures and admonitions. She could hardly believe how she had changed in her ways and her thinking.

Yet some of the old ways and habits prevailed. She simply had to bring some order to the comfortable tangle of her hair and make sure her face was clean and unsmudged. She hurried into her room.

She changed her blouse and skirt for others that bore no smudges or grease spots and cooking stains and pulled on moccasins whose toes bore a delicate design in blue beads and stained quills. The wampum headband she worked over her head, held her hair back from her face and forehead and she knew she looked as presentable as she would ever be in this wilderness Iroquois town.

She whirled around when she heard a step at the door and Corn Dancer's voice. But the red-coated officer was not with him and her face fell. Corn Dancer correctly read the meaning of her expression, grinned, then grunted and pointed down the corridor.

"The whiteface waits outside the Long House. He is ready to ride with his friends, the Tuscarora, but not before he talks to you."

"Praise God!" Abby breathed. "I was afraid he didn't want to see me."

"He does. He thinks we hold you a slave-captive, like those other women who first came with you. He didn't say, but I know he does not believe my word. Tell him my tongue is one and true, not forked and crooked."

"Oh, I will! But why is he outside?"

"This is house for our *Owachira* and our firesides. It is not house for guests—even of the other Nations. So he waits outside."

When she walked through the door just a step behind Corn Dancer, the officer instantly swung out of the saddle, removed his lace-trimmed tricorne hat and made a short, jerky bow. When he straightened and eyed her, she read a peculiar mixture of curiosity, concern and dislike in his expression.

He was a slender man, not very tall, but he had the squared shoulders of a soldier, the arrogant set of jaw and mouth, the proud lift of the head of the professional. Up close now, Abby saw that he was not of a provincial, colonial militia, but an officer of a regular British regiment. Gold trimming on cuffs, collar and hat marked him as a senior officer, confirmed by the tasseled sash in which he wore flintlock pistols. His sword, in an ornate scabbard, hung by beautifully tooled leather from the saddle horn of his saddle.

"I am Major Emmet Roberts of His Majesty's Somerset Regiment, presently stationed in New York," he said in a dry, noncommittal voice. "I glimpsed you the other day and asked about you."

She curtsied. "Thank you, Major. I am— was—Abigail Brewster, late of Westover in Connecticut Colony."

"Never heard of it."

He pulled a snuffbox from a greatcoat pocket, opened it and put a pinch to his nose. All the time his blue eyes swept over her from moccasins to headband. He had corn gold hair, smoothly combed back into a short queue caught by a watered ribbon of red and gold to match his uniform. He evidently made up his mind about her status in colonial life, for the notes of politeness and respect left his stance and he almost slouched.

He irritated Abby, almost to anger, but she bit it back. "Westover is a small frontier village, Major, close to the New York Colony line."

His brow rose in sudden recognition. "Ah, now I remember. The Indians pillaged and burned it completely to the ground."

"Completely!" she gasped. "It's all gone?"

"So I was told in New York Town. The Indians took a few prisoners—young women and girls."

"I was one of them."

"Indeed!" A touch of pity softened his eyes for a moment. "Most of them were found dead, some raped and then murdered. They were traced to the Hudson River and then all trace of them was lost . . . that is, until I saw you the other day."

"Three of us were bartered off a while back. They were taken further west . . . not exactly slaves nor exactly adopted into the tribes."

"Then they are beyond reach?"

She made a lost gesture to show she couldn't give him any certain answer. His attention centered more closely on her. "Why haven't you been bartered or sold? I hear it is a custom among these savages."

"The Onondaga are not savages, Major."

"Indeed! Pray, then, what are they?" She started to answer but he lifted his hand to check her. "Forget defining the Onondaga. I gather you have taken a liking to them, eh?"

The faint suggestion of smirk in voice and in his lips irritated her further. She drew back her shoulders. "I have lived with them for some time now, Major."

"Slave? Or adopted? I take it, neither word fully applies here."

"No, Major." She indicated the slight scar on her wrist. "I have been made blood Onondaga by their rites."

"That is unusual."

She told him what had happened to her. He listened with no comment other than a smiling "Bravo!" when she told him of her actions in running the gauntlet. But that was almost the only time he showed interest in her story. Otherwise he treated it as a chronicle of adventure in a land and among people whom he considered in another world than his own of family, tradition, regiment and service to a man on a throne somewhere afar off over the ocean.

Abby finished her story almost down to this very moment. He slapped the bridle reins in his gloved hand. "You married this—this—bug—" He caught himself. "This Indian chief?"

"According to the Onondaga ways and customs, yes."

"You've found a way to comfortably live with him as a wife and among the rest as you would've back in Westover had it not been raided and destroyed?"

"I've had to, Major. Thanks to the adoption, the secret society of the Hawk and the Owl and Corn Dancer, I have found a place, such as it is."

He slapped the reins again. "But you'd rather be with your own kind, what?"

"I—" She thought of Corn Dancer and the nights spent with him under the skins of the Fireside. She thought of this smooth-flowing, easy way of Indian life. She saw the wild-eyed and -haired *Shaman*, prancing about with his rattling gourd, and then saw the stern, hard-eyed disapproval and thundering jeremiads of the parsons she had known. She thought of the girls in Westover who had been as friendly and kind as any of her new friends in the women's society, but also of the dried-up, hatchet faced contemptuous sniffing of the women of Westover with their clacking tongues, disapproval, their certainty that in some manner they alone had earned the wings and halos that would be given them at the "Pearly Gates." They could never understand why the Mother of Mothers and the Father of All would not conform to their narrow individual definitions.

Major Roberts shifted his weight impatiently, and then exclaimed, "By Jove! I do believe you've turned savage yourself!"

"Not savage, Major. Not at all."

"Well, then, do I report seeing you when I reach civilization again?" He hurried on. "The raid, your captivity and eventual return to a civilized way of living is a colonial matter, you understand. Either New York Colony or Connecticut Colony will see to it when I make my report."

"But I thought—"

"I could take you with me after bartering bangles and beads or whatever these brutes demand for you?" He assumed a sad aspect and shook his head. "Alas Mistress! I wish I could! But I am on His Majesty's business. I am charged to make certain the Iroquois remain and will be our allies when we fight the French—and that will be very soon."

He sighed again and met her gaze a long moment before his eyes slid away. "I dare not anger them even by seeming to want your release. So you see, taking you off with me would be even more disastrous.''

''But I don't—''

''I'll report your presence at Albany or Kingston, Mistress, and insist that steps be taken to release you immediately. I would do it myself but first there are His Majesty's orders.''

''Thank you, Major.'' Abby hesitated and then slowly sought for words to make the major understand a land and its many, many peoples and races that he could not possibly imagine.

''Yes, Mistress?''

''There has been enough bloodshed and murder because of Westover, Major. I don't ask for rescue. That would only mean more and you tell me there will probably be thousands in a war that's close on us.''

''What with the Indians around here and in New France, the colonials here and in New France, the regular French armies and our own, that is undoubtedbly correct, Mistress.''

''Then if you report me, Major, make sure no more lives or efforts are spent on me.''

He stared at her, at the Long House behind her and then slowly around at the houses within the stockade, back to her. ''Do you mean, Mistress, you are willing to stay here? to live with . . . well, whoever the savage buck may be?''

''I want no deaths on my account, Major.''

He still could not fully understand. ''But the Iroquis are the most feared and cruel tribes in all the colonies! Everyone fears them, even the colonists.''

''Then why does His Majesty seek them as

allies, Major? I thought he is called, 'His Most Christian King.' ''

Roberts flushed, and then retreated behind official, majestic dignity. He gave her a curt bob of the head. "If it's not the part of a Royal Officer in His Majesty's army—and also an envoy—to question, then by what right does a renegade wench who has thrown herself away to a brutish native chieftain—if he happens so to be!—make judgment of matters far beyond her narrow mind to comprehend? This is for kings and nations. Good day, Mistress. I have wasted time!''

He did not even bother to bob his head, but swung into the saddle and spurred away. Several yards out, he reigned in, twisted about. Abby still stood speechless, shocked, her mouth open and wordless.

"Since you are one of them, you will see the final ceremonies of the Great Council of the *Sachems*. I was warned in New York to leave before they started if I wanted to retain my sanity. But, of course, you're one of them and used to it.''

Abby's mouth snapped shut and hot retort sprang to her lips. But Major Roberts had now spurred on, his Tuscarora guides running beside him, easily keeping pace with the trotting horse. He was beyond call now and Abby could not lower herself to shout after him. Instead, she turned back into the Long House.

Corn Dancer waited just within the door. He pointed out beyond her to the fast-moving officer and his Indian escort. "He does not stay?''

"No. He says he was warned to leave."

Corn Dancer grunted disdainfully. "It has happened before. Some paleskins do not understand courage." He grunted again. "Many of them do not have it—like Iroquois. But Strong Woman stays and watches, eh?"

"Of course. The white was washed from me."

He smiled. "Then you will dance with your *Owachira*. Today we have two blackfaces. It will be good to watch."

She smiled and nodded in anticipation. Onondaga ceremonies had fascinated her but now the great *Sachems* of all the Nations were here in the town. Such a meeting of importance would be filled with dancing, color, drums, *Shamans*, the Keepers of the Faith of every Nation and town. Abby doubted if she had ever seen anything that would be like it and probably would never see anything like it again.

"We will soon be ready," Corn Dancer said, "so now you wear beaded dress and moccasins, wampum band and carry the signs of the Hawk and the Owl."

"What will you wear?"

Corn Dancer drew himself up proudly. "I dress for warpath like a chief. I paint my face with the marks of the Wolf."

She knew the Wolf was the secret society of the Onondaga warriors but he continued to talk as he led the way to the rooms off their fireside. "All the Nations will speak of our town and of this *Owachira* and of the Fireside of Corn Dancer. You will take your skinning knife."

311

"Why?" she asked.

"You will use it."

So the dances and ceremonies would include pantomimes of the hunt as well as of battles and war, she thought. It sounded as though she would be dancing all day and into the night by the light of many fires. Well, she might be dropping from fatigue before the ceremony was over but Abby now knew positively she would never forget the tribal rituals that were about to start.

She hurried into the Fireside room with Corn Dancer. As she brushed her hair and he carefully placed the crimson slashes on his cheeks from the corners of his mouth to his ears, she examined her blouse, skirt and leggings. Though she had worn them but a short time while talking to Major Roberts, she wanted to make sure no smudge or stain would cause comment among the women of the society.

As she worked, she heard the eager voices of adults and children all along the corridor of the Long House and a constant bustle and movement. Apparently only the very, very sick or the extremely ancient and feeble would miss the ceremony.

XXIV

When Abby and Corn Dancer came out into the corridor, they found it filled. Everyone who lived in the Long House, each person of every Fireside stood waiting, facing the far door that Abby could not now see because of the crowd. Little, sometimes naked, girls and boys tried to wriggle through the crowd to the distant door but harsh, angry commands of the adults cowed and sent them scurrying back to their proper places.

Not a person, Abby saw as she looked about, but did not wear finery; the women beads and colored quills worked into their clothing, necklaces of claws of small animals or of glass beads, obviously bartered from traders along the distant Hudson River, or from the few braver and bolder ones who brought their packs of gewgaws into the Iroquois towns themselves. Some, Abby thought with a sudden wave of sorrow and memory, may have been taken from the bodies of the raided, burning towns like Westover. She hastily closed her mind against that thought.

The line started moving and at last Abby saw the door just ahead. A Keeper of the Faith stood to either side of the portal and sharply inspected each who came up. She found herself outside, still at Corn Dancer's side, Moon Willow and Howling Wolf just ahead.

Without a word of explanation, Corn Dancer, Howling Wolf and the other men of the Long House moved away from the women at an angle. Abby choked back her surprised question when she saw that the other women paid no attention to this abrupt separation of the sexes. She noticed the children remained with the women.

Instead of going to the open-sided, roofed meeting place of the Council, the procession turned sharply toward the distant stockade gate. The Keepers of each Long House led the way for the *Owachiras*, that gradually coalesced into one huge solid body. Now they approached the platform with its ring of cold ashes that Abby had seen when she first came to the town. However the burned posts had been changed and new ones now stood deep-planted, thick, strong and high.

She saw grass, twigs and small branches intertwined with larger sections of wood forming an irregular ring a few feet out from each post. The men and warriors had not reappeared but the women and children moved around the circle of wood and, as though a silent command had been given, all sat down at once.

Abby, at Moon Willow's silent motion, left the older woman and joined her sisters of the Hawk and the Owl. Two made room for her, saying nothing, but the friendly eyes that lifted to her, gave greeting. More and more came from the other Long Houses while the Keepers made a slow moving, impressive procession to the distant guest houses where the *Sachems* of the other Five Nations waited.

They disappeared within the house for a long time but finally emerged and came toward the circle. The *Sachems* followed as tall and dignified as the Keepers, but the visiting chieftains this time did not wear their full panopoly of headdress and feathers. Rather, they looked more like Corn Dancer, war chiefs ready for the battle, their faces painted with whorls, circles and slashes of many colors. Each bore a lance and some wore sheathed knives. Here and there

Abby saw a rifle or musket.

Once more a silent command was given in the strange, eerie manner Abby had experienced before. The woman seated beside Abby touched her shoulder, rose and moved back from the ring. The other women also moved away, leaving a cleared pathway between the ring of wood, and the Keepers, followed by the *Sachems* marched down the path, then seated themselves where the women and children had been but moments before.

A long silence ensued and then a drum started a muted, slow beat that gradually increased in tempo. A second drum joined, a third and then, one by one, every drum in the camp throbbed like menacing thunder.

The Onondaga Keepers stepped into the center of the ring, walked to the new stake and, as one, lifted their arms to the clear sky. One of the women started a chant, one that Abby had not heard before. First it called up the Father of All for abundance, the Mother of Mothers for progeny in every one of the Long Houses and Firesides in the Six Nations that the accumulative *orenda* of the Iroquoian League become even more mighty, that its foes everywhere and everyplace tremble with fear at the very name of the League or any of its tribes, that its power extend from the great inland seas to the north to that on the east, to the Beautiful River to the south and west.

"Beautiful River?" Abby asked herself but immediately forgot the puzzle as the ceremony continued.

Now the Keepers praised bravery, their own and that of their enemies and captives. Knowing the Iroquois respect for strength and bravery in self, tribe and the League and wherever found, Abby did not feel surprise at this supplication. Her own act at the gauntlet had gained her status among these people and privileges beyond the reach of Leah, Marion and Patience, wherever they might be.

The rhythm of the drums increased and suddenly the warriors of the Onondaga, her own town and her own Long House, burst out from behind the Long Houses bordering the cleared space about the rings. They shouted, sang defiance and danced, brandishing weapons at imaginary foes. Abby witnessed a war dance, one that always preceded a foray, large or small, upon an enemy.

Then her eyes popped wide. Young warriors bunched about two figures that they hustled forward to the edge of the ring. Abby saw one was Indian, the other white. Both were fully clothed, though stoutly bound and their faces had been smeared black with charcoal. Now she began to have some concept of what "blackface" meant.

The woman beside her pointed to the Indian. "Shawnee, that one," she hissed and her eyes gleamed vividly. "Maybe he brave but not like our warriors. We will see."

The white man was forced, still bound, to lie prone to one side of the ring but the Indian remained standing. Onondaga warriors surrounded him, blocking him from Abby's sight.

Across the ring the visiting great *Sachems* sat unmoving, watching, and their impassive faces slowly began to change. It started with covert exchanges of looks between them, a hint of lips moving, faint shiftings of their bodies. Abby felt a strange, mounting electricity all about her.

Suddenly the warriors about the Indian captive moved aside and Abby could not suppress her small sound of surprise. The Shawnee had now been stripped completely, even to loincloth and moccasins. His arms were roughly pulled to a tortured position behind his back and tightly lashed.

To Abby's amazement, the man started to sing in a voice that alternated between triumph, anger and pride. The words were of a different dialect and Abby could understand only a few. He boasted of his prowess as a warrior, as a Shawnee, of the warriors he had killed, the scalps he had taken. No one made an attempt to silence him until at last the Onondaga turned to the Assembled Keepers of the Faith.

"Do we test his strength and courage?" one of the warriors asked.

"Hai!" the Keepers answered with a single voice.

Now the visiting *Sachems* had abandoned all attempt at impassivity. They sat leaning forward, intently interested in every move. The Onondaga led the captive inside the ring of brush and wood and up to the stout post. Thongs from his lashed wrists were wrapped about the post and tightly secured. The captive's singing became stronger and he glared around the circle, hatred fairly blazing from his eyes.

"Why, that's his Death Song!" Abby exclaimed and the woman beside her nodded.

"He boasts. They all do at first. But for how long?" the woman asked, not so much as turning her head. Her hand fell to the hilt of her knife but she did not draw the weapon from its sheath. She waited for some expected sign or word.

One of the women Keepers stepped within the ring and took a stand beside the captive. He glared at her and continued his song. The Keeper paid no attention but looked very slowly about the ring and, except for the captive's voice, an utter silence fell on the assembly. But now every seated woman leaned forward, eyes agleam. Some drooled and many licked their lips over and over. Hands now grasped the knives at their belts.

The Keeper abruptly thrust her arm upward. "Mothers! This one and his people have warred with our Nations and our sons and brothers and warriors. His people have killed, taken the hair and weakened the *orenda* of many Firesides in the Nations. Do you want him!"

"Hai!"

The Keeper lowered her arm and stepped back out of the circle. "He is yours. Take him!"

Every woman jumped up as the drums thundered a deafening, mind-jolting rhythm. Abby came to her feet without conscious volition, moved by the general action of all about her. The women jumped the circle of brush and wood and converged on the man tied to the post. Abby started to move with them and jumped the low barrier. She knew that the women would beat the prisoner severely as they had the girls who had run the gauntlet. But she stopped short when one of the women bent down, a second joined her, heavy sharp knife blades gleaming in the sun.

The prisoner's song stopped in a gasp of pain but almost immediately lifted again. The knives had slashed and cut and now the prisoner's groin was streaming blood down both legs. The women held up his genitals with screams of triumph and began a grotesque dance about him.

Abby stood transfixed with horror. Other women wrenched the prisoner's hands about and the knives again went to their bloody work. Fingernails and first knuckle joints fell to the earth. The prisoner still sang his death song and defied the women, even though his voice shook with pain.

Now men's voices rose around the ring. The Onondaga warriors and the *Sachems* of all the Nations shouted and screamed at the prisoner. But, as though in a living nightmare, Abby heard not taunts but praise. The Shawnee was the bravest of the brave! Surely none of his tribe had his courage! The woman now drove splinters into the man's skin from head to toes, front and back and then striking flint to dry grass, set the resinous wood splinters aflame.

"Stop it! Stop it!" Abby heard a voice scream and realized it was her own. But none heard her. The women danced around the thick post, knife points jabbing small triangles of flesh and skin from his arms, chest, stomach, his legs, even his cheeks.

She suddenly knew what she must do and she slid her own knife out of its sheath. If she could reach the man and sink the blade to the hilt in his chest, his terrible torture would be over. She had to do it! Her horror-numbed brain dinned at her. She tried to reach him but the women had gone totally mad. They circled in a witches' gyration and time and time again, Abby received flailing blows that sent her hurtling back.

Through it all, the Shawnee death song continued, quivering, sometimes blood choked, but never stopping. He could no longer stand alone but had dropped back against the support of the wooden pillar. Everything had turned into a completely hellish nightmare for Abby as she tried again and again to reach the man and give him the blow of mercy.

Suddenly she was nearly swept off her feet, carried backward by a wave of blood-smeared, screaming women. She stumbled over the piled broken wood of the ring. Her toe caught on something, and she hurtled forward and down. She saw the earth coming up to meet her, and then her eyes and mouth filled with dirt as some unknown instrument smashed her face and head. A moment of swirling awareness and then everything turned black.

The darkness continued, warm and silent, and she did not want to disturb it. Slowly, slowly, she realized that she stood on the unsure edge of consciousness, and her desire to remain in blackness was a small stirring of awareness. She tried to cling to darkness and dropped completely back into it again. Then, slowly, she became aware of being—just "being." Somewhere afar, far off, she sensed something more than that she could not define. Then she sensed, but only sensed, that Abby was more than darkness that she had some sort of form.

Somebody screamed. That constant noise had snapped her senses back into full awareness. But still, she could not move her body, and her mind moved gropingly into memory. There had been the prisoners with the charcoal-blackened faces—one Indian, one white. She frowned, still unmoving and wished those constant screams would end. Her eyes slowly opened. She lay with her cheek on the ground, and the world she looked upon had a strange aspect.

She saw women's legs in the skin wrappings that protected them from briars, thorns and accidental bruises against rocks, logs or any object that could strike, cut or harm in any way. But what had happened to the rest of their bodies? If only that screaming would stop, she could concentrate and solve the problem.

Then it seemed as though another thick curtain lifted from her brain. Blood-smeared women sat cross-legged all about, but none near her. Not one woman looked at her but at something she chould not see beyond the soles of her feet. She smelled smoke and something else that she could not place, and she heard the constant whooping of warriors, the beat of drums, the shouted encouragement to somebody to endure. The screaming continued—a man's.

The whole gruesome scene snapped clearly into her mind—the tortured man at the post, her attempts to reach him and release him from his blazing, hellish ordeal with a single mercy plunge of her knife blade. In the rush of the women out of the ring, she had either stumbled or had been pushed and then fallen and lost consciousness. Now the Shawnee no longer sang or boasted. She heard his screams.

She suddenly knew the strange smell was that of cooking flesh. She became deathly sick and managed to roll on her side, away from the mess that had spewed from her throat. Her brain grasped the realization that she still had to somehow end the horror of the death at that tall, stout post.

She managed to come up on an elbow. She first saw that the ring of brush and broken wood had been set afire and flamed in a solid wall about the post. Onondaga warriors, shouted, whooped and danced in mad gyrations about it, each armed with some sort of weapon. She saw Corn Dancer, long war lance in hand, crimson painted face a devil's mask of terrible grimaces. He alternately straightened and bent, his legs pounding in a dance, knees rising high, his palm beating against his mouth as he yelled stridently.

That could not be Corn Dancer!

But, as she looked, he yelled again, whirled to face the flame and the post and hurled his lance with all his strength at the charred, smoking heap at the base of the post. The Shawnee! Then what—?

The man still screamed, but it was another over to one side, and not within the ring of fire. She saw the roped, trussed white man with the charcoal-smeared face. His eyes bulged and his mouth worked convulsively as scream after scream issued from his throat. He thrashed about, twisting to free his roped arms and legs, but they held fast. A young warrior suddenly went up to him, drew back his foot and smashed it into the man's face, then dropped heavily down on his thrashing body.

But the white man continued to scream, and the sounds were not only those of fear but of madness of a mind that no longer could function in the world of horror and death that the eyes had just witnessed.

An idea sprang full-born into Abby's mind; she could spare him. None of the women about her gave her the least attention. She started to blindly move her hand but realized she no longer had a knife. Just then a woman turned her head and looked at Abby. Scorn! Abby could read it.

Corn Dancer came into her vision again as he whooped, pranced and his war song mingled with those of his companions. But that could not be her husband! That could not be the strong warrior who had been so gentle with her, who had roused her as a woman! That was a blood-stained savage, red of hand and of mind!

She thought she saw a last quiver of the cooking flesh at the foot of the post that itself now was charred and blackened. The insane screaming continued and she wanted to block her ears against the sound. The Indian seated on the man spoke to a warrior standing near, who turned to the women.

At that moment one of the women Keepers agilely jumped through the flames and walked to the torture stake. She looked unconcerned down at the thing that had been a man and then up and around the circle of warriors and women. At her appearance all the shouting, drumming and singing stopped. The Keeper then looked over at the second bound prisoner, who continued to babble, bellow and scream. Then she turned about to face the visiting Great *Sachems*. She pointed to the horrible mound of cooked flesh and bones at the foot of the stake.

"This one brave Shawnee. He should have been Iroquois." Then she indicated the white prisoner. "I do not think that one brave."

One of the *Sachems* demanded. "Did he fight well when he was captured?"

"Hai!" another answered him. "We Tuscarora catch him riding north along the bank of the Great River. He fought well."

"Will he be brave and strong here?" the Keeper asked. "Do we try him now or wait until another sun?"

"Another sun," came the answer.

"So it shall be. Take the pale skin back to the Long House and change the post. Its *orenda* would be offended if, after the Shawnee, one of no courage touched it."

The white man was pulled to his feet and the man who had been sitting on him tied a dirty cloth gag about his mouth. Now Abby saw that he wore soiled, torn shirt and ripped, black riding breeches. His riding boots had obviously been taken from him, for he wore dirt-stained cloth that could hardly be recognized as the remains of stockings. He was whisked away but not before Abby, sickened as she was, knew him to be a colonial merchant or landowner of consequence who must have lived somewhere on the Hudson and been waylaid by the Indians.

Abby now sat erect but as yet did not have the strength to pull herself to her feet. She looked about but could not find her knife. The women about her started to move as the assembly began to break up. Suddenly Moon Willow stood before Abby and the older woman's mouth moved in anger and her voice dripped contempt.

"Strong Woman! Hah! You're a weak girl baby, no better than the frightened women who came with you. Once you were brave and strong, fit wife for Corn Dancer. Your *orenda* was good for his Fireside and for the *Owachira*. But now?" she pointed to the charred torture post and the rim of smoking ashes. "You are nothing. Corn Dancer has a weakling—not a woman. Go back to the house and hide yourself in your Fireside room. Corn Dancer will hear and know from every woman in the town before Howling Wolf or I can tell him. He will decide about you.''

XXV

By the time Abby had walked to her Long House and along the corridor to her own Fireside, she knew that Moon Willow had not exaggerated. Time and again women she knew turned their backs on her as she passed and, within the Long House, no one said a word.

Their expressions, when she threaded the long corridor to enter her dark room and bury herself under the pile of furs, were hard and impassive.

For a time she felt safe, though she could not stop her shivers as pictures of the horrible fire ritual kept coming to vivid life in her mind. She felt numbed with what she had seen, she could not fully believe the testimony of her own sight. She heard women talking outside, voices she recognized as belonging to those she had come to like. But she had seen two of them plunging the sharp resinous splinters into the bound man's body and setting them afire. The whole community had gone insane in an orgy of blood! These! Her friends, neighbors, sisters of the Hawk and Owl! How could they!

Then her own churning thoughts began to slow and she gradually gained at least mental freedom from the fear and shock she had just experienced. Still, she did not move, not wanting to look on neighbors who, as though by a wave of Satan's own wand, had changed to bloodthirsty fiends.

Then she began to hear men's voices and stirred, and with fear rolling over her again, tried to crouch into a small shape under the furs.

But she could not stop her ears. She heard Howling Wolf telling Moon Willow how strong and brave the Shawnee captive had been. Only a mighty warrior could have continued to sing his death song and defiantly call his tormentors contemptuous names. Howling Wolf regretted that the man could not have been adopted into one of the Nations. His *orenda* would have added strength to whatever *owachira* made him one of their own. But, of course, the Keepers of all the Nations had decided his fate and the black of death had been rubbed over his face.

Abby shivered at the memories Howling Wolf brought up and curled up into a tighter bundle under the furs. Then she heard Corn Dancer's pleased voice boasting how he had thrown his lance so that the spear point had pierced the thonged man's shoulder, pinning him to the post but not killing him. Only the flames could do that, of course.

His voice changed when he spoke of the white captive who would be stripped and tied to the new post tomorow. Corn Dancer did not believe the paleskin would prove anywhere near the brave warrior that the Shawnee had been. Look at how he had acted today! Now he lay trussed, his moans and screams silenced by thick rags and tight thongs across his mouth. Still, tomorrow, there might be some pleasure helping him die although he might not last even through the treatment of the women.

"Then he will be of no value," Moon Willow said.

"Not tomorrow," Corn Dancer agreed, "but his horse, pack and clothing had much and our Keepers allowed my own warriors to take what we wanted before the others could take what they wanted."

"You have something?" Moon Willow asked. "Perhaps a pistol or a knife?"

"Eh, the *Sachems* took those things! I have this."

"What is it?"

"I don't know. I thought it was one of those metal magic things that tell the paleskins where the sun stands in the daytime. But it's not. Look," Corn Dancer said eagerly, "there is only one pointer and it swings always to the same direction, no matter where the magic thing is moved. It is a plaything for paleskin children, maybe. Worth little but I brought it anyhow. Maybe the children of our *owachira* can play with it."

Then Abby heard him step into the room and she knew he stood at the door. She could almost feel his eyes boring at her through the furs. His soft moccasined step sounded close and suddenly he threw back the fur that covered her face.

Abby gasped when she looked up at him. He had blood on his cheek and his face was faintly smeared with white ash from the torture fire. Then she had a full look at his face. His tawny eyes looked more like those of a predator than a man. His jaws had slackened; his lips were loose and pulled back in a grin that looked more like that of a skull than of a living man. She realized that her gentle red warrior had changed into a near-animal, drunk even yet from the drums, shouts and dance of the torture.

As she shrank away his painted face twisted into a mask of anger. He dropped an object on the fur that partially covered her; it rolled down under the soft skin against her body. But she could not look away from the thing that was Corn Dancer in total, horrified disbelief.

"You did not help the Shawnee die," he accused harshly. "I did not see but many told me you tried to run away. You fell and lost your senses. That is the way of a cowardly paleskin like the one we will kill tomorrow."

"Corn Dancer! I just couldn't—"

She had reached out to touch him but he slapped her arm away with such brute force that it fell to her side, momentarily numb. "What happened to your *orenda!* Are you grown woman or papoose, wrapped up and carried on your mother's back? Strong Woman!" he sneered.

"Please, my beloved warrior—"

"There is shame at my fireside—you!"

She tried to plead, "I have never before seen anything like that. My people—"

"Your people!" he roared and his moccasined toe kicked out, striking her ribs and knocking her back and down, so she gasped in pain and out of breath. He glared at her, turned on his heel to cross the room and drop on the furs against the far wall. He rolled on his back, threw his arm across his eyes; Abby could hardly blink before he was sound asleep.

It was a horrible kind of drunkenness, Abby knew, brought on by blood lust and all the excitement of the death by fire ritual. And there was to be yet another tomorrow. This time a white man, probably a worthy Yorker who lived beside or near the Hudson, would die. What had he done!

Her erratic, dazed thoughts returned to Corn Dancer, the blood-drunk man who slept just across the small space from her, and with whom she had lived all this time, who had awakened passion in her, whom she had loved. But . . . ? But . . . ?

Abby sank back and again pulled the furs over her body, shutting out the sight of him but unable to completely shut off the continued laughing, triumphant, pleased voices that echoed and re-echoed down the long corridor. Suddenly she saw Major Roberts, saw and felt the contempt in his eyes and manner when he learned she had taken an Onondaga as her man. She remembered his harsh strictures about the Iroquois, the Onondaga. Beasts, he had suggested, loathsome beasts! Blood-thirsty marauders who could not be trusted. How she had tried to defend her adopted people, her Corn Dancer!

Now her hand struck something round and metallic, the object Corn Dancer had dropped as he angrily stood over her, the wine of another man's blood in his brain blotting the incident from his mind.

Her fingers circled the object. It did feel like a watch, a "thing that marks the sun," and she eased back a corner of the furs and lifted her hand. What she saw was a gold-case compass, the single black needle quivering with every slight move of her hands. She dropped the instrument as though it was contaminated, looked over at Corn Dancer and pulled the furs up over her head again.

The morning noises of the Long House awakened her after a night of broken sleep, periods of full consciousness followed by nightmare dreams in which the ritual death fire of Onandaga town became confused with the flames that crackled about her cabin in Westover. The screams of the white captive -blended in her sleep with those of the citizens of Westover as men and women had died from lance, war club and arrow. Then she would awaken drenched in sweat, and sit upright to blackness relieved only by the red eyes of dying embers out in the corridor.

Abby threw aside the furs and arose, realizing she had not really gained any rest at all. Corn Dancer now lay on his side, back to her, sound asleep. She knew he had not bothered to remove the bloodstains and ash smudges from his hands, arms and body and the very thought revolted her. She suddenly wondered how she could face him, having now seen the cruel, untamed, primitive savage in him.

As her hand touched metal she instantly gasped and drew it out from under the skins. The needle, barely discernible in the false dawn that was more night than day, quivered as she strained to see it clearly.

Sounds in the corridor startled her but a second later she knew it to be the first stirrings of the women who soon would build up the fires and start the morning meal, once they had returned with the full pots of water to set aboil over the flames.

Habit had her throw the furs completely aside until her brain fully functioned. Light just outside and slightly beyond the doorway suddenly grew stronger and she knew that it must be her neighbor or perhaps Moon Willow already up and about. Then she sat quite still as a new fear struck her. Moon Willow had made it clear enough that Abby no longer met the harsh standards of an Onandaga woman. What would Moon Willow say or do?

She discovered soon enough when she walked out into the corridor and shaped the mound of grass, twigs and small bits of wood to start her own morning fire. When she twisted about to pick up her water pot, she faced Moon Willow. Neither woman moved for a long, long moment.

"Are you Strong Woman?" Moon Willow asked in a scornful voice.

Abby replied with forced evenness, "I am Strong Woman, Mother."

"Do not call me 'Mother' until my warrior son gives you the right."

"He does not have the right. I am also of the Hawk and Owl and the Society—"

Moon Willow's angry, repulsing gesture cut Abby short. The old woman said, "Many of your sisters saw you yesterday and they have told me you are no longer worthy. But, of course, we will wait until after the Great *Sachems* of the other Nations have left to meet and decide on that." Moon Willow's voice grew vitriolic. "We test the paleskin today and every mother will be watching you. Can you keep your stomach in place? You couldn't yesterday."

"I will try," Abby answered shortly, then jumped up, snatching the water jug from its corner and pushing by Moon Willow.

Outside, the sky had just a hint of light to the east over the stockade and the gate had not yet been opened. This was, as she had learned, the favorite time for the Indians to attack an unsuspecting camp, cabin or village of the paleskins. Other women gathered at the well for water and Abby expected an outbreak from them much like Moon Willow's. But they only looked sleepily at her, even those from the Hawk and the Owl. None accused her of faintheartedness.

Relieved, but still not certain that angry accusations would not be hurled at her from anyone at any moment, Abby filled the jug and returned to the Long House. Safely inside again, she walked along the corridor, circled Moon Willow's fire though the old woman did not even look up. Howling Wolf gave her only a glance; Abby thought he looked half drunk. Had Major Roberts brought the paleskin's firewater when he had parleyed? But Abby had seen no sight of it.

At her own fireside, she started the morning meal. In the midst of it, Corn Dancer came from the sleeping room, yawning, scratching his ribs. His face paint had cracked and he had nothing for her but a grunt as he plopped down beside the fire. She realized he, too, looked drunk, though she knew he had not had anything like firewater, the raw corn whiskey of the frontier colonies. But the white captive had come from the Hudson. Had his horse or his wagon, both destroyed when he was captured, carried liquor jugs? She surreptitiously studied him as she worked and decided no liquor had caused his stupor.

He growled at her to hurry the meal; he was hungry. She answered shortly and then said that she could see no reason to rush. He glared at her. Had she forgotten the meeting of the *Sachems?* The sleep left his eyes, replaced by an avid gleam. He touched his face, smoothed his fingers along his cheeks. He would have to redo his ceremonial make-up. Corn Dancer, a minor war chief and potential war *Sachem,* could not appear before the *Sachems,* the Nations and the Keepers in his present condition. He would re-paint his face, see to his weapons and the feathered decorations while she finished the meal.

When he left Abby continued to work before the fire. But now she had the answer to the stuporous gaze of both Howling Wolf and Corn Dancer: both men were drunk on the torture they had witnessed yesterday—and the torture they anticipated today! She remembered an incident that had happened years ago, when she had been hardly more than a toddler, before she had been brought to Westover.

A man had beaten a dog for some fault Abby could not recall. But she could remember the tortured, crazed cries of the helpless animal . . . and its final bloody death-throes under the pounding of the club and the kick of the man's heavy shoes. She remembered the man had turned away with the same dazed, stuporous look she had seen this morning on both Howling Wolf's and Corn Dancer's faces. Though she didn't have a word for it, both Indians had actually become drunk on the drawn-out horror of the fire and the stake!

She couldn't believe it and tried to deny what her brain and logic told her. But each passing moment made her more and more certain she was right. No wonder the Iroquois were feared. Now she could more fully understand Major Roberts' desire to leave the Onondaga town and the Council of the *Sachems* of all the Nations. He must have witnessed these ceremonies before and could not face another.

Corn Dancer reappeared and sat down, accepting the bowl of combined rabbit and squirrel stew Abby handed him. Using a carved wooden spoon, he hungrily ate the chunks of meat; then he simply put the bowl to his lips to finish the remainder. He put the bowl down with a pleased grunt, frowning at Abby.

"What will you do today? Will you run?"

She shook her head and his scowl lessened. He looked beyond her at the fireside where Moon Willow and Howling Wolf broke the night's fast. "Mother is angry that you are not all

Onondaga. Maybe there is more paleskin to be washed from you."

"Maybe," she conceded, not wanting to get further into the discussion.

He nodded at her single word. "Then, after the *Sachems* have gone, the Keepers will again take you to the river."

"I will go."

He stood up, pushed his tomahawk in his belt and made certain his knife and sheath were secure. He smiled then, and even through the crimson slashes on his cheeks, she once again detected the Corn Dancer who had brought her to full womanhood and whom she loved—*had* loved until yesterday and this morning, she corrected herself.

"When the drums signal and the Keepers come, we will go to the fire circle. The paleskin might be a brave man after all—even though he cries like a woman or a crazed wolf. We will see."

He started round the fire, stopped. "I will look for you when the drums call the women. I will watch you test the paleskin beside the other women, eh?"

"You will watch," she agreed.

"And see?"

"Yes, and see."

"I will tell my mother and the Keepers. They will be pleased."

He walked beyond her then and Howling Wolf joined him as they went to the distant door and out. She looked up when a step sounded near.

Moon Willow stood looking down at her. "My son says you will be Strong Woman again today, eh?"

"I told him I would."

Moon Willow's grim face softened slightly and her eyes held a gleam of understanding. "The wash in the river by the Keepers, the blood bond, the Owl and the Hawk—maybe they are not enough to make you full Onondaga. You were born paleskin. That is hard to leave behind?"

"It is, Mother. But I try."

Moon Willow finally nodded. "It would be hard for me to become paleskin, I think. Do your people wash the red out?"

Abby thought of the baptisms in the creeks she had witnessed. "Some do, Mother. Others pray that the Father of All clean out the red."

Moon Willow had started to nod but when Abby mentioned cleansing by the Father of All, Moon Willow looked shocked and disbelieving. "But He could not do that! He is red Himself! Ah, paleskins crazy, eh?"

She turned on her heel and spoke over her shoulder as she walked away. "I go with my Society. You come with Hawk and Owl?"

"I will come with them."

Abby did not move after Moon Willow left. She heard the others leave, even the children, and she knew that soon the drums would start beating their summons. Silence held the Long House, the only sounds coming from muted voices and shouts outside as everyone gathered around the fresh wooden pillar that awaited its victim.

Her thoughts moved in a dark, turgid circle and she wondered helplessly what had brought on the course of events that had so wildly changed her mind and emotions. Fear, terror and bloodshed had overwhelmed her at Westover. She would never know how her father or Daniel had died but she had seen the shaft of the arrow protruding from her mother's breast. She had heard the crackle of flames and seen her friends killed. Then there had come that long, horrible march through the forest to the Hudson, across it, and the plunge into the woods on this, its western bank.

She knew that only Corn Dancer's care and concern had saved her from the skull-crushing clubs time and again. She knew that in his way, he had come to think of her as more than captive and paleskin, an object to be worked or bartered, however Fate decided. "God's ways," she heard her mother's voice say, as she had heard it so many times during the long miles, days and now months since Westover.

She remembered, and her body grew warm at the thought, how Corn Dancer had awakened her to an amazing, unexpected enjoyment of her body. She had not known what a man could do to fulfill a woman until Corn Dancer had taught her. She had come to love him and, with that love, she had been able to accept the fact that her life had changed and had become restricted to this Onondaga town.

But now, alone in the silence of the empty Long House, she knew that her heart and her body's desire had created an illusion.

And now she slowly awakened from it, slowly and painfully. She tried hard to hold to the gentle caresses and fiery passion of Corn Dancer. She tried to hold onto the way of this new forest life, of the fact that the paleskin had been washed from her.

She held up her arm and studied the barely discernible scar of the knife that had mingled white with red blood. She reviewed the companionship of the women and Mothers of the Hawk and Owl, their secrets of healing, of pleasing their men, their secrets of childbirth and the many other functions of a woman's body. She had become immersed in this world of the Onondaga and the Six Nations. She had become awed by the dignified, aloof Keepers of the Faith, by the folklore, hero tales and children's jokes and pranks of the Iroquois, never known to the paleskins or even hinted when one of them was around.

Illusions!

She bent her head and buried her face in her hands. Tears streamed down her cheeks and she did not bother to brush them away. Yesterday's horror of the Ritual by Fire had torn her apart as completely as the attack on Westover. As that had changed her life from Abby Brewster to Strong Woman, so yesterday's sacrifice, the sadistic drunkenness of every Indian warrior, mother, Keeper and even child, had changed her life again. She could no longer be Strong Woman. She could no longer be Abby Brewster, who had really died months ago.

Who was she? What was she?

Her head jerked up as the drums began to sound. She listened as the steady sound continued, soft but with an ever-increasing tempo that would build until the summons became louder and more insistent. What of the poor paleskin—she changed the word in her mind— white man? Would they treat him as they had the Shawnee? Could she stand it? Could she take part with knife or burning splinter as she knew would be demanded of her?

What could she do?

She looked wildly around. She could not go alone and unarmed into the woods. She lived each day with expert trackers and she had nothing with which to fend them off, any more than she had her sheathed knife to fend off the smallest of animals.

Abby knew that she had to appear at the loathsome ceremony. She had to. She jumped up, looked wildly around again but could find nothing. If she was not there within minutes, Moon Willow, a Keeper or even Corn Dancer himself would come looking for her. Maybe she could watch just the first ceremonies before they brought out the victim. Maybe . . . she prayed . . . maybe she'd find some means—surely God would not allow her to go through another such ordeal!

She hurried along the passage and out the

door. Now the drums sounded louder, deafening. Men, women and children hurried by, toward the great central space where the post stood. No one paid any attention to her as she fell in and was swept along.

Abby came to the area of the great council house where the high, raw wooden post was surrounded by the ring of yesterday's ashes. New grass, twigs and branches had been carefully placed and made ready. She glimpsed Moon Willow far over to the left among the crowd and the woman's smile flashed clearly even at this distance.

Abby edged to the rear of her sisters of the Hawk and the Owl and sat down. Corn Dancer moved to the front of this section of onlookers, walking close by the inner ring. He saw her and, though his expression did not change, his head made a short bob of acknowledgment. So far she was safe, and as yet the prisoner and victim had not been brought out.

Then she saw some movement at a nearby hut; the Keepers of All the Nations emerged, signifying it would begin soon. Abby shivered and touched the hilt of her knife. Could she save the poor man's agony if the blade sank into his heart or throat? She knew she would die an instant later.

Then the Great *Sachems* came solemnly out, following the Keepers, and the chant started. She saw a stir at another hut and the victim, bound hand and foot, was carried out. He was still clothed except for shoes and a thick gag covering his mouth so that, if he still screamed in terror, no sound could be heard.

The drums increased in tempo as the Keepers began their chant, arms raised to the sky. The Sachems found their places. Warriors gathered about the victim, now lying prone, and some of them even now danced and pranced, brandishing lances, clubs, knives, rifles and muskets. The warriors around the victim bent over him and their knives slashed his clothing from his collar to his stockings. He was soon as naked as the Shawnee had been the day before.

Then Abby forgot the victim as she saw that one of the Indians had dropped his rifle and bullet pouch to the ground to further free his movements in stripping the captive. Both still lay where he had dropped them.

The captive, who had been lifted to his feet, collapsed and sagged like an empty bag. Abby knew that if the gag was removed, his screams would again echo through the town. She now looked at the straining procession that forced him to the rings of wood, lifted him over and carried him to the post. No one paid any attention to the rifle and pouch. She stood up but no one looked at her, all eyes fixed on the tragic drama playing out in the circle. She edged toward the objects she wanted and then squatted down beside them.

In the circle the Keepers moved in a swaying half-dance, arms still lifted. About them the captors pulled the sagging captive to the post. When they released him, his knees hinged and he fell prone. Hands lifted him and this time the Indians lashed his whole body to the stake, bonds about his chest, waist, legs and ankles. She saw that his face had another coating of black ashes. His eyes looked glazed and Abby doubted if the poor man saw anything. If he did, it was only a haze of unreality.

Now the dancing started, the warriors swirling round and round the stake. No one came for the rifle and pouch. Abby wrapped her fingers around the gun barrel and slipped the thong of the shot and powder bag over her shoulder. She looked around.

A mass hypnotism held everyone's attention riveted on the action in the center of the ring. Now one of the women Keepers came to the victim. As her knife flashed the gag dropped from his mouth, but no sound issued from him. His head was hanging low and half swinging, symptoms of his catatonic state caused by continued fright. His mind must be completely gone, Abby thought.

But she certainly couldn't help the poor devil and time ran out on her with each tense second. The Keeper's knife then moved to the man's crotch, and the blade whipped once across it. The cut of the knife brought him into awareness of pain, though of nothing else. He started to scream and the drums truly roared and thundered, drowning out his shouts for a moment, until his keening wails arose even over the drum thunder and the savage, pleased cries of the Indians.

The Keeper turned, stepped back, and motioned the women to have their share of the ceremony. In a solid wave they swept over the rings of wood; their knife blades gleaming in the sun.

Abby had now backed away. The hut which had imprisoned the captives stood right at hand. In less than a moment she whipped around the corner, gun and leather bag still tight in her fists. She closed her ears to the mounting screams and the rising shouts and songs of the torturers. Her eyes swept the street ahead. Empty! Even the guards had gone to the ceremony. She raced to the next corner, turned it, and saw the stockade gate at the end of the long street. She and a slinking Indian cur dog were the only living things not at the ceremony.

She ran. She feared a shout, an alarm, a challenge or even an arrow or bullet. She arrived at the gate untouched, gasping for breath, but she sped on through it and along the trail that led to the river. The canoes pulled up on the bank added to her hurry, her first goal now almost near enough to touch. The rifle and heavy leather bag of powder and ball slowed her but she knew she dared not leave them behind.

At last she came to the line of canoes and stopped at the nearest one. She saw the paddle lying below the seat ready to hand. She swung rifle and bag into the craft beside it and bent to the task of pushing the canoe out of the gravel and sand into the water. Once the current began to grip it, she could jump in, grab up the paddle and help the slow-moving current take her downstream to the Hudson. So near to release!

"Hai! Hai!" a voice shouted a challenge.

She swung around. The guard must have been dozing in one of the other canoes and she had been so intent on escape that she had not seen him. But now he rushed at her and was hardly more than an arm's reach away. For the rest of her life the next few seconds would always be a blur. She could not be caught now. She could not go back to the savagery of the Iroquois and the Onondaga. Corn Dancer, Howling Wolf, and the Keepers would have her face ash-blackened, her clothing stripped, and she would be tied to the stake and fall victim to the torture and fire herself.

Without thought, Abby's hand jumped to her sheathed knife and drew it even as she twisted away, avoiding the warrior's clutching fingers. But he wheeled with her, thin lips pulled back from his teeth, his eyes gleaming circles of alarm and hatred.

She ducked under his arm but could not wholly avoid his rush. His knee struck her and his hand grabbed her shoulder. Her knife blade glittered and blurred as she brought it upward in a powerful blow. The point sank deep into his chest just above the stomach. He uttered a strangling cry and fell backward. The gunnels of the next canoe struck him just behind the knees and his arms flailed out as the toppled back and out of sight.

Horrified, Abby stood looking down at his

twitching body. He tried to speak but blood suddenly flowed out of his throat and he died without further sound. Abby, stunned, realized her knife blade dripped blood onto her fingers and hand. She threw a terrified look back at the distant town stockade and the open gate. No one had appeared and, even in her horror, she could faintly hear the drums thundering and thundering over there where a man was dying slowly and horribly.

She caught herself up and her mind snapped back into clarity. She whipped about and once more bent to the canoe holding her stolen rifle and pouch. She pushed and shoved and at last the gravelly sand broke its grip. The craft moved out and she jumped into it, swept up the paddle and used the blade to propel her deeper into the water.

A terrified, sweeping look told her the man she had just killed had fallen out of sight and only the line of canoes innocently bobbled slightly in the water. By some miracle no one had seen her, all held by the torture ceremony in the town beyond the stockade.

Now she moved well out and the current already sluggishly turned the prow of the canoe eastward. The Hudson lay in that direction and there would be paleskins—she caught herself up, white people—New York colonists, who would speak her own language, welcome her. She'd never again see a human being roasted alive after flaming splinters made his body look like a porcupine.

The Hudson—how far? Would she be able to reach it before the Onondaga discovered her missing and found the dead man in the canoe on the riverbank? She almost faltered when she thought of what Corn Dancer might do to her before he allowed the Keepers and the *owachiras* to strip her and—

Her crazed, fearful thoughts suddenly stopped and logic took their place. She turned the canoe toward the bank of the slow-flowing stream and heard it grate against sandy gravel. She sat long moments, paddle across her lap, her mind racing from factor to factor that she had not considered in her haste and fear. Corn Dancer would be the first to guess she would flee toward the nearest white farm or settlement along the Hudson. She would never be able to outrace the swift paddles that sinewy Indian muscles could wield. She had still to run another risk and it had to be done.

She took a deep breath, pushed out from the bank and turned the canoe back toward the town. When she rounded the bend, she hugged the far bank of the stream. The row of canoes still quietly lined the river bank and the stockade and its gate still stood empty and open. But she delayed only long enough to be sure she had not yet been missed or that the ritual of fire had not ended. She pushed her paddle deep and bent her full strength to the task of moving against the current.

Slowly, too slowly, she worked her way at what seemed to her to be a torturous snail's pace on beyond the canoes, the town and its open fields. She finally made another turn so that bushes and trees hid her from at least immediate discovery. Now she moved westward and the mountains slowly grew higher as she approached them.

During her time at the Onondaga town she had heard talk of the westward country. She knew before long this stream she travelled would narrow and finally become too shallow and small even for a canoe. She would have to abandon the craft then and strike out afoot.

But westward and southward she would find another stream flowing to the south. It was called the Allegaway by the Iroquois and it was the northern branch of the great stream they called "The Beautiful River." The Seneca Nation lived that way and so they called themselves the "Keepers of the Western Doors." More to the point, somewhere down the Allegaway was a post at the forks of the river which had been named Fort Prince George, where she'd find white men, colonists, even soldiers.

And it meant refuge for Abby.

If she could live through to find it.

XXVI

When the gloating voice sounded and
Edouard looked to the rim of the depression to
see the coarse, leathery face of the courier and a
pair of avid narrow eyes under a blue tricorn
hat, he reacted with the instinctive speed of a
soldier. Spotted Doe moved just as swiftly, her

Indian training triggering her into explosive action. Both of them moved as one.

As Edouard's hand darted to his sash and pulled his pistol, Spotted Doe grabbed the rifle lying next to her hand. Both weapons barked flame, smoke and lead as one. The buckskin-clad courier jerked spasmodically to his knees and toppled forward. The other man, struck squarely in the forehead, made no sound at all but his body made a jumping motion and then he slid down the slope to the bottom of the depression. Edouard heard the frightened whinny of a horse from some spot out of sight over the lip of the depression.

Then silence. The courier had twisted to one side in his fall, and then slowly rolled over. But the motion was only a reflex of muscles. Edouard saw the hole dead center in his chest and the small seepage of blood from it. The other man twitched a few times and then lay still and his small motion had also been mere reflex. Both men had died before they stopped rolling.

The sound of the simultaneous shots made flat echoes and then died away, leaving only the deep silence of the forest. Small curls of blue powder smoke made momentary ribbons from the muzzles of the weapons and then disappeared. Edouard looked, half stunned, at Spotted Doe.

"Who are they?"

"Of no importance now," she answered shortly. "More of them maybe, eh?"

"I'll see. Reload the rifle."

"They had guns. They will be up there; get them," she spoke swiftly and Edouard hurried up the slope, pausing just below the rim to cautiously peer over. He first saw the horse, bearing a military saddle, frantically tugging at reins wrapped and tightly tied about a small tree. Then he saw a musket lying almost to hand. His sharp, hurried and alarmed look swept the thin line of trees. But nothing moved, nobody appeared. He could see a portion of the wide trail to De Troit beyond the trees though not a thing moved into his vision between the trunks.

Satisfied, he scrambled the remaining few feet to the rim of the depression. He scooped up the musket and, checking his impulse to rush, moved slowly to the horse so as not to frighten it more. It tossed its head, rolled its eyes and moved skittishly. Edouard spoke soothingly to it and it finally stood still so he could untie the reins, gather them up and lead the horse back to the depression.

Spotted Doe had reloaded the rifle and examined the two slack bodies. Her husky voice held scorn. "That one is of the woods. Maybe outlaw, *non?*" Her expression became grim when she pointed to the second. "But he is *soldat*. He will soon be missed in Quebec or in Montreal."

Edouard answered with a brief, sharp, "Wait," and turned to the horse.

A long-barreled heavy flintlock pistol still rested in a saddle holster and thin blankets had been rolled and strapped under the pommel. His eyes even more bleak, Edouard loosened and swung the saddle bags off the animal, dropped them to the ground and started loosening the buckles. Spotted Doe stood over him as he opened the bags and brought out their contents.

One bag carried provisions for travel, already partially consumed, but the other held a small, thick roll of paper sealed with wax. Edouard opened it and dumped letters and folded dispatches, all wax-sealed and imprinted with the lily of the king and the insignia of the Royal Governor.

"A messenger! But what would he be doing with a *canaille* such as that one?"

He indicated the courier. Spotted Doe answered, "There are many of his kind at De Troit as well as Montreal and Quebec. They travel together. Two such ones would—how you say? discourage?—outlaws."

"But they are outlaws themselves."

"Maybe so. But that one *soldat,* too. You and me—we are in trouble, *mon Sieur.*"

He hardly noticed that under stress she had reverted to the formal terms between Indian and *habitant.* He looked up at the depression rim and then squatted down beside the man in the dirt-stained blue uniform. The tricorn hat with the little white feather had rolled to one side. He looked at the dead men, then up at Spotted Doe. She apparently read his thoughts.

"We cannot go to De Troit."

"We can't go back."

They sat in silence, each deep in troubled

thought and each looking up to the rim as though expecting vengeance-seeking soldiers or couriers at any second. Edouard broke the silence.

"Then what do we do? Where do we go?" His face lit. "To your people—to the lake you call Huron!"

"We will never reach it before these are found and then we will be hunted throughout the forest. It will not take long, that."

His face fell and he tugged thoughtfully at his earlobe. New France threatened to be no place of refuge at all. He spoke slowly, "We can't go forward. We can't go back. What is north?"

She shrugged. "Woods, wolves, bears. Indians and trappers who would knife us in a second for what little we have—and for me. Women are few, I become—how you say? Rape? Harlot? What is it?"

"Your choice, and little difference," he answered dully and then another thought struck him and new hope. "But south! The English! War already brews and they won't turn us over to His Excellency because we killed a French soldier and a *courieur du bois* of New France. They will welcome us."

She frowned, not comprehending, and Edouard repeated his thought, more slowly. "That is English country to the south. Empty, though—forest and rivers and streams, like here. But no French governor. There is a fort somewhere south. We find a river and follow it and come to the fort, eh? We are safe!"

She considered it. Her face lit up and, for a moment, Edouard thought he had the answer for them both. Then she frowned and he waited for her reply. So much depended on it.

"Spotted Doe Huron tribe. Safe here but—" she indicated the dead soldier "I die for that, *non?*"

"Both of us," he agreed and she fell into deep thought again. Then once more her face glowed.

"Eh, first there are the Erie tribe. They rule lake—big water down there."

"Lake Erie!"

"*Oui*. Erie tribe not war with either French or Britain, eh?"

"I don't know."

"Spotted Doe know. They not afraid us. They have long war and trade canoe. They take us across big water Erie, eh? That is, you have *louis d'or?*"

"I have."

"*Bien!* They take us over big water. But on other side Iroquois live. Seneca. Keepers of Western Door they name, eh? Seneca—Huron they enemies. But may be we find river Allegaway. Part big river far down there. It called part Beautiful River." She made a sign indicating distance beyond Edouard's comprehension. "Fork in Beautiful River, I told. English fort there. We find it, eh?"

"Then *I'm* in trouble. I'm French."

"You wear skin shirt. Fringe." She touched his shoulder and sleeve, then the trousers stretched tightly over his knees and his moccasins. "You trader, eh? Trapper, eh? You not care for French, maybe. They not good for you traps, eh?"

He studied her and then beamed. "Spotted Doe, maybe you're a savage of New France but you have plenty of brains."

"Eh? *Je ne comprends—*"

"Understand or not, no matter!" He jumped to his feet and indicated the horse. "Can you ride?"

"I Indian—Huron. I don't ride."

"You will." He dumped the saddlebags and the roll of blankets, then swung into the saddle. He held his hand down to her. "Up . . . behind me."

They came out of the copse of trees that hid the depression and soon had crossed the main west-leading trail and disappeared into the woods to the south. Spotted Doe clung so tightly to his waist that he thought once or twice she would break him in half. Then, slowly, her first fright began to wane.

"Good!" he exclaimed over his shoulder. "You'll soon be a good rider."

"But I sore."

He suppressed a chuckle and kept his voice even and soothing. "Of course. But that will pass."

"But too much hurt. Not good for you and me at fireside."

He burst into laughter and tightly clasped her hand as she clung to his waist. "We'll make up for it, *non?*"

"*Oui*, but not for long time."

"I'll wait," he promised. "I will be delicate, eh?"

She said some words that sounded like a Huron curse.

Though the main east-west trail lay behind them, they soon came on secondary trails leading south or north. Spotted Doe said they were Indian paths to the great lake of the Eries to the south and to Tionoti villages to the north. Edouard learned from her, between groans, that these trails formed what he would call trade routes as well as warpaths. Whatever their use, he felt thankful for them.

Spotted Doe had scanty knowledge of the countryside southward, since she had seldom ventured far down in this direction. She knew of the Ottawas because they were neighbors of the Hurons, but far less of the Eries except for their barter objects that occasionally came to her village or even to Montreal and Quebec. She had only a faint idea of how far away the Erie lake was.

So Edouard did more walking than riding to save the horse's strength and, after a time, Spotted Doe was glad to ease out of the saddle and walk slowly and painfully beside him. They travelled mostly through beech and white birch forest and only twice encountered anything living other than high-flying birds or small animals that disappeared into high grass and bushes with a quick dart or jump.

Spotted Doe tried the saddle several times but

the chafing sent her sliding to the ground. Still it was she, despite her pain, who suddenly spoke a warning and they moved off the trail into a screen of bushes. They watched a courier stalk by, long rifle in his hand, a heavy load of bundled skins over his shoulder held by a wide, stout strap. As they watched, he suddenly stopped short just at the point where they had left the trail. The man swung up the rifle and Edouard could clearly hear the click of the hammer as it was pulled back to fall on the flint.

He and Spotted Doe stood quite still, Edouard's hand over the horse's muzzle. The trapper sharply searched the bushes, his eyes slowly passing the very spot where they tensely waited, and then on along the trees. He stood a long moment until he again shouldered the rifle and moved on northward, back toward the main trail. Spotted Doe checked Edouard's impulsive move to hurry on south and put her finger to her lips. She continued long after Edouard knew they could never be heard but her fingers clutching his arm held him. Then at last she nodded and they moved out onto the trail again.

Late in the afternoon, when they thought they were far from any watching, hostile eyes, an Indian suddenly appeared in the path, stepping from behind a tree. Edouard started to swing up his rifle but Spotted Doe checked him. "That one Erie. He not hurt us. He want talk and maybe camp, eh?"

She lifted her eyes to a sky that was rose tinted with the final touch of evening sun. Then she lifted her hand, palm out, and spoke a single word. The Indian answered in kind, eased the tight bend of his bow and the poised, deadly arrow dropped into his hand.

"He go to Tionoti. Trade wampum for pale-skin knives and cloth, maybe. He want make camp then hear us and wait to make sure we pass him or we friends. He cook pot stew. I'm hungry, eh?"

"So am I."

For the first time in his life, Edouard ate without knife, fork or spoon. His fingers dripped and his hands felt sticky. They ate well off the trail, all three of them squatted around the flames of a small fire. Edouard followed the examples of Spotted Doe and Slick Otter, the Erie, in licking his fingers, then wiping his hands on the grass and along the buckskin legs of his trousers.

They spoke in a strange mixture of tongues—French, Huron, Erie—often searching for words and phrases, just as often substituting signs and gestures. Edouard knew that they must have bastardized the Erie and Huron tongues just as all of them did the French, but they managed to communicate.

Just as the fire began to die down, the Erie spoke to Spotted Doe, picked up his warbow and arrow quiver and disappeared in the darkening woods. She explained, "He go see no one close, eh? We—how you say?—safe. No enemy."

"How far are we from the lake?" Edouard asked.

Her pointing finger made an arc from the east to midheaven. He translated that as half a day at the most and then asked, "How do we get across the lake if it's so big and wide?"

"Maybe get canoe. You, me, paddle, eh? Paddle long time—all day, maybe night."

"Just you and me?" He had to point to her and then himself and make the motions of paddling before she understood. She shrugged, and that was troubling answer enough for him. Slick Otter returned, smiled reassuringly and dropped prone before the fire. Edouard looked over at Spotted Doe and then pointed to the Erie.

"He can row us across? Iroquois over there and Erie friends?"

She finally fully understood that and queried Slick Otter. She turned back to Edouard and shook her head. "He go north. Barter and trade, *non?* Not go back to lake and his village. He give us token that we travel in peace. His—how you say?—family treat us good."

"Across the lake?" Edouard insisted. "How about that?"

She spoke to Slick Otter, then shook her head. "Seneca, Erie maybe friend, maybe enemy. No know until meet. So Erie no cross lake with us."

Edouard sank back, frowning at this disappointment. Here he was a few miles from some sort of wide lake and across it lay safety from the *lettre de cachet* and the vengeance of the royal governor for the death of the soldier-messenger. He dared not show his face in New France but he could not escape from it.

Just then the captured horse, staked out beyond the firelight, stomped and blew. Edouard jerked upright, eyes alight. "Spotted Doe, would Slick Otter or his people want our horse?"

She stared a moment, then translated for the Erie. He answered instantly, swiftly, all excited anticipation. Then his eagerness vanished and he slumped.

Spotted Doe translated. "Slick Otter—Erie—want horse like paleskin. But too much barter, eh? Too much trade, eh?"

"Tell him," Edouard leaned toward her and spoke slowly, "if his people take you—me across lake, horse is theirs. That is all."

Spotted Doe asked him, "How you say? You mean it?"

"I mean it."

She studied him, brows raised, and then slowly she looked around as the horse stomped again. An expression of bright hope touched her face and she spoke rapidly to Slick Otter. The Erie also looked stunned, disbelieving, and then jumped up, clapped his hands as he answered, the words pouring from his mouth.

"He say go back his village. He say you cross lake. Big war canoe. Many Erie. Seneca see and hide, eh? If not, Erie fight 'em."

Now Spotted Doe showed delight but Edouard remained stern. "They guide us south, *non,* to stream or river that will lead to English fort, *non?*"

She queried Slick Otter, turned to Edouard.

"He say Allegaway not far in Seneca land. Erie take you there. Steal Seneca canoe. You be English place fast, eh?"

Edouard nodded, his problem solved. But when had he ever seen so much joy as Spotted Doe displayed? He dropped to the ground, rolled over so she could see only his back and then allowed his shoulders to shake in silent laughter. He knew of one saddle-sore Huron maiden who would never ride a horse again.

XXVII

He had never seen a canoe as long and large as the one the Eries used to transport him and Spotted Doe across the lake. Nor had he ever seen a lake so much like a fresh-water ocean and just as wide and mighty as Erie. The huge canoe not only carried the warrior paddlers, Spotted

Doe and himself, but provisions, weapons.

A strong cross-wind blew constantly and the crossing was almost as pitching as the *Demoiselle's* crossing of the Atlantic. But at last the high prow struck the southern shore. Eries snatched up lances, bows, arrows and even two smooth-bore muskets before they jumped ashore. They hustled Spotted Doe and Edouard out. Then, at the command of their leader, they pulled the great craft up the sandy beach at the foot of a low escarpment. They dragged it into a deep cleft choked with bushes and vines. The craft was out of sight in a matter of minutes.

A scout, who had jumped out of the huge canoe before it even touched the shore, swiftly scaled the low cliff, paused a moment at the crest to peer ahead and then disappeared. Edouard climbed out more slowly and the Indians pointed to the cleft in which they hid the canoe.

"We hide there," Spotted Doe explained. "If no Seneca, we go that way."

She pointed inland. Edouard crouched beside her under the concealing brush over the canoe. He heard scurryings for some moments as the Erie found hiding places and then all became silence.

The scout soon returned, making a low wailing sound at the crest of the escarpment to identify himself, and then jumped down. Instantly the Erie appeared, conferred with the scout and then turned to Spotted Doe. She spoke with them, partially by words, partially by signs and then she turned to Edouard.

"No Iroquois close. So we go fast, eh? They take us to Allegaway. They call it north fork of Beautiful River."

"Then?"

"English down that river at fork. We go there. Erie come back here. Cross lake other side and their village."

Edouard and Spotted Doe scaled the low cliffs with the Indians. Atop them, Edouard saw a wide area of grass ending in a tangle of bushes and trees that marked the beginning of the forest. But the Erie leader angrily spoke and hustled them across the open ground and to shelter under the trees. Once they were many yards into the forest the pace slowed and finally halted.

The Eries immediately clustered about their leader and conferred, their voices hardly more than a low murmur. A warrior pointed in one direction, southward, but the leader shook his head and pointed to another angle. Edouard touched Spotted Doe's arm.

"Lost?"

"Not lost. How you say?—decide how quick find Allegaway. No let Seneca find us, eh?"

"Decidedly *not*—from what you tell me."

At last the discussion ended and the leader made a sign to Edouard and spoke to Spotted Doe. She translated. "We go now. Soon now find river—maybe tomorrow, eh?"

Her guess proved right. They made cold camp in the woods that night but were up at dawn and again marching south. Edouard wondered how they kept direction for the trees were thick and one looked exactly like all the rest. But the Erie moved ahead with confidence. They stopped once and crouched down. When Edouard started to ask a question, Spotted Doe clamped her hand over his mouth. Wisely, Edouard did not try to jerk his head away. He could see nothing ahead but bushes. A scout crouched low beside them made a signal by waving an arm and then pointed to the left. Edouard saw the man's head also turn in that direction. It slowly moved in a half circle to the extreme right and Edouard actually felt the tension in the Indians about him. Some of them tightened their fingers around lance, tomahawk or bow. One man reached over his shoulder to touch the feathered butt of one of his arrows, but he did not draw it, standing frozen, poised, ready.

The man ahead moved at last, dropping his hand from the arrow as the tension flowed out of his body. He made a signal to the group and Spotted Doe touched Edouard's shoulder. "We go now, Seneca hunting go by and our trail open. Come."

Once more they moved forward but with increased speed. The advance scout had again disappeared. Edouard could not guess how many miles they had traveled when the advance scout again appeared. He made a signal for the band to come up and pointed back over his shoulder, smiling.

"River!" Spotted Doe breathed.

In less than a quarter of an hour, Edouard stood on the banks of a narrow, winding stream, its surface broken by jagged rocks around which whitewater boiled. On either side, oak, maple and chestnut trees climbed high, steep slopes. White birches relieved the almost solid dark brown of the other tree trunks and along the crests of the cliffs Edouard saw an occasional pine.

"Allegaway," the leader said to Edouard.

Just then the scout made another peculiar call and Edouard was jerked back into bushes, Spotted Doe falling in a sprawl by his side. He started to get up but an Erie almost knocked him flat again.

"Seneca!" Spotted Doe whispered. "Canoe."

She placed her finger to her lips and Edouard, now well trained, remained silent and frozen. The Eries ahead of him, peering out the bushes toward the river, did not move. Then one of them very slowly stood up. He arched his hand over his shoulder, swung out an arrow and fitted it to the bow. It arched as he sighted. Edouard heard the slight twanging whisper and then, at some distance, a choked-off cry.

The archer turned his head, grinning, waved the party forward and then darted south at an angle. When Edouard broke through the bushes and could see the narrow wild river again, the scout pulled up a canoe. A red body lay loosely across the gunnels near the bow and the long shaft of an arrow protruded from his back.

The canoe was pulled to the bank and the body lifted out. It was hidden in the bushes and the Erie leader turned to Spotted Doe and Edouard. He gestured to the empty canoe and Spotted Doe translated for Edouard.

"You—me . . . we now have canoe. Take us downstream to the English. Fort Prince George, the paleskin call it. Erie now go back to lake and across to their village. Use horse good, eh?"

"Yes, and tell them they're welcome to it. Tell them trade good. We are happy and hope they are happy."

Spotted Doe listened and her frown of puzzlement increased as Edouard spoke. Then he shrugged, turned to the Erie leader and held out his hand, making the sign of peace with his right one. The man immediately understood and red fingers crushed Edouard's for a moment.

Then they were alone with the canoe. The Erie had vanished as though swallowed. Edouard cautiously examined the vessel. He saw the paddle the dead man had dropped lying across one of the two seats and then discovered there was a second in the bottom. He helped Spotted Doe to a seat and she picked up one of the paddles. Edouard shoved the bark craft free of the riverbank, snatched up the other paddle as he took two splashing steps and hopped in. The current found them.

In a matter of moments, Edouard thanked his Gascon luck that Spotted Doe handled a paddle at the bow. She not only avoided the sharp rocks that protruded from the river but she recognized the sworls of water in the current that marked the jagged boulders beneath the surface which would have ripped the bottom out of the frail craft. Time and again she would sit with poised paddle as the canoe swept down on a rock. Then, just as Edouard knew for certain they would crash, she would thrust outward, blade catching an angle of the stone, and the danger would whip by to left or right. They avoided catastrophe by inches.

In split seconds she would judge which channel to take as the stream split around obstructions and only once did they come to a near miss. To his surprise, as they swung right around a boulder, she jumped out of the canoe. The lightened craft immediately became more buoyant and tried to pull free of her tight grip on its rounded rim. She stood to her armpits in water but even so, Edouard heard a momentary frightening clawing-scratching sound along the bottom. Her added weight would have destroyed the canoe. Beyond the shallow stretch, she guided the craft to the bank and came up out of the water, adrip down from her armpits.

Now Edouard himself could step out of the canoe without fear of tipping the thing over and swamping it. He helped Spotted Doe pull the prow to the bank where the pebbly sand could securely grip it. Spotted Doe unconcernedly pulled her soaked tunic over her head, stepped out of her dripping skirt and spread the garments over the canoe that she had pushed over to one side.

She stood before him wearing only headband and soaked moccasins, reminding him of the way he had first seen her in Madam Demain's Snow Fox. She pointed to his wet skin trousers, indicating he remove them and put them beside her own garments.

"Sun will dry before long. We camp, wait, rest, eh?" She laughed at him. "You no good boatman, and that no good, fast river with white water."

"Nothing in France like it that I've seen." His smile suddenly vanished and he turned to the canoe.

The rifle and powder and shot bag lay on the inner curve of the tipped canoe, out of the damp sand and gravel, and, as swift examination showed him, untouched by water. He let out a great sigh of relief, picked them up and handed them to her. Then he handed her the wet garments and pulled the canoe completely out of the water. Since its sides were bark and its ribs and seats formed of light wood, it had no weight despite its length. It took little effort to swing it upside down over his head and carry it across a few yards of open bank and into a fringe of bushes. Out of sight of the river, he lowered it.

Spotted Doe returned rifle and pouch to him, spread their garments once more over the rounded, nearly flat keel. She smiled at Edouard.

"Maybe so you go Huron. You—how you say?—learn to hide canoe. We go into woods—far back so we make fire that will not be seen. Then soon dry out everything. Rest."

He followed her lead, knowing that she was by far the better woodsman. They found a hidden spot deep in a thick copse of bushes. The sun streamed down unimpeded and Spotted Doe nodded approval. They stretched out to let the sun warm their bodies and evaporate the last vestiges of river water.

For the first time Edouard could forget fast water and rocks, an uncertain craft beneath him, a paddle that fought him more than it helped propel the canoe down the river. Banks, forest, bushes and all had been only a blur, but in this moment of isolated peace he could at last look up. Beyond the trees he saw a high wooded ridge that formed the west side of the river gorge. Again, birch, oak and maple covered the slopes. He heard an unseen bird singing from somewhere deep within the woods beyond the copse.

He touched the grass at his side and then rubbed his hand over good, solid, unmoving ground. Suddenly he saw a movement between two of the distant trees. As he came upright in surprise he saw a small deer look directly at him. His movement startled the animal, which vanished as with the snap of a finger. A squirrel chattered from somewhere nearby and Edouard saw a small branch sway as the animal apparently made a leap from one tree to another.

His sudden movement brought Spotted Doe to her knees in alarm. She grabbed up her hunting knife and sheath that she had dropped to her side and her eyes darted here and there.

"It is nothing," Edouard assured her. "A

deer, a squirrel, that is all.''

"This is Seneca—all this.''

"No Seneca. Just animal. We are alone . . . safe.''

She looked relieved for a moment and then slowly squatted back on her heels. "Maybe alone. But we need eat, eh?''

"What? The Eries left us nothing.''

"They know me Huron and can hunt. They think you courier and there is rifle and shot. So they think we hunters, eh? I fix fire and maybe we catch rabbit.''

"I'll hunt one.''

"No! You shoot, bullet make sound and if Seneca close they come see us. They see we not Seneca and—'' the edge of her palm slashed across her throat and Edouard needed no translation.

"But how do we catch a rabbit, then?''

"I show you how to make trap.'' She drew her knife and held it up. "But first, I make fire.''

He checked her move. "You make the trap and teach me while I make fire.''

"But it is woman's—''

"Next time you make the fire and cook. But now you hunt, eh?''

He arose before she could remonstrate and strode to the edge of the woods. Twigs, small branches and some larger ones, old and dry, lay about. He gathered them up, cautiously looking about for the faintest suspicious movement, his ears strained for sound. But nothing disturbed the silence. He saw Spotted Doe go to the canoe

374

and examine the clothing spread over it. Then she also slowly moved along the edge of the woods.

Edouard brought grass and material to the center of the glade, retrieved his rifle and emptied the barrel of its round shot and patch, poured black powder from the pan onto the grass. He held the weapon over the grass, pulled back the heavy, ornate hammer holding the flint and pulled the trigger.

The spark flamed the powder and it exploded with a small sound that hardly carried beyond the first row of trees. He added twigs to the flaming grass and then larger and larger bits of wood. In very few minutes the fire was ready for any kind of cooking, but . . . ?

"First, catch your rabbit," Edouard chuckled at the old joke.

He joined Spotted Doe, finding her several yards within the trees, squatted cross-legged, knife trimming a thick but springy long stick. She only smiled when he came up, dug a hole and firmly planted the stick. She had brought a strip of deerskin, jaggedly cut from the edge of her skirt, and she tied one end firmly to the tip of the bough, making a noose of the other end. She bent the sapling so that the noose touched the ground and she anchored it with a rock, looked around and then started digging up what seemed to be no more than wild plants to Edouard. But she pulled out what appeared to be some sort of wild radish. She placed one on either side of the bent sapling without removing the dirt.

"Maybe soon we have food, eh?"

She arose, looked about. Edouard saw she had placed the noosed trap on a very, very faint path, almost indiscernible. Satisfied, she turned back to the fire and dropped to the ground. "We wait, no? Nothing else, eh?"

Edouard drifted off to sleep with the ease of a small child, unaware that he slept. A sudden squeal jerked him awake and he sat up, hand reaching for his rifle. Spotted Doe already had come to her feet and her smile flashed. He ran with her to the trap. A rabbit, attracted by the bait, had been caught; it dangled and kicked, the noose tight around its neck. Spotted Doe's small sharp blow ended its kicking and her knife swiftly skinned and cut it up to be spit in small pieces over the fire.

Edouard looked at her in admiration and in self-derision again repeated, "First catch your rabbit."

"Eh?" she said, looking up from her work.

That night they slept close together under the arch of the beached canoe that protected their bare bodies from the wind that, though gentle, blew constantly along the river and grew more and more chill as the night progressed. Spotted Doe pressed closer to him for warmth. They had managed to partially don their shrunken skin clothing but the deerhide held the damp cold of the river water. At last they had discarded them as garments, and simply pulled them up around their shoulders to ward off the sharpest of the night breezes.

Once more, naked body touched naked body and, with one accord, they turned to each other, Spotted Doe met his love-making with her own. At last they slept but only restlessly as the chill grew more and more penetrating and no amount of closeness could make them entirely comfortable. Edouard was glad to see the dawn at long last and later sit under the sun rays and let the cold marrow of his bones become warm once again.

The next day, they continued their journey, but not before Spotted Doe's knife had cut loin cloths of a sort out of the shrunken, fringed garments they had worn in Quebec and across the lake of the Eries.

The river had many twists and turns, the banks always changed appearance—sometimes smooth with grass and wide, again no more than an abrupt rise of steep, harsh rock cliffs. Always trees, Edouard thought. How many hundreds of little French village houses could be built from a single league of the thick lumber he saw all about him!

Spotted Doe turned the canoe to the bank long before sundown but instead of making another noose trap, she plied her knife with skill, cutting small supple switches from the trees. She bent and intertwined them into a funnel shape: one end was wide and open, the other small and tightly closed as she bent the switches and bound them together with a thin swath of deerskin cut from the shrunken skin clothing. She used more skin to attach heavy stones to the contraption.

She had Edouard gather material for a fire that she built in the narrow cove formed by a fissure in the high cliff banks along this stretch of the river. She paddled a short distance out in the stream and dropped her weighted funnel overboard. It sank from sight but a long length of thong kept it attached to the edge of the canoe. Then she settled to patient waiting and Edouard understood she had made a fish trap.

Edouard himself squatted at the edge of the water to wait, amazed at Spotted Doe's ingenuity. He began to understand how the Indians survived in a wilderness environment without musket, pistol or any weapon. A European, including himself, would quickly perish. Her sudden soft exclamation broke his thoughts and he looked up to see her pull in the trap with a swift jerk. Fish flopped within the net of saplings and Spotted Doe's hand tightly closed the wide-open end, preventing their escape.

That night, canoe pulled well up on the small, narrow beach, fire burning far back in the cliff fissure, they ate lean fish, picking bones from their teeth and then, smothering the fire, slept intertwined as they had the night before—but this time desire could not arouse their weary bodies, muscles aching from constant rowing.

They came awake again at the first touch of dawn and pushed the canoe out into the Allegaway's current and its twists, its turns and rocks and rapids. Spotted Doe constantly searched both banks as though fearful of ambush. She answered Edouard's statement that this far south of the Lake of the Eries, they were well beyond danger.

"This Seneca country. Erie arrow kill Seneca and we in Seneca canoe. We not—how you say?—safe before we come to English paleskin post."

"The one they call Fort Prince George," Edouard said and she nodded. "But, still, we are far south, and the post can't be far."

"Not safe until we inside," Spotted Doe insisted, and Edouard saw there was no point in further discussion; besides, a bit of jagged rock protruded above the current several yards ahead.

There seemed to be far more of those jagged perils than there had been yesterday. Once they came on a line of them, that formed a broken, jagged dam across almost the whole stream. Spotted Doe at the prow had to choose a passage between any two of them in a matter of seconds as the white water boiled higher and higher about the boulders, and both she and Edouard had to fight and strain to keep the canoe from being whirled around and slammed broadside against stone that threatened to shatter the bark craft.

They whipped between rocks so close to either side that Edouard's blade scraped against one and Spotted Doe's against the other. Miraculously, though still swift, the current became smooth and they looked down a long stretch of river unbroken by rock or bent by curve. Without a word, Spotted Doe turned to a long stretch of smooth sandy beach on the east bank and a moment later the prow scraped gravel. They both jumped out, pulled the canoe up out of the current's treacherous grip.

Edouard understood the move without a word or sign from Spotted Doe. That last speeding flight through the barrier of rocks had left him breathless and almost unnerved at their narrow escape. He flung the paddles to the beach and swung the canoe above his head, carrying it to concealment under the trees and behind bushes. Spotted Doe swept up the paddles and followed him.

She dropped them beside the canoe when Edouard lowered it and he noticed the slight trembling of her hands. If the Indian girl is that shaken, he thought, we were even closer to disaster out there than I thought.

She held up her hands, spreading her fingers to show how they shook. Her eyes had rounded and her breathing was irregular. "No more canoe today," she said.

"No more," he agreed.

"We rest. Get so not—how you say?—shake, eh? Then maybe trap or fish and make fire. But first—rest, eh?"

"Rest," he nodded.

They moved deeper into the woods and found a thicket that would conceal them a few yards from the canoe. Spotted Doe simply sank to her knees for a moment, head hanging and breasts lifting and falling to her erratic breathing. Then she sat down, stretched out on her back and threw her arm over her eyes.

"Sleep, eh?"

"If we can."

"Spotted Doe can," she assured him.

He dropped down beside her, lying on his stomach, head cushioned on his arms. He could still picture the foam of white water, the deadly jagged boulders, the blur of their passage between them. Now, being able to think a little more clearly, he wondered if Spotted Doe had actually chosen the only safe passage or if sheer chance and the arrow-fast current had blindly taken them through to safety. There had been no time for choice, he finally decided.

He wished they were closer to the English post or to the settlement of any paleskin, but his brain moved sluggishly and he drifted into deep slumber before he could even envision the full implications of safety the thought evoked.

He did not know how long he slept, but from the changed and acute slant of the sun's rays he knew it had been some time. Spotted Doe was still asleep but had turned on her side and he could see only her smooth, naked, bronze-red back. He drowsily noted the muscles just below her skin and, for the first time, realized how great her strength must be.

Now fully awake, he could no longer just lie prone here on the grass. His nerves, though much more calm, still had not fully subsided. He came carefully and silently to his feet, watching Spotted Doe. She did not awaken. He studied the southward flow of the river out beyond the trees and the beach and wondered how much farther they had to travel to the post.

The thought aroused his curiosity and he felt restless so he decided to attempt a small, circumscribed exploration of the immediate area. Perhaps he would come on some sign of white man's presence long before either he or Spotted Doe expected it.

He walked slowly south, keeping the river in sight through a constant, never-ending screen of small bushes and trees. If there was to be trouble from Spotted Doe's dreaded Senecas, it would undoubtedly come from the stream. In this world, he thought, it's the rivers and lakes that are the highways. Mayhap it had been that way centuries ago in Europe, before the Roman legions had set their harsh but civilizing feet on the land north of the Italian boot. Caesar's didactic statement that "All Gaul is divided into three parts" popped into his mind. In how many parts was this immense land divided?

He paralleled a curve of the river and pulled up short. Just ahead, a wide brook flowing out of the east emptied into the Allegaway. He studied it a long moment and then shrugged. No use vaulting that barrier. He also checked his impulse to explore up along it. He'd return to Spotted Doe and as soon as she had recovered, they'd launch the canoe and continued on to the post that could not now be too far south. He wondered how the English garrison would treat him.

He turned back and soon came on the place

where Spotted Doe still slept behind the curved bottom of the canoe. He looked out at the river, empty as far as he could see in either direction. Just then Spotted Doe stirred, awakened and sat up, fully conscious in a second as Edouard learned all Indians could be.

"You leave me, eh?" she asked.

"Just around the next bend. A brook empties into the river there."

She spoke in anger and he felt the disgust in her voice. "You—how you say?—crazy! Seneca everywhere. We stay together, eh? Safe. Now we go back to river." She pointed south and then to the current of the stream. "We go fast now."

He flushed to the rebuke in her voice. She gathered up rifle and powder bag as he grasped the canoe and swung it up over his head. He walked toward the river, his vision limited by the great hood the canoe formed over him but he knew Spotted Doe would be close behind him, alert, searching in every direction for the first sign of danger.

He came to the edge of the stream and placed the birchbark craft on the wet gravel. Spotted Doe handed him the rifle and shot bag, then turned back to the thick bushes where she had hidden the paddles. In a moment she handed him one and, for the first time, read his shamed expression. Her broad face lighted with a smile as she touched his arm.

"I sorry. I forgot you are not a *courieur* or *voyageur,* eh?"

"It's all right. I was a fool. This is not France

or my Gascony. I'll not wander off again."

She looked puzzled and he apologized and explained again in more simple words and with signs. She understood and waded in the shallow water to the bow. She extended her hand for the rifle, which she placed in the bottom of the canoe with the skin bag. Then she swung a shapely leg over the side and stepped into the craft, taking her place on the narrow seat.

Edouard placed his paddle in the boat and then began shoving the craft out to where the water would be deep enough to float it. He felt the sudden bouyancy of the canoe and his muscles bunched for his quick jump and swing. Something whipped by his head and he saw a long, straight shaft bury itself in Spotted Doe's back between the shoulder blades. He had a confused glimpse of feathers as she cried out, came half erect and then fell over the side into the water, face down.

Edouard whipped around, glimpsed Indian warriors emerging from the bushes. One of them lowered a bow while a second leveled a rifle. Edouard saw the black muzzle pointing directly at him. He glimpsed a fierce, red-bronze face, a hawk nose and a bald head except for a single line of stiff high black hair. Then fire and flame spat at him from the rifle muzzle. A giant iron fist struck him in the chest, spun him half around, and he felt himself falling, unable to prevent it.

As the sand and water rushed up to meet him, the blackest of black night snapped over his brain.

XXVIII

He next looked up into a strange woman's face and could do no more than stare. He knew he lay flat on his back on something soft and dry—not the water that had rushed up to meet his fall. Then he felt a searing, stabbing pain in his right shoulder. Gasping with the overwhelming spread of it through his body, blackness snapped down again.

Gradually he sensed light coming from somewhere. Then dully he knew it was not light but for some magical reason his consciousness had wrapped him in it. He felt an iron stake drive into his chest and shoulder and something grip his throat. He heard, as at a long distance, a strange sound that repeated over and over again and with each repetition the agonizing pain shot through him. Nothing existed but the grip about his throat, the repetitive sound and waves of pain.

He felt that he struggled forward through the layers of pain but that, somehow, he gained a very, very small bit with each fighting breath. Somewhere beyond the pain was a different kind of world, somehow familiar, somehow a world to which he had to return. All sensation left him once more.

When he opened his eyes the third time, he still gasped with each move of his chest but now he could see after a fashion. And he could hear sounds at a great, great distance. A man said something somewhere but the meaning escaped him. Then he saw the woman's face just above him. He had seen her before. Who was she?

For a second his brain became clear and acute. A man said, "He just might live, Mistress."

"Pray God he does!"

It puzzled him that they did not speak in French and yet he understood them. He had been just a child when he last heard that language. His old tutor's face came bright and clear in his mind. But he could not be back in Bearn and reciting lessons again! The tutor had died many, many years ago. In an impersonal way, he thought that he, too, was dead. But that heavy male voice sounded too real.

"Maybe we saved one of those Frenchies who drove us out of Fort Prince George."

"It doesn't matter," the woman's voice answered. "If you hadn't come when you did—"

"Mistress, you'd already killed one of those red devils when I—"

His senses left him.

When next he became aware of a world other than his own pain-wracked body, he saw a wavering, flickering light-point and darkness that threatened to swallow it up. But vague things moved in the blackness and then something smooth and soft touched his forehead, moved down his cheek. The touch was cool, healing and he needed to feel more of it.

"Doctor! He moved his head just now!"

That woman's voice again. Suddenly, a bright, painful light exploded before his eyes and he closed them tightly. His body felt light and unreal but the pain had somehow become less a deep, penetrating, all-pervasive thing. It ground into his shoulder and he heard a moan—his own. The pain did not go away and he moved his head from side to side to avoid it. Then he felt a cold soothing on his forehead, a jerk and a touch on his shoulder that made him scream.

Everything vanished.

So Edouard gradually returned to life, fighting for every moment, fully aware one instant, completely insensible the next. He heard babblings at times. He felt at times that his head and shoulders had been tightly wrapped in unbearably hot blankets. No . . . it was a strange heat that came from somewhere deep inside himself. Then he felt that water streamed over his face. But it was hot and warm, an unhealthy moisture that he had to swim up through. He had brief seconds of clear sight and thoughts, but only seconds. Sometimes he opened his eyes on Stygian darkness except for that flickering, wavering yellow light. Again he looked on sunlight, a rectangle of it at a distance. He could not quite understand and his brain exhausted itself with the effort.

Something snapped open his eyes. The strange woman again bent over him. But she was no illusion. He had come to a stable world again. He knew it. He had left nightmare and death behind him. That was enough to know for the moment. He felt pain but it would pass. He slipped into sleep with a feeling of thankfulness.

When he awakened, it was late afternoon, judging from the soft golden color and slant of the sun's rays through a distant window. He lay in a bunk, one of several built in tiers, and a blanket over him made him feel snug and warm. The bunks were, for the most part, empty. He heard muted commands from somewhere outside the building, and then came a soft, steady thump that grew louder, resolved itself into the march of many feet. Commands grew louder as the steps approached, thudded in a steady rhythm and then slowly lessened as the group marched on. Edouard, from past experience, knew that the building stood on the edge of a drill or parade ground of some sort.

He tried to sit up but could only half roll to an elbow. He heard a step close by and the woman of the half-dreams and nightmares appeared. Her dark face lit up when she saw him and he realized that sun had burned her skin to that Indian tone. Her nose was high-bridged but straight and finely-formed, and her hair was a dark auburn red. She was tall and her coarse gray linsy-woolsy dress could not conceal an excellent figure. Slender hands lifted in surprise and clasped, long fingers interlacing. Her voice sounded like low-pitched music to him.

"You've thrown off the fever!"

English! So that had brought on the fantasy of his long dead tutor and the classes in the ramshackle, sprawling house his father had called a "chateau." But he could no longer support himself and he dropped back down on the bunk.

She made an exclamation of concern and fright and called over her shoulder as she rushed to him. "Doctor! Doctor! He has awakened! He'll live!"

She now had come to the side of the bunk. She held his shoulders and he winced with the sudden pain that cut through his arms and chest like a sword. She gently lowered him.

"Don't move if you can help it. The doctor will be here in a minute. We've fought so hard to keep you alive that you can't rip the bandages and start bleeding again. Lie down. Please! Lie still."

He lay looking at her with stupefied surprise. His tongue passed over dry lips and he managed to say, "Who are you? I've seen you before. Where am I?"

He had groped for some of the English words and even in his uncertain state he knew that some of them had come out wrong. But the woman did not seem to mind. She looked at him, high-planed face aglow, and her smile seemed to him like a heavenly beacon.

Then a heavyset man with a leathery skin the color of an old lemon pushed her aside. "Let me look at him, Mistress Abby. Let me see that wound. Pray God he hasn't done harm with twisting about and sitting up!"

She dropped back out of Edouard's sight and the old man, with wrinkled face and gray hair, touched his shoulder. Edouard choked back a half-smothered cry of pain. Dark old eyes grew gentle though they still narrowly and sharply studied Edouard. He spoke with a strange burr to his voice.

"This will hurt some, but I have to see that wound. You have been close to dying, lad."

He worked slowly and as tenderly as he could to unwrap the heavy wad of bandages on Edouard's shoulder. But each light touch of finger, every faint loosening of bandage made

Edouard gasp and bite his lip. The old doctor stopped once to wipe the cold sweat from Edouard's face and neck.

"You've been a soldier, lad, it's plain to see. Hold steady now if ye can and we'll have a look at the hole the musket ball left."

"Musket?" Edouard gasped.

"Aye, Indian. Seneca, I think. Had it not been for Mistress Brewster, ye'd have died face down in the river water just as the Indian woman did."

He gasped with pain but in his mind he suddenly saw Spotted Doe spilling loosely over the side of the canoe, the long arrow buried deep in her back. He felt new moisture on his lips and chin as the old doctor finally pulled off the last turn of blood-encrusted bandage, soiled and dirty now, stained with the yellow pus that had seeped from the wound. Edouard heard a scream that he finally placed as the horrified gasps of the girl. But the old doctor now touched the swollen wound itself and looked pleased.

"We knifed out the musket ball, lad. There's red inflame all over your shoulder but that will pass with luck." He looked beyond Edouard at someone out of sight. "Lass, can ye bring landanum from the medicine chest and bring new, clean cloth? Sleep and fresh dressing will help the lad."

Edouard gritted his teeth, trying to hold to his senses for just a moment or two longer. He forgot his English when he asked, "Where am I?"

"Ah, French be ye? From the new defenses they make of our Fort Prince George?"

"French. Not from Fort. From—"

It was the next day before he could complete the sentence and then to the girl rather than the old doctor. The moment he opened his eyes, she removed a cloth from his forehead and replaced it with a cold compress. She ordered him to lie quietly while she left him for a moment. "I'll be back in a few minutes. You're in need of food."

He could only weakly nod in gratitude. She returned with bowl of steaming, golden liquid and a spoon and soon ladled warm chicken broth into his mouth. The taste, the warmth spread through his body and he eagerly accepted each spoonful she extended. Finally she placed the empty bowl on the floor, pulled a blanket up about his shoulders but not before she critically examined the new bandages around his shoulder. The wound burned and stabbed like a thousand knives but some of the inward heat had left his shoulder.

The girl sank back on the stool beside the bunk and curiously eyed him. "You *are* French?"

He found the old, nearly forgotten words that his tutor had so laboriously drilled into him long ago. "I am. Gascon. Sieur Edouard de Fournet. You're English?"

"I suppose I could be called that. Connecticut Colony near the New York Colony boundary line. I am Abigail Brewster. I was captured in a raid by Onondaga Iroquois and taken to their main town. I lived there some time. They called me Strong Woman.''

"Where is Connecticut? What is it?"

She explained then asked, "Who was the Indian girl? She was beautiful."

"She's dead," Edouard's statement was also a hopeless half-question.

Abigail nodded. "We saw the Senecas kill her and shoot you. We were able to save you but she was undoubtedly dead by the time she struck the water."

"We?" he asked.

"I wanted to exercise after all the time I've spent in the fort. I was with three Virginia Colony militia officers."

"Then this is Fort Prince George? Spotted Doe—the Indian girl—and I were trying to reach it."

"You, a Frenchman, trying to reach your own people? Oh, no! You *have* to be a soldier at Fort Duquesne!"

"I don't understand, Mademoiselle. I am a fugitive—a *lettre de cachet* bears my name and I fled Quebec and Spotted Doe came with me. She took us around Montreal and then—"

He swayed and she caught him before he tumbled from the bunk. "You've talked too much. You're too excited." She turned her head and called over her shoulder, "Doctor! Hurry! Please!"

He heard nothing more as his senses swirled away from him, and girl, bunk, room and all spun around faster and faster and then snapped into blackness.

He awakened to bright morning light and intermittent but terrible pain in his shoulder and chest. The wrinkled doctor sat by the bunk and bent over him, once more working on the bandages, each little tug a knife slash. Edouard cried out and then bit his lip but the doctor's head sharply lifted.

"You've come around again! Damme! But I think I'll manage to keep you alive. Colonel Washington will want to talk to you."

"The girl?" Edouard gasped as he shook his head. "The girl who was here before?"

"Abigail?" The old man pursed his lips. "Yes, Abigail and her hot soup will do you more good than the colonel right now. His questions can wait. I'll get her."

But first the wrinkled old fiend had to further torture him as he changed the pile of bandages. He made a soft whistle of approval when he saw the wound and then bound it up again with clean strips of cloth. Then he called the girl and she came quickly. Cold sweat beaded Edouard's forehead as waves of pain rippled through his chest but the soup was hot and soothing, the girl's smile and soft words encouraging. Before long he could, with effort, rise above the constant grinding pain. But even so, neither the auburn-haired girl nor the doctor would allow talk and the old man must have mixed a sleeping potion in the hot soup. Edouard's consciousness alternated between dull awareness and sheer nothingness time and again.

However, the next day proved to be different.

From the instant he opened his eyes he felt more alert even though the slightest movement sent a hot poker driving from his shoulder deep into his chest, making him gasp for long moments of time. Abigail appeared with the doctor and then—Edouard never knew what time of the day—a tall young man with steady level eyes, a high-ridged boned nose and a square jaw that looked to be carved of granite, replaced the doctor on the stool.

"I am Colonel George Washington of Virginia Colony, Sieur de Fournet. Since your country and ours are at war, you can understand the need for questions."

Even in pain, Edouard knew that this tall British colonial officer's steady eyes would instantly detect deception. He shrugged. "Colonel, I am an outlaw from my country. That is why I fled Quebec and sought this Fort Prince George."

"Outlaw?" the deep calm voice asked. "Whose purse did you rob? Whose throat did you slit?"

"Neither one nor the other, Colonel. I became too enamoured with the doxie of the Duc de la Verre. A *lettre de cachet* sent me flying to the nearest seaport and across the ocean to New France. I thought I would be safe enough with the governor's license to seek peltry but a new governor came and then unfortunately that *lettre* frightened me when I learned the Marquis de Montcalm came with a war fleet and army directly from France."

Edouard could not quite be certain if Washington's firm lips did not slightly soften though he could not detect laughter in the calm firm voice. "New France is many leagues away, Sieur de Fournet, and you were hardly dressed as a man of title. I have heard that a *lettre de cachet* and an ardent attention to the wrong woman can lead to trouble in your country." Edouard almost heard a soft chuckle as Washington continued. "Ardent attention can also lead to trouble here, though English and colonial laws differ. But that is hardly explanation enough in times of a war that rages from these forests to far-off India, you'll agree."

Edouard then told the story from the chateau of the Duc de la Verre, to the *Demoiselle*, Quebec and the Snow Fox where he met Spotted Doe. The colonial officer listened without impatience, only asking an occasional sharp question. He showed surprise at the journey across Lake Erie with the dry comment, "You were lucky on a treacherous lake, Sieur de Fournet. Storms blow up without warning."

"The Erie Indians seemed to know it would be safe," Edouard explained. He answered questions about acquiring the Seneca canoe and Colonel Washington's suspicions seemed to lessen.

"You say the Erie killed the Seneca and gave you and your Indian girl the canoe? What did they do with the body?"

"Just threw it overboard, Colonel. Spotted Doe and I did not object too much, you understand."

"I do—and it explains their attack. The dead body finally surfaced, the tribal canoe did not reappear. They must have trailed you, wanting your scalps for their dead tribesman. Two advance scouts caught up with you."

"And Mistress Abigail and her escorts appeared at the right time. It must be true what is said about the luck of all Gasconards. Here I am safe at Fort Prince George—"

"And there you are wrong, Sieur de Fournet. Your countrymen captured Fort Prince George, rebuilt and renamed it Fort Duquesne. They defeated a British army and its commander, General Braddock. I commanded the Virginia militia that accompanied the Regulars. I stopped the retreat and brought my militia and some of the Regulars here. This is Fort Necessity, as I call it."

Edouard stared, read the truth in the grim, carven face, then shook his head. "How could Hurons and their Indian allies and regular French troops defeat you?"

"Wilderness warfare, Sir. Despite all I could say or plead, Lord Braddock maneuvered his men as though they were on parade or a European battlefield. In fact, some of his officers made my men leave the protection of trees. 'Stand up like soldiers and fight,' they ordered." Washington sighed. "Thank God, few of them obeyed and they lived. The Regulars stood shoulder to shoulder in plain sight and the whole thing was more a massacre than a battle. General Braddock was killed, many captured and taken to Fort Duquesne. Mistress Abigail told me what has undoubtedly happened to them, for she knows Indian ways for handling prisoners."

Colonel Washington gave Edouard news of the activities of the Marquis de Montcalm in this western country, who was building posts at key spots and preparing to drive the British behind the mountains, as the Colonel put it. Edouard listened with but half an ear, biting back stabs of pain as he tried to assess his own position.

When Washington paused, Edouard said, "Colonel, I have no part in this quarrel between monarchs. It happens part of it is here about us but of what matter is that to me?"

Washington looked searchingly at him and Edouard hurried on. "If His Majesty, Louis of France wins. I will still be fugitive. The Royal law and arm is long. It almost touched me in Quebec and we had to avoid Montreal. But if your King George wins, I am enemy, eh? Prisoner, eh? Will I be returned to New France?"

Colonel Washington tugged at his ear lobe and frowned. "You could be a spy with a very clever story."

"Spy?" Edouard started to laugh but it changed into a near scream of pain. He regained his breath. "What do I know about this country or anybody in it? Make me your prisoner, Colonel! I will be grateful and feel safe from the royal guillotine."

Colonel Washington arose, paced to the far

window and looked out, fingers beating a light march on the sill. Then he turned.

"At the moment, I'll do naught, *mon Sieur*. I'll give Doctor Gregor time to heal you if he can and Mistress Abigail time to feed you, which I hear she does very well. Once you can leave that bunk, we will decide what to do with you."

"You have my thanks, Colonel."

"I'll also send you clothing that you can don when you're able. I heard you resembled Adam a great deal when you were found on the river Allegaway."

"I did, Sir, and thank you."

"The clothing will be more coarse than your taste would like, sir. The shirt, stockings and the rest are American colonial—Virginian, specifically—but you will be able to do with it."

"You have my gratitude, Sir."

"I want one more thing, Sieur de Fournet. I doubt if you could get far in this land and in these woods and waterways, but you might try. It would save me and some of my soldiers a great deal of trouble if I have your parole to remain in Fort Necessity until we can further discuss the matter."

"You have my word, Colonel. I will not step foot beyond the fort stockade."

"I accept." Washington fully turned then, strode back to the bunk and, extending a long uniformed arm, took a tricorn hat from the bunk above Edouards's. "I have much to do, Sir. If you will excuse me now that we have come to at least a temporary solution of your problem."

Washington had his hand on the door catch when Edouard suddenly blurted, "Colonel! May I ask another favor?"

"Another?" Washington's stern face softened and Edouard looked on a different person, one not of military aloofness but one who gave Edouard a sense of human understanding beneath the formal mien. "For a prisoner, you ask a deal, Sieur de Fournet."

"I know. But this—" Edouard broke off and blurted, "Is it possible that Mistress Brewster could attend me now and then when Doctor—Gregor, is it?—is busied?"

Those direct eyes bored deep into Edouard and then that amazing change came again, even a smile. "Mistress Brewster? Of course, and allow me to compliment your taste, sir."

XXIX

The shoulder wound made progress and healed rapidly for a time, so much so that Dr. Gregor began to talk of seeing Edouard up and around in a matter of two or three weeks. Abigail Brewster reappeared, not only with her soup but now more and more often she brought plates of food on a great platter, so heavy that a soldier carried it for her.

Finally, Edouard could sit up and move his torso very, very slowly. But something deep within the wound would not respond to treatment, no matter what Dr. Gregor tried. It puzzled the old man and he was not at all reluctant to discuss his uncertainty. He bled Edouard several times, an unpleasant process in itself, made more so when he would take a shotglass of blood to the window and hold it up in the sunlight.

"It does not look poisoned. It holds no pus. But there is often something deep in the body that, when the air touches it, causes trouble. I've often thought it's evil little lives but my fellow doctors have laughed at me for that."

"It may be the evil little life of the patient," Edouard suggested. "I've commited enough sins myself."

The old man sighed. "Someday maybe we doctors will be smart enough to find out."

The days slowly passed but the healing seemed to progress only at a snail's pace. Abigail Brewster came each day to visit Edouard and the formality between them became less and less a barrier. She told him of her life in Connecticut and her childhood in the frontier settlements before she came to Westover. It fascinated Edouard, just as his life in France intrigued her.

Each had reticences. Edouard did not mention the many dalliances he had in the villages of Gascony before he was sent to the royal military instructors in Paris. He managed to gloss over the old duke's anger that had brought on the *lettre de cachet*. Spotted Doe, though completely naked when she was killed, was more easily accepted by Abigail than the mistress of the Duc de la Verre. After all, Abigail had lived among the red savages of these forests and knew many of their ways. A Huron surely could not differ greatly from an Onondaga.

But she, in turn, said as little as possible about Corn Dancer. She gave the impression he was just one of the many warriors and minor leaders among the Iroquois, though there were times Edouard wondered if he might really have been more. Then he'd dismiss the thought. Abigail spoke and acted too much the pioneer daughter raised on the precepts and under the strict control of parents and the harsh strictures of the parsons and circuit-riding exhorters of the English colonial frontier.

Now and then Colonel Washington paid a visit to his unexpected prisoner. Like Abigail, he grew less and less formal, although his innate dignity always remained. He seemed to enjoy talking to someone more travelled than the men and most of the officers of Fort Necessity. From the Colonel, Edouard learned of the Virginia colony, the estate-like farms that sprawled along riverbanks accessible to merchant vessels which brought English and European products to exchange for tobacco and the other products of the colonies. Both Washington and Edouard had read many of the same books, though of course in different languages. Edouard had not only travelled over France but had also visited England, Spain and many of the small Italian and German principalities, city-states and palatinates.

In time Edouard could slowly though painfully dress and walk about his room with the support of a young orderly the colonel placed at his disposal. Quite often Abigail would watch his uncertain progress as she sat straight and lovely in a chair against the wall. She would encourage him by her enthusiasm.

The orderly, a young soldier from Pennsylvania colony, told Edouard about the Quakers abounding in his colony and Edouard had the opinion they were a strange, queer lot. But the young man disagreed.

"Not all, Sir. Have you heard of Benjamin Franklin, for instance? He came to us from Massachusetts and now is one of the most important men in Philadelphia. In all the colonies, for that matter. He proposes an alliance among us for protection from the French and the Indians, and for trade and exchange of knowledge of farming and other such things. We are very proud of him, Sir."

"You have every right to be, from all you say about him."

"Indeed, Sir. He publishes a weekly journal of news and also an almanac that he calls 'Poor Richard's.' You should read him, Sir. I could bring you a copy of his almanac, if you care."

"I do—and you have my thanks."

But it was Abigail who brought the tattered little booklet that had obviously been read time and again by many people. He found the aphorisms pithy and to the point, though he did not particularly care for the constant note of frugality and penny-pinching that ran through them. Abigail took exception, however.

"This is not your France with all its elegance. We are a poor collection of colonies and an ocean separates us from the palaces and cities and finery you're used to."

Edouard chuckled. "That ocean is no wider than the one that separates my purse from *louis d'or*."

"What are they?"

He explained the coins and she in turned explained pence, farthings and crowns as well as Pine Tree shillings and the dizzying variety of paper money issued by the various colonies.

So time passed and at last Dr. Gregor brought partial freedom early one morning. He finished his examination, thoughtfully stroked his chin as he considered Edouard. "Colonel Washington tells me you have been given parole."

"I have, Doctor."

"Then, there's no reason to restrict you to four walls when you need exercise, sunshine and air. Have your Pennsylvania Dutch boy help you walk about the post compound tomorrow."

"Do you mean I'm that much improved?"

"That much, but hardly more. Understand, you are not to tire yourself." Dr. Gregor smiled. "I'll inform Mistress Brewster. I'm sure she'll be pleased."

"Does she have the freedom of the post?"

"Of course. In fact, if we weren't so deep in Iroquois country and the French weren't so near, she could return to her Connecticut country." The Doctor's face saddened. "Though she says she has no family back there anymore."

"She's all alone in the world?"

"That she is, except for those of us she's met since escaping the Onondaga. So you see, she needs protectors and from simple private to the Colonel himself, that's what we all try to be for her."

"And you can count on me—that is, if she'll accept a Frenchman now that our countries war."

"I doubt if that means much to her these days. In fact, you make us all forget you're French except for the sometimes strange way you shape your words and sentences. Abigail—Mistress Brewster—has often mentioned that herself."

He waited impatiently for his orderly to appear the next morning and gulped down his breakfast only because the doctor made a point of being present and forcing him to eat. But at last, holding tightly to his orderly's shoulder, he stepped out the door onto soft, springy earth. Even though he wore heavy-soled buckled shoes made here at the post, he felt the wonderful resilience of grass rather than the unyielding feel of thick wooden floors.

He took a deep breath, winced at the sudden

stab in his shoulder and the orderly saw it. "Be ye all right, Sir?"

"It is good to be outside again, Jan. We'll walk slowly, *non?* I will be strong enough for it."

But he found that he could not stride out as easily and as well as he had thought. He became grateful for Jan's supporting hand or dependable shoulder a dozen times in this first, short journey. He looked out over the barren parade and drill ground surrounded by a high log stockade that was broken by a closed wide gate on the east. Blockhouses towered at the corners and he knew they must give an unobstructed view of whatever kind of terrain lay out of his sight beyond them. They also provided points of enfilading fire through small rifle holes along the walls. That would be deadly for any foe attempting to scale them from the outside. A high peeled pole in the middle of the parade ground bore the British flag, now almost wholly limp in the faint breeze that occasionally touched Edouard's cheek. Along each stockade wall, lean-tos of logs had been built, some of which looked like barracks for the soldiers. Others appeared to be storehouses and one was obviously a small stable.

Looking back, Edouard realized he had been living in a small lean-to, one of a row that must be officers' quarters. A few men in the rough clothing of colonial militia mingled with a few others in the red uniforms of the British army. Jan explained the regular soldiers were men of

Braddock's defeated army who had later straggled out of the woods, lucky beyond luck to
have escaped capture by either the French or
their Indian allies.

A young militia officer came out of a cabin,
saw Edouard and hurried over. He forgot the
military formality of a salute and he looked uncomfortable in his blue uniform of coarse
weave.

"You'd be the Frenchie? I'm Lieutenant
Butler, at your service, Sir. I hear you're not to
go near the gate."

Edouard bristled slightly and then realized
this lad hardly knew how a soldier, let alone an
officer, should be addressed. So Edouard faintly
smiled. "I'll not go near the gate, Sir, since I
gave Colonel Washington my parole and he accepted it."

Butler flushed then, sensing he had blundered
in some way. Then he brightened and indicated
his cabin. "I'd be pleasured if you'd visit me,
Sir. I have good, smooth whiskey."

"What is that?"

Butler stared a second and then laughed.
"Come, find out, Sir. Even some of our lobsterbacks didn't know what whiskey was until we
gave them a drink. We make it from the Indian
corn we grow."

"A liqueur?"

"Likker, yes. Sour mashed and jugged its
easier to handle than loading up carts and
wagons with the grain."

So Edouard had his introduction to a purely

colonial drink, a brew as hot and as heady as anything he had ever tasted. He didn't like it but did not tell Butler so and made excuses as soon as politeness would permit. The lieutenant insisted on returning with him, despite Edouard's protests, and pressed a jug of the raw liquor on him as a gift. Instead of a cork, it bore a frazzled corn cob that looked as bad as the contents to Edouard.

Jan carried the thing as Edouard started the return journey to his own cabin. But the visit had not been entirely wasted. Edouard learned that "lobsterback" was a colonial term for the English regular soldiers and referred to their red uniforms. He learned that Colonel Washington had ridden out yesterday to meet a General Forbes and a Colonel Bouquet, who led fresh troops to retake Fort Duquesne, and that Mistress Brewster resided in the last cabin to the left on officers' row.

He looked over that way as he progressed along the parade ground but the door was closed and a heavy drape covered its window. He shrugged off his disappointment at not seeing the girl but Jan answered his casual question.

"She goes walking beyond the fort with a guard every day, Sir. I understand that's how she saved you from those Indians."

True enough, Edouard thought, and thankfully enough. He entered his cabin and dropped onto a chair, more tired than he had realized and with his shoulder aching abominably. When Jan asked about the whiskey, Edouard wished the stuff could be poured out but Butler might be angered if he discovered his gift so little appreciated. So he ordered the jug pushed out of sight under his bunk.

He stretched himself out, glad to ease his shoulder and chest. From his bunk, he could look out the now opened door onto the parade ground and he wondered if he could see Abigail return.

Suddenly he realized with surprise the intensity of his feelings about her. He was grateful for her presence when the Senecas had attacked, killed Spotted Doe and put a musket ball in his own shoulder. He thought of the way she had come time and again to help Dr. Gregor, to spoon hot soup down him when he hardly cared if he lived or died, conscious only of the searing pain.

He had vivid memories of the sunlight's reflection in her auburn hair and he could see her slim figure moving gracefully from the bunk to the window or to the door when she threw a shawl about her shoulders and departed. He could hear her voice.

But he had seen many another graceful figure and many another girl's face with high-planed cheeks and soft eyes that held pity and care. He had seen girls wearing jewels and in dresses made especially for balls in châteaus or ducal courts. Why did Abigail Brewster, fugitive from Indian raids and Indian life, so attract him?

He sighed, not finding an answer and started

to turn on his side. Then, there she was—at the door, smiling at him.

"Can I come in?"

"Of course!" He started up but had to grab his shoulder and choke back the painful sound at his lips.

She was at his side instantly, hands supporting his as she gently eased him back. He gasped for relief from the pain, trying for breath to speak. She looked accusingly at him.

"You try too much too soon."

"I forget," he gritted through clenched teeth. "Where's Jan?"

"Here Mistress Brewster. I had just gone out to see the Colonel and all those officers ride in."

Abigail whirled about to face him and spoke, her voice stern. "You should not leave Mr. Fournet in his condition—not until Dr. Gregor gives you permission."

"It's all right," Edouard found his voice at last. "It was just a passing spasm."

"It's *not* all right!"

"I'm sorry, Mistress," Jan started but Edouard cut him short.

"She's here now, Jan. Maybe she can stay a bit, eh?" He looked at her.

She hesitated, then surrendered. "All right, for a bit."

"Then find what you can about the Colonel and the new officers, Jan. I'm in good hands." The young man hesitated and Edouard snapped, "Bring me news, if any. Do you mind, Mistress Brewster?"

411

"Well . . . I had come to inquire of you anyhow."

"Then, please stay. Before you go, Jan, a pillow to my back? One at least sits up to speak to a lovely visitor, *non?*"

Jan carefully lifted him and placed the pillow. Though Edouard winced, he saw the pleased flush on the girl's face. Pulling up a stool to the bunk, Abby sat down when Jan had at last left. She tried to give him a very severe frown but did not quite succeed. Instead she made a mock little gesture of petulance.

"I don't know what's to be done with you, Sir."

"Easy answered, Mistress. Talk to me and permit me to look at you."

"Now that is bold, Sir!"

"But not offensive?" When she didn't answer, he gained courage. "I walked the parade ground and saw the cabin where you live. It's not far."

"You were outside!"

He told her of his small expedition and of his visit with the young officer, of the jug he had perforce to carry home. He made a face. "This whiskey—it's a hot and hard thing to swallow. I don't like it, but Lieutenant Butler seems to."

"He's American and probably much used to it. But I am glad you are not a drinking man, Sir."

"Not of your whiskey that I never encountered before today. But the wines of France are more to my taste."

"Oh?" Her eyes shadowed. "I did not know you imbibed."

"A good, fine wine is not imbibed, Mistress. It is sipped delicately so one enjoys the flavor of the grape and the sun that is in the liquor."

"I would not know. Only the wealthy have wine in the colonies."

"A pity! But should both of us escape this wilderness to one of your colonial cities, I could . . ."

"The parsons preach against it, Sir."

"Again, a pity. But let us say we talk of an uncertain future day and time. Right now, was your stroll along the river enjoyable? Did you rescue any more Frenchmen under Indian attack? I hope I'll always be the only one."

"Once again, you are too bold. If I rescued you by sheer chance of happening along at the right time, that is enough, isn't it?"

He started an ardent reply but checked it. This was not France or any part of Europe and there was a most inexplicable stiffness to these girls of the American colonies. He sensed she was pleased but she was also close to feeling offense. What did one say! He mentally shrugged. Only the impersonal things, apparently. But, then, how did it happen that men and women married, seemingly having fallen in love before the ritualistic words were spoken that made them man and wife? How long a time did it take to break down the barriers that he constantly felt with Mistress Brewster?

"My apologies, Mistress. I simply wished to

express my gratitude again!"

"I did not understand. I have offended you."
She looked so contrite that Edouard wished time
and circumstance would permit him to swing out
of the bunk and gather her into his arms. He
mentally berated himself. Gascon . . . hot
blood . . . how often had it put him in trouble
before he had so much as dreamed of crossing
an ocean!

"Not at all, Mistress." His words sounded
strained and false, even to himself. "It is only
that you do not understand the French and I do
not understand the English—especially here in
America."

When she smiled he said, "My stroll was
uneventful, as it almost always is, but you are
wise to go with a guard. There are always Indians about and . . . do they look for you?"

"The Onondaga might, but they are a far
distance from here. The Seneca are Iroquois,
part of the Six Nations, but I doubt if they know
me or even seek me."

"Then you are safe?"

She had a sudden vivid picture of Corn
Dancer and answered slowly. "I think so—as
long as I remain in this country of the Allegaway
and the Ohio. The Seneca are Keepers of the
Western Gate. They would have no interest in
me."

XXX

The officers who had so excited Jan arrived at
the Fort and a short time later their troops
marched in to the sound of fife, drum and
bagpipe, British flags aflutter along with
regimental and colonial colors. For the most
part they encamped outside the stockade since

the small fort could not accommodate them all, but their presence destroyed the even, monotonous flow of the days. The new arrivals mingled in off-duty hours with the regular troops of the post and there was a constant coming and going, a constant babble of voices in all accents, some of which Edouard had never heard before.

Jan became round-eyed with excitement and each day he had a dozen or more stories of men he had met from Scotland, the Carolinas, New York, and even Maine and Georgia. Abby no longer came to visit amidst all the hubbub, except for brief moments with Dr. Gregor when he called.

"There is too much male ogling," she answered Edouard's complaint, "and sometimes these strangers do not care how they speak. The regulars are the worst of the lot. They treat all colonials with contempt, even a lady."

"Have you said aught to Colonel Washington?"

"I prefer to handle my own problems, thank you, Sir."

"Do they lay hand on you?"

"They dare not!" she blazed.

"She's right, Sir." Jan put in. "No Fort Necessity man would allow for that."

The day after the arrival of the officers and troops, Edouard managed to dress with Jan's help and, with the boy's shoulder and hands as support, he left the cabin. By then, some of the furor had subsided and he could hear the bark of commands beyond the stockade as sergeants put their men through drills that seemed to last from morning to night. The crowd within the stockade grew miraculously smaller as order was brought out of chaos.

But there had been noticeable changes in officers' row. Now a General Forbes occupied Colonel Washington's former quarters and Edouard himself was moved to a smaller cabin across the parade ground to make place for one Colonel Bouquet, a surprising name for an English army officer. Edouard surmised that Bouquet's family may have fled from France a century before when the Edict of Nantes drove the last of the Protestant Huguenots out of Catholic France.

Colonel Washington could not confirm the guess when he finally took time from feverish activity to pay a call, but he had news of importance. He saved Edouard chagrin by taking no pleasure in the telling of it. The French had tried to invade the northern part of New York Colony but had been driven back into New France. An English general, Wolfe, had arrived with an army fresh from Europe's battles and had boldly sailed up the St. Lawrence.

"He'll get no farther than Quebec, Colonel."

"On the contrary, General Wolfe captured Quebec though he lost his life doing it."

Edouard gasped then recovered his voice. "But that is a high rock, Colonel, bristling with fortifications. You English must have lost thousands fighting up that slope almost foot by foot. Besides, the Marquis de Montcalm had a new army from France. It arrived just as I left.''

''Your General Montcalm and the Governor of New France should have questioned the washerwomen, Sieur de Fournet.''

''I don't understand.''

''For many years the army laundresses have been using a narrow passage from the fort to the river. I heard it was hidden by trees and rocks and hardly anyone but the washerwomen know of it. However, scouts for our General Wolfe discovered it and one morning your Montcalm awakened to find our regiments on the Plains of Abraham lined up for battle. Quebec fell into our hands but, as I said, we lost our general. Your Montcalm was also killed. Montreal is in our hands and I hear soon Fort De Troit will surrender.''

''But . . . but . . .''

Colonel Washington shrugged. ''I think France has only a very weak hold on Fort Duquesne, Fort Vincennes and some posts along the Mississippi, including Fort St. Louis. General Forbes plans to capture Fort Duquesne as they now call it, and the whole of the Ohio is open to us when the smaller posts are taken. The war draws to a sudden close, here in America at least.''

Edouard stared glumly out the door at the parade ground. He looked up when Colonel Washington gently placed a hand on his shoulder. "Fortunes of war, Sieur de Fournet, or mayhap Destiny. Perhaps you are fortunate to be here with an Indian wound in your shoulder rather than an English musket ball in your heart. I know how you must feel and I am sorry I am the one to bring you the news."

Edouard managed a rather sickly smile. "Colonel, you did not do this to my country and king."

"No—but I plan to continue to harass him."

"As any officer and gentleman would harass a wartime enemy, Colonel. I bear no ill will."

"Thank you, Sir. But I have brought you more than enough bad news. Would Mistress Brewster's presence be of cheer to you?"

"It would, Colonel, but even she is not certain how to consider me. I'm French and therefore enemy in her mind. I also speak much too 'forwardly,' she calls it."

The tall man's square jaw and thin lips broke into that surprising sunny smile he used so seldom. "I think our wars and nationalities would mean little if they ended."

Edouard grunted his disbelief. "Mayhap. But, even so, when would that be?"

"How can you suggest defeat and also promise hope in a single sentence?"

"Do I?" Washington's brow lifted in a high, quizzical arch. "Perhaps I am more of the Virginia gentleman than anyone suspected, even myself."

"The tides of war rise high and also fall, Colonel. But, whichever side wins, what will happen to the prisoners of either side? Those on this side of the ocean will be far from home."

"Such matters are always considered in the peace treaties. We—" He caught himself up at Edouard's sour expression. "All, I imagine would have transport across the Atlantic if it is so desired. Or to New France, which we call Canada—or to their homes here in the American colonies. It would be arranged."

"And I?"

Washington spoke slowly and carefully. "You were rescued from marauding Indians, sir, not captured on the battlefield. Was your regiment among those the Marquis Montcalm brought with him?"

"I had not been mustered in, Colonel. I don't know."

"I doubt if Fort Necessity is on any European map either British or French. Except for that punctured shoulder of yours that refuses to heal, I'd wager you're free to stay, go back to France or Canada, or wherever you choose."

"If your war plans are successful, would this country become another British colony?"

"Who can say what parliaments and the King's ministers may decide? Would you like to remain?"

Edouard did not hesitate. "I would, Colonel."

"Then it might happen. But, first, let us see how our war ends. General Forbes and Colonel Bouquet might have doubts about the wisdom of Sieur de Fournet remaining in the Ohio country, but there's a deal of rivers, lakes and forests in which to find him.''

"Thank you, Colonel."

"Would Mistress Brewster have an influence on your questions?"

"She detests me, Colonel. I am too forward."

Washington chuckled. "Another point that awaits the end of our war. Too many protests often have surprising causes. Good day, Sir. Recover speedily. I'll not see you until after we have reduced Fort Duquesne."

"You leave that soon?"

"I am not in command, Sir, and you come perilously close to the questions of a spy even though I have your parole."

At the door, he made a small, formal bow and started to turn. Edouard impulsively called, "Encounter no harm, Sir."

Washington turned back, showing faint but pleased surprised. "I shall certainly try."

Two days later, the soldiers moved out, leaving only a sparse handful to guard the post under the command of Lieutenant Butler. Abigail Brewster also remained and took the place of Dr. Gregor, who left with the troops. She called daily and had Jan change Edouard's bandages when she felt that was needed. She would walk with him when Jan had dressed him and they made monotonous circles of the stockade around the empty, dusty parade ground. Butler accompanied them several times, all attention and eyes for Abby, but he soon sensed the futility of that and Edouard had more and more time with the auburn-tressed colonial maid in her coarse-woven gray dress.

The days passed in slow monotony and they had no word from the soldiers who had left to retake Fort Prince George from the French. Edouard persuaded Abby there would be little danger for them outside the stockade and Butler had to agree that the French and their Indian allies would be much too busy fighting to be scouring the country seeking an occasional scalp.

So their strolls were extended. Edouard, Jan and even Abby were armed with pistols and knives, but the weapons were never used. The only intruders into the trees were sunlight and small wild animals and birds. Edouard had the constant and growing feeling that the war in this portion of the country would soon be over and he wondered if some of old Captain Jouvier's psychic vision of the future had touched him. Certainly, the master of the *Demoiselle* had been correct in saying rivers and waters—did he mean the lake of the Eries would play a major part in Edouard's life. Would that continue?

Sometimes he mused aloud to Abby about the prophecy and she became intrigued. She agreed. "There are all sorts of rivers and streams everywhere in this country. Some, like your lake Erie, will bear large ships someday. Others are even too small for a canoe. But wherever you go there is a brook or river—something."

"And westward also?"

"So far as I've heard," she answered. "But

what did your sea captain say you would do about them?"

"He didn't."

"Well, water or dry land, you had best plan your future, Mr. Forny. That is—"

"What did you call me?" he broke in.

"Forny. It sounds less Frenchified than Sieur de Fournet. It sounds better to our English and colonial ears."

"So it does—and all of you are suspicious of a French name as well as person, *non?*"

"Since this war began. But even afterwards, if you stay in America, 'Forny' would suit us better. But it's not a name that should be of bother to you, sir. It's your future."

"I know, but I have this arm that Dr. Gregor says will take a long time healing. I'll decide my future after that."

She took several steps before she spoke uncertainly to him. "I'm certanily not a doctor and I've seen but few in my life. None have ever treated me."

"You're lucky to be so healthy!"

"Well . . . maybe. But I've been sick many a time and I've had cuts. The Indians gave me several scars before they decided to adopt me."

"Adopt you!" He stopped short. "You never told me that. I thought they only killed, tortured and scalped."

She flushed. "They do a deal of that, I admit. But they liked the way I fought back against running a gauntlet. I thought they'd kill me certain for knocking a half-dozen or more of their women flat and breaking some bones."

"You!"

She flushed at the surprised admiration in his voice. He had stopped short, stunned that so quiet a girl had such a story to tell. She took his unbandaged arm and urged hm to continue walking, her cheeks fiery red with embarrassment.

"That's a story I may tell later. But now I'm saying that regular doctors, in or out of the army, in or out of the towns and villages, do not have all the knowledge. Dr. Gregor is very good and is doing the best he can for you, I know."

"Well, then?"

"There are cures we use in Connecticut, family remedies, I think they're called. I hear they're used in all the colonies—in places like Westover, in the woods and mountains where a doctor's seen maybe once in five years if at all. Then, the Onondaga shamans have secrets that Dr. Gregor knows nothing about. They'd probably set his dear gray hair on end, but so many of them work! I've seen it."

"Do you mean to say that this shoulder of mine—"

"I don't think it needs all that bandage and bleeding and probing. I know of herbs that can be blended into liquids and salves that have healed many an ax cut or lance thrust that looks worse than your bullet hole. That should have covered over and healed weeks ago."

"Will Dr. Gregor permit you to treat me?"

"He's busy now with the French fort and

heaven knows when he'll be back at Necessity. We could try. Of you could keep the bandage and go on with your pain.''

"I've had enough of *that*, Dr. Abigail Brewster.'' He touched the bandage to remove it but she checked him. "Give me time to find the herbs and then blend them. A few days more can make little difference, can it?''

They returned to the nearly empty post and the next morning Edouard learned that Mistress Brewster had left the post earlier with Jan. He had a glimpse of her crossing the compound when the sun had almost reached meridian. She carried a small covered basket and went directly to her quarters. A short while later, Jan came in and answered Edouard's questions as best he could.

"She dug up roots, Sir. That's all. But she was very particular. Sometimes she walked around and looked at the ground weeds for near an hour before she'd have me spade one up. And then I had to be careful not to cut or bruise a root or a leaf. It made but little sense to me!''

Late in the afternoon, the peace of the post was shattered when a hundred hard-looking, hard-muscled men marched in. Edouard awkwardly walked out to watch Butler meet their leader, a sergeant who proudly proclaimed himself and his men to be "Green Mountain Boys'' from Vermont and said they were to construct a new wilderness road north and west to the Forks of the Ohio.

"But the French are there!" Butler remonstrated.

The sergeant grinned, spat to one side and widely grinned again. "That's as may be, Left'ent. But give us quarters for the night, a stable for our horses and wagons and tools and we'll at least start the road west come morning. We've had our orders afore Forbes and Bouquet marched west from Philadelphia and Ligonier."

Butler could only shrug and send off a courier toward Fort Duquesne and General Forbes to confirm the sergeant's news. He spoke disparingly to Edouard when the Vermont sergeant was out of earshot.

"A road! Who knows who'll march along it—Frenchies or us."

Abigail came at her regular time to supervise Jan's supper cooking. She had another basket covered with a cloth that she placed on a lone chair against the far wall and then invited herself as a guest to the meal. After it was finished, she made certain Jan's dishwashing was thorough and then sent him to visit new arrivals from Vermont. He left without demur, pleased to escape.

Abby immediately took her basket from the chair and forced Edouard to take its place. She had to courageously force her backwoods propriety into abeyance and ask him to remove his shirt, helping him remove the sleeve from his injured arm when he winced. She made him twist about so that the sunlight through the window fell fully on the wound and then she examined it.

She uncovered the basket and lifted out a small bowl of sticky yellow ointment and covered her finger with it. "This will hurt each time it's applied for a time. But that will pass."

"Is the wound pussed?" he asked.

"Somewhat. But with all that wrapping, pussed and seldom changed, what could be expected? Now, let me be at work."

She was right. He had to bite his lip time and again when she touched him. But despite the hurt of the touch, the ointment almost immediately began to soothe. She finally sat back and wiped excess ointment from her fingers and replaced the bowl in the basket.

"That will do this time, Mr. Forny. I'll douse you again in the morning."

"Douse?"

"The salve, Sir. This will take more than one treatment."

"You'll do each one?" He smiled when she nodded. "Then I'm grateful you're a doctor."

"Thank you, but I have little need of your French flattery."

As she promised, the next day she treated him again, after Jan had served breakfast and gone to watch the men start to build a new road to join the old one Braddock had used during his vain attack on Duquesne. Abby had made a padded square for Edouard to wear while he slept, but Dr. Gregor's stained, ragged bandage had disappeared the night before. Now she discarded the pad.

"It is only to keep your wound unchafed when you move in your sleep. The rest of the time you'll wear just your shirt or coat, if the weather turns colder or rainy."

Late in the day, Lieutenant Butler's messenger returned and the young officer dashed out of the post-command building with a shout that brought every soldier popping out of the cabins. Edouard jumped out just as Abby sprang through her own cabin door. Butler could not contain his excitement.

"The French are gone! They destroyed and burned their fort and moved up the north fork of the Ohio. Scouts say they're heading back to Canada. The war's over in these parts!"

No one could quite believe it but the messenger swore to the fact. Late that night another messenger, this time Christopher Gist, Colonel Washington's Virginia friend and partner, loudly called at the closed stockade gate for admittance. Candlelights flared along officers' row and a crowd gathered. Gist confirmed the news. He told the assembled crowd that gathered before one of the cabins.

"Some went up the Allegaway branch of the Ohio toward Erie and some westward down the river toward their posts at Fort Vincennes, and St. Louis. But here, at Necessity and Duquesne, the war is over."

As the meeting broke up and Edouard turned back toward his cabin, he almost walked directly into Abigail Brewster. He apologized but she waved that away.

"How is your chest and shoulder?"

He looked surprised as he carefully moved his left shoulder about. Then he touched it delicately and stared at her. She could read the puzzled pleasure in his face.

"*Tonnerre!* You are a magician. I can move and turn without pain!"

She smiled. "Dr. Gregor will be surprised—and if I know doctors, not too pleased at the potency of pioneer and Iroquois medicine."

"*Mon Dieu!* forget him. The war is over. That is what counts."

"So it does. Now what will you do?"

XXXI

Abby knew she could have very well asked herself that question. Colonel Washington and most of the militiamen from the various colonies soon reappeared at Necessity. But only Washington, Gist, and a few others remained, for the rest, typical of the colonial farmer-militia of the time, packed up and started for their distant homes as quickly as they could. A British regular detachment manned the post.

As Abby learned from a dozen sources who had marched on Duquesne, the French had burned and destroyed it before they moved out so she, Mr. Forny and a few others had, of necessity, to remain while the old French post was being rebuilt. It was renamed Fort Pitt, after the royal minister who had directed the war in the name of King George, the third Hanoverian British monarch of that name.

She continued to see Edouard each day, making sure that he exercised his arm and shoulder either under her supervision or Jan's. At first he had almost cried out with the pain of it, but that gradually passed, as she had known it would, and she almost wished Dr. Gregor had returned so that she could wring even grudging credit for the progress from him.

But Colonel Washington time and again acted as substitute as the doctor travelled to Vincennes or St. Louis. "He'd be astounded at the progress of Sieur de Fournet's wound," Washington commented to her one day.

They met by chance near the flagstaff and now they both looked toward the stockade gate where Edouard exhibited to Christopher Gist his ability to bend and straighten his arm and then lift it high above his head and lower it.

She explained what she had done and added that she wanted her patient to have even more use of the arm before she was done with it.

431

"Salves and balms and ointments from Westover in Connecticut and the Onondaga Indians," she answered his query.

"Old wives' remedies and Indian cures, the good doctor would call them," Washington nodded. "But many of them do work. I've used them back home in Mount Vernon and so has my brother. Doctors are too often far away in these parts when we need 'em."

They continued to watch Edouard for a few moments and then Washington abruptly said, "You and Sieur de Fournet are free to go and come as you please now."

"During your time at Duquesne, he has come to be known as Edward Forny."

He looked around and down at her in surprise. "Now that is a strange combination of French and English, Mistress. Better suited to our colonial English tongues."

"I thought so, Colonel. French names are not exactly friendly to our minds these last years."

"Your idea, Mistress? Does he agree?"

"Not fully, but he will. And I confess to the idea."

Washington looked back to the stockade gate but his friend and Edouard had walked on through it and out of sight. Washington continued with his line of thought. "You seem to have taken him well in hand, Mistress. Like him, I am also taken with the new name you gave him. But there is still the problem of what you will do and where you will live. Do you have kin in Connecticut or somewhere about like Rhode

Island Plantation or Massachusetts Colony? I would make certain you'd have place on a wagon train when our militia from the area leave."

"Thank you, Colonel. But I have no family."

"What then? Surely not the Onondaga!"

Corn Dancer and the Indian women of the Owl and Hawk suddenly came vividly to her mind and then instantly vanished as she saw the rim of fire around the charred stake and the burning resinous splinters, like porcupine quills, in the writhing skin of the tortured victim. She closed her eyes tightly against the vision, realizing that her lips flattened in a grimace against her teeth.

"Mistress, I've called up bad memories. My apologies."

She regained her composure. "It is all right, Colonel. But you are right. I cannot go back to the Indians."

"You and the Sieur—" he caught himself up. "I mean, Mr. Edward Forny—are truly orphans of war, then. We must decide what we can do for you."

"I'm sure both of us will find some way to take care of ourselves."

"Undoubtedly, but it would do me pleasure to be of help if I can. Do you mind if I give thought to it?"

"Colonel, I need help on the matter."

"And your Mr. Forny?"

"He is too proud to say, I believe. But that is the Frenchie in his blood."

"And his training, I'd vow. Well, I shall give thought on it."

"You will be much too busy rebuilding the French post, Colonel."

He smiled faintly. "Now and then I have time to consider other things, Mistress."

That may have been true of the Colonel but Abby had long, empty hours to while away—except for those short periods when she exercised Edouard's arm and shoulder or strolled about the post with him. Now and then they wandered beyond the stockade, Jan always with them, armed with a musket.

The land round about seemed to be a series of high, uneven ridges that separated small pockets of valleys. They now and then encountered brooks that trickled westward. The bright sun, the grass, the occasional patches of wild flowers made it hard to believe that only a matter of weeks or a few months before, men had fought and died anywhere near this area; but the constant movement of work parties to and from the abandoned French post gave lie to that thought.

Abby sounded out Edouard on his future, at first with no success at all. He would smile or laugh and make an airy gesture of dismissal. "There will be time enough for that before long, Mademoiselle."

"Mistress," she corrected sharply and then softened her voice. "But you rapidly mend. Will you go back to New France?"

"You forget, it is now Canada. King George rules there instead of King Louis and the British flag has replaced the Lilies.''

''Then there's no danger to you if you return,'' she insisted.

He stopped short and wheeled about to directly face her. ''There is not unless I'm counted a prisoner of war and I'm exchanged for those my countrymen have captured.''

''Where? When?''

He made a disgusted face. ''Spare me a little pride, Mistress. Surely we have not been so thoroughly beaten as not to have won a skirmish or two. I'm sure the Marquis de Montcalm's troops will return by transport fleet.''

''I did not mean to wound your esteem, Edward. I simply wonder what you will do and what will happen to you.''

His eyes sharpened. ''Does that mean aught to you?''

''Of course, after all both of us have been through together.'' She tossed her head half in anger. ''But that seems more than you think of me.''

His proud expression vanished and his irritation disappeared. ''But I do wonder about you—and I am concerned more than you think.''

Her eyes softened. ''But you are so far from your native land, Edward! You don't know our ways.''

''I have been to England,'' he said, still a little miffed.

''But England is not at all the colonies—and each one of *them* is different. Virginia is not at all like Vermont, nor is this colony of Pennsylvania like Vermont—any more than my Connecticut is like the Onondaga or Mohawk towns.''

''Nor my Gascony like New France, my Toulouse like Montreal.'' His irritation disappeared behind a wistful smile. ''You forget my king has signed an arrest order for me should I appear in any French colony.''

''Colonel Washington is right. We are both orphans of the war. He asked me our plans just three days ago.''

''I doubt if he can solve them, Mistress.''

''I am not so certain, Mr. Forny. The Colonel is a man filled with wisdom and ingenuity, I think. He will come up with something.''

''I am accustomed to solving my own problems.''

''I'm sure of it. But nothing is harmed should the Colonel have some thoughts to help us. I would listen. I hope you will also.''

''We shall see.''

She silenced him with a dry statement, ''What else can we do?''

Two nights later, the Colonel again returned from his work on the abandoned post, and invited both Abby and Edouard to sup at his cabin. His orderly served the simple but tasty meal, along with a red wine poured from a clean, well-corked bottle.

''A burgundy of sorts, Sieur de Fournet. But this was bottled and aged in Virginia Colony. I have it through the kindness of Governor Dinwiddie. I hope it may be somewhat to your taste.''

Edouard sipped from the glass. When he looked his pleasure, the Colonel beamed. Edouard suddenly laughed. "I must confess, Colonel. I had bad thoughts of colonial corn whiskey, which I recently encountered.''

"Then I understand your noticeable reluctance. Some of the colonies make a good distillation that is quite passable once the palate becomes used to the taste. Some European wines can be had in cities such as Philadelphia, Charleston, Boston and New York. Many of my planter neighbors have excellent cellars. Their factors buy it in London or Le Havre for them. But out in this wilderness, of course, we do it with our own grapes and fermenting, such as they are.''

"My compliments to your Governor, Colonel.''

Washington chuckled. "Dinwiddie will love that praise when I tell him it's direct from the lips of a good Frenchman.''

"More like a fugitive or lost one, Sir.''

Washington instantly sobered. "That brings me to the reason—beside your company—for the evening, sir. And for your lovely presence, Mistress Brewster. Would you like to see the progress we make at Fort Pitt?''

Abby clapped her hands in surprise and Edouard's smile revealed his pleasure but he looked quizzically at his host. "Is the post far enough along for a lady to visit?''

"Indeed—for a long day's trip there and back. If the lady agrees, I'll have one of our work wagons adjusted to suit her travel comfort. She seems to have mended your shoulder enough so you could mount saddle again."

"I could indeed, Colonel. Mistress Abby should be made the post's surgeon."

"She has the gift," Washington conceded, "but her sex prevents. But to a more important matter and question, Sieur de Fournet."

"Edward Forny," Abby corrected firmly.

"I forget," the Colonel smiled.

"Even I find it hard to remember, sir," Edouard said quickly.

Washington waved the apologies aside. "You told me you came down the north branch of the Ohio from the Lake of the Erie?" At Edouard's nod he leaned forward. "There is timber a-plenty up that stream, sir?"

"I fled New France and the Senecas, who had a murdered tribesman to avenge, though I did not know it at the time. I did not count the trees, but I assure you the forest—and the ridges—are abundant."

"That confirms my own knowledge."

"You've been up in the North Fork, Colonel?" Abby asked—in surprise.

Washington smiled thinly, signalled to his orderly to leave the cabin, closing the door after him. Then he dropped back in his chair, studying his guests, sighed when he reached decision.

"I've been up that stream many times, Sir, with my friend, Christopher Gist, before the

French dominated it. You see, under our royal grant from a king long since dead, all this land was granted to Virginia Colony from the Atlantic to whatever sea or Ocean lies to the west, no matter how far. Recently, Governor Dinwiddie along with a few other gentlemen of Virginia (including myself), and some men of rank at the court of King George, have decided to act on the grant."

He realized both Edouard and Abby, round-eyed, tried to envision the enormity of the grant and also their surprise at his own involvement. He smiled frostily.

"So we formed the Virginia Company. Kit and I crossed the mountains to explore and—"

"But this was French country, Colonel!" Edouard broke in.

"I know. Lord Celeron who nailed lead plates on trees and buried others at the mouths of streams endeavored to prove that. In fact, Celeron came down the North Fork with some four hundred men and drove us out of Fort Prince George." Washington made a wry face. "They built a better fort where the Ohio forks and called it Duquesne. Now we have it back, we will rebuild it and call it Fort Pitt."

"What is this to us, Colonel?" Edouard asked.

"I come to that, Sieur—" Washington's eyes cut to Abby and he said, "Mr. Edward Forny. What skills do you have?"

"I . . ." Edouard floundered and then threw back his shoulders in pride. "Soldier, Colonel.

Commander of a Royal Regiment. Swordsman of small merit, if you'll allow me. I was also considered as of some value in construction and planning of military bastions and trenches."

"Mathematics? Physics?"

"After a fashion, Colonel, as a soldier picks up such knowledge in the course of his duties. But why—?"

"Later, if you will bear with me," Washington demurred. "But now I am certain I want you to see the fort."

After he had left, Edouard escorted Abby to her cabin on officers' row. They walked slowly, each deep in thought. Edouard broke the silence.

"So we see the new post a'building on the morrow. To copy the Colonel, 'Mistress, what skills have you?' Is that too bold?"

She stopped short and he had to wheel about to the sudden tug of her hand on his arm. "Not too bold. But why do you ask?"

"Because I think the Colonel will also ask it and it has something to do with his plans for Fort Pitt."

"Well . . . I sew both a plain and fancy stitch. I can cook for many men or few, whatever is demanded. I can plan and plant a garden and see to its growth. I can handle flintlock, pistol, knife, lance or bow and arrow if the occasion demands."

"Write? Read?"

"A little. They are not considered proper for a young lady in the colonies. I did go to parson's school for a time."

"Now why does the Colonel ask us?" Edouard asked.

"I have come to believe," he answered himself thoughtfully, "that Colonel George Washington of Virginia Colony answers such questions in his own chosen time. He is one of many talents and one to keep his own counsel."

Abby sighed. "You and I think alike, Edward."

"I am glad to hear that, Mistress." He took a deep breath and plunged. "And, pray, what do you think of me as other than a puzzling Frenchman, recently an enemy?"

"You are bold, Sir!"

"Then I'll pose the question at another time."

A few days later, Abby rode on the hard wooden seat of a supply wagon to the distant fort. It had been built especially for her. Edouard and Colonel Washington rode saddled horses to either side and Edouard found it a pleasure to once more be astride a horse. He looked around and up at Abby with pride and she smiled in return. Christopher Gist and Jan rode guard at the rear of the wagon.

They did not use Braddock's old crossing of the Monongahela that he had used to advance on the fort, but Washington led them along the east bank north and westward until at last they broke out of the forest and looked ahead to the point of land where the fort had stood.

It stood there now, but vastly changed. Entrenchments had been dug around a stockade already partially built. Edouard saw many charred timbers lying along the bank of the river and, beyond the point, he saw another, much wider river flowing westward into distance beyond sight.

"The Ohio," Washington said. "Called La Belle Rivière by our late enemies. Even the Iroquois call it the Beautiful River in their language."

"Seneca dialect," Abby said. "They are the Guardians of the Western Gate. That is this country out here."

"Arrogant devils," Gist called. Abby started to protest but only sighed and kept silence.

At the post, Washington made Abby comfortable in a makeshift log structure and then took Edouard on a tour of the work in progress. They soon returned to gather around Abby and Edouard immediately broached the question in his mind. "Colonel, what have I to do with all this?"

"Perhaps much, perhaps little. It depends on your answers."

"Service in your army, Colonel?"

"Service *to* our army, rather. I've told you, long before the French came, Virginia Colony claimed this whole area, all land drained by the Ohio and its tributaries. Then the Pennsylvania Colony laid claim and came over the mountains. That explains why Kit Gist and I traversed from the post here northward almost to the Lake of the Eries and westward as far as we dared go. Now that our England has obviously won the land, the Virginia Company's claim will be validated.''

"I still do not understand how I can serve 'your' army, as you call it.''

"The Regulars will be recalled, Master Forny. Virginia militia will replace them and eventually Virginia settlers from this very region. We will need supplies. Right now, we need peeled logs for our stockades and buildings here. We will need fresh-killed meat for food. We will need lead for bullets and kegs of gunpowder, cloth for uniform repairs—flour, meal, and hundreds of items to keep the post here supplied, and other posts we plan to build. I must return to Virginia, so we need someone right here to know what we must have and where to get it.''

Edouard stared at him. "But, Colonel! I am only a soldier and from Gascony at that.''

"Soldier, used to command. If I know you French, you will have a knack for trade. You will know how to transport all the supplies we need by wagon or by boat or canoe. You will know how and where to build work camps and control the crews to fell the trees, trim the logs, make rafts. Oh, we have use for you, Edward Forny!''

"But I hardly know this land—''

"After your journey across the country from Quebec? After crossing the Lake of the Eries and down the North Fork of the Ohio? And we will need you up there in Canada, for you speak French.''

Edouard's stunned surprise held him

chless for several minutes, then he gulped
d found his voice. "Colonel, do you know
hat you do? You give me a whole forest
kingdom and all its people—British, French, Indian and all—to rule like a minor monarch."

"I'm aware of it and chose you!" Washington
nodded.

Abby startled them with her impulsive exclamation to Edouard. "Take it. You will be a
prince in fact if not in title."

"Not so fast, Mistress," Washington cut in.
"I have plans for you, and a question also."

"But where could I possibly fit into all you
have in mind?"

"Very simple, Mistress Brewster. A prince, as
you call him, must be above gossip and reproach
and he will also need help—constantly. I pro-
pose you as 'princess.' Does 'Madam Forny' sit
well to your mind and tongue as well as it might
to your heart?" Washington arose. "I think I
had best leave you now."

Abby and Edouard sat stunned as the tall man
strode out of the cabin to inspect the trench for
stockade posts that a dozen men dug a hundred
yards away.

Neither Edouard nor Abby had the wits to
stop him. They could only look round-eyed at
each other, turned speechless by the offer and all
its implications. Edouard finally managed to
whisper,

"Mon Dieu!"

XXXII

Colonel Washington did not press them for an answer, either on his return from the stockade construction or the whole of the journey back to Fort Necessity. He broke the silence only when they arrived at the post and he concernedly asked Abby, "Mistress, do you seek your cabin?"

At her nod, he motioned the driver on. Edouard had spurred off across the post grounds to the stable the moment he rode through the stockade gates. Jan caught up with him just as he dismounted and strode to the stable door.

"What has happened, Master Forny? Did Colonel Washington say aught to upset you and Mistress—"

"*Sacre bleu*! Out of my sight!"

"But I—"

"Go!"

Washington himself helped Abby down from her high seat on the wagon. The moment her toes touched the ground she raced into the cabin slamming the door closed behind her. She blindly took two strides across the room to her bunk but collided with the chair beside it and dropped down upon it with a thud.

She couldn't move, her racing thoughts making her dizzy and she gasped for breath as the implications of the Colonel's offer became more clear and, certainly, more involved. "Princess" to Edward Forny! By what right did Colonel Washington throw her so blindly at that French refugee from what must have been a scandalous love affair in France!

She jumped up then and this time found her bunk, dropped down upon it and buried her face in her arms. She heard the activity of the post, the sound muffled through the closed cabin door. What must Edward Forny think of her? Oh! But she should by rights snatch every hair from the head of that tall, supposedy dignified Virginia colonel! Certainly, she could never face Edward Forny again after this. Almost immediately a traitorous thought crept into her mind. Who would see to it that his arm and shoulder would completely heal? Unguents, balm and exercise had to be regular.

She flounced onto her side. Let Jan take care of that. Did Colonel Washington think that because of her ministrations to Edward, she could become his wife? This was wilderness and no parson would be within miles and miles and miles—perhaps clean over the mountains in Pennsylvania or Virginia. Did Colonel—

"Oh! how dare he!" She pummeled her fist into her pillow and heard the rustling sound of its straw filling. She buried her flushed face in her arms.

Slowly her thoughts ceased their tumultuous spinning. She became curiously detached from herself, as though considering one Abigail Brewster as she would have Patience, or Marion or Leah—wherever they were. That thought led her on to others—of Westover and the Hudson, and the Onondaga town and that horrible ring of fiery torture that had sent her fleeing from the Iroquois, Corn Dancer.

What of him? Alive? Killed in this horrible war by a French bullet or bayonet, or by Huron or one of the warriors of an Iroquois nation? Or mayhap standing tied to a post somewhere, singing his death song as bloodthirsty squaws set fire to splinters in his skin, or their knife blades grew red with his blood as they slowly and gleefully cut off his genitals? The picture sent a shiver through her and she blotted it from her mind, tried to erase that period of savagery she had known.

Her thoughts unwillingly returned to the fiery torture ring and she saw Corn Dancer, prancing his blood lust with the rest, his long lance ripping and slicing first at that Shawnee and then at that poor, unknown white prisoner with the ash-smeared face. No, she could not have remained in any Iroquoian town after that. She had been wise to flee.

She had been even wiser to abandon her stolen canoe upstream and watch it float away eastward. Mayhap it had bobbed and swirled its way to the Hudson, or mayhap it had been discovered before then. If so, Corn Dancer would have sought her along the Hudson, so her flight westward had saved her, bringing her here and to . . . Edouard, and that brazen Washington!

Brazen, yes, but . . . she took a time letting the admission enter her mind . . . wise, understanding and certainly he had the answer for so many problems. She turned her head so that now her arms formed a pillow rather than a blindfold. She forced herself to remember what he had proposed and the scope of his vision.

A light tap on the door aroused her. She merely lifted her head a trifle higher and called,

"Who is it?"

"Jan, Mistress Brewster."

"Go away."

A pause and then the lad's puzzled voice. "Ma'am, have I harmed you?"

"Of course not! Just go away."

"What of Mr. Forny, Ma'am?"

"Let him take care of himself."

"That's all I can do. He's like you, telling me to go away. I've never seen him so mean-mad."

"Really?"

"Yes, Ma'am. But that ain't why I come. What do I do with this present?"

"From whom?"

"Colonel Washington."

She almost snorted in renewed anger. "Take it back, throw it away, or do what you will with it. But just go away."

A long pause and she thought she heard a long sigh. "I'll leave it out here on the stoop, Ma'am. There's a note with it."

She heard a noise by the door and then Jan's receding steps. She tossed about on the bunk. Let the present and the note stay out there. Mayhap some passing militiaman or worker might see it and take it.

Then, despite all her resistance, she began to wonder what Jan had brought. No, she didn't care about that. But what had the Colonel written? Apology that he so richly deserved to make? Time passed and gradually the room became darker. She tried to remain in the bunk but, somehow, she could almost *feel* whatever sat on her stoop. It would soon be time to prepare for supper if she was to put in appearance at the officers' mess. Or to start her own small evening meal over the fireplace if she decided to stay right here and give the Colonel and Edward the treatment they deserved.

No, not Edward, she corrected herself. Washington was the one who deserved the cold snubbing of a proper young lady he had presumed to push into another man's arms. The near-presence of whatever sat on her stoop intruded in her mind. With an irritated flounce she arose from the bunk and walked to the door. She cracked it slowly and peered out. No one was near and she saw only three militiamen talking among themselves far across the parade ground. She opened the door wider and looked down at the stoop.

A small covered basket sat there and a wax-sealed envelope lay upon the white, coarse cloth. She looked up and out once more. No one near. With a swift flowing movement, she opened the door wide enough to grab the basket handle, step back and close the door. She placed the basket on her table and tried to penetrate the cloth and whatever message the sealed envelope contained merely by staring at them.

Daylight lessened and she struck flint to the fire that was laid and waiting. When the flames sprang up, she lit her candle in its holder and carried it to the table. Then she touched the basket, rejected curiosity once more and walked to her cupboard to see what she might prepare for her very small evening meal.

When she turned, there sat the basket and the note. And she could no longer withstand curiosity. She threw back the cloth, revealing a complete supper, ready cooked. It needed only warming and there was also a stoppered small clay jug, its mouth sealed. She knew it must be more of the Colonel's wine from Virginia. What did he mean by sending such a thing to her!

She broke the seal of the note, unfolded the single sheet with Washington's bold scrawl. *"Mistress,"* she read; *"I fear I may have offended you. If so, I make amends two ways herewith. My personal cook is excellent as you will find if you do me the honor of acceptance. The wine is for a guest you will have sometime this evening and I hope you will* both *do me the honor of acceptance, forgiveness, agreement and a toast for your sincere friend and counselor, George Washington."*

What guest? Christopher Gist? Then the thought struck her—Edward Forny! But she shook her head. The Colonel would not dare and Edward certainly wouldn't come. He'd be more likely to challenge the Colonel to a duel after that outrageous suggestion of this afternoon.

She replaced the cloth over food and jug. She would return them as soon as Jan put in appearance in the morning. And she had best plan on departing Fort Necessity. But where would she go?

She turned to the fireplace and placed wood

upon it and then started to prepare her mush and placed strips of bacon in a small pan.

A knock on the door interrupted her. She placed the uncooked ingredients to one side and impatiently arose and went to the door. She opened it and stood frozen, mouth agape. "Master Forny!"

He swept off his tricorn hat. "Mistress, may I come in?"

Without thinking, she stepped aside and he entered. It may have been the play of fireplace flames upon him, but he suddenly looked to have gained inches in height and looked amazingly more handsome than he had just this very day. He glanced back at the open door and closed it.

"No!" She suddenly could think clearly once more. "We should not give reason for gossip."

"Would you have every passerby stopping to gape at us and listen?" he asked. "The Colonel suggested you might wish to talk to me. Certainly I wish to talk to you."

So Edward *was* her guest! She made a vague move with her hand that he took as an acceptance and it emboldened him to come farther into the room. She stepped back, touched the rough corner of the fireplace and then could retreat no more. He smiled at her.

"Mistress, you surely can't be fearful of your own patient! I'll not harm you, but we have much to discuss." He looked about, saw a chair at the table and pulled it out. "Pray be at ease. We might be a time."

"We have nothing to talk about."

"We have much to discuss, Abigail. We have very much indeed. He made us an offer—both of us—and I think we should not pass it by."

"But—we're not married!"

"Is that all that stands between us and a future kingdom!" He saw her shock, took a deep breath and suddenly his voice became sharp, short and filled with command. "Sit you down and stop babbling! Stop thinking of anyone but ourselves, of anything but what we've been offered. What else *is* there to think about?"

"Our reputations and—"

She suddenly realized he spoke basic, solid truth. What else was there to talk about! She dropped into the chair and before she could move he had captured both her hands. "Mistress . . . Abigail! How many times have you ministered to me—and sometimes when I was too sick and too out of mind to know of anything but that soft hands touched me, took care of me and finally healed me?"

"I only—"

"You still babble. Listen! When I had my wits about me but had no strength to do more than watch you move about the bunk, tell Jan what to do to help you, change those damnable bandages, have you any idea what I thought? Don't just look at me. Answer!"

She could only speechlessly shake her head. Suddenly in his whiplike voice she heard Corn Dancer out in the wilderness, the snarl of his Indian word that then she could not understand. But this man Edward Forny did exactly what Corn Dancer had, using apparent cruelty of voice and harsh grip of hands to clear her mind of fear and cobwebs, to give her courage to face an unknown future here as Corn Dancer had given her courage to face the dangers and death of the forests and woods westward to the Hudson, across it and on westward to a haven in the Onondaga town.

He released one of her hands and his arm made a sweeping gesture westward. "Out there—you and I. Fort Pitt, the North Fork, Canada! The Colonel gives us the chance to build a fortune in this new land, to establish it before it fills up with Virginians, Pennsylvanians, *mon Dieu!* and who knows what else. This will not be Indian land always. It is too great and too rich."

"But . . . but . . ."

"First, Abigail! First! I may be a Gascon fool, but Gascony is a land of small farms and villages. It was once wild—ages back before the Romans came and tamed it. The savage Gauls had ravaged it and there have been wandering hordes from Spain, from the north—even Crusaders who cared for nothing but pillage and rape as they passed through on their way to free the Holy land. They taught us to face any adversity the Good God would send upon us."

He recaptured her hand. "That is what the Colonel offers us, Abigail, if we have the heart and strength my people had and I know yours had. Did your father and mother hesitate to strike out into Indian country and establish towns and farms?"

"They died for it."

"And so might we. But at least we will have tried to do something. Is a wagging tongue or a million of them more to be feared than what both of us have already faced?"

He fell silent and they sat unmoving for many minutes. Then he spoke more quietly and completely released her. "I've frightened you, and I've shocked you. I'm sorry but I have come to love you, Abigail Brewster. Both of us are without family and far from our homes. We can never go back. We have only one another . . . or we have nothing."

She jumped to her feet and he stood up with her, so close she could touch him. She looked up into his lean, dark face and suddenly she knew that she could not face the world alone. She was hungry for stability, for protection; she needed love that came from strength and this man before her had it. He seemed to read her racing thoughts for she caught a fleeting glimpse of change and softening in his face and read hunger in his eyes.

Then she felt his arms about her, holding her close and his lips crushed down on hers. The fires of her body, seemingly dead under the ashes of horror and war, suddenly flamed through her as his hard body pressed against hers. She did not fully realize that her arms had gone to his shoulders. She felt his fingers at her blouse and then his hand around her breast.

She uttered a little moan of hungry anticipation and in a mad confusion of emotions, thoughts, feelings, needs, she pressed his hand against her naked flesh and felt her nipples harden. This was no longer a cabin on officers' row in Fort Necessity, but the dark room of the Fireside in a Long House in Onondaga Town. The edge of the bunk struck the back of her knees and she fell backward.

Edward Forny loomed above her and she felt his hands on her bare legs, at her waist. The flames in the fireplace danced unheeded as Abby willingly lifted herself to him and felt him enter her, fill her. A great tremor shook her and she gave a muffled cry just before her fingers taloned into the cloth of his back and her nails ripped down his broad shoulders.

XXXIII

For the rest of her life, Abby could never decide if Colonel Washington knew that one of the men who labored so hard at the stockade at Fort Pitt was a parson from Rhode Island. The man had come west to work with and bring spiritual courage to his fellow colonists in a land filled with warfare between English and French, Indian and white.

The only thing Abby knew for certain was that the Colonel showed suspiciously little surprise at her acceptance of his offer of a parson to make her Madam Edward Forny. And she also had unconfirmed suspicions that the Colonel had a hand in bringing Edouard de Fournet to confess he was of a Huguenot family so that a marriage by a frontier Protestant rite did not particularly upset him.

In any case, it was swiftly done and their combined cabin home, trading post and Edward's office was quickly erected on the point of land in the shadow of the new post. However, it took a good deal of argument and discussion to allay her fears when Edward first hired Indians to canoe him up the North Fork of the Ohio to find the best spot for a lumber camp. She remembered all too well that her own flight from Onondaga Town had ended there, and that Edward and Spotted Doe had come to disaster along its banks.

But he returned safely and soon departed again, this time with a cutting crew. He returned on a raft of peeled logs, more sun-blackened than she had ever seen him before, and certainly far more of a frontiersman and American colonist. He reported the camp had been visited by several Senecas but none of them seemed to know that Edward had once been an object of tribal vengeance.

She felt less concerned when he made a more

extended trip, this time in a long canoe paddled by *voyageurs* who had lost their fear of British bullets now that the war was over. They went as far as the lake of the Eries and this time returned with a bundle of fur pelts that Edward exhibited with pride.

"And without the permission of His Excellency, the Governor of New France," he exulted to Abby. "Colonel Washington knew that with the end of the war, this whole country would open up. Any of us can travel from Fort De Troit to Montreal, Quebec or even the length of the St. Lawrence out to sea without so much as a by-your-leave. I heard tales of great western lakes I would like to see."

They had not yet arisen when early dawn light touched their bedroom window and Edward recounted that phase of his adventures. She laughed and placed his hand on her stomach and his eyes rounded in astonishment.

"If you can wait," she said, "perhaps the three of us could see them together."

"A baby! A son!"

"Always a boy!" she pouted. "Don't girls count for anything?"

"Certainement! You do."

And he twisted about to pull her close and kiss her. Then he pulled back and looked at her in wonder, but at the same time his eyes were on something beyond her or far distant in time. "A child! Abby, we will be a family, eh? And there will be other babies and—"

"Not so fast. This one first."

"And the children will have children," he continued as though he hadn't heard and his eyes remained on some far-distant thought. Suddenly they sharpened and he pointed to the window. "All that out there for us—all that river, and all the lakes to the north. All the rivers that flow into the Ohio. What is to the west, eh? How many more rivers and lakes?"

"Who can tell? What are you thinking about, Edward?"

He looked around at her. "The captain of *La Demoiselle* said he had some sort of second sight. He said something about being descended from the Albigensians. At the time I secretly laughed at him. But, see: out there, the Ohio. Over there, the North Fork—"

"Allegaway," she corrected.

"Whatever," he said impatiently. "There is also the big river you told me you crossed when the Indians captured you."

"The Hudson?"

"Are there rivers and lakes to the south?"

"I don't know. But Colonel Washington spoke of streams in his Virginia Colony, so there must be."

"Captain Jouvier said flowing waters and inland seas would always be part of my life." He held her shoulders and his voice lowered, but Abby instinctively knew his softer tone was the voice of prophecy. That distant something he saw beyond her was not a thing but a time—the future.

"Canoes, ships, boats for the rivers—boats of

many kinds, perhaps. *Mon Dieu!* Jouvier must have been the seventh son of a seventh son! Colonel Washington has started us.'' He touched her stomach gently. ''And this one will continue. Those to come later—our children and their children. Always on the rivers, sailing the lakes—eh? And the oceans, too, perhaps.''

''You're a dreamer!'' Her smile and touch on his lips took the sting away from her laughter.

He caught her hand. *''Oui!* Whatever has anyone done without a dream to lead the way?''

She put her arms around his shoulders and pulled him down into the bed beside her, snuggled close against him. Her lips pressed against his cheek and then his mouth. ''With all those dreams, my love, hadn't we best start right away? This instant?''

''But the baby! Will it—?''

''Not yet, Love. Let's dream.''

FICTION FOR TODAY'S WOMAN

THE FOREVER PASSION   (563, $2.50)
by Karen A. Bale
A passionate, compelling story of how a young woman, made hostage by a band of Comanche warriors, becomes captivated by Nakon—the tribe's leader.

THE RIVER OF FORTUNE: THE PASSION   (561, $2.50)
by Arthur Moore
When the beautiful Andrea Berlenger and her beloved Logan leave their homes to begin a new life together, they discover the true meaning of love, life and desire on a Mississippi Riverboat and the great . . . RIVER OF FORTUNE.

BELLA   (498, $2.50)
by William Black
A heart-warming family saga of an immigrant woman who comes to America at the turn of the century and fights her way to the top of the fashion world.

BELLA'S BLESSINGS   (562, $2.50)
by William Black
From the Roaring Twenties to the dark Depression years. Three generations of an unforgettable family—their passions, triumphs and tragedies.

MIRABEAU PLANTATION   (596, $2.50)
by Marcia Meredith
Crystal must rescue her plantation from its handsome holder even at the expense of losing his love. A sweeping plantation novel about love, war, and a passion that would never die.

Available wherever paperbacks are sold, or direct from the Publisher. Send cover price plus 50¢ per copy for mailing and handling to Zebra Books, 21 East 40th Street, New York, N.Y. 10016. DO NOT SEND CASH!

BESTSELLERS FOR TODAY'S WOMAN

MILEAGE　　　　　　　　　　　　　　　(569, $2.50)
by Toni Tucci
Let Toni Tucci show you how to make the most of the second half of your life in her practical, inspirational guide that reveals how all woman can make their middle years more fulfilling.

ANOTHER LOVE, ANOTHER TIME　　　　　(486, $2.50)
by Anthony Tuttle
The poignant story of Laura Fletcher, a 47-year-old woman, who rediscovers herself, her life and living, when her husband's arrogance drives her away from him and into the arms of a younger man.

THE AWARD　　　　　　　　　　　　　(537, $2.50)
by Harriet Hinsdale
When Hollywood star Jane Benson sees her fame begin to fade, she strives for something to revitalize her image. She buys Vittorio Bellini, the renowned European director, and together they fight to save her career, her life and to help her win . . . THE AWARD.

SEASONS　　　　　　　　　　　　　　(578, $2.50)
by Ellin Ronee Pollachek
The dynamic, revealing story of Paige Berg, a sophisticated businesswoman, who devotes her life to men, designer clothes and the Salon—one of the most exciusive department stores in the world.

MOMENTS　　　　　　　　　　　　　　(565, $2.50)
by Berthe Laurence
When Katherine, a newly unmarried woman, finds herself faced with another chance for love, she is forced to make an earth-shattering decision that will change her life . . . again.

Available wherever paperbacks are sold, or direct from the Publisher. Send cover price plus 50¢ per copy for mailing and handling to Zebra Books, 21 East 40th Street, New York, N.Y. 10016. DO NOT SEND CASH!